Lauren in Pieces

Published by Black Jacket Publishing
Farmington, UT

First Edition Paperback - November 2024

Paperback ISBN:978-1-962734-02-8
E-book ISBN:978-1-962734-03-5

www.LindsayHiller.com

This book is for my ADHD friends.
I see you, and I love you.

Lauren in Pieces

a novel by

Lindsay Hiller

Chapter 1

---Eleven years ago.

Gently twisting Mom's rusted door handle, I slipped into the living room of her single-wide trailer. She slept on the couch, curled under a blanket, head wrapped in a scarf to fight off the cold—she was always cold. Her latest scans had come back clean. So why hadn't her hair grown back yet? And why did she still spend most of her time resting?

At least she wasn't getting worse.

I sank onto the faded corduroy cushion beside her. The faint scent of cinnamon gum clashed with the ever-present smell of hospital clothes and medications. These barely registered, though. My thoughts were focused somewhere else entirely. On *someone* else. He hadn't called in three days. Completely disappeared. My body chilled as I fixated on the possibilities, each one worse than the last. Was he okay? What could have—

My fourteen-year-old sister, Hallie, crashed through the door behind me, spots of the never-ending Seattle rain speckling her shirt. She muttered into the silent room as her long ponytail swung behind her. Within seconds, she stopped pacing the narrow strip of fraying carpet. "Lauren," she hissed, "were you even listening to me?"

"Hmm?"

Hallie placed her fists on the hips of her jeans and glared at me from under the brim of her tattered Mariners ball cap. Oops, had I missed something? Hallie was nothing like other teenage girls; she didn't spend hours doing her makeup or searching the mall for the perfect summer outfits. With Mom asleep most of the time, Hallie spent her days playing street sports with the neighbor boys. I should have made her come home more, keep a closer eye on Mom. But I didn't live here—I lived on the couch in Jared's apartment.

At least, I *had.* Until he disappeared three days ago.

Hallie perked up, her scowl morphing into a hopeful smile that lifted higher on her right cheek. "Will you take me to your dorm today? You graduate soon, we're almost out of chances!"

My stomach tensed. How could I show off a dorm that didn't exist? At a college I'd dropped out of? Not that Hallie knew that. Besides, with Jared missing, I had no energy to take her anywhere.

Hallie groaned, then squished between me and Mom. "I know you're worried about Jared," she said softly, "but I'm sure he's fine."

She smelled like cinnamon gum. Her warmth seeped into me, holding me back from a full nervous breakdown. Jared wouldn't just leave, right? I couldn't go back to a life without him.

I wouldn't.

Mom had always said I could do anything I set my mind to, but from the first day of college, I'd known I would fail. The focus I needed in class wouldn't come. Essays gave me anxiety. Panic attacks hit daily. No matter how hard I tried, I never finished a single assignment.

Then, two weeks before the end of my first semester, I trekked to the stinky, sweaty, campus gym, squeezing the gold heart ring Mom had given me in my hand. How could I face her if I dropped out?

I ran on the treadmill for three solid hours, excruciatingly focused on pushing my body to exhaustion. If my body wore out, my brain would wear out too, right? Then it would finally let me focus on studying for finals? But during every one of those ten thousand seconds, the only things

I could think about were the million *other* things on my to-do list. Finally, my legs gave out and I stumbled onto the ground—

—and there he was.

Jared DiMaggio.

I'd seen him around campus. He stood out with his muscular build and confident stride. He walked like someone who knew precisely where he was going. But that day, he'd trained his focus on exactly one thing. One person.

Me.

While I was preoccupied by my failing grades, the temperature of the room, and trying to ignore the annoying show on the gym television, Jared had zeroed in on *me*.

I fell instantly in love.

"I'm Jared, what's your name?"

"Lauren Cross."

"I need to film a workout for my exercise science class," he said, pulling me to my feet. "Will you hold the camera?"

The second I nodded, he turned his focus to organizing his space and selecting dumbbells. My heart rate doubled, and I chewed on my lower lip, following his precise movements. Jared handed me a black digital camera. Then, he began his workout—

—and my brain flipped to overdrive.

I found the corner with the best view.

Adjusted for ideal lighting.

Zoomed in and out, calculating new angles as he moved through equipment.

The complexity of filming occupied every part of my brain. Never once, in eighteen years of living, had I functioned so effectively.

The next day, Jared sent me the footage, and I secretly uploaded it to this brand-new website gaining popularity around campus. It was called YouTube. For an entire week, our video went viral in an untapped market. Then I hunted Jared down.

I found him in the library, tucked into a quiet corner, deep in conversation with a neatly dressed woman with lightly curled, blond hair. Jared introduced her as Lily, an old family friend, and she scoured me with the kind of sharp, appraising gaze that missed no details. But when I showed Jared our channel, his gaze locked on mine, wheels spinning. "Have any free time?"

"Too much," I replied. "Want to make more videos?"

That was the day my life changed.

We uploaded five more workouts that first month—and YouTube started paying us. Instead of taking my final exams, I filed for a business license and crashed on Jared's lumpy couch. Three months later, we were earning enough money to pay for TV dinners and rent. I had every intention of telling Mom and Hallie that I'd dropped out of school. I hated keeping secrets.

But then Mom got sick.

The cancer was eating her liver. They caught it early and cut out the tumor, but she still needed treatment in case it had spread. Her hair fell out, and she had to quit work. Her pride in me was what kept her going. Her college kid, the daughter who'd escaped White Center to conquer the world. If those were her last days, how could I shatter the one thing keeping her hopes up?

So, I let her believe I was still working toward my fancy degree.

For four terrifying years, I lied to keep her happy.

Then her scans came back clean. She beat the odds and beat her cancer. But my lie had grown so big I couldn't untangle it. My shame burned hotter every time I came home. What would Hallie think when she found out I'd made it all up? The dorm. The roommates. The classes. Dad was a liar; I'd become just like him.

Now, four years had passed, and Jared was graduating, which meant we were losing access to the campus gym. We needed to buy our own weightlifting equipment. Set up our own studio. Upgrade our cameras. I vowed that as soon as we got set up, I'd tell my family everything. When they saw our success, they'd forgive my lies. All we needed was startup funding.

So, three days ago, Jared set out to ask somebody for a business loan.

But he never returned.

So here I sat on Mom's couch with Hallie's warm arm pressed against mine, my worries trickling down my spine, burning like acid. Why hadn't I thought to ask more questions? Was he nearby, or had he traveled outside our little corner of Seattle? Had he gone to a loan shark then lost the money? Was he arrested, or injured, or half-dead in a ditch? I still hadn't found the nerve to confess my feelings to him.

Jared, where are you?

I slipped Mom's heart ring off my finger and squeezed it in my hand. The last time I'd held it this way, Jared had strolled through the door of the campus gym. Could it bring him through my door again?

But the painful truth settled in my chest. Without Jared here to help run our company, all my lies were going to unravel.

I dug my nails into my palm until they pierced the skin. "Hallie," I whispered, swallowing hard. She looked up at me with wide, innocent, unsuspecting eyes. This would shatter her perfect image of me. "I need to tell you something—"

Someone knocked on the door.

Hallie jumped up, her long ponytail swinging behind her, and yanked open the door. There he was. Jared wore his nicest slacks and a navy polo, his hair combed crisply up in the front. He was alive! He was *here.* No one had beaten him and left him for dead.

"Told you he was fine," Hallie said with a smirk.

But I leapt off the couch and threw my arms around his waist. Jared's warmth cocooned me like a shroud, his familiar cologne soothing my nerves. My entire body sagged with relief. "Where have you been?"

He pulled away, but his hand trailed down my arm until his fingers intertwined with mine. He rarely touched me, preferring to focus on work. I'd always assumed our romance would happen as soon as we got the company up and running. But today, he gripped my hand and led me outside under the overcast sky. "Let's go for a walk."

Hallie made kissing noises as Jared led me down the steps. I swatted the bill of her baseball hat.

When we reached the crumbling sidewalk, I stopped. "Where were you?"

Jared leaned against Dad's old, busted car. He'd never once commented on the overgrown lawn or the rusty bikes. Not even after we visited his parents' mansion on Mercer Island. Instead, he pressed our clasped hands against his warm chest.

"One hundred thousand dollars." He whispered the words like it all might disappear if he spoke too loudly. "I got it, Lauren."

Tension drained from my muscles like water rushing over a cliff. With that much money, our company would explode overnight. If I could support myself, I could look Mom and Hallie in the eyes again. I could find success—*without* the college degree. Mom would still be proud of me.

"How?" I asked.

Jared's gaze focused on something behind me, and he shifted his weight.

Was he . . . nervous?

He shoved one hand into his pocket, took a deep breath, and pulled out a black velvet jewelry box.

When he popped it open, a large diamond ring sparkled in the sun.

"Jared!" I gasped.

"Do you think Lily will like it?"

My lungs froze. "Who?"

"Lily. You met her once, in the library, remember?" He shifted his weight again. "We grew up together; our parents were friends."

My smile froze into place, but my insides trembled violently. He was proposing to her? What about me? What about us? I tried to inhale, but my throat wouldn't respond, and when my smile drooped, I forced it back into place and cleared my throat. "You're proposing to Lily?"

"Her dad's our investor. We told our parents we're engaged and requested a two-hundred-thousand-dollar loan as a wedding present. Lily will take half, and I'll take the other half."

Were the trees lining the road tilting to the side? The trailers too. "You're marrying her?"

"Her parents only agreed once they realized we were serious about each other. But it's a scam, Lauren. It isn't real." He lifted my hand and pressed it firmly against his lips, warmth blossoming on my skin. "You and me? We're real. I just need you to play along for a little while."

Play along?

He tucked the engagement ring into his pocket, then he wrapped both hands around my waist, pulling me against his body but holding my gaze.

A hundred thoughts zoomed through my head. A fake marriage with *Lily?* When something real was sprouting between Jared and *me*?

When had they hatched this plan?

Was the money worth a sacrifice *this* huge?

"Jared, what if I don't want you to do this?"

He sighed, long and slow. Uncertainty crawled into the creases around his eyes. "I don't want to either, but I have to—for you and me. For our company. But I can't do it without your support." He paused. "A *trust-fall favor.*"

I sucked in a breath. A *trust-fall favor?* We'd made this up years ago, a code word for a life-or-death situation. An *everything hangs in the balance* favor that the other person couldn't say no to. I'd only asked Jared for one once, the day I asked him to lie to Mom and Hallie about me dropping out of college. He'd agreed without hesitation.

How could I refuse him now?

"How long will you stay married?"

"Just until we've paid back the loans." He said it casually, like it wasn't a big deal. "A few years at most. Hopefully less." His gaze turned serious. He leaned in close, one hundred percent of his attention focused on me, just the way I loved it. "Will you wait for me?"

His breath caressed my skin. Then, for the first time, he brushed his lips softly against mine. My heart fluttered like a hummingbird. Nothing existed but the heat of his breath mingling with mine. Was this really happening?

"Please?" he begged. "I can't do this without you—you're my rock."

I'd waited a lifetime for him to say those words, to finally kiss me. "I'd wait for you forever."

"Good, because there's a catch." Jared rested his forehead against mine. "As a wedding present, Lily's family is buying us a house . . . in St. Louis."

I jumped from his arms. "You're moving to Missouri?"

"Our entire business is online. It shouldn't make a difference where I live."

"How will that work?" A million problems erupted in my head. I paced across our overgrown yard at record speed, biting hard on my thumb. "I suppose you can email me the video files. I can edit and upload them from here—but Mom's internet is crappy. Maybe I could go to the library . . . but who will film for you? We'll have to hire a cameraman. I'll train them. But what if they don't have an eye for good angles? Or lighting? And if we're buying new equipment, I get to pick the camera—"

Jared stopped me with a hand on my arm, laughing. "I'll never understand how you survive with all those thoughts in your head. You've got to shove them down. Quiet all those voices! But I don't think you understood what I meant." He lifted his fingers to cup my cheeks. "You're coming with me."

I froze. "I am?"

"I don't trust anyone else."

The entire street fell quiet. Could I leave this place? Leave Mom? Hallie? What if Mom's cancer came back? What if Hallie needed me?

I'd come home, obviously.

And I'd call every week. Every day, if it helped. And we'd come home the second Jared and Lily called off their marriage—with a legitimate reason for Mom to be proud of me. A tangible success. No more fake degrees and lame excuses about skipping my college graduation. No more lying, no more pretending. This would be *real* success.

"Will you come?" Jared asked.

I took a deep breath, then nodded. "Of course."

Jared followed me back inside and told a smooth story about an investment opportunity in St. Louis. Hallie sucked in a sharp breath, covering her mouth with both hands. Mom huddled quietly behind her.

"If you move away," Hallie said, clenching her fists, "who will take me out for ice cream on the anniversary of Dad leaving? Or drive me to the hospital after I play hockey? Who will help me if Mom gets sick again?"

"Mom's fine," I assured, though her words sparked a flash of tension in my neck. "The cancer's gone."

"But I never got to visit your dorm. You can't leave!"

Mom nudged her aside and wrapped me in a feeble hug. "We'll be fine. I get stronger every day. I'm so proud of you. You're going places, Lauren. I can't wait to see how far you fly."

My tension increased, stabbing into the space between my ribs. I couldn't meet her gaze. She was proud of a person who didn't exist.

"I mean it," she said. "No matter what, you'll always be my hero."

This was why I had to go, why I had to follow Jared. Together, we could turn *me* into the person Mom already thought I was.

Hallie sniffled, and I slipped the heart ring off my finger and pressed it into her hand. "This is full of good luck. It calls people home who've been gone too long. Hang on to it for me?"

"But it's your favorite ring."

"It's a loan. Keep it safe until I come home."

Hallie rolled it delicately between her fingers. "You'll visit soon, right? Halloween? I'm planning out my *serial killer* costume."

"As long as you promise to take care of Mom."

Hallie threw her arms around my neck. "I promise."

Three weeks later, I gripped the handle of my suitcase and followed Jared onto an airplane. My family was proud of me. It was time to become the person who deserved it.

Chapter 2

---*Eleven years later.*

$22.42 left in my wallet

I, Lauren Cross, was the epitome of success. Gray pantsuit pressed to a crisp with a perfectly angled collar. Black dress boots, polished and sparkling like diamonds. Chanel perfume, spritzed just enough to smell pleasant but not overpowering. My white-blond pixie cut was artfully styled, every strand pointing at the exact upward angle I'd intended.

Thriving.

Perfect.

The wildly successful agent of fitness superstar Jared DiMaggio.

At least I was, until six months ago.

Now, no one would work with him.

"AAGH!" I shrieked, hitting *end* with all the strength in my pointer finger and slamming my phone on my desk. That call was from a no-name trainer who was trying—and failing—to climb his way into the supplement industry. He was the last person who might still sign Jared into a promo deal. The meeting had taken three weeks of begging to set up—

but he'd rejected us, same as everyone before him. And now we were broke. Bankrupt. Not a single prospect left.

Except . . .

The email's subject line taunted me from my laptop. I'd ignored it for days. A keynote speaker had dropped out of the Croft Power fitness convention in Seattle, and they needed a last-minute replacement. They wanted my other client, Fearless Felicity. She would refuse, of course—she refused every job—but maybe they'd consider Jared in her place.

But I couldn't make myself respond to the email.

Why did it have to be in Seattle—my hometown? And why did it have to be *Croft*?

It didn't matter. They'd never agree to Jared. *Never.*

Unless . . .

No.

Frantic, I dug through my desk drawer until I found a red cinnamon taffy—my favorite stress food. The stale candy crumbled when I untwisted the wrapper and crunched when I bit into it. The sharp pain of a cavity reverberated through my gums. I couldn't afford to get it fixed, which didn't help my anxiety. The cinnamon didn't help this time, either. Or Jared's empty work schedule. So, I crawled beneath my polished oak desk in my undecorated JD Fitness executive office, pulled my knees into my chest, clenched my teeth, and yanked a handful of hair with all the strength of a woman who worked for a fitness company but never found the time to exercise.

And then I screamed.

Ten seconds later, Bailey Dupree burst through the door. The lock on the knob gouged an ever-growing hole in the drywall. I held my breath, afraid to make a noise lest Bailey discover me hiding from my failures. The list of them bubbled up through my chest and snaked through my throat, higher and higher, fighting for space in my brain, all of them clamoring to be the one that finally pushed me over the edge.

Was it Jared's floundering career that was killing me? Was it my own? Was it that my phone hadn't rung a single time in the six months since I'd handed my company over to Bailey and become Jared's agent full time?

Or was it the fact that his reputation had only worsened since the world found out he cheated on his wife—despite his profuse apologies and his almost-finalized divorce?

It could also be my empty bank account, or my growling stomach. Thank goodness for the free supplements in the office cafeteria, otherwise my annoyingly petite body would have withered away weeks ago. How could I return home and face Mom and Hallie like this? I was supposed to be proving myself as a successful businesswoman, not a floundering catastrophe.

And of course there was one more failure: no matter how loyally I threw myself into turning Jared's life around, now that he was finally single, he still hadn't kissed me.

Not once.

Not since the day he first told me about his sham marriage, back when it was the two of us, Jared and Lauren against the world, climbing the fame ladder rung by rung, surviving on nothing but grit and Green Fizz energy juice.

The Polaroid I always kept in my pocket memorialized that era, but I couldn't bring myself to pull it out and see all the hope shining in our eyes.

I always fixed things, so why couldn't I fix this?

Maybe because six months ago, he'd accidentally confessed on live TV that he'd cheated on his wife with fitness blogger Fearless Felicity. Now, no one wanted to hire him. No one wanted to work with him. No one watched his YouTube videos. They spoke his name in whispers, like the word was laced in poison. A guttural yowl rose up from my lungs, and I yanked on my hair until a strand came out in my hand.

"Ow," I whimpered.

"Lauren?" Bailey poked her head behind the desk, her long brown locks brushing the floor between my curled-up body and my office chair, which had somehow ended up on its side.

Oops. I'd forgotten she was there. Bailey Dupree, the savior of JD Fitness, the one who'd rescued us all from disaster after Jared and I had leveraged every last penny on a new YouTube workout program. I'd thrown my own savings in there, then re-mortgaged my condo, and maxed out my credit cards. Without Bailey, we would have lost it all. Not only had she taken control of our company, but her existence kept our viewers coming back, holding their breath for the day when she'd make her own appearance on our YouTube channel.

Six months ago, she was our lowest-paid employee. Then the entire world—myself included—discovered she was secretly the world's most famous fitness blogger, Fearless Felicity.

For the record, she'd had *no clue* Jared was married when he kissed her.

And now everyone wanted to hire her.

But as her agent, they had to get through me first. The problem was, she hadn't let me sign her for a single fitness show, a single promotional deal, a single ad campaign. Bailey claimed she was holding out for a cause noble enough to be worth hitting the road and leaving her teenage daughter home alone.

Which was why all my eggs were firmly in Jared's basket.

My stomach growled.

I banged the back of my head against the inner wall of my desk. Hopefully the vibration didn't upset Francine, my pet angelfish, in her small glass bowl.

Bailey sighed, then rubbed her chin.

Oh yeah, Bailey.

"You okay?" she asked.

"What's wrong with me?" Her face blurred as my eyes crossed and lost focus.

“I’ll be right back.” She slipped out of my office.

“Alexa,” I said, “turn off the light.”

The room plummeted into darkness. Tomorrow, Jared would finish filming with the ZBC TV network, and our careers would officially end.

We’d failed. *I’d* failed.

My phone vibrated on the desk above my head. I reached up and flailed my fingers across the top, bumping Francine’s fishbowl until I found it, then opened the new message from Jared. He’d forwarded the same email I’d been ignoring.

Jared: *Did you see this? Croft Power Company’s fitness convention? Sounds like they’re desperate for a last minute replacement. It’s PERFECT! Can you make a call, get me that keynote spot? We could make a dozen promo deals. This is our big break. I can feel it!*

Make a call? Seriously? I opened a text and typed him a quick message.

Lauren: *You’re aware this is a* Croft *convention, right? In Seattle? You know who I’d have to talk to?*

He responded instantly.

Jared: *You worry too much. She’s your sister, she’ll forgive you.*

No, she wouldn’t. Pressing my head against the underside of the desk, I folded my arms around my stomach. Why would she forgive me when I’d done nothing to deserve it? Nothing to prove that I was more than a failure? The light flickered back on.

“Alexa,” I groaned, “turn off the light.”

“No, don’t.” Bailey’s voice had developed an authoritative edge in her six months running JD Fitness. Why did the light obey her and not me? Apparently, even my little black speaker considered me worth ignoring.

“Lauren, will you come out here?” she said.

“No.”

“Please.” She didn’t say it like a question. There was no point in refusing.

I gripped the cold, plastic arm of my upturned chair and pulled myself to standing. I straightened my suitcoat, then my collar, and wiped my hands on my pants. With a breath so deep the oxygen burned my lungs, I put on an overly bright smile and faced my friend.

But Bailey wasn't alone.

Marco, Bailey's diamond-selling, cane-carrying, ballroom-dancing, stunningly handsome Italian fiancé, stood to her left. Stella, our new fitness star, leaned against the wall to her right. Stella's three-month YouTube workout program had just aired its teaser episode and had already blown every one of Jared's massive viewership records out of the water. Stella was the most exciting thing to happen to JD Fitness since Jared's glory days a decade ago. If she and Bailey kept kicking ass, they just might pull the company out of bankruptcy.

My stomach growled again. When did I eat last? Everything felt a little fuzzy, like I couldn't think in a straight line. My blood sugar must be dropping. It did that when I forgot to eat. Or got too busy to eat. Or too stressed to eat.

"Hey, hi, guys." I tried to sound normal. Like my brain wasn't full of too many words zooming in every direction. But my voice came out an octave too high.

"You okay in there?" Bailey asked.

"Oh, yeah. Sure."

Bailey's nose scrunched up in that way that meant she didn't believe me, and Marco pressed a supportive hand against the small of her back. He was dressed from head to toe in designer black, the polished cane in his left hand shining as brightly as the Rolex on his right. Then Bailey gave him a *look*, the kind of silent communication that belonged only to lovers of an epic caliber. I used to daydream about Jared looking at me that way, especially in the beginning, before his miserable marriage. Back when he would linger near me after a workout and praise how well I'd directed from just off camera.

Where had those days gone?

I slumped back against the front of my desk, half-sitting, half-standing, and Bailey stepped in close enough that I couldn't escape. Did she really think I'd try to run away?

"You need a break," she said.

"That's the opposite of what I need."

"No one can go full speed forever. It's okay to slow down."

I didn't need a break; I needed more hours in the day. Years, even. More time to scour the internet searching for opportunities for Jared. More TV deals, more clothing lines, more fitness conventions—

—like the one that would start tonight. In Seattle.

Ugh. I had to call Hallie.

After all these years, she was my last hope.

The blank walls of my empty office closed in around me. Then spun in wild circles.

"She's going down," Marco said, all business. "Grab the chair."

Stella dashed behind me—in front of me? around me?—and grabbed my overturned office chair, then Marco and Bailey lowered me into it.

"Breathe," Bailey said, but I barely heard her.

My sister? I hadn't seen her in over a decade. Hadn't visited Seattle since Jared and I chased this dream into the suburbs of St. Louis. We'd never gone back. Never stopped by for a long weekend. Despite all our success, it had never felt like *enough.* It never assuaged the guilt from my lies, from years of hiding my failures by weaving an entire pretend life. It didn't take long before I only called every few months, then every few years.

What kind of person doesn't call home?

I loved my family more than anything in the world. I could hardly look at myself in the mirror without despising the face staring back at me. But even when I *did* call, Hallie eventually stopped answering. Then Mom's landline got disconnected—they probably couldn't afford it. Don't get me wrong, I sent them money plenty of times. But still, my calls wouldn't go through.

Now, I was too ashamed to face them.

Hallie would be twenty-four now. Or was she twenty-five? How could I reach out to her when we'd barely spoken in a decade? But what choice did I have? Hallie worked for Croft Power, the fastest-growing clean energy company in the world. Each month they held a massive international convention in downtown Seattle supporting an industry in line with their cause. Two months ago, it was *environmental cleanup*. Last month it was *renewable paper and packaging*. This month, *fitness*—and they were desperate for a keynote speaker.

On top of that, each convention included a massive competition. The winner earned a long-term publicity deal with Croft Power's CEO, and that was exactly what we needed. What Jared needed. But why did it have to be in my hometown?

"I've gotta make a phone call," I muttered. Bailey frowned, but I scrolled through my contacts until I found Hallie's name, and hit *call.*

Hallie didn't answer until the last ring, her voice hesitant. "Lauren? Is something wrong?"

For once, nothing came to my mind. No voices, no ideas, nothing to quiet down. Bailey watched me carefully, then touched my arm for support.

"Hey, Hallie, it's been a while."

She said nothing.

"Sorry to call like this, but you work for Croft Power, right? They invited Fearless Felicity to speak at their convention this week, but I need them to hire Jared DiMaggio instead. Do you know who runs these things? Could you get them to agree to a different speaker?"

Still, Hallie's silence stretched on.

"Please? I'm desperate." If only she knew about *trust-fall favors.*

Hallie sighed into the phone. "I'll see what I can do." Then she hung up.

Bailey leaned against the desk, pressing her arm against mine. "Want to talk about it?"

My heart pounded too quickly to reply. Within ten seconds, my phone beeped.

Hallie: *He speaks Thursday night.*

Tomorrow.

I stared at Hallie's words. Should I be elated? Or terrified?

Maybe both.

Then my brain turned to overdrive, hurling questions with no answers. How would we get to Seattle? How would I pay for it? And once I got there, did Mom and Hallie still live in the same house, with the cafe at the end of the street? A lot could change in eleven years. What if they'd paved over our block and rebuilt? What if Mom was ashamed of who I'd become? What if she didn't want to talk to me—was that why she'd disconnected her phone? And what would Hallie say when I apologized for disappearing?

What if she wouldn't forgive me?

Bailey dug through her purse, then handed me four crisp hundred-dollar bills. "From petty cash. Think you can make it last? It's all the company can spare."

Four hundred dollars? It was a fortune.

"We have two travel vouchers too. Enough for two one-way tickets and a hotel. Can you and Jared get yourselves home after?"

Jared and I would be together at a convention.

Alone.

My nerves settled.

I pulled out the old Polaroid I'd refused to look at only minutes before.

Jared waved back at me, next to a younger version of myself at the first convention we'd ever attended. That one had been in Seattle too. He'd charmed his way into the hearts of the entire fitness community—and I'd followed behind with my laptop, working out promo deals. Those were our glory days. Everything had come so easily.

What if we could revive that momentum at this convention? What if I talked to the fitness community face-to-face and explained Jared's situation? Described his unhappy marriage, explained his impending divorce. Then, when he blew them out of the water with his speech, they'd be ready and willing to give him a second chance.

And with our careers back on track, I could finally face Hallie.

She would understand why I'd stayed so focused on my job.

I scooped up Francine's small fishbowl and set it carefully in Bailey's hands, followed by a three-quarter-empty bottle of fish food.

"Take care of her? She gets lonely." I pulled a few dollars from my wallet and handed it to Marco. "In case you need more fish food. Be sure to buy her this exact kind, she has expensive taste."

This was it. My one shot.

My chance to fix everything.

I glanced at my watch. I'd need to hurry to Seattle to make it to tonight's opening banquet. Sure, Jared usually did the schmoozing, but he wouldn't arrive until he finished filming tomorrow. Why wait? I was our master researcher. I had files and spreadsheets documenting every person in the fitness industry. For fifteen years I'd fed Jared information and pointed him in the right direction.

Tonight was my turn.

A few quick meetings and Jared's reputation would be back on track.

With our careers on the rise, Hallie would forgive me for staying away so long.

And when Jared arrived tomorrow?

He'd finally remember how much he loved me.

Chapter 3

$422.42 (thanks for the cash, Bailey)
-$8.00 fish food
-$4.50 disposable water bottle
-$14.49 phone charger in the airport
$395.43 remaining

Despite the annoyingly strict rules about using phones on airplanes, I texted Hallie mid-flight.

Lauren: *Meet me outside baggage claim?*

I'd bounced in my seat for the last two hours, a confusing combination of terror and excitement to face her. I finally did the math. Hallie was ten when I enrolled at the University of Washington, still ten when I met Jared and dropped out, and fourteen when we packed everything up and moved to St. Louis. That made her twenty-five this year.

Would I recognize her?

A text popped in from Bailey.

Bailey: *When you get a sec, we got the trailer for Stella's new show. Let me know what you think! Can't believe it's finally happening!*

I locked my phone without watching it. It used to be *me* producing our shows, but now that job belonged to Bailey—and she was a kickass producer—but I still missed it.

Fortunately, I was a kickass agent too.

During the flight, I'd blocked out all the airplane distractions and laid out countless ideas in my notebook. How many vendor contracts could I realistically fit into Jared's schedule? Should I prioritize larger upfront payments or longer-term contracts? Jared preferred in-person appearances, while I pushed him toward photo shoots and pre-recorded videos. Not that I didn't trust him during live appearances—I did, completely, he'd only messed up that one time—but with photo shoots, I could control the final product.

But I kept flipping to a page I'd titled *Hallie.* I'd been working on a similar one in my phone's notepad for years. I'd see my little sister in half an hour. Should I jump right in with an apology, or was sister-abandonment a delicate subject that needed to wait for just the right moment? Was there a *right moment* for that sort of thing? Or could we both pretend like it never happened?

I'd scribbled columns and columns of notes. Conversation starters, apologies, excuses. Hopefully when I saw her face, I'd know which one to use. The fact that she was picking me up had to be a good sign.

So as the plane soared toward that inevitable conversation, I forced my attention back to Jared's career—or lack thereof. My knee bounced, shaking the row and earning me a glare from the man in the aisle seat with a buzz cut and red-framed glasses. My fingers tapped too, so I dug through my oversized purse and found a disposable water bottle I'd bought in the airport. It had cost nearly five of my precious dollars, plus fifteen because I forgot my phone charger too. I snapped the seal on the cheap plastic lid and added a packet of green powder. It bubbled as I shook it, then settled into a solid neon green. Courage in a bottle. Liquid energy.

Green Fizz.

My lifeline. The thing that pulled me through every rough day. Green Fizz was our patented blend of caffeine, beta-alanine, and creatine—the perfect combination of pre-workout supplements. I never picked up dumbbells, but to me, every day was a workout. When all else failed, Green Fizz kept me going.

Thanks to my empty stomach, it kicked in within five minutes, the beta-alanine spreading down my arms and prickling my hands and face. Yes, this was exactly the boost I needed.

Ideas for Jared flowed into my head and out through my pen. I didn't know who would attend the convention, so I listed every fitness influencer who might make an appearance, then made another list of likely vendors. Beneath them I jotted every detail I could remember about their interests, hobbies, and favorite types of promotional deals. Some wouldn't want to work with Jared no matter how cleanly I scrubbed his reputation, so I crossed them off. But I pondered over the rest, jotting down any notes that might help. Under *the Twins* I wrote *loves whiskey from St. Louis*. I'd packed a bottle in my suitcase especially for them.

But the guy with red glasses kept peeking over my shoulder, scowling, so I glared straight at him until he angled his entire body away. Not my fault his life was boring while mine was on the verge of the most spectacular comeback in human history.

Jared would be here tomorrow, and our lives would make a complete one-eighty. Until then, I'd talk to every fitness influencer at tonight's banquet, then I'd spend tomorrow schmoozing every vendor in the convention hall. When Jared arrived tomorrow night, he'd be amazed.

Amazed with *me*.

Ten minutes before the plane landed, my notebook ran out of pages. I'd need to buy a new one, ASAP, then transfer all my notes into my phone. But for now, I'd sufficiently prepared, so I read the short speech our PR specialist had insisted I recite anytime Jared's reputation got in my way. Unfortunately, JD Fitness couldn't afford to hire her full-time, but hopefully this would get me through the weekend. All I had to do was memorize it.

Jared and Lily DiMaggio appreciate the concern you've all shown over their marriage. They are working closely with their attorney and their marriage counselor to make this drama a thing of the past. Jared is excited to turn his attention back to his career and back to bringing high-quality exercise programs straight to his fans. He is especially grateful for—

The plane landed with a deafening rumble. As we taxied toward our gate, I watched through the window, taking in the gray clouds that made three in the afternoon feel like evening. In the middle of April, rain in Seattle was a given, and the steady drizzle darkened the surrounding sea of cement.

A text popped into my phone from Hallie.

Hallie: *Meet at Baggage Claim 2.*

Hallie was here. She was at the airport. The reality of it sucked the air from my lungs. After eleven years, I'd finally see her! *Please forgive me, please forgive me.*

My knees wobbled as I hoisted my red roller bag from the overhead compartment, dug my jacket out of my suitcase, then followed Red Glasses off the plane. Spring in Missouri rarely required a heavy coat, but Seattle rain was something different. It came nonstop. The smell permeated the air—even indoors, like the scent had soaked through the walls.

A sign pointed down the escalator to baggage claim, and my hands started jittering. Hallie would be down there, waiting for me. I pulled out my notebook and skimmed through my apology options. How would I begin? Compliment her, maybe? A gift. That wasn't even on my list! I should have brought a gift. Maybe I still could. Except that we'd maxed all my credit cards on JD Fitness stuff. I had Bailey's cash, though. What did Hallie like? Probably not street hockey anymore. Oh! She'd developed a thing for slasher films after that boy moved in next door. What was his name? But they wouldn't sell movies inside the airport, and she'd stream them now, anyway. Why did I know so little about my sister? What kind of person was so bad at keeping in touch?

My legs stopped moving, two feet before the top of the escalator.

Red Glasses crashed into me from behind then flipped me the bird as he stalked around. But I still couldn't walk. The crowd split behind me like a zipper, reforming as they descended. My stomach heaved. I spun to my left and bolted, shoving through the crowd, tumbling onto a bench and leaning my cheek onto the frigid surface of a bronze sculpture of three sockeye salmon. Their eyes were wide, mouths open, like they were gasping for air, same as me. Where had the oxygen gone?

I overturned my purse and dumped the contents onto the tiled floor. A heavyset female security guard took two steps closer, watching me with shrewd eyes, but I ignored her. The room was turning fuzzy, and I still hadn't found—

There! I twisted the lid off my tiny prescription pill bottle and swallowed a Xanax with the last gulp of my Green Fizz. *Thanks, Dad, for the curse of anxiety.* Instantly, my breathing slowed, stomach unclenched, the dark around my vision abated. What would I do without Xanax? Realistically, no medication could cure me so quickly. But knowing what the pill would do as it seeped through my limbs was usually enough to ebb the onset of a panic attack.

Yes, much better. I could do this.

One by one, I stuffed my things back into my purse, waved to the security guard, then bought another disposable water bottle from a vending machine. I rejoined the crowd funneling down the narrow escalator. When my turn came, I squared my shoulders, then stepped onto the top stair.

What would Hallie look like? She wouldn't be wearing roller blades with dirt smudges on her cheeks. She was twenty-five now, not fourteen. I should have asked her to send me a picture, but that meant admitting how many years had passed since I'd seen her. Instead, I peered into the crowd below as the escalator descended. Hired drivers waved whiteboards while

TSA agents weaved through crowds exuding an air of annoyance. It was surprisingly busy for a Wednesday afternoon at three o'clock.

But where was Hallie?

At the far back, behind Baggage Claim 2, leaning against a white wall tarnished by years of fingerprints, was the only unmoving person in the flurry of chaos. He was another hired driver—except his whiteboard wasn't dry erase. He held a crookedly cut rectangle of cardboard that read *Lauren Cross* in hastily scrawled permanent marker, and he stood apart from the other drivers.

His attire didn't match theirs, either. His black suit pants held their crease too stiffly. The sleeves of his white button-up weren't rolled to the elbows, but rather cinched at the wrists with cuff links that refracted gold light. He wore no jacket, despite the cold breeze blowing through the automatic doors, and he'd combed his mildly curly hair sharply to the side. His skin was dark, though not as dark as Marco's. Latino, perhaps? Half, maybe a quarter? Just enough to give him olive skin and a dark goatee. Only a few wrinkles surrounded his eyes, so maybe late-forties? His black dress shoes were polished, not utilitarian like the other drivers' who hefted luggage all day. And he stood stock-still, unmoving, like those photos that captured a serene face while everything around them blurred out of focus. But this man was anything but serene. Frozen, yes, but bored to death.

No, not bored. Annoyed.

Where was Hallie?

My escalator spit me out, and I stumbled, falling hard on my already-bruised knees. My notepad of apologies skidded across the floor. People zippered around me again. No one offered to help. That was fine. Great. Everything was okay. Hallie would have a solid reason for not being here, something incredibly important. Maybe she got stuck at work. Maybe she was helping out her billionaire clean-energy boss. Maybe she hated me so much she couldn't face me.

Or maybe she'd realized that I'd only called because I needed a favor. I needed her connections. An apology right now would sound contrived.

Forced. Like a lie. The idea hit like a punch to my lungs. I *wanted* to apologize, to make up for running away, to erase the memory of her begging me to stay—and me promising to visit.

I wanted my sister back.

I *missed* her.

Until this moment, I hadn't realized how much.

I climbed to my feet and called her phone, but it went straight to voicemail. So, I marched straight up to the driver, and said, "You're not Hallie."

"No, I'm not." His low voice scratched like gravel in my ears.

When he didn't move or say anything else, I held out the handle of my red roller bag. He stared at it for three long seconds. This close, no trace of wrinkles laced his eyes—I'd mis-guessed his age by a decade. Late thirties at the most. If his face hadn't morphed into a scowl, I might have called him handsome. But he took my suitcase, spun on his heels, and strode silently out of the airport.

Chapter 4

$395.43
<u>-$4.50</u> vending machine water bottle
$390.93 remaining

Cold air rushed at me the second the sliding doors opened, the spring afternoon sun completely hidden by black clouds. Rain pelted down and the frigid air pierced straight through my coat. It didn't smell fresh, it only smelled cold. Miserably cold.

"It sure rains a lot here!" I yelled over the wind.

The driver didn't answer, just kept walking. He didn't pull out an umbrella, either. In fact, no one carried umbrellas. He led me to a black Tesla in the dark parking garage and lifted my suitcase into the trunk. Then he slid into the driver's seat without looking at me once.

Was I supposed to sit in the back? Or the passenger seat? Was there a protocol for this sort of thing? No one had ever hired a driver for me before. When Jared and I traveled, he always rented a muscle car. My hand hovered between both handles, closer to the first, then the second. This shouldn't be so hard.

He rolled down the passenger-side window. "Is there a problem?"

I reached for the back door, then switched at the last second and dove into the front. If I'd chosen wrong, the driver gave no indication. He lifted a bag of dog treats and a curled-up leash from the edge of my seat, placed them in the back, then started his silent car and drove the spiraling road down to street-level.

The Tesla still smelled new, like fresh leather and recently dried paint. The black seat cushion enveloped me with all the luxury of a brand-new car. But my awe was overpowered by the animosity rolling off the driver in waves. Or was it anger? Annoyance? He'd angled his body away like he might catch something contagious if I breathed on him. Maybe I smelled bad? I leaned to my right and discreetly sniffed under my arm. Nope, my deodorant was doing its job. He scowled and leaned farther away. Maybe I wasn't that discreet.

"You have a dog?" I asked. Dog owners intimidated me. It took all my effort to keep Francine the angelfish alive.

After a long stretch, he said, "A husky."

The silence lengthened until I squirmed. Maybe I could smooth things over with a compliment. "This car seems pretty nice for a professional driver."

He grimaced like he was in pain. What was I doing wrong? Couldn't he see I was trying to fix it?

"Are you the boss? Is that how you afford a Tesla? Or is that inappropriate to ask? Of course it is. Sorry."

My knees started bouncing, my heels tap-tap-tapping on the black rubber floor mats, my hands drumming on my thighs. The tension in my spine jumped painfully up into my neck and shoulders, so I poured another packet of Green Fizz powder into a disposable water bottle—my last one, I'd have to buy more ASAP. But how to smooth over the conversation? "It's just that no one's ever hired me a driver before. I'm not sure what to talk about."

Or maybe I wasn't supposed to talk at all?

"I'm not a driver." His knuckles turned white as he gripped the wheel.

Then who was he? And where was he taking me?

"Do you work for my sister?" All my worries came crashing back. Where *was* she? I took a big drink from my water bottle.

"She works for me."

I spit Green Fizz all over the dash.

"I'll clean it!" Scrambling out of my jacket, I used the sleeves to dry every inch of the dash and glove compartment. This was the gazillionaire clean-energy guy? No wonder he was seething about having to pick me up. Fortunately, this wasn't the first time I'd exploded Green Fizz, so I knew how easily it came off furniture. "Don't worry, there's no sugar in there. It won't leave behind any sticky residue. I would know, I engineered the formula myself." My words came out before my brain had time to think them through. "Well, me and Jared DiMaggio. Do you know him? Fitness guy, does YouTube workout programs. He's filming with ZBC right now." *I'm rambling.* "Today's his last day on set, then he'll come to Seattle tomorrow. Here, to this convention. With me. His show airs next month, you should check it out."

Shove it down, quiet the voices.

I clamped my lips shut with two trembling fingers, one of them speckled with Green Fizz. Thank goodness his car was black.

Hallie's boss still said nothing. From the corner of my eye—I didn't dare look at him straight on—he clearly spent time in a gym. He was tall, wide-framed, and his muscles bulged beneath the fabric of his button-up. But unlike Jared, who wore skin-tight athletic shirts, this guy wasn't attempting to show it off. Like, sure, he lifted weights sometimes, but his mind lived perpetually at the office, hence the creased slacks and cufflinks.

And he remained excruciatingly silent.

His car didn't make a hint of noise either as we glided onto the freeway, unlike Jared's muscle cars that roared everywhere we went. The only sounds were the drumming of rain on the roof and the whirring of his tires on the pavement. Not even his radio peeped.

I wrapped my now-wet coat over the strap of my purse, shivering against the cold. Should I apologize again? Or talk about Jared? Important people liked knowing about each other. Better yet, I could start pitching their partnership right now! No need to wait until the convention. But what was his name? The entire country knew his name, why couldn't I remember? Or maybe I should bring up Hallie. She was our only mutual connection, after all. Maybe he could tell me why she hadn't picked me up. Or just how much she hated me.

But my mouth moved before I had time to process my words. "What's it like being the billionaire owner of a major power company?"

He finally glanced at me, touching his goatee with his thumb and pointer finger. "Excuse me?"

My knees bounced faster. Of all the things I could have opened with . . . And why did he look so confused? "You're Hallie's boss, right?"

"The Marketing Director."

"Not the billionaire?"

"No."

I relaxed the tiniest bit. "That makes way more sense. That other guy wouldn't be picking up random people from the airport. What's that guy's name again? Lincoln? Lawrence? Wait, if you're her boss, how did she rope you into this?"

He turned his gaze back to the road. "I owed her a favor."

"Must have been a big one."

"You have no idea."

My fingers twisted together in my lap. "Where is my sister, by the way? I thought she'd be the one to pick me up. It's been"—I gulped—"a while since I've seen her. Not that you're not great company. You're great. You're perfect. Who'd complain about being picked up from the airport by a handsome guy in a sparkly new Tesla? Not that I'm judging you by your car, but you have to admit, it's pretty nice. You knew that already, of course, it's your car. And these seats are amazingly comfortable. But where is she? Tonight? Like, right now?"

He took a long inhale, then blew it out slowly. “She’s working.”

“Ah. Does she work a lot?”

“Yes.”

“And she does marketing? With you?” The more information I could glean from him, the less out-of-the-loop I’d look when he brought me to Hallie. “What’s your name, by the way?” My knees were doubly bouncing now, completely out of sync as I twisted my ring around and around my knuckle. “And what’s the name of the big boss, the guy I mistook you for?”

He exhaled a loud gush of air. “Do you say everything that pops into your mind?”

Was it that obvious? The Green Fizz boost hit my veins right then, my hands prickling, energy settling, my mouth and my thoughts finally syncing into the same pace. My entire body calmed. “Only when I’m anxious. Can you tell me when I’ll be seeing Hallie? Please? Or where you’re taking me? I don’t exactly have a car, but I’ll need to get to the opening banquet tonight.”

He pulled off the freeway into downtown Seattle, the Space Needle towering in the distance. Somehow, in the recesses of my brain, the knowledge emerged that the billionaire powerplant guy had bought the entire complex surrounding the Space Needle and rebuilt it into his clean energy empire. But for the life of me, I couldn’t recall how I knew it.

“I’m taking you to your hotel,” he said, “then I’ll pick you up in time for the banquet. Hallie asked me to keep an eye on you while you’re in town.”

“Oh . . .” I slumped back into my chair. So, this was it, then? She did me a favor by getting Jared the keynote spot, but that was as far as she’d go? I suppose I shouldn’t have expected more from her. Not after disappearing for so many years. But still, I’d hoped she’d at least see me once. Give me a chance to beg for forgiveness.

“Can you tell me why she’s not keeping an eye on me herself?”

His gaze leveled at me for a long moment before he faced back toward the road. "She won't see you until you get *my* stamp of approval. Something about skipping town when she was a kid."

My lungs deflated, and I crossed my arms, squeezing my ribs. She officially hated me. I couldn't blame her, but how would I change her mind if she refused to see me in the first place?

"I don't need a babysitter," I said. I pulled out my phone and called Hallie for the second time in an hour. It went straight to voicemail.

"I promised Hallie that I'll babysit you until you've impressed me, or until you're back on a plane to St. Louis."

Ugh. I had to spend my entire trip with this guy, to earn the right to talk to my sister? Who put him in charge of my life? Oh right, Hallie did . . . And he looked as excited about it as I felt.

"Also," the driver grumbled, "we don't seriously have to go to tonight's banquet, right?"

"Not *we.* Me. And yes, my entire future hinges on it." I slipped the Polaroid out of my jacket pocket, Jared's face smiling back at me. "You didn't tell me your name."

He did a double take when he saw the photo in my hands.

"Watch the road!" I screamed.

He swerved, his tires screeching as he yanked at the steering wheel, both of us careening to the right as he veered back into our lane.

"You almost hit that guy!"

He gripped the wheel, glowering straight forward like he couldn't wait to be rid of me. "Caspien," he hissed. "I'm Caspien Martell."

We both breathed heavily until he turned onto a side road with less pedestrians.

"Is that you in that picture?" Caspien asked, eyeing my photo.

"Sure is." My heart throbbed looking at it.

Jared wore a yellow tank top that accented his rippling arms, and blue leggings that matched his glorious 1980s sweatband. His costume didn't hold a candle to mine, though. From bottom to top: yellow tights, baby-blue leg warmers, a neon-green leotard, green sweatbands around my wrists, and my crowning glory was the turquoise, pre-pixie-cut hair that puffed around my shoulders with the perm I'd gotten for the occasion. The invitation had said *80s throwback themed* and we'd delivered.

"Are those crowns on your head?" Caspien asked.

"Definitely. We won the Fit-And-Fab Award that night, like being crowned Homecoming Royalty in the fitness world. We had no idea we were famous yet. Well, Jared was famous. I kicked ass behind the camera."

"He's your . . . husband?"

"No, my business partner. But after this convention . . ." It was a loaded sentence, but how to end it? *Things might change!* Or *He'll finally notice me!* Or *He'll see how much I'm worth!*

Instead, I blurted, "He's married."

I slapped my hand over my mouth.

"What?" Caspien swerved to the side of the narrow street and stopped in the shadow of an ultra-modern, gray tower. "You're chasing a married man?" He swiped the Polaroid from my hand. "Hang on, I recognize him. Isn't he that fitness guy who went viral on Instagram last year? He cheated on his wife, on camera, with Fearless Felicity?"

"Off camera," I snapped. "And he's divorced."

"Are you sure? I saw him on a morning talk show with his wife."

Why did people believe everything on TV? This was exactly why I was here, to set the record straight.

"Only because they're trying to play nice for the cameras. They filed for divorce months ago, they're just waiting for the official documents before they announce it to the world. It's not a secret, rumors are spreading, but they're waiting for it to be official before they discuss it publicly."

Caspien peered at me. "So, you're saying he *didn't* cheat on camera with Fearless Felicity?"

"No, he didn't." I yanked back my photo. "He kissed her off camera, one time. And his marriage had already fallen apart. And for the record,

Fearless Felicity didn't know he was married. And she never kissed him again. In fact, she's now engaged to my friend Marco."

"Hang on, you know Fearless Felicity?"

"Of course. We became friends after all that drama."

"Didn't she totally disappear?"

"Sure, but only because she's hard at work for JD Fitness. She's waiting for the perfect time to get back into the spotlight. And that's not the point—Jared's the point. He's nothing like what the media says. Their marriage was already dead. He made the mistake of kissing a few girls before their split was officially announced, but that's in the past, and he's not proud of it."

Caspien twisted the knob on the heater and his own small photograph of a woman fluttered from his dash. He plucked it up quickly and shoved it inside the center console. "You say that like it's no big deal."

"Of course it's a big deal—*was* a big deal—but they've been separated for months now."

"And you're here to fix his reputation? Why isn't he doing that?"

"Gah!" I pushed the photo back in his face. "He is! But he won't be here until tomorrow, so I'm going to the banquet tonight in his place. Getting a head start."

"But you two never dated?"

The question froze me in my chair, but only for a second. "We sort of did, but it wasn't the right time. Lily was exactly the wife he needed back then—her dad had deep pockets. But their marriage always sucked. They shared no common interests, she only wanted his money, and he wanted to spend all his time in the gym. By the end of their first year, they hardly spoke."

"And you fell in love with him?"

"Oh, Cass—can I call you Cass? I fell in love with him long before Lily came around. Jared and I have been a seamless duo forever."

Caspien glanced at me, brown eyes turned down at the edges. "But he still married another woman?"

"You say it like he had a choice! Parental expectations are a big deal, especially when you're still a kid." I leaned in, lowering my voice. "Besides, we were desperate for an investor. But now that JD Fitness has grown, a marriage for money no longer matters."

Caspien stared at me like I'd grown an antenna and six eyes.

"What?"

"You're claiming Jared doesn't deserve his reputation as a womanizer, but you're also trying to convince him to leave his wife for you?"

"That's horrible! Since the day they married, I've never once hinted about an affair. But now that they've split up on their own . . ."

"Yes?" Caspien urged.

I sat taller and lifted my chin. "Maybe when his head clears and he's ready to settle down again, he'll realize who's always been here for him."

"You?"

"Obviously." I groaned at the ceiling as I said it, hiding from the way Caspien's gaze bored into me. "He's a good person."

He snorted. "You're lying. You didn't look at me when you said it."

I glared into his eyes and growled, "I trust him, *completely.* And once I explain this to everyone at the banquet tonight, they'll trust him too, and I'll spend the rest of the weekend signing deals and rescuing our careers."

He shook his head. "You're naïve."

With a sharp gasp, I faced forward in my seat. Caspien was wrong. Completely wrong. Wasn't he? I paused for a moment too long. No, he knew nothing about Jared, about us. Who was he to make any sort of judgment about people he'd never met? "You sound like one of those grumpy loners who got your heart broken by some girlfriend, and now you don't trust anyone. Am I right?"

"Pretty much," he said. "Better than being the *other woman* to a man known for having affairs. I'd rather trust no one than trust him."

"Will you just take me to my hotel?"

Caspien pointed one finger to the gray building above us. “Front lobby’s that way. Banquet’s in three hours, I’ll pick you up out here.”

I almost demanded to go alone but clenched my teeth at the last second. As much as Caspien made my skin crawl, my desire to see Hallie was stronger. But that didn’t mean I had to cling to his side at the banquet. I needed to devote every second of my time to mingling, chatting, and charming every vendor at the convention. But how could I do that with the grumpiest man on the planet following me around? I’d have to ditch him at the first possible second.

“You’re the worst,” I muttered.

“Call me whatever you want,” Caspien said. “But if you have any hope of reuniting with Hallie, you’ll be ready to go at seven o’clock.”

My fingers wound into fists. “Just tell Hallie you followed me around. Tell her we became instant best friends. She’ll never know.”

“Oh, she’ll know. And I won’t lie, especially not to Hallie.”

I paused. “Why? Are you two dating?” I’d missed so much of her life. What if she was married? Did she have kids?

“Definitely not.”

Good. Anyone would be better than him. I pushed open the door and stepped out into the rain. “Of course you’re not. You’d have to trust her to date her, and you don’t trust anyone.” But if I didn’t convince him to trust me, I’d never get to apologize to Hallie. I slammed the door as hard as I could. At the exact same second, he popped open the trunk, from inside the car, without getting out to help.

Whatever. I didn’t need him to carry my suitcase. I hefted it onto the wet sidewalk, then dashed into the hotel lobby as Caspien sped off toward downtown.

I didn’t look back once.

I suspect he didn’t either.

Chapter 5

$390.93 remaining

The second I entered the hotel lobby, Caspien vanished from my brain. Bailey had outdone herself with this one.

Thank you, company reward points.

The lobby? Full of velvet sofas. To my right, a bartender in a stiff black suit served martinis to an elegant couple on high-backed stools. A glittering chandelier with thousands of sparkling crystals hung three stories above. And beneath my feet lay a lush green and purple carpet. Carpet! In a hotel lobby, in the rainiest place in the world.

Before I had the chance to approach the counter to my left, a bellhop in a red jacket with gold tassels took my suitcase and led me to a waiting receptionist.

"Do you have a reservation, Miss?" the woman asked. Her red lipstick matched her hair that draped dramatically behind her shoulders.

"I think so. For Lauren Cross?"

The lobby smelled like roses, the scent wafting from the vases of red flowers on every available countertop. Where had they found so many this early in spring? Bailey must have used every last reward point to book a room here. My stomach twisted. Or perhaps it growled. Fifty-fifty chance I was guilty or hungry. Maybe both. When did I eat last?

"Found you," the receptionist said, her voice as sweet as the roses, "and there's a package here for you." She handed me a brown package the size of my purse with a department store logo stamped on the side.

The bellhop led the way up the mirrored elevator to the second floor. He opened my door, handed me my keycard, then whisked away before I had a chance to tip him. Good thing, because I couldn't spare the cash.

The room was significantly more average than the lobby. A queen bed in the corner, a small sofa that likely pulled out into a second bed, and a tiny desk along the far wall. Normal. Not at all pretentious. It smelled faintly of lemon-fresh cleaner, and the faucet in the small bathroom dripped a steady rhythm into the porcelain sink.

I dropped my suitcase one foot inside the door and opened the mysterious box. Inside, I found a vacuum-sealed bag of bright clothing and a square, typed message.

I heard the banquet's theme is Throwback. Knock their socks off! Wish I was with you!

-Jared

I ripped open the bag and out tumbled yellow tights, blue leg warmers, and a green leotard. *No way.* I held out my Polaroid to compare. The colors didn't perfectly match, but they were close. I'd be a spitting image of the first time we did this.

Plus, he'd gone out of his way to research tonight's banquet and buy me this outfit. Giggles bubbled from my stomach, and I crushed the clothes against my chest. Jared sent *me* a gift! How could I not wear them?

The clock said 4:15 in the afternoon. The party would start at 7:00. That gave me a little under three hours to transform myself into a blast from the past that would blow everyone's minds. I could do it—but where to begin? So much depended on tonight, on the next twenty-four hours.

On the next five hours.

To make this work, to *really* make this work, I had to be all-in. No holding back, no going halfway.

A small convenience store sat across the street from the hotel, and I sprinted through the cold rain. Getting wet didn't matter, I wouldn't be wearing these clothes much longer. A bell jingled as I pushed through the door into a quiet bodega with only six rows of snack foods and grocery essentials. A hint of cigarette smoke laced the air, and shelves of pet food lined one wall, an assortment of wine covering the back. With a quick glance at my watch, I scanned the meager cosmetics rack until I found what I needed—twenty-or-so boxes of hair dye. Five were shades of blond and brown, while the rest were fabulously bright shades of metallic pink, blue, and green.

"Thank you, Seattle," I whispered, swiping the brightest turquoise box of temporary dye. "Time to go all-in."

The cashier looked barely twenty-one, with dual-toned hair—half orange, half red—and tattoos lacing down one arm. She sat behind a tall desk with a large fish tank on one side. A silver angelfish with violet stripes swam near the top.

"You look just like Francine." A sliver of homesickness tingled through me. "She likes Ocean Feast the best."

"Who?" the cashier asked.

"The angelfish. I have her twin at home. Ocean Feast fish food is more expensive, but she'll love you for it."

The girl smacked her gum and held out a hand as I forked over twenty painful dollars for the dye, three for a blank notebook, and four more for a case of water bottles. Then I lugged it all back to my hotel room and went straight to work. Towel around my neck, dye in my hair, I let it sit while I furiously scribbled down plans for tonight's banquet. Then I rinsed my hair out, admired its new color (gloriously turquoise!), blew it dry, then hair-sprayed it straight up.

Yes.

Yes, yes, yes!

Just like the photograph. Jared would be so proud.

Next, I set a phone alarm for 6:30 p.m.—so I wouldn't forget to get dressed in time—ripped out a dozen pages from my new notebook, then wrote a word on top of each in bold permanent marker.

Vendors.

Gym rats.

That billionaire guy.

I needed to schmooze all three, which meant knowing how to impress them all.

Fortunately, research was what I did best.

The rest of the world faded away as I opened up my phone and searched for hashtags related to the convention, then skimmed the feeds of anyone who might show up. Each time someone posted something relevant, I wrote their name on my list. Once I'd gathered a long group of names, I started digging. I searched their feeds on Instagram, TikTok, and Facebook. I scoured their YouTube channels, personal blogs, and any other site they posted updates to. I watched videos, noted their favorite colors, family members, and whether they had any pets. And most importantly, whether they preferred to partner up with men or women, influencers or products. Then I made a special mark next to anyone Jared had worked with in the past. If they'd taken a chance on him before, they'd be more likely to do it again.

The only answer I didn't have was how to charm the owner of the power company—the internet said his name was Lucas Croft—but Jared would help me with that one.

Goosebumps raised on my arms as my plan came together on paper. What mattered most was spending tonight chatting about Jared with every person who'd give me the time of day. I rehearsed my PR speech again and again until I could recite it without trying. Hundreds of people would be at this banquet, maybe thousands. Every one of them needed to leave the party convinced that the media was wrong about Jared. He'd made one teensy mistake, and they'd branded him with a scarlet letter. But he was different now, a solid business partner for their future advertisements.

As long as Michael Kay wasn't here, I could do it.

Michael Kay . . .

The sword-slashing, cape-wearing French idiot who constantly bashed Jared in his exercise videos. Well, not actually French. He only pretended to be for his online persona. Women loved a man with an accent. Unfortunately, he'd managed to raise his YouTube ratings up to neck-and-neck with ours. Despite being a moron with a cheesy costume, he and his clichéd, celebrity-themed fitness shows drew hundreds of thousands of viewers, every one of whom knew exactly how much he hated Jared—which was almost as much as we hated him.

If he stayed away, I could turn Jared's ship around.

Fortunately, his social media said nothing about being in Seattle right now.

My 6:30 alarm beeped, but I snoozed it for ten minutes. I had one more thing to do: I typed *Caspien Martell* into my search bar and scanned the results. There wasn't much. His only social media account was a Facebook page, but he'd never posted. And while he was tagged in a few friends' feeds, the posts were more than five years old. His only recent mentions were in Croft Power press releases, which told me nothing about his past or his interests.

I set my phone down and frowned. There had to be more about him out there, and if anyone could find it, I could. But my alarm beeped again, telling me to get dressed for the banquet. Researching Caspien would have to wait. It was time to turn into Jane Fonda.

Piece by piece, I put on the gear Jared had sent. The tights were too big, but the leg warmers covered them. The leotard was too small, but so was my body. No big deal. With a splash of blue eyeshadow and bright-pink lipstick, I'd transformed into a whole new person. Tonight, I'd glow like a pastel sun, dazzling everyone exactly like we had at that first conference. Thank you to the fitness gods for the banquet's *throwback* theme!

Unfortunately, it wasn't a warm costume, so I dug through my suitcase for my formal, knee-length black jacket and tied it snugly around my body. No reason to endure the cold until I arrived at the party.

My phone rang, a shrill chime chosen specifically because sometimes only the most obnoxious noises could pull me out of a focused research session.

Jared's name popped up on the screen. My heart triple-jumped, a tingle racing down both arms and swirling through my stomach. After fifteen years together, my reaction to him never changed.

"Hello?" I said breathlessly.

"It's me!" Jared's voice boomed, and I grinned like a junior high kid getting a call from her crush.

"Hey, you! How was your last day of filming?"

"More importantly, how's your trip? How's the convention? Are you surviving?"

I bit my lower lip, my cheeks warming that he'd thought to ask. Thank goodness he couldn't see me. "I'm in my hotel room getting ready to head over. These clothes you sent? They're amazing!"

"*Throwback* is my favorite theme."

"Mine too." My heart thrummed. "Wish you were coming with me."

Jared drew quiet, silent, the seconds dragging on. "I wish I was there too. You and I are always stronger together."

I closed my eyes, letting his words sweep through me. "Do you remember our first ever convention? That banquet?"

Jared let out a booming laugh. "We were brilliant! We tiptoed in there like newbies, no clue that our YouTube videos had whipped the fitness world into a frenzy. We left like royalty."

"I still have the picture, crowns on our heads and everything."

"Man, those were the days," Jared mused. "Do you think we'll ever get them back?"

He had no idea how much I'd already planned for this week, the deals I'd land for him before he arrived tomorrow. "Absolutely. This convention will change everything, you'll see."

"You think so?" Jared's voice sounded brighter. "Because no matter how hard I try, the press keeps hammering my reputation. Everyone thinks I'm a cheating scumbag. We need this week to go well. I need it. I need *you.*"

"I'm positive." I sat crisscross on the hotel bed, the purple comforter silky smooth beneath me. "This costume is going to dazzle the crowd. The only thing missing is you."

"Tomorrow," he said. "We'll be together again tomorrow."

With a heavy breath, I lay back on the bed, the pillows enveloping me. "How are things with Lily?" I asked softly. "How's the divorce settlement?"

Jared answered quietly too. "Not great. No matter how much mediation we sit through, we still can't agree. I think the judge will have to divide our assets for us."

"You hanging in there?"

"It's weird. We smile and hold hands to make the press like us, but deep down, we both just want this to be over."

They'd stuck it out for so long, it was hard to watch their marriage finally crash in such a public way—even considering my own feelings for Jared. But at least soon he'd get to escape the drama for a couple of days. "I can't wait until you're here."

Jared perked up immediately. "It'll be like the old days. We'll be king and queen again. I owe you everything, Lauren. You know that, right?"

"What? You owe me nothing." But heat still rushed into my face.

"Of course I do. You're out there saving both our careers—and I always pay my debts." His voice lowered, focused and professional. "You've written a marketing plan, right?"

I stared at my lists of notes scattered across my hotel room floor. "You know me, I've been researching all afternoon."

"Wish I was there to help. Will you have it organized before you go out in public? So you don't accidently fly off script?"

He knew me so well. "Don't worry, it's coming together."

"Never once have I doubted you," he said. "Just remember when you're feeling overwhelmed, shove it down, quiet the voices. You've got this. And tomorrow we'll be together again, like we always should have been."

His words settled over my body like tiny flakes of snow, melting into my skin. Together again. *Always should have been.* We should have been together from the start.

Then a deep, familiar voice vibrated through my door from the hallway outside.

"Aw, hell," I grumbled, "he's early."

"Who is?"

"My babysitter. Hallie stuck me with some guy until I convince him I'm not going to run off on her again."

Caspien's voice rumbled louder.

"Wait, you haven't seen Hallie, yet?" Jared asked.

"It's a long story. But sorry, I've got to go."

"At least send me a picture of your costume, so I can live vicariously through you."

I grinned down at the leotard poking through the top of my jacket. "Absolutely." Then I hung up and tiptoed to the door, pressing my ear against it as Caspien spoke. His voice wafted back and forth, like he was pacing the hall while he spoke on the phone.

"But do I have to attend the entire banquet?" he said.

Silence as he listened to the voice in his phone.

"So far? She spouts off whatever's on her mind, even if it shouldn't be said out loud. She's weird, Hallie. I don't know how you two came from the same parents."

Ugh. He could have told Hallie that everything between us was splendid and ended this whole mess hours ago. I opened my door and leaned against the frame, glaring at Caspien's back. The next time he spun my direction, he jumped, dropping his cell with a thump.

"Give me the phone," I said, holding out my hand. "I want to talk to her."

But he scooped it off the ground, hit *end*, and stalked straight past me into my room. "She doesn't want to."

"So what? Why don't I get an opinion? She's *my* sister."

He sank onto my couch, making himself comfortable, so I stopped right next to him, grabbed the hard back of the sofa, and pulled it away from the wall with all my strength. With a groan, the couch heaved forward and launched Caspien onto the floor in a heap of cushions and pillows.

"What the hell was that for?" he growled.

The sofa fell back into place with a thud. "Don't act all high and mighty and then think you're welcome on my couch," I growled back.

Only when he climbed up to standing, cursing under his breath, did I soak in his appearance. He wore a black pinstripe suit and matching vest and pants, accessorized with a pocket watch, a top hat encircled with a gray ribbon, and shoes as shiny as water. He'd jumped straight out of the 1920s, though his scowl was more gangster than flapper.

"Interesting hair," was all he said. Then he replaced one of the cushions on the couch, slumped back down, and clicked on my TV.

Seriously?

If he could ignore me, then I could ignore him too—though a flurry of curse words blew wildly through my head.

Shove it down, quiet the voices.

Thank you, Jared, for that excellent advice.

I dug through my case of toiletries, then twisted the cap off a water bottle and dumped in a packet of Neon Nutrition—another of our brilliant supplements. This one was a full meal in powdered form, shockingly healthy and filling. But as soon as I took one swig, my gag reflex kicked in and my stomach flipped over. Yup, too many nerves for my body to handle food. This happened when I was nervous. Or anxious. Or upset. So,

I tossed the bottle in the trash and plopped down on the floor in front of my papers, between the TV and Caspien's feet. I'd done my best to predict who would be there tonight, I just needed to transfer my notes into my phone. Then I could sort them by who was most likely to partner with Jared.

The twins were my first choice. Sheila and Sherry were the first fitness-industry friends we'd ever made, and the four of us had weathered some horribly rough times together. A couple decades older, they'd mentored us when we desperately needed them. Surely, they would still be on our side. I created a tab in my phone's notepad with their names, then wrote *whiskey* on the top line. Sheila could never turn down quality alcohol.

In the next tab I typed *Jenson Haskin: text him, no chatting.* He wasn't sociable in-person—kind of like the grump sprawled out on my couch—but he liked making deals via text message. In fact, I would text him as soon as I finished these notes.

Next came Doug, Bailey's old boss at the Lucky 13 Gym. When she left and his gym went belly up, he invented a fancy blender and marketed it to the fitness community. He and Jared went way back. Every few years they'd partner up again for promos, and they were overdue. He always came to these things. I'd have to save enough cash to buy a blender from his booth, butter him up so he'd work with us again.

Right as I transferred the last of the information into my phone, my alarm went off, alerting me it was time to leave.

"Ready?" I asked, swiping the remote from Caspien and flicking off the TV.

His gaze dropped to my shoes. "You're wearing sneakers?"

"It's all part of the plan."

Caspien opened his mouth to speak but closed it again. Then he shrugged, put his hat back on his head, and rose from the couch in one fluid motion.

My phone beeped with a text from Jared.

Jared: *Good luck tonight. I'm so lucky to have you in my corner!*

My excitement increased at the same rate as my anxiety. We'd failed at everything the last six months, but tonight Jared needed me to succeed. He was relying on me. I would *not* let him down. Where was my purse? My sweatband? My notes? No, not my notes. Why would I walk around a banquet with a stack of loose papers? Those were in my phone. I swiped two new powder packets of Green Fizz from the giant stack in my suitcase—make that three. Oh! And Jared had requested a picture.

"A selfie?" I said to Caspien.

He refused to play along, so I scooted right up next to him. He held stock still while I took a picture of us, he in his flapper suit, and me with my long black coat tied tightly around my body. I'd remove it at the banquet, surprise everyone. But even with the coat covering my costume, I grinned with the confidence of a superstar fitness queen—not that I ever went to the gym. Chasing Jared around the country the last fifteen years burned plenty of calories. But this picture perfectly captured Caspien's annoyance and my excitement, so I texted it to Jared with the caption *Bringing back our glory days!* Then I waited anxiously for his response.

My phone beeped seconds later.

Jared: *Who's that guy again?*

Lauren: *The babysitter.* Caspien was reading over my shoulder. *Ugh.*

Jared: *Don't have too much fun without me.*

Lauren: *I promise I won't.*

"That's the fitness guy?" Caspien asked, leaning against the door while I grabbed the final things I needed. My phone, for sure. And Xanax—couldn't forget my Xanax. My nerves had me bouncing between my feet, anxious to get going, a little dizzy each time I changed directions, searching through my increasingly chaotic hotel room.

"His name is Jared." I threw my phone into my purse then dumped it out and filled a different one. Smaller, less in the way.

"I know his name; I just didn't think he deserved to be called by it."

"He's not what you think."

"Yes, he is."

Spinning full circle, I stalked straight up to Caspien and pointed a shaking finger at his nose. "You're as bad as the rest of them, listening to the trashy media that rakes his name through the mud. He made *one* mistake. Can you honestly say you've never made a mistake? Never done something you wished you could take back?"

Caspien raised both hands. "Okay, okay, I see your point. While I still wouldn't trust him as far as I could throw him, you seem to genuinely believe what you're saying. Don't worry, I'll stay out of your way tonight."

I paused. "Does that mean you won't follow me around after all?"

"Hallie's instructions were very specific—I can't leave your side." His mouth twitched. "I'm to observe you in your natural habitat. Discover your secrets and report back."

This could not get any worse.

"Do you have a plan?" he asked.

"For helping Jared? Yeah. Talk to every single person at the convention and vouch for his character until they give us another chance."

Caspien's almost-smile dropped. "You're talking to *everyone?*"

"All of them." I inched closer. "In fact, Hallie tasked you with getting to know me, right? You may as well help me."

Caspien paused, one hand on the door, the other on his goatee.

"Help me meet everyone. Chat, mingle, get some autographs from the fitness celebrities, then convince them to work with Jared. You're the marketing director, right? Market the hell out of him! You'll get to know me and Jared, I'll salvage my job *and* get to see Hallie sooner, and before you know it, you'll be rid of me."

Caspien studied my face, his eyes narrow, piercing, searing into my skin. Then he set his jaw like he was gearing up for a long night of misery. "No." He swung the door open and marched out into the hall. "I'm your babysitter," he called over his shoulder. "Nothing more."

I followed him out with a scowl. "Asshole."

Chapter 6

$390.93
-$3.75 case of water
-$3.00 blank notebook
-$19.45 turquoise hair dye
$364.73 remaining

True to his word, Caspien did nothing helpful the entire drive. He didn't speak at all, not once, all the way to the Croft Power business complex.

After Caspien parked the car in an enormous underground lot (thank goodness for no rain!), I gathered my purse, then followed him into an oversized lobby with tile floors. Endless hallways branched off in both directions, and the ceiling opened up three-stories high. Music vibrated through the ten-foot double doors in front of us.

The party was already booming? That couldn't be right; it was barely past 7:00.

Without a word, Caspien pulled open the doors and I stepped into the banquet hall.

No. No, no, no.

Every single person was clad head-to-toe in 1920s flapper gear. Top hats, tassels, and short dresses lined with rows and rows of beads. Canes, heels, black tights.

This wasn't happening. I couldn't breathe.

What happened to *throwback?*

I hurried back out into the lobby, closing the door tightly to separate myself from the party. Then I wrapped my coat as tightly around my body as the belt would go, knotting it under my arm. It only covered to my knees, though. Nothing would hide my legwarmers or bright white sneakers. Or turquoise hair.

"Everything okay?" Caspien asked, following me out.

Jared had sent the costume, and I'd trusted he'd done his research. I'd never checked the website. Now as I pulled it up on my phone, it did say *throwback . . . to the 1920s.*

Shit. Shit. Shit.

How to fix this? Maybe the shop with the angelfish sold costumes? No, it had barely counted as a convenience store. They didn't offer more than basic snack foods. Maybe I could borrow Caspien's hat, bury my mistake? No, that wouldn't conceal the legwarmers and tights, and I'd overheat in thirty seconds. Plus, I refused to give him the satisfaction of asking for his help.

Shit.

What would Jared do if he were here, and we'd worn costumes from the wrong decade? He'd march into that party like he'd done it on purpose, like he was *above* their 1920s tassels and top hats. He'd stride in there with so much confidence the rest of the room would wish they'd dressed like him, instead of the other way around.

It was brilliant. *Brilliant.*

"Everything okay?" Caspien asked again.

I flexed my fingers before I untied my coat and slid it off my shoulders. "Never better." Caspien's eyes widened, his gaze sweeping over my pastel leotard. But my smile grew, and I pulled open the giant double doors.

Then we stepped inside the ballroom.

The closest dozen people on the dance floor paused their movements to stare at my outfit. Blue and yellow, tights and leotard, turquoise hair encircled by a sweatband. I stood taller, hands on my hips.

But as they absorbed my outlandish outfit, my brain absorbed a hundred other details. Michael Kay—Jared's nemesis—lorded over the exhibition hall from the stage at the far side of the ballroom. He was *here?* He'd mentioned nothing about this conference on any of his social media accounts. Yet, there he stood, in a pin-striped suit and bowler hat, with his classic sword tucked into his belt. And between us, a thousand people gyrated to music pumping from loudspeakers.

No. Not speakers. A live band.

Guitars and a bass and someone on a saxophone filled the stage to Michael Kay's left, singing "House of Memories" as the crowd moved in rhythm with the drums. It was a *Panic! At the Disco* cover band.

Wait, was that the *real* Brendon Urie? The lead singer in the flesh?

But that wasn't all.

An invisible line split the crowd down the middle, dividing the room into two. Only, instead of a boy/girl divide like at a high school dance, gym rats and influencers filled one side, partying like wild animals unleashed from their cages, while vendors cowered in the other, timidly watching the party unfold.

What the vendors didn't know was that most of these celebratory vibes were artificial. Michael Kay was here, which meant he'd supplied just enough drugs to get the party started. It tinged the way the gym rats moved, too loosely, unnaturally cheerful, too unabashed for only 7:30 in the evening. It was difficult to pinpoint the source—unless you *knew,* of course. It all came from Michael Kay. At every banquet he attended, the lights sparkled a little brighter, the wine tasted a little richer, the liquor a little harder, like seeing the room through the lens of a disco ball. And though no one would ever witness it with their own eyes, somewhere, somehow, he would be slipping white powder to anyone with a zipped mouth and deep enough pockets.

I hated him.

Until a few years ago, he'd supplied drugs to Jared too—he gave Jared a black eye when he went clean. But the final straw came when Jared beat him in a bodybuilding competition a few years ago. Ever since, Michael Kay made it his personal mission to ruin our careers. He smeared Jared's name, bad-mouthed our show, and stole vendor deals out from under us. Everyone knew he had *scumbag* etched into his soul, but no one could deny that his shows were wildly popular. And he supplied the drugs at parties.

Not that every gym rat here was stoned, of course. Only his closest friends—the rest were clueless. Like that young, barely twenty-something couple hanging around the edges of the dance floor, weaving through the crowd with phones in their hands and stars in their eyes. They were streaming the entire party on Instagram like they'd never imagined life could be so glamorous. I'd researched them back in my hotel room. Kindy Young and Cameron Pratt, adorable, young Instagrammers on the rise with four new puppies and twenty million followers between them. Those two would never catch a glimpse of anything illicit, but when you knew it was there, hidden in pockets, slipped into sleeves, you couldn't miss it.

"This is . . . different," Caspien shouted over the music.

Which detail was he referring to? The costumes? The live band? The fact that the party was in full swing when it wasn't yet dark outside? With Michael Kay in the room, they'd keep going for hours. Croft Power hosted a different convention every month, right? Perhaps their previous opening banquets hadn't had quite this much . . . energy.

"Marco would love this," I said, pointing to a row of canes lined up along the wall.

"Who's Marco?" Caspien asked.

"Fearless Felicity's fiancé." We moved farther into the room, and I pretended no one was gaping at my pastel outfit. "He has a thing for canes. He wouldn't like the cocaine though."

Caspien stopped. Froze completely. Not one muscle moved except a twitch in his cheek. "Cocaine?"

"Nobody has this much energy without Michael Kay around."

"Wait, who?"

But Michael Kay had disappeared from the stage. Before I could relocate him, the two most beautiful faces I'd ever seen bee-lined straight toward me.

Sheila and Sherry, the twins, our mentors. The tension in my shoulders finally ebbed, like the water at the highest tide had suddenly drained after one quick pull from the moon. If anyone could help me conquer this weekend, it would be these two. Sheila reached me first, enfolding me into a hug so tight my body melted into hers.

"I'm glad you're here," I said.

The twins had launched their careers only a few years before us, though they were in their sixties now. At first, they rose through the ranks as Jared's competitors, but after a late night of bonding at a convention similar to this one, we'd become close friends. Sheila had taught Jared to navigate the bodybuilding circuit, and Sherry had introduced me into hundreds—if not thousands—of lucrative partnerships.

They'd barely changed, despite the time that had passed. Thanks to years of steroid use, their voices had deepened, their shoulders broadened, and their overdeveloped jaw muscles had etched their chins into squares. But their wide smiles were exactly as I remembered. Tonight, their foreheads were both accented by 1920s circlets. Sheila wore a burgundy cocktail dress with rows of dangling black beads, and Sherry wore the opposite, black fabric trimmed with burgundy. She hugged me the second Sheila let me go.

"I hoped you two would come," I said. "I texted, but you didn't respond."

Sherry, the organized one in their duo, pulled her phone from a slender black bag and skimmed through her messages. "Are you sure? I don't see one."

I searched through my phone too. "Maybe I didn't. But I meant to." Then I reached back into my purse, turning to Sheila. "And I brought your favorite whiskey from St. Louis." My hand came out empty and I glared at the ceiling. "It's in my hotel room. I wrote a reminder to bring it and everything."

"Same old Lauren," Sherry said, and she squeezed me from the side. "Now tell us about your outfit. What's your angle?"

"My angle is, I didn't bother to read the website," I said without thinking.

Caspien watched me with one brow raised, like he'd expected me to brandish a stellar excuse. If Jared were here, he would have had an instant explanation, a perfect reason, like it was all intentional, part of a bigger scheme to win back the hearts of the fitness crowd.

"Well," Sheila said, "you look as perfect tonight as you did the first time you wore this. You've barely aged a day." She kept eyeing Caspien, but when I didn't introduce him, she didn't ask.

The band stopped playing as the ballroom lights brightened, and a tall, dark-haired man in a crisp '20s suit tapped the microphone. A lavish European woman clung to his arm. Her hair hung perfectly to her waistline, and she wore four-inch, ruby-red heels that matched her red beaded gown with a slit to her hip.

"She's stunning," Sherry said as the crowd drew quiet, but I couldn't pull my gaze from the man. The arch of his nose and his narrow cheekbones—how did I know that face?

"Who is he?" I asked.

Caspien answered first. "Lucas Croft. He owns Croft Power Company."

Ah. The billionaire head honcho who owned this entire city block. "Why's he so familiar?"

"He was on the cover of *Forbes* last month and a dozen other magazines. Or you've seen him on the news. He's totally changed the clean energy industry."

"That must be it." But an itch in the back of my mind said it wasn't.

"Hello, everyone," Lucas said into the microphone, clearing his throat and pulling at his tie. "A couple of things, and I'll let you get back to your party." He shook his girlfriend off his arm and ran his fingers through his short, straight hair, which fell lazily to one side. "First of all, thanks for coming. I'm Lucas, the host of this convention. We've been doing these for a handful of months now, and I won't lie, I've never seen one quite this wild."

A roar of cheers erupted, and Lucas laughed until they settled.

"Second, as a clean-energy provider, I'm a sucker for supporting other industries that make our world a better place. Two months ago, I hosted a convention for all the folks cleaning up our oceans." He pointed to the wall behind me, where three long, vinyl banners hung from the ceiling, ending above a narrow refreshment table. The first banner sported a picture of a dazzlingly clean beach, with Lucas Croft shaking hands with a woman in a maroon business suit.

"Last month," he continued, "our convention hosted the renewable paper and packaging industry." A giant pine tree covered the second banner on the wall, with Lucas posing beside a gray-haired man a solid two feet shorter than him. The man wore a plaid button-up and a puffy vest, and he displayed seed packets like a hand of playing cards. "That crowd had nowhere near your energy."

Someone whistled from the front of the ballroom and several others hollered.

"This month, I chose the fitness industry because taking care of our bodies is as important as taking care of our planet." Lucas pointed to the third banner, completely blank and ready for printing. "That one is reserved for one of you. At each of these conventions, I choose one company to star in a televised showcase, followed by a long-term publicity partnership. If you want that spot, I'll be here for a couple hours tonight. Find me, introduce yourself, and schedule a slot in my calendar for the next two days. You'll have a thirty-minute meeting to convince me to pick you."

"Are you pitching for Jared?" Sherry whispered.

"He'll be here tomorrow. We'll do it together. What about you?"

The twins shared a quiet glance but didn't answer my question.

"And finally," Lucas continued, "let's give it up for this incredible band, and to Michael Kay for flying them in to play for us tonight."

Amidst a rush of applause, the lights dimmed, the band started back up again, and a brand-new wave of energy rolled through the crowd. I, however, focused entirely on my mission.

"Who are the main contenders for Lucas's partnership?" I asked the twins.

"There are lots of hopefuls," Sheila said, "but only a couple of big fish. You've got Michael Kay, who's already making friends with the boss."

"Figures," I grumbled.

Sheila then pointed to the young couple, Kindy and Cameron, still streaming the party live to the world on their phones. "They have a good chance too. They remind me of you and Jared when you first started."

"What do you know about them?"

"Instagrammers. Dating, not married. They live next door to each other in side-by-side apartments."

"Next door? Not together?" I hadn't caught that in my research.

Sheila shrugged. "It's part of their brand. They live-stream everything, their workouts and their shopping trips and their vacations. They post their whole lives. Between them, they have twenty million followers." That part I *had* uncovered.

The kids were completely adorable. Kindy's flapper dress was turquoise with sleeves that just covered her shoulders, and her chin-length straight hair perfectly framed her petite nose and heart-shaped face.

Cameron had already ditched his suitcoat, rolling his sleeves up to his elbows. Both were short, Kindy almost as short as me, and when Sherry motioned them to join us, they came right away.

"You're Lauren!" Kindy squealed, her cheerfulness lighting up every inch of her tiny body. Her hair bounced as she held up her phone in front of us with one hand, carefully balancing her wine glass in the other. "Hey, Instagram world, you'll never believe who I found. This is Lauren Cross, the mastermind behind Jared DiMaggio himself!" She focused on me, silent, as if waiting.

"Oh, should I say something?"

"Of course! Millions of people are watching right now. Is Jared here too?"

Cameron cleared his throat, just off camera. Then he went so far as to stop his own live stream all together, before he reached over and clicked off Kindy's phone too.

"Hey!" she squeaked. "Why'd you do that?"

"You know Jared's not good for publicity." Cameron grimaced at me, eyes wide. "No offense, I don't mean to be rude. You seem super nice." But he spun back to his girlfriend, who'd folded her arms, all signs of cheer evaporating. "We talked about this, remember?"

"Cam, you can't turn off my stream like that."

"This was important. What you say affects us both."

"But two million viewers were watching. You can't just interfere!" Kindy's bottom lip quivered.

Cameron wrapped his arms around her while she cried on his shoulder. "You're right, you're right. I'm sorry."

But all I heard was *two million viewers.* If they'd stream me again, I could explain to two million people how the media had blown Jared's mistakes out of proportion. Cameron and Kindy just needed to get on board. But how to convince them?

"Listen, guys," I said, catching their attention. "The biggest reason I'm here is to clear up the rumors about Jared's personal life. He's nothing like people believe." Then I jumped into my practiced speech from the PR lady. "Jared and Lily DiMaggio appreciate the concern everyone has shown over their marriage. They are working closely with their attorney and their marriage counselor to make this drama a thing of the past, and Jared is excited to turn his attention back to his career and back to bringing high-quality exercise programs straight to his fans. He is especially grateful for everyone who has reached out to him with their encouragement and support, and he hopes that he'll get the chance to someday meet and thank each one of you in person."

"They're putting it behind them?" Cameron asked, rubbing his chin. A few more people joined our circle, listening closely.

"He'll be here tomorrow; you can ask him yourself."

"Okay, sure," Cameron said, nodding. "I grew up on his videos, I'd chat with him tomorrow. Give him another chance."

Kindy's smile returned. "Do you think he'd stream with me?"

My heart pounded as loud as the music. This was working. "Absolutely."

Then a thin man with a thick mustache slid into our circle holding up a small glass bottle of pills.

"You all look like you care about being strong," he said. "Have you heard about the new steroid?" He shook the pills and they rattled. "It's fresh off the boat from Russia, twice as strong as anything found in America, and completely untraceable in your blood. It's a pill, no syringes. This is the first batch ever smuggled into the country."

Kindy's eyes grew so wide it was as if he'd offered to assassinate her mother. "I would never put that garbage into my body."

His gaze dropped to the glass in her hand. "But you'll drink alcohol?"

"It's sparkling cider!" she gasped. "I'm not even twenty-one!"

Sheila slid her wide frame between the horrified Instagrammers and Mr. Mustache, glaring down at him like she'd grind him into meat for dinner. "Michael Kay will murder you, chop you into chunks, and leave the pieces in a ditch if he hears you're reselling the same steroids you bought off him half an hour ago. No one will find your remains."

Kindy shrieked, and Cameron pulled her close against his chest.

But the man with the mustache squinted one eye and scowled up at Sheila. "He'll never know if you don't tell him."

"Unlike you, I'm not stupid enough to double cross that guy."

Sherry leaned close to my ear. "Michael Kay's been selling those new steroids left and right since last night. Rumors about it have trickled out of Russia for months, but he's the first one to get his hands on it."

"Explains his oversized muscles," Sheila said, gesturing at Michael Kay as he circled the banquet hall like a vulture, stopping occasionally to whisper in someone's ear. "He begged us to buy some and try it out."

"I've read every speck of research about those pills," I said. "Not only does it have the usual steroid side effects like uncontrollable anger, but if you use it long-term, it breaks down the cells lining your organs and your joints. Sure, you'll gain loads of muscle at first, but it will literally kill you. Why do you think it wasn't approved in the US?"

Mustache Man huffed then flashed a packet of white powder. "Then are you interested in this instead?" It disappeared a second later.

"Are you kidding?" Kindy shrieked. "Get that out of here!"

But before he could respond, Michael Kay muscled into our circle. "Twins!" he boomed in his deep voice. Mustache Man vanished instantly. "I've been looking all over for you. I have an idea—"

But he froze, six feet of steroid-induced muscle rigid and tense as his attention zeroed in on me. Then the giant mouth on his tiny head split, ever so slowly, into the wickedest of grins. "Please tell me Jared had the nerve to come with you."

"Leave her alone, Mikey," Sheila said.

"Never." He leaned his head all the way back and let out a high-pitched laugh that bellowed above the music. Then he slung his beefy arm around my shoulder, the metal sword at his hip digging into my ribs. "Love the outfit. Let me guess. He's too scared to show his face in public, so he sent you in his place." Michael Kay's breath reeked of garlic and wine, his skin radiating heat like a halogen lamp.

"I thought he was French?" Kindy mumbled.

"He fakes it," Cameron replied. "Didn't you know? Viewers love a guy with an accent." My gaze stayed glued to Michael Kay's face, but I could hear the eyeroll in Cameron's voice.

"Jared is filming today." I spoke loudly, so our whole circle could hear, and squirmed out from under him. "He'll be here tomorrow."

A dozen other gazes followed my movements, a crowd gathering to watch.

"I can't wait." Michael pulled off his bowler hat and rubbed his short blond hair.

Then Kindy and Cameron lifted up their phones.

So did three other people. Then four. Then ten.

They were streaming live.

This was my chance.

I stepped out from Michael Kay's shadow—what kind of weirdo goes by his full name?—and spoke to the growing crowd, including the streaming cameras. "I want to clear the air, right now." My fingers tapped rapidly against my legs under all the attention, but I launched into my memorized speech, changing it up just enough that it didn't sound identical to the last time. "Jared and Lily DiMaggio appreciate so many people worrying about their relationship. They are working closely with their marriage counselor to move past all the TV drama, and Jared is excited to turn his attention back to producing high-quality exercise programs . . ." When I reached the end, I smiled for the cameras. "He'll be here tomorrow night. He'd love to talk to you all, one by one, and clear up any misunderstandings."

My phone beeped instantly with a text.

Bailey: *I saw that! Perfect!*

I tried not to grin, but I stood an inch taller as the twins both nodded in approval.

"You're saying he's not a cheater?" Michael Kay asked, folding his thick arms across his wide chest.

"I'm saying those days are long gone."

"Does he still make guest appearances on other people's fitness shows?" someone asked.

"Absolutely. Find me later, let's schedule a day."

"Did he really kiss Fearless Felicity?" Kindy asked, her high-pitched voice full of awe.

"He kissed her once, a long time ago. He's *never* cheated since."

"What about that Romanian ballerina a few months ago?" someone yelled. "Nicoleta something."

This one was easy—I'd already drilled Jared about these rumors. There wasn't an ounce of truth to them. "Nicoleta never happened."

But Michael Kay stepped between me and the crowd, pulling out his own phone. It looked like a child's toy in his giant hands. "Yes, she did. I was there, check this out." He played a video of Jared backstage at a concert, a slender brunette on his lap. Jared's entire tongue dipped into her mouth.

"Where did you get that?" I gasped.

Michael Kay's smile widened. The band hadn't resumed playing so everyone could hear us. "I took it myself, six weeks ago. That's long *after* he admitted to kissing Fearless Felicity."

"That can't be right," I insisted, but the room started to spin. I dug my nails into my palms, focusing on the pain, trying to hold the world steady. If he'd cheated after he kissed Felicity, after he'd sworn to us all that those days were over, what else didn't I know about? How could I fix a problem if I didn't know it existed?

The room spun faster. Cameron raised his phone and zeroed in on the video of Jared, still playing on Michael Kay's phone. Kindy stepped closer, her camera pointed at my face. The walls whirled, like a tornado had sucked them up. Someone had to fix this. His career depended on it. *My* career depended on it.

Me.

That someone was me.

I glared hard at Michael Kay, my entire body quaking. "Please, turn that off. I'm trying to get Jared's reputation back on track. Don't play that for the whole world to see."

Sheila rested a hand on my arm and squeezed, her own phone open to Instagram in her other hand. "Five million people are watching, honey. The damage is done."

Kindy lowered her phone halfway, like she couldn't decide to turn it off or keep it on. "How can you fix his reputation if he's still cheating on his wife?" The innocence in her voice competed with her horror toward his infidelity.

"There are no more secrets," I insisted. But was that even true? Then I peered straight into Kindy's camera. "Do you hear that, everyone? There are no more. I trust Jared completely."

But Michael Kay took two steps back, widening our circle as he relaxed against the refreshment table piled high with candy bars. He folded his arms across his broad chest. Then he, too, looked straight into Kindy's camera. "But how can we be sure? Sounds like he's only fessing up to cheating when he gets caught. Not exactly the 'putting it all behind us' you say he's doing."

Every face turned toward me.

The room spun wildly now, the tornado picking up speed. I couldn't make my eyes focus on any one person, and I teetered, grabbing onto the closest thing for support—Caspien's arm. He stiffened but didn't pull away.

"All of that is behind him!" It was, wasn't it? I gripped tighter to keep from falling over. Even if it wasn't true, our careers depended on everyone *believing* it was. "I know it!"

I was losing them. Their eyes widened, their jaws hung open, thirteen—no, fifteen—cameras pointed at my face, filming or streaming or broadcasting. This wasn't supposed to happen, it wasn't supposed to crumble like this. I was supposed to come here tonight, blow them all away with my nostalgic costume and my solid defense of Jared's honesty, and they were supposed to fall all over me begging to work with him.

"You really don't think he'll cheat again?" Kindy asked with the sweetest, most encouraging nod. "Be honest. You would know better than anyone." She was throwing me a bone. Giving me the chance to tell it how it was.

But I didn't have notes in my phone for this. Didn't have a pre-written answer from a PR specialist. Jared was the one who could speak off the cuff, not me! So, my mouth opened, and words sprayed out, like a faucet on high. "I mean, he loved his wife and they tried hard to make it work."

"*Loved?*" Kindy gasped. "He doesn't anymore?"

Shit. They were still telling the world they were together. I leaned into Caspien, giving him more and more of my weight so I didn't fall over. "Loves. He loves her."

"Are there any other women?" Cameron asked. "Any more secret videos out there?"

"Of course not! He made a mistake—a couple of mistakes—but he's not that person. He's only human, same as you and me." I pointed at Michael Kay with my free hand. "Same as you."

"But I never cheated."

"You're single!"

"Exactly. The standard for someone in a committed relationship is higher. And he blew it."

I tried to pull away from Caspien, only to immediately stumble and grab his arm again. The room wouldn't stay still, and my stomach twisted, a wave of nausea rolling through me.

"You have to trust me on this. You all could benefit from partnering up with Jared." I tapped the arm of a man in front of me, the only one I could reach without releasing my vice grip on Caspian. I'd read every word on the man's Facebook page; he and his teenage daughter had started streaming their workouts from their garage last year. "You have a kid, right? Jared does too, a daughter. She's the sweetest thing, same age as yours. You could team up, fly back and forth to film. You'd gain each other's followers if you streamed together."

The man's eyebrows raised, but he didn't immediately say no.

Yes. He was listening.

It didn't matter that Jared preferred partnerships where he promoted physical products. He liked keeping his stage all to himself. But right now, we'd take anything we could get. The ideas flew faster, louder.

"You could have themed workouts. Your kids are in middle school, right? Sports day, nerd day, cheerleader day." The man frowned and cocked his head. "Scratch the themes. Bad idea, but you see what I'm saying? People love workouts with kids."

I pointed to Kindy, who grinned, and Cameron, who peered to his right and left like he couldn't decide if he wanted to be singled out. "And you two! You're anti-drug, right? He'd love to team up for an anti-drug campaign. Maybe stream a gym class for homeschool kids. Exercise mixed with health lessons. Like D.A.R.E.! Did you have D.A.R.E. when you were young?"

I'd designed a program like this ages ago, but Jared had voted against it. The idea was solid, though, I was sure of it, even if my delivery was terrible.

This was why I needed Jared. This was why I always funneled my ideas to him, and he presented them as his own.

"Anyway, Jared used to do steroids, then quit. You two would represent healthy choices, and he'd talk about what he learned from hard experience. You need both. Oh! You could bring bunnies on stage to keep the kids' attention. The cute factor, you know? Or baby goats? They could wander around the stage while you worked out. An entire petting zoo! Nope, not that. But maybe my old health teacher! Uh, nope, not him either. He's in his eighties by now. But maybe yours isn't so old? Did you have a good one? Was he attractive? Attractive people help draw a crowd—not that it's necessary. Doesn't matter. I'm rambling."

I stopped.

No one made a sound.

Kindy pressed her hand silently over her mouth. Caspien's gaze burned holes in my cheek. Why did he have to witness this? Couldn't he see that my ideas were solid? Couldn't they all see? But no, not one of these people would work with Jared now. With all those phones watching, his reputation would be in shambles—because of me. I'd come here to fix everything, but I'd only made it worse.

Nobody spoke.

Nobody lowered their phones.

Then the crowd parted, and Lucas Croft stepped through, his European girlfriend still clinging to his arm. Lucas! How had I forgotten about Lucas?

Jared didn't need these people. He didn't need vendors or lifters or fitness celebrities.

He only needed Lucas.

My entire body filled with helium, floated off the floor as my tornado settled back into nothing. With Lucas as his partner, Jared's credibility would skyrocket. They'd be on the cover of every magazine, interviewed on every talk show, their faces plastered on the sides of city buses.

The only one I needed to convince was *him*.

"Here, honey." Sheila handed me a skinny glass of red wine. I clenched it, channeling all my anxiety into gripping the stem until it snapped in my fingers—then I held my hand perfectly still so the glass appeared intact. With Lucas, Jared still had a blank slate. It was my job to write on it, starting now.

Leaning my head back, I downed the wine in three large gulps, pulled away from Caspien's steady grip, and stepped right up to Lucas with my hand out.

"Hello, I'm Lauren Cro—"

My stomach revolted. It flipped in a full circle and projected the wine back out, onto my hand, onto the floor between us.

Gasps thundered through my eardrums.

Lucas didn't move.

The room spun and I fell forward, vomiting again all over Lucas's black, leather dress shoes—and his girlfriend's four-inch heels. I should have known better than to drink while anxious; my gag reflex always ran in overdrive. But why was I so dizzy? Food. I hadn't eaten in . . . too many hours. Damn low blood sugar. And their shoes? Ruined.

Why did I always do this? Why couldn't I stand calmly like the others, chatting and sipping wine? Why did my anxiety always screw everything up?

"Hello, Hallie," Caspien said.

My head snapped up.

There she was.

Hallie. *My* Hallie, exactly how I remembered her.

She'd tied her long brown hair back in her usual ponytail, her narrow face too soft for a kid raised in a White Center trailer park. She'd replaced her old dirt smudges with mascara, but no other makeup graced her face, and in place of cut-off jeans she wore a simple, black, floor-length dress with a few beads around the cap sleeves. Minimal frills, just how she liked it. Eleven years had passed since I last saw her, and yet she'd barely changed, a taller version of the girl who'd trudged dirt through the trailer between rounds of hockey with the boys.

But now? Standing above me with confidence in her shoulders and heaviness in her eyes? She'd grown up.

And I'd missed it.

Everything I needed to know about this older Hallie could be summed up in the fact that her white sneakers stuck out under the edge of her formal gown. Those shoes told me exactly who she still was, and who she wasn't—because the four-inch sparkling heels of Lucas's glamorous girlfriend stood right beside hers. The women leaned away from each other like they were afraid to share the same air.

But what did Hallie see in me, on my knees in retro workout gear, surrounded by regurgitated wine? Our first interaction in eleven years? We were supposed to reunite with my head held high, with a flawless excuse for why I'd stayed away.

But this?

"Lauren?" Even her voice lilted like it used to, steady and calm. "Are you all right?"

Slowly, I lifted my gaze. Hallie watched me with a tilted head, concern etched into the soft arch of her forehead as she hid her face from the cameras. She opened her mouth but no words came out. Did she feel like me? Consumed by so many apologies, so many questions, but she couldn't decide where to start?

"Hey, little sis." My voice scratched against my ears, the sound tangled up by an avalanche of emotions. "I'm okay."

But after a long moment of silence, Hallie's shoulders sagged, one slightly lower than the other, and she pressed her lips together. Why couldn't I read the words behind her eyes? For a moment I'd thought we . . . but a hardness crept into her lips, a tension in her jaw. Was she embarrassed? She must have called in a favor to bring me here, and now she had to deal with *this*. With *me*. Did she regret answering my call?

Hallie peeled her gaze away and focused all her attention on Caspien. My sister and my babysitter, locking eyes in a silent argument. He shook his head, but Hallie folded her arms.

Wait, what were they arguing about? Was it who would be stuck taking me home? Whose responsibility I was?

It dawned on me like a crash of lightning through the dark banquet hall, a quake of thunder shaking the ground—neither of them wanted me.

Then Hallie exhaled so heavily her torso crumpled in on itself. Her gaze danced across my outfit, my turquoise hair, the pool of spoiled wine on the ground beside me. "I'm sorry, Lauren; I can't do this." Then she spun around and pushed into the crowd.

She was gone.

Caspien had lost the fight.

Lucas gave me one last glance, then he followed her out, his glamorous girlfriend on his heels.

"Hallie, wait!" I pressed my hands against a clean spot on the cold floor and tried to stand, to chase her, but my legs gave out. High anxiety and minimal food meant my traitorous body wouldn't cooperate. I crashed back onto the floor, landing hard on my hip.

Slowly, Caspien stepped around the puddle of wine, took my arm, and lifted me to my feet, as silent and brooding as always. Then a second realization shook through me. Ever since I'd arrived, since he'd shown up at the airport with his cardboard sign and grumpy attitude, I'd been annoyed to have a babysitter, to be saddled with a chaperone that slowed me down and refused to be social.

But I'd had it backward.

I wasn't stuck with him. *He* was stuck with *me*.

He'd picked me up, helped me find my hotel, attended a party he'd dreaded, and then kept me standing when the room spun too fast. And now he had to take me home, covered in vomit, in his brand-new car, and it was killing him. I was an anchor chained to his leg, dragging him deep underwater to his own personal hell. How had I become . . . *this?* I didn't want to drown him. I didn't want to drown anyone.

But I couldn't walk on my own. I could barely stand.

So, I let him take my arm and wrap it around his shoulder, and the entire crowd parted as we hobbled from the room, his body supporting my weight, solid and strong as I craned my neck, searching for one last glimpse of my little sister.

But she was long gone.

Caspien opened the door to the parking garage and helped me climb down the stairs to his car. When was the last time someone had touched me longer than a handshake or a nudge?

Up this close, Caspien smelled like grass after a rainstorm.

Chapter 7

$364.73 still in my wallet

By the time we reached my hotel, my anxiety had settled into a slow tide of regret and mortification. They came at me like waves, in and out, one after the other, with a pause of numbness in between. Why couldn't I do the simplest things? No one else had struggled tonight. No one else had made a fool of themselves. Had I really said all that about Jared? Puked on Lucas while broadcasting live to millions of viewers? I'd never open social media again.

Caspien helped me to my room and lowered me onto the small sofa. He didn't bolt screaming from the hotel like I'd expected, but instead hesitated at the door.

"You okay?" he finally asked.

My anxiety had ebbed, but the room still spun, and my clothes smelled like soured wine.

"When did you last eat?" he asked.

I wanted to laugh, to say, *Of course I'm okay, I eat all the time,* to wave him out of the room and pretend like nothing happened.

But I needed help.

"Last night, I think."

He watched me with such heavy eyes, like he couldn't decide between annoyance and pity. Hatred from him would have been easier, or disgust or even frustration—if he'd glared at me, I could have glared right back. But his expression hovered too close to concern, like I was a child who needed her hand held.

He pulled a candy bar from his pocket, the caramel kind from the refreshment table at the banquet. He must have grabbed it on our way out. "Can you eat?"

"I think so."

"Are you sure? Last time you swallowed something, you threw it up."

My head fell back onto the couch. "That was my anxiety. My gag reflex goes haywire when I get worked up."

He took a step closer. "Then why'd you fall over?"

"That would be my blood sugar. It's unstable all the time, I can't go more than a few hours without food. Anxiety and low blood sugar are a terrible combination." Suddenly, inexplicably, I needed him to understand. "I'm not always like this. I usually have my job under control. I do the research, give Jared my notes, then he sells the products, and everything goes smoothly. But ever since he cheated, no one will talk to him, so I've had to do both jobs—but I can't speak on the fly! I make a fool of myself *every time.*"

My voice hushed to a whisper, my breath going out in enormous gasps that made the room spin again. I dug through my purse until I found my Xanax and popped a pill into my mouth, but it didn't calm me instantly like it had in the airport. This wasn't something a pill could erase. Tomorrow morning I'd have to face the conference attendees again, I'd have to own up to all my mistakes.

Caspien stepped closer and took the pill bottle from my hand, reading the label. Then he unwrapped the top of the chocolate bar and handed it to me. "You should raise your blood sugar."

I took a bite. As soon as the chocolate and salty caramel filled my mouth, my stomach growled. "This is so good."

"It's my favorite," he said, then he dug through the pile of powder packets on the desk in the corner until he found a Neon Nutrition. "Will this help?"

"Probably. But maybe start with a Green Fizz."

He read the label, then raised an eyebrow. "An energy drink? After a Xanax?"

"Okay, maybe not. But a Neon Nutrition would be great."

He pulled a water bottle from the case, filled it with powder and shook vigorously, the water sloshing in the silent room.

"Why are you helping me?" I asked as he handed it to me.

Caspien lowered himself onto the black, wood coffee table across from me like it was a chair. If he could smell the sour wine on me, he hid it well.

"First, explain something. Kindy asked if you thought he'd cheat again, but you avoided the question."

"No, I didn't."

"You fumbled, then said that he loved his wife. Why didn't you just say *no*?"

I paused, my entire body slumping. "Because it wouldn't be the truth."

"That doesn't mean you had to say it."

I took a long drink of my Neon Nutrition shake then twisted the lid back onto the bottle. "Have you ever met my mom? Hallie's mom?" Caspien shook his head. "I haven't seen her in, well, a long time. But when I was a teenager, I had panic attacks all the time. Terrible ones, where my lungs would stop working and I'd hyperventilate, gasping for air until I passed out. Mom was always so patient, she'd see it coming and would move me to the couch so I wouldn't hurt myself when I fell. She was the one who figured out I had an attack every time I lied to cover something up. As long as I stuck with the truth, the anxiety wasn't so bad."

He sat perfectly still, listening closely. "You had panic attacks as a teenager?"

"Only after my dad walked out. He'd lied to my mom so many times, covering up all the awful things he did. Mom thought my attacks were a psychological reaction to the way he treated us. Like, deep down, I didn't want to become like him, or something." I pressed one knuckle against my teeth and grabbed a handful of hair with my other hand. No, Caspien would think I was crazy if I yanked my hair like that. I slid my fingers through it instead. "Is that how Hallie sees me? Like I walked out on her? Just like *him?*"

The realization crushed me like an avalanche. A mountain of boulders cascading over me, stealing away my air. After years of anxiety over being abandoned, I'd become like him anyway. No wonder Hallie ran away from me in the ballroom.

I collapsed back against the couch and rubbed my eyes as the sugar from the candy finally crept into my veins. The room held still, no longer spinning each time I moved. "You still haven't told me why you helped me home."

With a deep sigh, Caspien scratched his head. "First, tell me about that anti-drug campaign you cooked up for Jared and the Instagram couple. What plans do you have in the works for it?"

"Anti-drug campaign?" I wracked my memory, trying to remember.

"You said it back at the banquet."

I unlocked my phone and scrolled through my old lists of show ideas until I found the one about drugs. "I came up with this years ago, but it never went anywhere. Jared vetoed it."

"He didn't like it?"

"When I get in the mood to plan, I come up with way more ideas than Jared has time for, so he picks his favorites and the rest sit untouched in my phone or my computer." My heart picked up speed and I sat straighter, scooting to the front of the couch. "See, my entire job revolves around studying Influencers or fitness companies and discovering what they like to put in their feeds or ads. Then I find a way for Jared to fulfill that need for them. My plans are so fleshed out that by the time I present them to

Jared, he only has to regurgitate the information. They agree ninety-nine percent of the time."

"Why do you give the information to Jared? Why not pitch it yourself?"

"People like Jared's flair." I squinted, scrunching up my nose. "Besides, did you see me tonight? I'm excellent at following my notes on my phone, but the second I go off script my anxiety takes over. My thoughts won't think in a straight line—even when my ideas are brilliant."

"Like your anti-drug campaign?"

"Exactly." I held out my phone so he could skim through my notes. "In Jared's early years of fame, he'd go to LA and get caught up in the drugs and parties. He was deep into illegal steroids too, the heavy-duty stuff. But he quit all of it when he realized what it was doing to his body and his family. If Kindy and Cameron are anti-drug, they could make a six-episode fitness show that combined exercise with healthy living. Jared would talk about the realities of drug use and the Instagrammers could teach about healthy diets. Obviously, they would also lift weights together. They'd draw a bigger crowd if they brought in one of those dogs that sniff drugs. Jared did a running show once where a dog ran on a leash beside him. His viewership doubled that month."

"You've planned this already?" He scrolled through my endless pages of typing.

"Sometimes when I focus on my research, I get a little obsessive."

"A *little?*"

"All six episodes are scripted, including prop lists, stage crew requirements, and travel arrangements. I'd need to adjust it for Cameron and Kindy, instead of the guy I'd originally planned to be with Jared, but that's easy."

Caspien handed my phone back. "Why didn't you film it already?"

"Jared didn't love it." I shrugged one shoulder. "I have hundreds of these that'll never see the light of day. If Cameron and Kindy wanted it, I'd just give it to them."

"But aren't they your competition?"

I tapped my forehead, then pointed at him, resting my elbows on my knees. "Absolutely, but I have a theory about this. Back when the only option to get your name out there was landing a TV deal, there were a finite number of slots, right? Fitness stars had to protect their ideas in case someone stole them." I'd tried to explain this to Jared a dozen times, but he'd never grasped my idea. "Now that anyone can stream a fitness show, there's unlimited room for sharing the market. Viewers don't only watch one YouTube channel, they bounce around. They want variety."

Caspien scratched his short beard. "So, the people who try to keep their viewers all to themselves—"

"—get way less views than those who collaborate. In the words of Fearless Felicity, 'There's room on the first-place podium for everyone.'"

"Seems obvious when you explain it that way. But Jared doesn't agree?"

"Eh, halfway. I'm trying to teach him."

"Tell me honestly," Caspien said, folding his arms, "does he use drugs anymore?"

I almost said *no,* but my spine tensed, and I paused. He'd lied about cheating with Nicoleta, and he'd slipped back into drugs a couple of times when life grew too stressful. But that was years ago. He wasn't using now, right? Of course not. I would know. I'd recognize the signs. "No," I said. "Never."

But was that true? My fingers clenched and my breath sped up. I wasn't sure.

Caspien peered into my eyes. "You're lying."

I pulled back under his scrutiny. "Maybe he does, I don't know. I have suspicions when he goes on long trips. He parties, but he knows how I feel about it, so he doesn't tell me any details."

"You don't do drugs with him?"

"What? Put drugs into *my* brain? When it's already racing a thousand miles a minute? I'd probably turn telekinetic and blow everything up. I tried it once, at a party in college with Jared. Some little blue pill, I don't know what it was. The experience was horrifying. My brain felt like a toddler with a set of drums inside my head for an entire day. *Never* again."

"I believe you," Caspien said, almost like he was surprised.

"You do?"

"It's obvious when you're lying. Very obvious. But what I don't understand, is why people like Jared and that guy with the sword do drugs. They're fitness people, seems like an oxymoron."

"It's not all of them," I explained. "Only a few. The famous ones who let their success get to their heads. The majority don't have a clue."

"Lucas will explode when he finds out," Caspien said. "We've never had a banquet crank up the energy like that."

"That was definitely the drugs. You could feel the energy zinging through the air."

I stuffed my candy bar wrapper into the empty Neon Nutrition bottle. I couldn't remember finishing either, but my energy level had immediately increased. What hadn't improved though, was the stench of sour wine wafting off my clothes. "I should shower."

The corner of Caspien's mouth turned up as he rose to his feet. "Good idea. I'll get out of your hair."

I planted my feet on the ground, but my legs wobbled as I stood, and my stomach growled. A few more Neon Nutritions sat on the stack, but most of the heap was Green Fizz. When I took another step, my legs wanted to give out.

With an inward groan, I said, "Maybe you could stay?" How much more could I ask of him tonight before the humiliation killed me? "Just until I finish showering, in case I pass out. I'm still pretty shaky."

He checked his watch then lowered himself into my desk chair. "Sure."

Safely inside the bathroom, I stripped off my exercise gear. The purple wine stains would come out, right? With some miracle detergent and a lot of scrubbing? But for now, I desperately needed to cover up the smell, so I pulled the clear liner from the garbage can and dropped my clothes inside, then tied it tightly shut. But I paused at the mirror before stepping into the shower. Mascara smudged the skin around my eyes and traveled a path down my cheeks, and a purple stain dripped down my chin like vampire blood. And my hair. My hair! I couldn't wait to wash out the turquoise dye.

The warm shower soothed my tense muscles, and though Caspien was waiting to leave, I let it soak into my skin for a long time. As soon as my body calmed, worries inched their way into my head. After my ridiculous exhibition tonight, would anyone give me a second chance tomorrow? The twins were long-time friends, maybe they would. But how could I face Jared? Even if he hadn't viewed it live, he would see clips. Was he watching them right now? Did his wife see? Did I blow their 'happily married' façade into smithereens? I fled from the shower and wrapped a towel around my body—then I froze, mid-step, gaze glued to the mirror.

My hair was still turquoise.

No. No, no, no, no, no.

Clinging to my towel, I sprinted into the bedroom where I dug through the garbage can. Where the hell was the hair dye box? I yanked it from beneath the pile of empty water bottles and frantically read the label.

Permanent hair color.

How could that be? I'd made sure to buy temporary dye! Or . . . I'd planned to buy temporary dye, but had I forgotten to check when I picked out the box? Was my mind too distracted by a million other things?

Why? Why was I like this? Why couldn't my brain stay in one place long enough to do something right? Or at least to not screw up this bad?

Caspien cleared his throat, standing above where I crouched on the floor. "Everything okay?"

I handed him the box and covered my head, like maybe my neon hair would return to blond if he couldn't see it. "I'm a blue-haired idiot, that's all."

His eyes scanned the box, then flicked to my hair. "Can you dye it back?"

"I'll need a professional to fix this mess, but I won't have time until after I go home."

"You're still going back to the convention tomorrow?" He sounded surprised. Or impressed. Or maybe just bewildered. I did, after all, humiliate myself in front of more people than I could wrap my mind around.

"What choice do I have? I can't let Jared's career tank. And I still haven't talked to Hallie."

After digging my cozy pajamas from my suitcase, I ducked back into the bathroom to dress. Every time my turquoise hair flashed in the mirror, my stomach clenched tighter, so I kept my gaze glued to the floor.

When I slunk out of the bathroom, Caspien was leaning against the door frame that led out to the hall, his arms folded, brow furrowed like he couldn't figure something out.

"Why do you keep fighting for Jared when videos of his lies keep popping up? What if he's cheated on his wife again? Or what if people find out their fitness idol uses cocaine on the weekends?"

"They won't." My voice wavered.

"After tonight, don't you want to race back home and move on to something different?"

"I can't—I have to fix this! I made a fool of him with millions of people watching!"

"No, you didn't. Jared made a fool of himself. It wasn't *your* behavior that made tonight a disaster, it was the video of Jared cheating, after swearing to the public that he'd turned a new leaf. You went into that fight already doomed to lose—because of *his* actions, not yours. So, I ask again, why do you keep doing this?"

"Because I believe in him."

"Still?"

"Yes! He's pathetic sometimes, I know. But look at me—I am too, yet he has stuck with me for a decade and a half. The least I can do is repay the favor."

Caspien studied my face, glancing at my unmoving fingers. They didn't tap or twist or shake. I wasn't lying.

When he finally spoke, his voice was so low I could hardly hear him. "The fact that you're not hyperventilating means you genuinely believe what you're saying. But you're wrong about one thing. No one who puts herself out there for someone again and again is pathetic. There must be something special about him to deserve this kind of loyalty."

"There is," I said, squaring my shoulders. "I promised Jared I would fix his reputation and resurrect his career. And I never break a promise."

"Not even to Hallie?"

I sucked in a breath. How could I explain without sounding like a terrible person? After lying to her for years, how could I visit without facing my horrible past? I'd have to tell her the truth—but I was too much of a coward. Too ashamed. Just thinking of it made it impossible to meet Caspien's gaze. No, I couldn't try to explain.

"I didn't mean to hurt her." I held out my hand into the space between us, my fingers steady, no shaking or tapping. No hyperventilating. "I'm telling the truth."

Caspien smiled, but it didn't reach his eyes. "You're a puzzle, Lauren Cross."

I almost laughed. He had no idea how right he was. Like my entire body was a one-thousand-piece puzzle, but all the pieces were flipped backward and upside down, then twisted into chaos by a hurricane. Occasionally, I could piece a few back together, just enough for a stroke of brilliance to keep me and Jared afloat. But then nights like tonight would resurrect the storm, and my moment of clarity would be upended.

"Shit!" I screeched. "I never made an appointment with Lucas! How can Jared convince him to work with us if we don't have a meeting?" I pressed my palms against my eyes. First the banquet, then the hair dye, and now this. Sure, I threw up on him and had to leave, but this was *important*. I should have asked him before I humiliated him. "I forget every freaking thing."

Caspien squinted, his gaze following my outburst. "Are you sure it's anxiety causing your forgetfulness?"

"No, it's the other way around. The forgetfulness causes the anxiety."

He opened his mouth, then closed it again, like he wanted to say something but changed his mind. Instead, he pulled up a calendar on his phone. "Lucas still has one open slot. The day after tomorrow, ten in the morning. Want me to stick your name in there?"

The tension washed out of me, and I dropped my hands to my sides. "Yes, please. But you still haven't told me why you're helping me."

"Because you tell the truth."

"You're helping me because I'm a bad liar?"

"I've been lied to a lot of times in my life." Caspien shrugged into his jacket.

"By who?"

He paused, studying me, his face contorted like he was dredging up painful memories. "Someone I loved. But you're an open book."

What was I supposed to say to that? He was praising the quality that dragged me into this mess in the first place. "Well, thanks, I think. I couldn't have made it home without you."

Caspien nodded, then opened the door. "Pick you up in the morning? Eight o'clock?"

I almost said no, but different words left my mouth before I could stop them. "That would be great, thanks."

"Can I give you some advice?" He pointed to the soiled workout clothes I'd squished into the garbage bag and dropped on the floor. "You're doing Jared's job this week, right? Maybe you're having anxiety because you're trying to do it *his* way, even though he's not here. When you go to the convention tomorrow, try a new approach—*your* approach.

Use those ideas you've saved up in your phone. You'll impress every single vendor."

He slipped out before I could respond, and I crashed onto the couch, lying flat with my feet up over the arm. Do things *my* way? How could I do Jared's job without channeling his flair? Could it be done differently?

Speaking of which . . . I needed to call him. Chew him out for cheating again, on camera, and not warning me. How could he expect me to cover for something like that? I also needed to beg his forgiveness for screwing things up with Lucas. I fumbled my hand across the carpeted floor until I found my phone tucked halfway under the couch. I held my breath, then dialed his number.

Ring.

Ring.

Ring.

It went to voicemail and the air rushed from my lungs. Maybe this was for the best. Perhaps I needed a game plan before we spoke, some written notes. Without thinking, I dialed Bailey's number instead. Someone answered on the second ring.

"Bailey?"

"Nope, Marco. Bailey's backstage with her daughter, who's getting ready to go on. How's Seattle?" He spoke with his typical confidence, enthusiasm, energy. And the way he said Bailey's name? Like she was made of solid gold.

"Will she be back soon?"

"Not for an hour." The cheer left his voice, and he exhaled before speaking again. "How are things going? You holding up?"

"Yeah. No. Not at all." I couldn't even lie to Marco. After being groomed to take over his father's diamond business, Marco had rocked the boat by splitting off and fabricating his own synthetic diamonds—and found wild success. I used to think he and I were the same, each separating from our families, forging our own paths with thriving careers.

But now?

I'd made a royal mess of mine.

"I saw the videos from tonight," Marco said, his voice quieter.

"Did you see *everything*?"

"You mean Jared cheating? Then you puking on Lucas Croft? I'm so sorry, Lauren." My shame burned hotter under the blanket of his pity. "What are you going to do?"

"I'm not sure yet."

Marco stayed quiet for a long time, no sounds but his breath echoing through the phone.

When he finally spoke, his tone was somber. "Do you remember how I got the scars on my hands?"

"Your dad's diamond mine in Africa, right? You wanted to experience it for yourself."

"I spent days in the hospital while they repaired my hands, and my dad stayed calm through the whole thing. But when we returned to America and we were alone, he let me know how much I'd embarrassed him."

"What did he do?"

"He had an antique cane, an heirloom from his grandfather. He beat me with it, all across my hands and arms, until my wounds had split back open, and half my fingers were broken. At the hospital, they assumed the foreign doctors had done a crappy job fixing me. Only Bailey, and now you, know the true story."

"Wow, Marco, that's horrible."

"Want to know the real reason I carry a cane?"

I held my breath, waiting.

"To remind me what scares me most. After I left my dad's company, his memory still haunted me—until I went back as an adult and punched him in the nose. I started carrying the cane to remind me of what it felt like to confront him. If I can face my dad's cane, I can face anything."

I clutched my phone with both hands, willing his courage to surge through it, to wash over me. "You're telling me to face my fears?"

"I'm telling you that if a scrawny Italian kid can stand up to his overbearing father, you, Lauren Cross, can do anything. If those people scare you? Face them head-on. Show them you're not afraid of a little bad press."

"Stand up to them?" The words carried weight. Solid. Sturdy.

"You can do it, I know it."

"You're right." A hint of my resolve returned. If Jared could make deals using my notes, why couldn't I? "Thanks, Marco, I needed this."

By the time we hung up, my mind had already jumped three steps ahead. The phone dropped to the floor, my papers spread out across the table, and the pen in my hand scribbled faster than it had in ages. I skimmed the convention website, pouring over the newly-posted vendor list, studying them one by one—and, of course, taking copious notes. The ideas poured from my brain to my fingers to my notebook so quickly I giggled like a maniac as I wrote.

I only stopped briefly to grab a water bottle—and at the last second, a Green Fizz. I was going to need the clarity. This might take all night.

Chapter 8

$364.73 remaining

The next morning, my alarm went off promptly at 8:00 a.m., and I texted Caspien that I'd meet him at the conference. I wanted to walk the two blocks to wake up properly and pick up breakfast on the way. It didn't matter that I'd miss the morning session of classes, since I hadn't planned to attend them anyway. My sights were set on the vendor tables—on the people who would hire Jared to promote their products. While everyone else sat through lectures, I'd spend my day in the vendor hall schmoozing. I'd stayed up half the night researching each one, and I had a phone full of notes to prove it.

On the little hotel notepad beside my bed, I jotted down my to-do list for this morning.

Step 1: Shower.

Step 2: Check the conference schedule.

Step 3: Don't forget Sherry's whiskey.

The hot shower woke me up the rest of the way, though my hair still shocked me every time I looked in the mirror. Afterward, I downed a Green Fizz to settle my racing thoughts, slid into nice jeans and heels, and slung my purse over my shoulder, sending my pages of notes flying across the floor.

Whatever. Everything I needed was in my phone.

Time to take up my proverbial cane and face my fears. I'd impress the vendors, I'd amaze Caspien, and I'd earn my way back into Hallie's life. Today, I'd win at everything.

The map on my phone led me east through the rain, while I typed a careful text to Hallie.

Lauren: *Sorry if I embarrassed you in front of your boss. I promise, I'm not typically like that.*

I lurched to a stop halfway to the convention center as the drizzling rain morphed into a downpour. I'd forgotten the whiskey—and I needed to be on the twins' good side today. Across the street was the same store I'd bought my hair dye from, so I ducked inside, safely out of the rain and searched through their whiskey selection. A nice bottle would cost nearly one hundred dollars, but I couldn't spare that much cash, so I settled on a medium-quality pint. It would have to do.

The same woman with red and orange hair sat behind the counter. She perked up when I approached. "It's you. Dig the hair."

"Thanks." I pulled out two twenties, but she didn't take them.

"You were right about the fancy fish food."

"I was?"

She pointed to the angelfish darting between fake coral rocks in the tall aquarium. "I've never seen her so active." She took my pint of whiskey and swapped it out for a different brand. "This one's better, trust me."

"Hey, thanks." Then I took my change, wiggled a finger at the silver and purple fish, and ran back across the street. I barreled into the convention center, my feet squeaking on the hard floor with every step. The vendor hall was upstairs, so I sprinted up, then lurched to a stop at the end of the hall where the narrow space opened into a wide reception area. Every table was void of people. Each vendor's wares were spread out, with signs and samples and business cards. But where was everyone?

Step 2: Check the conference schedule.

Crap, I'd forgotten. I dug the schedule out of my purse, wrinkled and rained on, then checked my watch. At 8:30 the entire conference had gathered in the banquet hall for a Vendor Showcase, so each vendor could have a couple minutes to show off their product to the other attendees.

My phone vibrated with a text from Caspien.

Caspien: *Where are you? I saved you a seat in the front.*

I was an hour late. Crap. Crap. Crap.

I sprinted back downstairs, then shoved through the oversized door with a crash. Half the room stared at me, and I hunched down as I crept between circular tables, my heels simultaneously clicking and squeaking. Caspien waved me toward him. Halfway to the front I stopped again. Where was the whiskey? Not in my hand. Not in my purse. Had I seriously left it on the counter in the liquor store? I spun around, but banged into someone's chair, the crash echoing through the room.

Caspien stopped waving.

I stalked toward him anyway—the whiskey could wait—then slunk into the empty chair to his right, sliding as low as it would let me.

"Everything okay?" he whispered. He folded his arms across a forest-green polo, above his pressed, gray slacks. He lounged back, completely at ease, though he leaned slightly away, like my embarrassment might rub off on him.

"I'm perfect," I glowered.

"How's your blood sugar this morning?" He slid a packaged muffin toward me from a pile of breakfast snacks in the center of the table.

"Perfectly fine." He didn't need to know that I'd forgotten to buy breakfast on the way. But I snatched the muffin and scarfed it down, only caring a little that the wrapper made a ridiculous amount of noise. Chocolate chip. Unbelievably delicious.

While I focused on eating, a man with a fancy blender demonstrated its extraordinary blending abilities by making a smoothie and distributing it to everyone at the center table: the twins, Michael Kay, and Cameron and Kindy—who turned on their Instagram live-streams as they posed with the vendor and tasted the smoothie. Kindy smiled adorably for the camera and gushed about its deliciousness (*Not one chunk in the bottom of my cup*!) Lucas Croft himself also lounged in a metal chair at their table, looking bored.

Had he seen my late entrance?

Of course he had.

Everyone had.

Hang on, did I know the blender guy? Yes! He'd shaved his head and tattooed his left arm, but he was *my* blender guy! Doug—Bailey's old boss at Lucky 7 Gym! The second this meeting ended, I would get on his good side by buying one of his blenders, then I'd schedule a meeting. What other past relationships could I resurrect? And why wasn't Jared here to sit at the hotshot table and taste those smoothies? It should be vendors sucking up to Jared, not me sucking up to vendors!

Soon. Jared would be here soon. In fact, he should be boarding his plane any minute, then this conference would feel just like the old days. I'd feed Jared information about vendors, he'd land the deals, and we'd spend all night celebrating. Jared would finally gaze at me like he used to, like I'd handed him the world on a platter. My stomach fluttered just thinking about it.

Doug cleared off the stage and someone new took his place, a woman sharing samples of collagen supplements with fabulously flowing hair. She gave one to every person at Michael Kay's table. But when she handed one to Lucas, she also set one at the empty seat beside his. Whose chair was that?

"Have you seen Hallie this morning?" I whispered to Caspien.

"No, but I talked to her. She checked in, made sure you got home okay."

I pulled out my phone and texted her again.

Lauren: *Did I get you in trouble last night?*

For the next twenty minutes, I stared at my phone. Yes, I needed to study the vendors, but I couldn't pry my gaze away.

"She's at work," Caspien finally said.

"Who is?"

"Hallie. She has a busy job; she can't spend her day texting."

Of course.

Of course. Of course. Hallie had a job and real responsibilities. But I at least wanted her to text me back. Let me know if I got her in trouble when I puked on her boss's shoes . . .

But I had responsibilities too, so I spent the next two hours adding notes to my lists about each vendor who took the stage, their personalities, their products, and the best angle from which to approach them. Jared would want to read over this list once he'd arrived. That was our system: I scoped them out, researched their products, then pointed Jared toward the ones we could work with. It was efficient and productive. Many would be easy sales.

But when the last vendor cleared off the stage, I stayed in my chair. I should eat another muffin. I grabbed one and unwrapped it—free food, after all—but Hallie still hadn't texted, and my stomach cramped.

"You look stressed," Caspien said.

"I'm not." A pathetic lie, considering my fingernails tapping wildly against the table.

"Did something happen this morning?"

"No." No reason to bring up running through the rain, leaving the whiskey behind—twice—or my embarrassing entrance. At least my clothes had mostly dried. "I'm just anxious for Jared to arrive. He's better at schmoozing important people like Lucas."

"Schmoozing?"

"It's a word."

Caspien almost smiled. "I know it is."

I stuck a bite of muffin in my mouth and immediately gagged. Caspien slid his chair away, and I spit the food into a napkin.

"I'm not going to puke," I said.

"I believe you." But he didn't scoot closer.

Surprisingly, I laughed. "Am I that predictable?"

"You're an open book. So, what's your plan for today?"

"Schmoozing vendors and making deals."

Caspien laughed outright, a dimple dipping into his right cheek.

"With or without Jared, I'm taking my cane by the handle and facing my fears. I'll win some deals today, then I'll win Lucas's promo contract, then I'll go home as a brand-new me."

"Do you have a plan for your pitch tomorrow?"

"Of course."

Anxiety erupted through me like a wrecking ball. My legs started bouncing and my breathing picked up until I was panting like a dog in the scorching sun.

"You're lying," Caspien said, squeezing my arm. I focused on his touch, on the steady way he held perfectly still. "Stick with the truth and you'll be okay. Do you not have any ideas for that meeting?"

I did. Well, sort of. "Jared always just . . . walks in and dazzles people. He'll give his big speech tonight, then tomorrow morning will likely be the same."

The air flooded back into my lungs and my body calmed—a little.

"That's your whole plan?"

"What's wrong with it? It's worked for us hundreds of times. He's the king of schmoozing."

Caspien pointed to Lucas, one of the few still lingering in the ballroom, who scrolled his phone, bored, while Michael Kay chatted with him. No, Michael Kay chatted *at* him. "Lucas isn't a fan of people sucking up. You might want to think of a backup plan, in case Jared's doesn't go well."

"It will." I checked my watch, though my eyes didn't register the time. Was Caspien right? Did I need a backup plan? No, not with Jared already on a plane headed this direction. "But I do have my own agenda for this afternoon. I'm going to impress Jared by fixing his reputation and making deals before he even arrives. Time to get to work."

In the vendor hall, noise boomed through the wide space. The jockeying for partnerships was well underway. Dozens of influencers mingled with hundreds of vendors, talking, laughing, and demonstrating their products. And, sometimes, making affiliate deals.

"We're late," I muttered.

There were other attendees too. Regular fitness folk who wanted to buy—or at least see—everything. A clump of them posed for pictures with Sherry and Sheila, leaving barely enough space for Caspien and me to squirm through. Well, I squirmed. Caspien skulked, his bad mood from yesterday returning.

How could I forget, he didn't like people.

My bad mood returned too, because the loudest person in the room was Michael Kay. He'd brought an extra sword and a photo-booth backdrop where anyone could attempt to fight him, then take a selfie after. At the moment, he was mid-fight with the big-haired collagen lady, both of them cackling, drawing half the room's attention.

I hated that guy.

But at least his audience cleared space on the other side of the hall for me.

I dumped a packet of Green Fizz into a water bottle and chugged the whole thing. Time to focus.

But who to target first?

The closest table was a couple selling yoga mats made from recycled materials. Jared hated yoga, so I skipped to the next one as Caspien peeled away and leaned against the wall. Two young men selling vertical dumbbell racks smiled at me. I pulled up their tab on my phone and read everything I'd learned from their social media videos. College kids, one an engineer, one a weightlifter. They recently won a hundred-thousand-dollar investment but needed to make massive sales to pay their investor back. The engineer's apartment was currently overflowing with their product. Yes. They'd be perfect for Jared. Bachelors filled a big chunk of his market. One demonstration on his show and they'd sell out all their inventory—and we'd get a cut.

"What's your product?" I asked.

They jumped straight into their well-practiced speech. "After four years of living in tiny dorms or sharing rooms in rented apartments, we grew tired of gym equipment that took up all our space," one said. "I'm a weightlifter."

"And I'm an engineer," the other continued. "So, I built him a vertical rack that takes up minimal space but won't tip over if you bump it."

On cue, I jumped into my own less-practiced speech. "This is brilliant. I'm Lauren Cross, I represent world-famous super-trainer Jared DiMaggio. Every once in a while, we find a product he loves, and he promotes it on his shows. With over two million subscribers, he can bring a significant increase in your sales. This vertical rack seems like exactly the kind of thing he'd love."

The young men exchanged a glance. "Isn't he the guy who cheated on his wife? I don't think he has two million subscribers anymore."

"I recognize your hair," the other one said. "Didn't you puke on Lucas Croft's shoes last night?"

"Yeah," the first guy said, "I don't think Jared is the kind of publicity we're interested in. Thanks though."

Okay. Sure, not the outcome I'd hoped for. But could I blame them? They were young, too internet connected. Too new to appreciate Jared's history in the industry. All they knew was what social media told them. I needed people who may not have seen my embarrassing moment on Instagram last night—or any of Jared's from the past year.

But I knew what these guys needed too.

I pointed to Kindy and Cameron at the far end of the row. "See that couple? They live in apartments with a bunch of roommates, and they've complained multiple times online about not having space for their equipment. When they walk by, tell them what you've made. They may not cut a deal with you, but I'm positive they'd each buy one. And the next time they stream their workouts, the whole world will see. Out of anyone here, their audience is your exact target market."

The boys exchanged glances, then high-tailed straight for Cameron and Kindy. I grinned as they showed off one of their weight racks and Kindy squealed with delight. Then I moved on to the next table.

"Hello," I said to the women behind it, but I paused, calculating what to say next. Why hadn't I looked them up in my notes before I approached? They were older, in their forties maybe, so it was possible they hadn't seen any of our embarrassing videos. But should I avoid Jared's name for now, anyway? Yes, the best strategy was to get them hooked on the idea, then tell them his name once I'd sold them on the partnership.

"I'm Lauren Cross," I said, but they stopped me.

"We know who you are. We heard your speech to the weight rack guys."

"We don't want Jared," the second one said.

This wasn't how this was supposed to go. But the first woman scratched her cheek the same way I sometimes did. Was she nervous?

"You rep Fearless Felicity too, don't you? We want her."

I took a slow breath, preparing myself to go off-script. "Yes, but she's not taking on new partners. Jared, however, is very interested in your products."

Both women glanced down at their table: pink exercise bands, bath salts, flowery lotions. Yeah, I should have reviewed my notes.

"Are you sure?"

My stomach flipped over. "Sorry, guys, wrong table."

I fled around the corner, down the hall, into a whole new row of vendors, and pulled out my phone to text Bailey.

Lauren: *I met some women who want you to sponsor them. They sell spa gear; it would be fun! Interested?*

I crossed my fingers and waited, my gaze glued to my phone until she replied.

Bailey: *Sorry Lauren, things are too busy trying to get the company back on its feet. Eventually I'll have time, I promise!*

"Eventually" was too far away. I needed something now. *Come on, Lauren, you've got this.* But Michael Kay walked by and knocked into me with his elbow, his other arm draped around the blender guy.

My blender guy.

No, you don't.

I followed them until they stopped at Doug's table, covered in fruit and ice and protein powders.

"Doug!" I exclaimed, shoving between him and Michael Kay. "Long time no see, how's your family? Do you still live down on Honeyhart Lane?"

Michael Kay's eyes went dark as Doug shook my hand. Doug's company was huge. A promotional deal would be highly lucrative. Fortunately for me, he'd worked with Jared a handful of times already. They'd been friends for years, we were practically neighbors, and I knew exactly what my notes said about him.

"Lauren and I live in the same town," Doug explained to Michael Kay, his grin lighting up. "My gym, Lucky 7, went out of business a few years ago, so I used my engineering background to design this little lady." He held up a clear blender with a turquoise base. "Best thing that ever happened to me." Doug's smile split wider as he took in my hair. "Did you dye your hair just for this?"

I matched his blender perfectly.

"Of course! I think we need a picture."

Doug asked Michael Kay to take the photo and I grinned at the venom in his eyes as we posed. I almost texted the picture to Jared, but I paused. Maybe I'd hold off until I landed the deal.

"How's your boss?" Doug asked, and I bit back the urge to correct him to *business partner*. "It's been a while since we've met up," he continued. "What's the name of that French restaurant he likes?"

"Le Chateau."

"That's it! He used to take me there all the time."

"I'll make sure he takes you again soon." My heart rate picked up as I prepped for what came next. "How are blender sales going? Want to partner up with Jared again?"

Doug's face twisted as he hesitated. "He's getting a bad rap lately. And our wives are good friends. Mine would kill me if Jared and I partnered and then they, you know, divorced."

"You have nothing to worry about. Their marriage won't affect your partnership in any way." It wasn't exactly a lie—I had no idea if the divorce papers had finally gone through. But after Michael Kay's video yesterday, their official split would likely be a relief to them both.

"Even after last night?"

I tried not to wince. Or blush. Or run away crying.

Shove it down, quiet the voices.

"He'll be here tonight; you can ask him yourself. The media's having fun with him; they'll move on to someone else soon. In fact, why don't I buy a blender? This one matches my hair, after all."

He gave me half off, but it still cost a painful one hundred and fifty-four dollars. The expense was worth it, though, because Doug offered me his hand. "I've always liked Jared, let's plan on another year together. I'll have my attorney send over a proposal."

I did it!

I shoved down any signs of giddy laughter. *Stay calm, stay cool. Shake his hand, offer samples of Green Fizz from your purse. Then walk away slowly.* I turned carefully but ran smack into a giant wall of muscles—Michael Kay.

"You'll regret this," he hissed, "wait and see." But I pushed past him and kept walking until I reached Kindy, who was laughing hysterically over something Cameron had said to a vendor selling protein bars. Her cheeks had brightened to the color of tomatoes.

Caspien sidled up beside me, his face grim. "Thought I lost you," he muttered. "No ditching the babysitter."

"I made a deal!" I squealed, showing off the giant blender box in my arms, but the man selling protein bars drowned out Caspien's response.

"Listen, guys," he said, handing Kindy and Cameron a free box of protein bars. "I appreciate your attention. I even appreciate you streaming about my product on your channel. You're both nice, and I'm sure you'd be fun to work with, but you live-stream *everything.* Sure, you gave me all that publicity, but you're giving it to a hundred others too. If I stick your name on my box, or give you a cut of my sales, it feels like I'm paying you to do something you're doing for everyone else for free."

Kindy and Cameron's faces fell. Even Kindy's bob looked flatter, like her glow had diminished.

"They're so adorable," I whispered to Caspien. "I want to hate them, but I can't."

"Who, the Mormons?"

"They're Mormon?"

"I'd put money on it." He leaned closer. "The wonder in their eyes, the way they never stop smiling."

"I've never met a Mormon. Are they all like that?"

"Like you said, I want to hate them, but I can't. They're too damn nice."

Cameron and Kindy backed away from the protein bar guy, their whole bodies slumped from his rejection.

"They're nice, sure," I said, "but definitely not salesmen."

"What do you mean?"

"The protein bar guy *wants* them to convince him."

"I agree completely," Caspien said. "They need to explain how they'll give his product special treatment, but they don't get it."

"I could show them. I could set up the deal, I already have a similar plan written out in my phone."

"You think you could do it?"

"I know I could."

Caspien motioned me forward.

Maybe it was my confidence from my deal with Doug, or maybe I just knew my stuff, but I accepted Caspien's dare and set down my turquoise blender box so I could open the appropriate notes on my phone. A crowd gathered, expectantly. Cameron and Kindy watched with interest, like they couldn't fathom why I'd step into the limelight again after last night.

"It's simple," I proclaimed, and as I skimmed my notes, the floodgates of ideas opened in my head. Hundreds of them, laid out in a row so I could grasp whichever ones I liked best. "Your protein bars are good, I've had them. Low carbs, decent flavor, and macros ideal for anyone who counts them." I glanced at my phone, rapidly reading an old marketing plan, then flipped to my vendor notes about the protein bar company. "You also recently opened your own factory in the cutest town in Illinois—but you're producing more bars than you're selling. What you need is—"

A text popped up, blocking my bullet points.

Jared: *I'm watching Kindy's stream on Instagram! I love those protein bars. Can you get my face on their box?*

I froze. Jared wanted this deal? Halfway through my pitch for Kindy? Jared was a terrible match for this guy. He'd want a bigger cut than they could afford, and they mostly sold in big-box stores. Jared never made money from those deals. Soccer moms didn't like him.

And he'd still said nothing about my disaster last night. No comments about his video with Nicolete. Or my run-in with Lucas.

"Lauren?" Kindy said, nudging me with her elbow.

Focus.

I closed Jared's text and returned to my phone's notepad.

"Cameron and Kindy, he's right, you give publicity to everyone. If you want him to sign with you, he needs special treatment. You need to go above and beyond."

Another text popped up.

Jared: *Sorry to do this to you, but Michael Kay's video caused drama at home, and I had to push back my flight to early tomorrow morning. I need a favor . . . I just got off the phone with the conference coordinator. I talked them into letting you take my place as Keynote. You'll nail it! Thanks for understanding. See you bright and early.*

A second later, another text came through.

Jared: *You know I wouldn't ask if it wasn't important. It's a trust-fall favor.*

I blinked slowly as the weight of his words settled in, like chains dragging me underground. He wasn't coming? I had to give his keynote speech? And he'd texted me while he *knew* I was streaming on Kindy's feed? My gaze shot up. Everyone stared at me, waiting. What was I saying? I tried to reopen my notes, but my brain couldn't remember where to find them.

He asked for a *trust-fall favor?*

I had to give a speech. Tonight?

Where was that damn tab about their protein bar factory in Illinois?

Kindy cleared her throat, trying to reclaim my attention. But without my notes, what was I supposed to say? My right leg bounced. My left leg too.

"Do you need to pee?" Kindy asked, her nose scrunched up.

"No, why?"

"You're doing the potty dance."

I shook her off, trying to stay focused. My ideas for her and the protein bar guy would work, without a doubt. But how to articulate them without my notes? Without looking stupid?

"Airplanes," I said, clinging to what remained in my memory. "Fly out there. See it all."

"See what?" Cameron asked.

My ideas started bouncing, no longer in order. They ricocheted off the inside of my skull, fighting for my attention, clawing their way to the front. They could publicize his protein bars in so many ways—but one idea was better than the rest, if only I could cling to it.

Shove it down, quiet the voices.

My stomach clenched. Then flipped over.

"Protein guy, fly them out. Mormons, stream the whole thing. You're cute, wide-eyed, play off it. Make everyone as excited as you are."

"Excited about the protein bars?" Kindy asked.

I glanced back at Caspien. Thankfully, he was focused on his phone, typing furiously. Maybe he'd stay distracted enough to not see any of this.

"Factory, machinery, the whole ten years."

My stomach heaved.

"You mean nine yards?" the protein guy asked.

"That's what I said. I mean, that they're so, wonderful eyes—"

I was going to puke.

But not on camera, not again. So, I took off running toward a garbage can I'd spotted in the next aisle over. I stopped beside it, leaned forward, hands on my knees, panting. Oxygen still wouldn't absorb into my lungs, but the urge to throw up passed as quickly as it came. Caspien arrived a second later, the twins on his heels.

"What was that?" Caspien asked.

"My stomach."

"So, you ran out on the Mormon kids?"

"I was screwing it all up," I muttered.

"Were you? The overall concept was a viable idea."

"Sure," my voice rose, I was panicking, "if I could make coherent words come from my mouth. And if Jared hadn't—" I covered my face.

"Jared hadn't what?"

But I couldn't say the words, like speaking them might make them real. He genuinely wanted me to give a speech? *Me?*

"You're in marketing," I said, forcing myself to breathe. "How would you have sold Kindy's deal?"

"Pretty much the same," Caspien said, "but without the half sentences, or mentioning their wonderful eyes."

I scratched my neck beneath my chin. "Did I say wonderful? I meant *wonder,* as in, they should play up their innocence—the wonder in their eyes—make the trip seem like the most life-changing thing they've ever experienced."

"Ah, that makes more sense," Caspien said. Sheila and Sherry nodded.

"But my notes on my phone disappeared. There's so much on the line right now, and then Jared texted me in the middle of my pitch!" I dug for my prescription bottle and popped a Xanax into my mouth. Only a few remained in the bottom. "No one else would have panicked when they couldn't find their notes. And did I seriously sprint away from Kindy?"

"You're pale," Caspien said, and Sheila pressed a hand against my back.

"I'm fine," I gasped, but the room spun like it had last night.

"Do you need food?"

"No. Just water, with a lot of caffeine."

Caspien placed a gentle hand on my arm. "I'm not sure that's what you need."

I pulled away, stepping back as the room kept twirling. "I need to sit down, then I'll be fine. A bench in the hall, I'll be back in a few."

Then I sprinted away. But when I reached the closest bench, I couldn't stop. The noise from the vendor hall closed in around me, pushing me onward, down the stairs, into the rain, two blocks up until I burst into my hotel room and crashed on the bed, unlocking my phone to call Bailey.

If anyone could fix this, she could.

But a text from her waited on my screen.

Bailey: *BIG news! We signed another full-time trainer! Her following isn't huge yet, but she's so chill and fun. I won't lie, I'm nervous making these decisions alone. You always think of details I'd never come up with on my own. How will I produce a full show without you?*

A second later, she sent another one.

Bailey: *Sorry, ignore that last text. I'm not trying to guilt you for leaving. Enjoy your week with your family!*

Bailey, I hate you.

Not true, I loved her. But how could I ask her for help when she was swamped trying to save *my* company for me? What was I even doing here? I threw my phone on the bed beside me and covered my face with my hands. I could never call Bailey now, not with *failure* written all over me.

For now, I just needed to breathe.

And write a speech.

I lurched up, sitting on the bed. Hang on, a speech? To the entire fitness community, on a mic where Michael Kay couldn't interrupt me?

This was my chance.

I could write a speech all about Jared and the mess that the media had made of our lives. This was my opportunity to clear the air, to make Jared look like a saint.

I could do this. I really could.

Couldn't I . . .?

I scribbled notes for hours, but they appeared on the paper in random order. My mind kept wandering to how Jared had pushed this on me. He'd asked for a *trust-fall favor.* I couldn't refuse him when he used those words, the same way he would never refuse me. But I took a swig from Sherry's whiskey bottle from St. Louis—still sitting on my desk—then chugged my third Green Fizz of the day to help me focus.

But each time I filled a page, I ripped it from my notebook and threw it on the floor. When I ran out of pages, I gathered them up, then flipped them upside down to write from the bottom so my new thoughts wouldn't mix with the old ones.

Maybe it was the deadline, or maybe it was my ever-growing fury at Jared for dropping this into my lap, but tonight, I could barely write a coherent sentence.

My phone rang.

Caspien. "Where are you?"

It took a minute to figure out the answer. I still sat on my bed, surrounded by dozens of pages, but I didn't have a speech. Yet. But I would soon.

What time was it? 6:30.

No, no, no. My speech was at 6:30! Why hadn't I set an alarm? I knew better! *Never* focus on a task without setting an alarm for the next activity. Plus, I'd come up with millions of ideas, for tonight and tomorrow morning, but nothing cohesive. The ideas were there, good ones, brilliant ones. I had pages and pages of lists of possibilities.

But no speech.

"You need to get down here," Caspien said. His words sounded clipped, urgent. "Why did they just call your name to give a big speech? What's going on? Where's Jared?"

"He's been delayed."

"And you're taking his place?"

I wanted to reply, to give any sort of response, but tremors shook my body. How could I go on stage right now?

"Shit," Caspien said, his voice dropping to a whisper. "You're not here, so Michael Kay volunteered to take your place."

Chapter 9

$364.73
-$37.65 bottle of whiskey
-$153.99 ridiculously expensive blender—50% off
$173.09 remaining

I lurched to my feet, dropping my phone and cracking the glass in its corner. Great, another problem I couldn't pay for. When I scooped it up, a text waited on the lock screen.

Jared: *Good luck with your speech!*

"Seriously?" I screeched into the air. "Who do you think I am? *You?* I can't give speeches on the fly, asshole!"

My phone rang, Caspien again, but I didn't answer. I shoved my feet into my heels, took another swig of Sherry's whiskey (sorry, Sherry, it belongs to me now), then sprinted down the hall, down the stairs, and down the street as the wretched rain pelted me from the sky. Did it ever let up? Ever? And what the hell would I say when I stepped onto that stage? Or had Michael Kay already filled that spot and made a fool of Jared yet again?

Caspien waited for me right inside the dark banquet hall, and he pulled me aside as soon as I entered, his hand wrapped security around my arm.

"You can let go," I said, once he'd hidden us in the back corner.

"Not yet." His gaze stayed glued to the stage where Michael Kay was at the lectern, a wide smirk on his narrow face as he droned on about raising the quality of fitness influencers.

"It's time for the has-beens to retire," he demanded, as if he weren't from the same generation as Jared, "and leave the lucrative partnerships to the people still making waves in this industry. If you're not getting viewers, it's time to bow out and pass the torch to those of us who are."

"Should I run up there?" I asked. "Stop him, before it gets worse?"

"Do you have a speech planned?" Caspien tore his gaze away, a spark of hope in his voice.

"No." My stomach flipped over. This could only end terribly. "Jared always wings these things. I could . . . try."

That hope disappeared. "That might not be wise. What would you say? You're better with pre-written notes."

"You're right. I'm better with notes."

On stage, Michael Kay pressed a button, and a video flickered onto the giant projector screen—a scene I knew perfectly well because I'd been there. I'd lived through it.

I'd barely survived.

But how did Michael Kay get this footage?

"I've been waiting for the perfect moment to share this video," Michael Kay said. "And I think I've finally found it. If you're out there, Lauren Cross, this one's for you."

"No," I whispered. "Please, no."

The whole world had seen the video when Jared admitted to kissing Bailey Dupree. It was the same day the world found out her secret identity as Fearless Felicity, because the stage crew had forgotten to turn off the video camera. That clip had circulated the world, ruining Jared's marriage, ruining his reputation, and ruining both our careers.

But this video was different. It was the same moment, but from another angle, like someone had filmed from their phone—which meant it wouldn't cut off where everyone expected.

And Kindy and Cameron sat in the front row, streaming it live to the universe.

"Please no," I whispered again, pulling us farther back into the shadows. "This can't be happening."

"What is it?" Caspien asked, but I couldn't reply. My gaze stayed glued to the screen as my nightmare unfolded. Who had recorded this?

On the screen, Jared stormed through the doors of the JD Fitness gym and marched onto the stage, where Bailey was leading a group workout. She stood at the front with a row of dumbbells to her side, and a dozen people behind her, mimicking her movements as she lifted weights for the camera.

Jared marched straight up to her, panic in his eyes. "Where's my jacket?" he cried, then he practically groped Bailey's body.

She stopped exercising and squirmed away. "What jacket?"

"The one I put on your shoulders this morning."

"I left it in the fabrication room. Why?"

"It's gone!" Jared wailed. "My wedding ring's in the pocket, and Daisy announced to the world that I kissed you. I can't go home without it."

Bailey leapt back like he had an infectious disease. "Jared, you're married?"

"I need that coat!"

Murmurs filled the entire banquet hall. Everyone had seen this video; it had circled the internet millions of times last year. Not only had Jared cheated on his wife, but he'd kept her existence a secret from our entire office just so he could have flings with the fitness girls.

But the video didn't end where it normally had. It blacked out for a moment, then jumped forward ten minutes and zeroed in on a pale face beneath a pixie cut. My hair. With Bailey by my side. Who the hell filmed this? They were *so* fired.

"You knew he was married, didn't you?" Bailey said to me on the giant TV.

"He made me promise not to tell."

"Sometimes we do stupid things for people we love." In the video, my entire body slumped until Bailey put her arm around me. Love? Bailey said *love.* Was Jared watching this?

"I deserve better."

"Yes, you do."

Then it spliced ahead again, only ten seconds this time, and zoomed in on our faces as I said, "The real Jared is . . ."

"A dick?"

"Yeah."

The lights in the banquet hall popped back on as Michael Kay held his stomach, laughing with his entire body.

"There you have it, guys," he said. "From the mouth of Lauren herself, she's madly in love with a slimy, skeevy, skirt-chasing dick. And she's known all along that he was sleeping around on his wife. The next time she tries to tell you he's changed, remember this magical moment." He bowed low, though not one person clapped, the sword in his belt swinging behind him.

Michael Kay continued talking into the mic, something about his upcoming exercise program, but I didn't hear him. Something was wrong with my body. Terribly, horribly wrong. My chest lit on fire; lava climbed up my throat. I clutched at my neck, squeezing.

"Breathe," Caspien said, still grasping my arm while wrapping the other around my waist. "You're panicking. Take a deep breath. This will be over soon."

I opened my mouth, and air flooded my lungs as Michael Kay left the stage and the room erupted into chaos. Everyone talked over each other, dozens of phones streaming the madness. The twins found us first, in biker shorts and tank tops that showcased their muscular bodies, expressions dripping with pity.

"There's no way Jared didn't see that!" I groaned. "Now he knows exactly how I feel about him, and his wife knows, the whole world knows!"

"The world already did, honey," Sheila said. "It was obvious from the day we met you two."

Sherry offered me her wine, but I couldn't move. "We all thought you'd finally leave him when he married Lily, but instead, you packed up and followed them across the country. You deserve better, you always have."

"But now the whole world knows that I covered for him," I gasped. "No one will ever believe me."

Sheila rubbed my arm, but she didn't disagree. "Michael Kay's video was a dick move."

Sherry nodded. "He went too far."

"Did I though?" The phony Frenchman himself strolled up, his tiny head swiveling on his thick neck as he smirked at each of us in turn. His form fitting tank top displayed just how muscular he'd grown since our last event together.

Instinctively, I coiled back into Caspien, who wrapped his other arm around me. Sheila and Sherry moved to block me from his view as a full entourage followed behind him, cameras streaming, ready for a show.

Cameron and Kindy were among them, one on each side, but they filmed with less enthusiasm than usual. Exhaustion had etched itself into my bones. This crowd had witnessed enough gossip tonight. They wouldn't get any more drama from me.

"The fitness industry used to be about becoming better versions of ourselves," Michael Kay said, his voice booming. "People like Jared DiMaggio rake our reputations through the mud."

"Says the guy who carries a sword?" To my surprise, the outburst came from Caspien, who still held me close.

Michael Kay laughed, swishing the sword through the air between his crowd and mine. His thick fingers engulfed the narrow hilt. "There's no shame in a little flair."

But Sheila rolled her eyes. "You have no room to talk about reputations. You tried to sell me illegal steroids an hour ago."

He slid the sword into its sheath and winked at the streaming phones. "I would never. I would, however, happily steal Jared's clients." He slid to the left revealing Doug, *my* Doug. "Nothing's yours until you sign a contract."

"Sorry, Lauren," Doug said. "You understand, right? Jared's too big of a risk."

I unfurled from Caspien's cocoon and stepped forward, directly between the twins. "You think Michael Kay's any better than Jared? He's not, he's just better at doing it off-camera. He'll turn on you as quickly as he turned on Jared."

"Y-you think?" Doug stammered, his forehead creasing.

But I wasn't finished, and I didn't need notes for this one. "Use the twins instead. They're reliable, they have a huge following, and they sell their own line of protein powder. How do people make protein shakes? In a blender, just like yours. It's a no-brainer."

Doug's gaze flew to the twins. "Is that true? Call my people, let's chat about it."

The humor dropped from Michael Kay's crooked mouth. "No way. We have a deal."

"Nothing's yours until you sign a contract," I said, and Michael Kay balled his giant hands into fists, his pale skin reddening like a pimple ready to pop. "And even then, you're easy to wiggle away from."

"Don't you dare mess with my contracts, you home-wrecker!"

Something snapped inside me. I was possibly the *only* woman at JD Fitness that Jared *hadn't* fooled around with. "Then don't mess with mine!"

Michael Kay lurched across the gap and smashed into me. His shoulder bashed into the side of my face, and I flew backward, crashing flat onto my back on the cold, hard ground. The air knocked out of my lungs. Did I hit the back of my head? Not sure, but stars burst across my vision. My jaw popped; pain split through my cheek. And Michael Kay crashed onto the floor at my feet.

Then silence.

The entire conference room held perfectly still, cameras poised and rolling, everyone holding their breaths. Kindy hid her face in Cameron's shoulder. Her phone still streamed in her other hand, trained on Michael Kay. Everyone's cameras were.

Caspien dropped to his knees. He slid one hand beneath my back and gently helped me to my feet. Then he touched my cheek, inspecting for injuries, but I pushed his hand away.

Michael Kay was on the move.

He climbed to his feet, his chest heaving, fists flexing. Veins bulged down his neck and arms. Barely contained fury broiled in his narrow eyes. The only sounds in the silent room were his panting breaths. They picked up speed. Then his nostrils flared, like a bull ready to charge.

"Roid rage!" Sherry yelled, clinging to one of his giant arms and holding him back.

"She's half your size," Sheila shrieked.

Then everyone erupted at once. Wild chatter came from every direction. Someone screamed, Kindy sobbed into Cameron's protective arm. But none of their words made it to my ears. Nothing penetrated my own bubble of fury building up in my chest. My lungs. My fists.

Unlike Michael Kay, I hadn't done any steroids, but I still wanted to kill him.

A million methods stormed into my head as my vision cleared, and my rage built up. I could poison his precious protein shakes, drop him in a lake until his oily skin bubbled and peeled off, smash his tiny little head in his sleep. Bribe his bellhop to give me a key, climb through his window, or just blow up the entire building. The ideas had no beginning, no end, they roared through the room like a steam train, barreling over the people until all that remained were me and Michael Kay and the train's whistle, screeching louder and louder, burning my ears, clawing at my brain, filling me up with bubbling, boiling acid that couldn't do anything but—

—I exploded.

I launched myself across the room, my entire body aimed at his chest. My shoulder connected first and he crashed out of Sherry's arms, falling onto his back. I landed on his stomach, straddling him, smacking his face with both hands.

"How dare you?" I shrieked. "How dare you ruin my career, my life? And then attack me!" Hands in fists, I punched his ribs—it hurt like hell, but the steam exploded from my hands and my mouth and the tips of my hair, and I couldn't stop until Michael Kay shoved me off like I weighed less than a ladybug. He staggered to his feet, wiping blood from a cut on his lip. Then he turned and pushed his way into the crowd. Caspien grabbed one of my arms and someone else grabbed the other. I kicked wildly, trying to connect with his back, his legs, whatever I could reach. But Caspien wrapped both arms around me, locking me against his solid chest until Michael Kay disappeared completely—and someone else slipped into his place.

Hallie.

Again, Hallie.

When I was at my worst.

I gasped for air, but it wouldn't stick. I sucked in, and out and in and out and in. Couldn't breathe. Hyperventilating. I stuffed my hand into my purse and yanked out a Xanax—my second to last pill—but the moment it touched my tongue my stomach roiled.

Caspien grabbed a garbage can and slid it before me, and I puked every drop of liquid into the bin. My adrenaline drained away with it, my injuries rearing their ugly faces. My jaw ached, my cheek bone, the spot between my spine and my right shoulder blade. Caspien handed me a napkin, and I wiped my face to an audience of hundreds.

Or millions, if you counted the viewers at the other end of their phones.

But I was only aware of Hallie, her long ponytail hanging down her back, her forehead scrunched up in worry.

"Are you . . . okay?" she asked, her small voice uncertain. She wore a maroon suitcoat and black slacks. Had she come straight from work?

"I think so." My rage disappeared. The steam evaporated. "What are you doing here?"

She eyed all the streaming cameras then turned her back to them, hiding her face. "I saw Michael Kay's video; I came straight over." She lowered her voice and rubbed the back of her neck, never once meeting my gaze. After a tense silence, she pulled a piece of gum from her pocket and popped it into her mouth. Cinnamon. "I wanted to know, have you really loved Jared all this time?" At last, she met my gaze. All her prior hostility had vanished, replaced by uncertainty. Or perhaps curiosity. "Is that why you left?"

But before I could answer, someone circled around and shoved their camera in Hallie's face. "What is your relationship with Lauren Cross?" the man asked. "Do you work for Jared too? Have you had an affair?"

Hallie's arm shot up, hiding her face. Then she darted from the room. I wanted to chase her, to answer her question. But I didn't have the strength.

"Need a doctor?" Caspien asked.

The second he mentioned it, the throbbing in my cheekbone grew stronger. "Fresh air."

He nodded, then put his arm around my waist and led me from the room. A few would-be paparazzi tried to follow, but the twins stopped them at the door.

"Thanks, guys," Caspien said.

"Take care of her," Sheila replied.

I leaned into Caspien as the big doors shut behind us. I could breathe now, but the shock of my first ever fist fight had my entire body shaking.

"It'll wear off," Caspien assured, and by the time we reached the street, and I'd inhaled a lungful of cold, rainy air, the jitters were draining from my system. But what must Caspien think of me? How pathetic, that I'd chased a man all these years, moved across the country for him, covered for him when he cheated with other women. I'd humiliated myself again and again.

Caspien stopped me under the first streetlight, the nighttime sky cloudy and dark, the rain a light drizzle. When he faced me, I stared firmly at the ground.

"Look at me," he said. But how could I meet his eyes after everything I'd done? Caspien put one hand under my chin to lift my face. His brown eyes lingered on mine.

Pain shot down my shoulder. "Ow." Not too bad, though.

He frowned then moved my torso side to side while watching my reactions. "Was that your first fight?"

"Was it obvious?"

"Only a little. Can you open your mouth all the way?"

I did, with only a hint of pain back by my ear. Caspien ran his fingers tenderly over my temple, then my cheekbone, then my jaw. Everywhere he touched came alive. Shivers trailed down my neck, goosebumps across my collar bone. My breaths grew shallow. I studied his face as he searched my eyes for signs of a concussion. Light freckles dotted the tops of his cheeks, and a hint of a scar marred the left side of the bridge of his nose. Did he wear glasses? He narrowed his dark eyes as he cupped my chin with both palms. "Does any of this hurt?"

"Not too much."

His breath tickled the tiny hairs on my cheek. "I can't believe he attacked you. Nothing seems too injured, but you may end up with a headache and a black eye."

"It's a fitting end to this terrible day." Not to mention, I'd just puked my guts out. Again. Could he smell it on me? I held my breath.

Caspien smiled a little then dropped his hands. The temperature outside dropped with them. He started walking, but in the opposite direction of my hotel room.

"What happened in there?" he asked.

"Honestly? I wanted to kill him."

"I get it. He never should have attacked you like that."

"It wasn't just that." The memory of it swarmed through me. The anger, the betrayal, the humiliation, too many emotions, too much to process all at once. "It was everything piling on top of each other. Jared's video with Nicoleta, humiliating myself with Lucas, failing to sign any deals. Then I focused so hard on writing my speech I lost track of time—not that I'd finished—but then this new video? And Hallie keeps seeing me at my worst! I'm *trying*, Caspien, I'm really trying. But when Michael Kay shoved me over, all those failures erupted inside me and I just . . . I needed an outlet, or I was going to explode."

Caspien listened quietly as we circled the block and approached a tall skyscraper. "I have an idea," he said, using a keycard to open the dark building. "Will you try it? It might help you."

"Where are we? Is this still the conference center?"

"It's connected to it. This is the Croft Power corporate office. There's a staff gym in the basement."

"The gym? Seriously?" I'd had enough of gyms to last a lifetime.

"Give me five minutes. If you hate it, we'll leave."

I agreed, and Caspien led me down a staircase, across a long hall that smelled like chlorine, and into a wide workout space similar to Jared's back home. Cardio machines filled one half, weight racks filled the other, and the familiar odor of sweat and rubber lingered in the air. But instead of a central stage, like in Jared's gym, rows and rows of punching bags hung from the ceiling. Caspien grabbed a pair of green gloves from a rack and handed them to me.

"Lucas likes kickboxing," he said, as if that explained what we were doing. "Put the gloves on."

"You want me to box?"

"You promised me five minutes. It's an experiment, that's all."

With a groan, I slid out of my heels and kicked them against the wall, then dropped my coat and purse on top of them. "For the record, I hate exercising. And I hate gyms."

But Caspien shrugged out of his jacket and led me to the nearest punching bag. "Have you ever boxed?"

"Never. And I want it to stay that way."

Caspien smirked, then he pointed to the bag. "Go ahead. But start slow, in case you're more injured than I realized."

I punched, once. Then again with my other hand. The bag swayed and Caspien stood behind it to hold it in place. He added a few cues to fix my form and tighten my core.

"How's your shoulder?"

I shrugged it a couple of times. "Feels fine." My head did too.

Caspien nodded and motioned for me to punch again. Immediately the muscles in my stomach and shoulders burned, but my raging thoughts slowed.

"Keep taking swings," he said. "But now I want you to tell me more about what happened with Michael Kay."

"Honestly, when I spiral out of control like that, it's hard to remember."

"Try. And don't stop punching."

"Well, remember what you said last night? About me being a puzzle?" I punched the bag again and again, letting it distract me from my uncomfortable explanation. "You were more right than you realized. It's like my entire brain is a puzzle, an ocean of pieces in a torrential storm, crashing around so I can never find the pieces I need." I stopped punching and met Caspien's eyes. "It may not seem like it, but I'm smart. Like, really smart."

"Keep punching."

I did. "The problem is that I have all these great ideas, but the storm in my head keeps me from focusing on the right pieces at the right time and completing the puzzle. It's why I constantly write notes in my phone and make lists to keep things straight. If I can refer back to those, I function pretty well. But when I'm thrown off guard, like when Jared texts me that I have to give his speech in the middle of my pitch for Kindy and Cameron? Or when Michael Kay shows a video I wasn't prepared for . . . My brain chucks responses at me, like baseballs through a pitching machine set at the highest speed. I know all the answers, but I lose them as quickly as they come. They sail right past me."

I attacked the punching bag, throwing all my weight into it. My muscles came alive in my shoulders and my core. I felt powerful, strong, no signs of lingering injuries from Michael Kay. Each time my fist connected, my body craved another punch. And with half my brain occupied with punching, the speed of my thoughts settled to manageable pace.

"The only thing I've ever done right, my entire life, is Jared's career. Selling his program was easy because I mostly hid behind my computer writing promo emails. I could get into the zone and write a month's worth in one day. Jared did all the in-person stuff."

I threw my weight into my punches, leaning into each one until Caspien had to brace himself to steady the bag. "But ever since I got here, I've had to cover for Jared's half of our job and I'm failing!" Sweat poured down the back of my blouse, but I didn't stop. I pummeled the bag, over and over, pouring my frustration into every punch. "When Michael Kay played that video, the only thing I've ever done right disappeared before my eyes. I panicked."

Caspien circled behind me and pressed a gentle hand against the small of my back. "Slow down," he said calmly. "You're injured, we don't want to make it worse."

I slowed my punches, settling into a rhythm. Caspien kept his fingertips lightly on my waist. His touch grounded me, soothed the panic that continually welled up inside.

"I wish it would stop," I said. "All of it. Everything. We were a perfect team until Jared's cheating became public." I spun around and faced him, my arms dropping to my sides. "I've never once tried to break up his marriage. I've never tried to flirt with him or dress sexy for him. I even like Lily. She's smart and hard working. I respect her too much to be so cruel. But do you want to know something? He's kissed almost every girl in our entire office, except me."

Never me. Not once. Was something wrong with me?

Caspien cocked his head. "Hang on, you knew he'd cheated more times?"

"Yes, I knew. Our whole office knew, and I still wanted to be with him. Why do I still love somebody like him, Caspien? How can I be so stupid? I've told myself over and over to move on. I've dated, I've tried one-night stands. But every time, when I return to work the next day, the second I see him I turn to mush."

"Lauren—" He slid his hands softly around my forearms, just above the gloves, but I pulled away. His touch was too humiliating after a confession like that.

"Why doesn't he want me? Is it because my brain doesn't work like a regular person's? Is it because I'm too much baggage for someone to love? He doesn't even like his wife, but she still gets more of his attention. I've been telling myself for years that those other girls are just keeping his bed warm while his marriage is in shambles, that he's saving *us* for after they split up for good. So we can be together for real. But that's stupid, right?"

"Maybe," Caspien said softly. "But maybe not."

"Or maybe I'm just an idiot." I dropped to the floor and pulled my knees to my chest, hiding my sweaty face in my arms as a sob heaved up into my throat. Caspien knelt in front of me and pulled the gloves from my hands, one at a time.

"I've never met Jared," he finally said. "There's clearly a complicated history between you two. But I do know that you spoke in full, coherent sentences for the last ten minutes. Not one sign of a panic attack."

When I lifted my head, a hint of smugness hung at the corners of Caspien's lips.

"I did?"

"Can I tell you my theory? The reason I brought you here?"

"Sure."

"My favorite aunt had anxiety. She was kind of like you, brilliant woman, but her brain worked too fast. She'd start a million projects, but never finished a single one."

I dropped my knees until I sat crisscross. "How did she cope with it?"

"Very poorly, for a long time. When she was in her forties, she finally talked to a doctor about the panic attacks and learned she had ADHD. He first suspected it because she tapped her fingers all the time. She'd tap with one hand, doodle with another, hum, and bounce her legs, all at once. If she stopped, her brain would go haywire. Turns out, the anxiety wasn't the root problem. The ADHD was keeping her from functioning, which then caused anxiety and panic attacks. He put her on ADHD medication and found her a therapist who explained the quirks in her brain that she'd always seen as defects. She became a different person, like her life finally began."

Caspien sat quietly while his words soaked under my skin, the pipes humming their gentle vibrations in the walls. My brain had too many defects to keep track of. Was he saying they weren't actually defects? Could they be symptoms of something else?

"What did she do?" I asked, scooting closer until our knees touched. "After she could function again?"

Caspien smiled, his most genuine expression since we'd met. It reached his forehead, his eyes, his posture. "She read books. Thousands of them. For the first time in her life, she could concentrate long enough to get to the end. I don't know if this fits your situation, but when this is all over, run it past your doctor. See what he thinks."

Deep inside my chest, amidst my flurry of chaos, one of my tiny little puzzle pieces . . .

. . . clicked into place.

"That's why you had me punch while I talked?"

"You couldn't seem to get it out otherwise."

"Thank you, Caspien. For paying enough attention. And for caring enough to tell me."

He smiled again, softer this time, and my legs tingled at the exact points where our knees touched, and where the tip of his finger rested against my calf. He angled his body closer toward mine.

Was I breathing?

No.

Breathe, Lauren. Breathe.

My gaze dropped to his lips, the ones that had just smiled at me—really smiled—only seconds before. There was an indent in his plump bottom lip above his closely-trimmed goatee. Something crackled in the air between us, something alluring and powerful. I swallowed.

"We should go," I said, clearing my throat. "Tomorrow's a big day, my meeting with Lucas and everything."

Assuming Lucas even still wanted to meet with us. After Michael Kay's video, it might be pointless. And how could I prepare before Jared arrived tomorrow? He likely had something planned already, but what was it? Should I call and ask him? Definitely not, now that the world had watched the video admitting how I felt about him. I mean, Jared knew this. He'd always known. But we hadn't ever actually discussed it. That video brought it out in the open.

So, how could I plan for our pitch without Jared?

Caspien had mentioned that Lucas hated schmoozers like Michael Kay. What if we did the opposite? What if we walked into that meeting and candidly laid our situation on the table? Our desperation. He might appreciate the honesty.

Worth a try? Maybe.

But when I looked up at Caspien, all thoughts of Jared's meeting fled. "What?"

He grinned. "Your brain is already ten steps ahead, isn't it?"

"I can't help it. There's so much to do."

He offered a hand and pulled us both to our feet—then dropped my fingers quickly. But neither of us moved. The air felt different now, lighter. Standing there with Caspian felt so . . . comfortable. So safe. Like I could be my messy self and he wouldn't shame me for it.

"Jared has this phrase for me," I said. "*Shove it down, quiet the voices.* It used to help, but it doesn't anymore."

"He wants you to trap it all inside? You'll go mad!"

"That's kind of where I'm at"—I crossed my eyes—"a bit psycho."

Caspien chuckled. "Honestly, I'm jealous that you can survive so many feelings. I've spent years trying to face mine, but . . ." He shoved both hands deep into his pockets, gaze planted firmly on the floor. "It's too much."

"Is this the girlfriend that broke your heart?"

"Yeah, sort of. Listen," he pulled one hand out to rub the back of his neck, "there's this restaurant I go to sometimes . . ."

"I'm hungry." I had no money, but this feeling of not having to hide wasn't one I could walk away from just yet.

Caspien smiled and his dimple popped out. "Me too. Let's go."

Chapter 10

Still $173.09

The direct route to the restaurant required us to cross through the conference center. I cringed. How could I face the people in that ballroom? Fortunately, Caspien led me through a maze of hallways, my heels clicking with each step, until we made it to the main doors. Rain poured earnestly from the night sky. Caspien grabbed an umbrella from a staff closet, then we darted outside.

"I thought Seattleites don't use umbrellas," I shouted. Our faces stayed dry, but the wind blew the rain sideways, soaking everything from our waists down. And the cold? It seeped through my jacket like all I wore was a bra. Why didn't anyone warn me about the weather? Oh yeah, I grew up here. But clearly, I'd forgotten.

"They don't." We hurried down the dimly lit street. "But I didn't grow up here."

"Where are you from?"

"St. Louis. I moved to Washington three years ago. That's why Hallie called in the favor I owed her. She thought you'd open up better to someone from home."

Home? The word did backflips inside my chest. My childhood house was only ten miles away. But home had always seemed like wherever Jared was. His couch in college, then St. Louis for the last eleven years. Plus, Bailey was in Missouri. And my company. They were my family. But Hallie was too. What would it take to rekindle that flame? Or light it in the first place? We could be real sisters if she'd let me try. But what about when I return to Missouri in a few days?

And Mom . . .

The one person who'd never shamed me for being . . . different. But she'd stopped calling three years ago, and the times I'd tried to call her, the call wouldn't go through. If she changed her number, why didn't she tell me? Mom was *home* more than anywhere else, even if we hadn't spoken in ages. Did she feel the same way about me that Hallie did? The answer scared me too much to dwell on.

"You never told me you were from St. Louis," I said.

"You never asked."

I stopped halfway across the empty street. It took Caspien a few seconds to hurry back with the umbrella, but I didn't continue walking.

"You're right," I said. "I never asked. You've been helping me flounder through the last two days. I've puked—twice, I've had panic attacks and blood sugar crashes and jumped into fistfights. You've heard my entire life story—probably three times by now—but I've never once asked about yours. Caspien, I'm so sorry."

He didn't move, he just studied me like I might scurry away if he waited a few more seconds.

"When we get to the restaurant," I said, "will you tell me about yourself?"

His voice dropped an octave and came out scratchy. "What do you want to know?"

"Everything."

"I was born at eleven-oh-two in my mom's bathtub." A slow smile crept across his face.

"Not that," I said, pushing his chest and laughing.

He pointed at a shop on the next corner, a frilly little café called Marigold's Splendid Sandwiches. My watch said it was nearly 10:00 p.m., but the lights were still on, and pink and purple flowers filled the windows.

"This is your favorite restaurant?"

"Nope," he said, heading toward the door. I hurried to stay under the umbrella and fell into step beside him, my shoulder pressed against his. "But I eat here every day, so maybe someday it'll grow on me."

The interior decorations contained more frills than the exterior. Someone had scrawled the soup of the day in pink calligraphy across a blackboard framed by flowered garlands. Bouquets of artificial roses sat at the center of each white, linen-draped table. The air smelled like potpourri or too much perfume. Swirly patterns were even etched into the silverware. Needless to say, every patron was female.

I leaned close to Caspien. "Why do you eat here?"

"Hello, Caspien," said an elderly woman in a yellow frock. She'd piled up her hair in a heap of stringy curls and wore bright pink lipstick. "You're later than usual, and you brought a friend." Her gaze darted briefly to my turquoise hair, then her plastered smile shined brighter. Or faker.

"Hey, Connie," he said tightly. "Table for two, please."

She gave us a maroon vinyl booth in the corner, far away from other patrons, like they might catch my turquoise hair disease if we sat too close. Did I look beat up too? Fine by me, I preferred less distractions. Caspien sat across the table and slid me a menu.

"Why are we eating here?" I asked again, once our server walked away.

"My therapist says it's good for me."

"Getting in touch with your inner grandmother?"

He laughed, relaxing for the first time since we'd entered this ridiculous room. "Something like that."

When I read the prices, I grimaced. Twenty dollars for a grilled cheese sandwich? Forty for grilled chicken and rice? I couldn't even afford an appetizer. Connie returned and Caspien ordered a plate of tacos.

"I'm fine with water," I said, pulling a Green Fizz packet from my purse. When food failed me, I stuck with caffeine.

"You need to eat," Caspien insisted.

"This is plenty." I wiggled the little packet.

"Pick a meal or I'll pick one for you, and it'll be gross."

He stared at me, and I stared back. Connie leaned away with her hand over her heart, like we'd offended her horribly. Had my eye blackened yet? That wouldn't help make a good impression.

"Grilled cheese is fine," I grumbled.

"A bag of ice too," he added, "for her eye."

The server scurried away, then took a long drink of his water. "Can I give you some advice? About your fight with Michael Kay?"

"What? No." I had zero desire to relive that terrible moment.

But Caspien set his jaw. "This is important."

I grimaced, snorting up flowery air that sent me into a fit of coughs. How could anyone eat real food in a place that smelled like perfume? "Fine," I said, once I got my coughing under control.

"The conference coordinator texted me. They banned Michael Kay from all Croft Power property. But even without him around, there are things you should know about fist fights. First, if you're going to pick one—"

"Hey, I did *not* pick that fight. He attacked first." I gingerly pressed my fingers to my cheek bone; it was getting sore.

"You're right. If you're going to *participate* in fist fights—"

"That's better."

"Rule number one, always throw the first punch."

"Wait, what?"

"Rule number two, make that punch count."

"I don't get it."

Caspien leaned closer. "Pretend for a minute that you and Michael Kay were the same size. Real fights aren't like TV where everyone takes a million punches and then walks away unphased. In a real fight, advantage goes to whoever lands the first punch."

"Especially if it's a solid hit?"

"Exactly. And when you're half the size of your opponent, like with you and Michael Kay, you need to do the bulk of your damage before he hits you once and you can't recover."

"Or better yet, go straight for his balls."

Caspien laughed, the corners of his eyes crinkling. "Sure, if you can land it."

"Solid advice. Next time I attack a man twice my size, I'll remember that."

"Hopefully it's not for a long time."

"No kidding. Is my eye purple?"

"It's getting there."

Connie practically tossed our plates and a thin bag of ice on the table, then sprinted away. I bit into the corner of my sandwich and moaned. Had I eaten anything today besides that chocolate muffin? I genuinely couldn't remember, but the warm bread, cheese, and butter melted in my mouth, and I scarfed down a second bite. Then a third. As soon as I swallowed the last of it, Connie chucked another one at me and ran.

"What's this?" I asked.

Caspien nudged it toward me. "You seemed hungry."

"When did you order it?"

"While you were devouring your first."

I bit into it. "Thanks, Caspien." He always seemed to know what I needed better than I did.

He hadn't touched his tacos. When I finished my second sandwich, I slid my plate away and pulled my feet up onto the seat, my knees against my chest. I wrapped the ice bag in a napkin. Pressing it gingerly against my cheekbone, I stiffened from the cold, then slowly relaxed as my nerves responded to the soothing chill. Perhaps I'd been more uncomfortable than I'd realized. "No more avoiding it. It's your turn. Tell me about yourself."

He froze, his first taco halfway to his mouth. "What do you want to know?"

"Let's start with why your therapist thinks you need to eat at this obnoxious restaurant—with delicious grilled cheese, by the way. Ten out of ten."

"How about something simpler?" He finally took his first bite.

"Sure. Why'd you move to Seattle?"

"Hallie offered me a job." He said it too quickly.

"Okay, but why'd you leave St. Louis? People don't move away from home for nothing. And how do you know my sister?"

Caspien set down his taco. Wiped his face with a napkin. Swallowed some water. Straightened his overly decorated silverware. I waited. I could be patient when I wanted to. Really, I could. All ten of my toes wiggled in my shoes.

"I was married," he said, straightening his silverware again. "Her name was Samantha. She was a nurse, a brilliant one. We had a daughter, Maddie. She was six."

"*Was*?" My body went completely still.

Caspien stared at his plate. "They were killed in a car crash."

How could I possibly respond to a revelation like that? "I'm so sorry. Was it a drunk driver?"

"Drugs." He looked up, met my eyes. "My wife was the one using."

I lowered the ice bag to the table and pressed my hand against my chest. Was this why he'd worried about Michael Kay's cocaine? And asked so many questions about my anti-drug program? "What happened?"

"She became addicted after her C-section with Maddie. She was a nurse practitioner, so she didn't need a doctor for prescriptions. She and a friend wrote them for each other."

"Did you try to help her?"

"I didn't know. She hid the pills, only took them when I wasn't around. I was Sales Director for a multi-state company, so I traveled a lot, and our marriage wasn't amazing. We loved each other, but we both worked full-time. I guess I was distracted." Caspien squeezed the handle of his fork until his knuckles turned white. "They called me while I was out of town, saying there'd been an accident, Samantha and Maddie were gone. I rented a car and drove all night back to St. Louis thinking someone else had hit them. Someone had to pay."

After sucking in a long breath, he placed the fork carefully back in its row.

"Only when I went into the police station did they tell me about the blood workup. My wife had taken too many pills, then tried to drive Maddie to dance class. They didn't make it a mile on the highway before she swerved into oncoming traffic. They both died instantly."

Slowly, I inched my hand across the table and rested it on his forearm. He stared at my fingers without looking up.

"The hardest part was discovering Samantha's secrets. The years of medical records she'd hidden away, the pharmacy receipts for the pills, the bottles hidden inside our box spring. She had dozens, still full. Looking back, I remember so many times she'd seemed off, fuzzy. Like she wasn't all there. I'd assumed she was distracted by work or drama with her siblings. So many times, I'd asked her what was wrong, and every time she'd looked me square in the eyes . . . and lied to my face."

Everything about Caspien clicked into place. His disdain for drugs, his lack of trust, his relief that I couldn't tell lies. And every time I'd struggled, he'd seemed determined to help, like he never wanted to repeat what happened with Samantha. But the amount of grief built up behind his eyes, the well of it, the chasm. My heart ached for all that torment.

"That was five years ago." He shook his head, coming back to reality. "For a long time, I shoved down my grief. I tried to avoid it by burying myself in work. But eventually, I couldn't stand seeing the same house every day, Maddie's school, the kids on our street getting older without her. That's when Hallie called me, three years ago. She'd been college roommates with my niece, and I'd consulted for Croft Power a few times when Lucas first started the company. Hallie said she'd heard about my situation, and they were hiring a marketing director. The job was mine if I needed to get away. I left everything behind and flew out the next day."

"Is that the favor she did for you?"

"She saved my life."

"And here you are."

"Here I am."

I lowered my voice before I spoke again. "That doesn't explain your friendship with our delightful waitress." Connie was leaning against a table on the far side of the kitchen, arms folded, glaring at us.

Caspien almost smiled, I was sure of it. "When I first arrived, I may have been depressed."

"May have?"

He shrugged one shoulder. "Hallie and I worked close together back then. Eventually, she called me out and connected me with a therapist, a friend of hers. First, he required me to adopt a dog. Best decision I ever made. Then he said I needed to stop hiding from the grief and face it instead."

"So, you came *here*?"

"Samantha had a favorite restaurant back home, pretty similar to this one. She used to take Maddie there for breakfast when I was out of town. The therapist thought it would help me grieve if I spent time here. But honestly, it just makes me hate the color pink." Caspien shot me a self-deprecating smile.

I scrunched my nose. "Don't worry, I'm hating pink more with every passing second."

"Glad it's not just me." His smile faded. "So that's my life story. Now I'm just hanging around Seattle, missing my daughter and trying to convince myself not to hate my late wife. It never changes."

I tilted my head to the side, the same way Caspien did when I said things that didn't make sense.

"What?" he asked.

"It sounds like your therapist is trying to force the wrong emotions out of you. You're angry at Samantha, but he's telling you to shove down the anger and feel something else. That's exactly what Jared always tells me to do. But until . . ." I swallowed. "Until *you* showed me that hiding my feelings wasn't working, I didn't realize how much anxiety that was causing.

"Your therapist wants you to come to *her* favorite place and bask in *her* memory in order to stir up grief that doesn't exist. Grief isn't the emotion you need to process, it's anger. It's her betrayal. It's her ultimate breach of trust. You put your daughter's life in her hands, and she lied to your face."

I leaned back in my chair, studying the uncertainty in Caspien's eyes. "Go to Maddie's favorite places and mourn there, not Samantha's. Go to the graveyard, find a park similar to one back home, hang out at elementary schools—no, don't do that. Please don't get arrested for being a creeper. But mourn your daughter, then give yourself permission to be mad at your wife."

Caspien inhaled slowly. "But doesn't it make me a bad person? To hate her after her tragic death?"

"Maddie's death was tragic. Samantha's was terrible and heartbreaking, but also selfish. If you bottle up your anger, guess what will stick with you forever?"

"My anger?"

"Exactly. If you want it to fade, you first have to feel it. Bask in it. Let it soak through your skin until there isn't any left."

"That's kind of gross."

"It's true though. You can't bottle up all those emotions."

"What's that line Jared always tells you?"

"Shove it down, quiet the voices."

Caspien shook his head. "That's terrible advice."

"It really is." I laughed. "But I am so sorry about your family. Every bit of that story is heartbreaking. I'm glad that Hallie recognized you needed help. Sometimes we can't fix everything on our own."

"She's amazing," Caspien agreed. "I've been here three years and she's still my closest friend. But what really convinced me to take this job was Lucas. He wanted to found a non-profit division, to open an assortment of charities; he said I could run the whole thing. I asked if his foundation could support the children of parents addicted to drugs, and he said yes right away—that's the real reason I moved here."

"Did you start it?"

"No, the entire non-profit division never happened. It's been three years, but here I am, still running Sales and Marketing."

"You must be good at your job."

"Or Lucas is too distracted. He's been a mess the past couple of years. He lost that flair that made him brilliant, but no one knows why. Either way, my foundation for kids never happened."

"But doesn't Lucas's fancy clean electricity company help people? It's good for the environment, right? Revolutionizing the world, or whatever? Your job still makes a difference."

"Sure, Lucas is a brilliant engineer. But I just sit in an office pushing papers."

"That sucks," I said, sipping ice water. Caspien had still barely touched his tacos. "If you want to commiserate, my life isn't what I'd planned either. My high school career was perfect, 4.0 GPA, honor roll, a scholarship to the University of Washington. Growing up in White Center, I had a one-in-a-million chance of getting out, but I did it. Then anxiety happened, and depression, and I dropped out of college halfway through my first semester. If Jared and I hadn't started JD Fitness, I don't know where I'd be."

"That's why you moved to St. Louis with him?"

"I'd go anywhere for him. Or, I would have. I'm not sure what we'll do now."

What would happen to our careers if we didn't land the contract with Lucas tomorrow morning? What could we possibly say to convince him to hop onto our sinking ship? Perhaps it was time to think about alternative career paths, or at least finding new clients to represent. But my career had always been so wrapped up in Jared's, pressing forward without him was . . . daunting.

"You're friends with Fearless Felicity, aren't you?" Caspien finished his first taco and moved on to the next. "Why don't you represent her, instead?"

"I already do, but I keep lining up jobs that she turns down. She's a devoted mom to a busy daughter, she doesn't want to jeopardize that."

"Makes sense."

"Sure. But I could use the money. I'm flat-out broke, and last year we maxed out a bunch of credit cards in my name to keep JD Fitness afloat. I can't even borrow money now."

"Does she know?"

"About the company debt? Of course. That the cards are in my name? No, I couldn't put that on her. And she doesn't want to partner with any random vendors, she wants principled companies that share her values . . . unless it's fancy water bottles. That woman loves water bottles. Fitness people are so weird."

"Have you reached out to any water bottle companies?"

"She partnered with most of them on her own, long ago. Clothing companies and fitness venues reach out every single day, but she doesn't want any. She wants to stand for something. I get it. In fact, her scarcity makes people want her more. And her blog is ridiculous, like thirty million subscribers now. Meanwhile, Jared wants every job, but not one person will sign him. How is it that I have my dream job and I'm still completely failing? I'm like a cancer, screwing up everything I touch. You know what's ironic? Jared's currently doing a show for a *family* network. They're probably groaning every time a new video pops up online."

"Do you work for them too? Are you getting paid?"

"No, I only work for Jared. I get a percentage of his sponsorships and promo deals, but the network stuff goes through JD Fitness—which I technically own, but I don't have a day job there anymore, so I don't get a salary. And they're too broke to send out owner's distributions. Someday I'll earn money from it, but not until they pay off their debts."

"Sometimes what we think we want isn't what we thought it'd be."

"No kidding. Like your non-profit gig?"

"Exactly. Though that one will happen, eventually. Lucas promised."

"Do you get much time off? To go home to St. Louis?"

"I don't know." Caspien scraped his fork across his plate, scooping up the bits that had fallen from his tacos. Connie swooped in and rescued the dish, inspecting it for scratches before clucking her tongue and hurrying away. "I've never bothered to read my vacation package. I bury myself in work, so I don't have to think about Maddie. But living here, I can almost convince myself that I'm on an extended work trip, that Maddie will still be waiting for me when I get home."

"You haven't gone back a single time?"

Fire flared behind his eyes. "No, and I *never* will. Before this week, have you come back here to Seattle?"

I winced. He'd hit the hammer right on the nail. His three years away were nothing compared to my eleven.

"When are you planning to visit your mom?" he asked.

I winced again. So much baggage hung from that question. "Maybe never."

"Never? Seriously? Doesn't she live close by? I'll drive you there, we can go right now!" Caspien rose but I pulled him back down.

"Their only phone is Hallie's cell, so I can't exactly call ahead. And how can I face Mom when my life is falling apart?" My gasping breath returned for the first time in hours. Truths I'd spent years avoiding bombarded me from all sides. "If Jared and I were still ruling the world, that would be one thing. I'd have something to show for my time away, proof that I left for a reason. An excuse for all the lies I told them. But now? With a failed business and no prospects? I put my career and my love for Jared above my own family, made him my highest priority, and it crashed and burned. I abandoned my family for nothing!

"What if Mom doesn't want to see me? What if she hates me the same way Hallie does? I promised to visit two months after I moved away, but I've been gone for *eleven* years!" I dug through my purse for my Xanax, but only one pill rolled across the bottom of the bottle. I'd need it tomorrow morning. "I'd rather not know how Mom feels than face her rejection."

"If I could go back in time," Caspien said slowly, like he was choosing each word carefully, "I'd give anything for one more day with my daughter. One more hour. I'd forgive my wife for everything, beg her to get help. And if she refused? I'd still cherish every last second together. Maybe your mom was mad when you left, but I promise you, her perspective has changed. All she wants is to spend her time with you. Even if she only gets you for one hour."

My fingers trembled, but not from anxiety. From the way each of his words touched straight into the memories I couldn't face. "She wasn't mad. She hugged me right before I stepped on that plane, then kissed my cheek and told me she believed in me."

"You should go visit."

"How can I face her?" I pictured her rambunctious smile, the warmth of her cheek against my skin when she'd hug me. My voice dropped to a whisper. "It's not even that I didn't want to keep in touch. I didn't *intentionally* stop calling. But when people move outside the realm of my everyday life, they sort of . . . disappear from my mind. What kind of person does that make me? Who *forgets* to call home?" My face burned as my confession lingered in the air between us. "I'm so ashamed. I don't blame Hallie for avoiding me. She must hate me."

The center of Caspien's brow creased as he studied me. "If that's what you think, you don't know her very well."

"Yes, we've already established how little I know her."

"Why do you think Hallie's making you prove yourself to me before she'll see you? It's because she *wants* you back in her life. If she didn't, she would have turned you down the moment you called her. But Hallie is . . . complicated. Her fear of rejection runs deep, probably from your dad running out on your mom."

"And me leaving?"

"Maybe. But she's the kindest, most genuine person I know." A smile curled into the corners of his mouth. "The fact that she brought you here means there's a chance."

A chance. That possibility trickled into my heart like sunshine peeking through storm clouds. Could Hallie be hoping to reconcile? Could she be wishing I'd convince Caspien that I wouldn't abandon her again?

But a sliver of worry crept beneath my hope. What if I *couldn't* remember to stay in touch more often? My track record the past eleven years wasn't great, and the last thing I wanted was to hurt Hallie.

"What if I let her down again?" I grabbed the salt shaker and slid my finger along the ribbed edges. "I can't seem to keep in touch with anyone."

"My aunt was similar," Caspian said. "She moved to New York when I was a kid, and we barely heard from her for ten years. My mom was so hurt and angry. But when she finally moved back home, she explained to me that a symptom of her ADHD is that she forgets to keep in touch. Her therapist said it was an *out-of-sight, out-of-mind* sort of thing, but with people. She doesn't forget about them, she just doesn't think to reach out regularly unless she sees them all the time. Does that sound like you?"

I held perfectly still. "Her ADHD made her forget?"

"She didn't forget her family; it just didn't cross her mind to make the phone calls."

Could that be true? Was there more to my mistakes with Hallie than just me failing again and again? It was like Caspien had dissected my brain. Not only had he put one of my deepest shames into words, but he'd framed it in a way that didn't imply that I was *bad* or *wrong* or *broken* because of it. He'd described it like it was normal, not shameful.

"Yes," I whispered.

"Have you tried describing this to her?"

I shook my head. I'd never described it to myself so clearly—I'd never even been willing to face it—how could I have explained that to Hallie?

"You should," Caspien said. "She'll understand."

"Do you think so?"

Caspien nodded earnestly. "Hallie is understanding. Once you guys work things out, if she knew you struggled with keeping in touch, she'd take that responsibility on herself. She's not close with many people, but once you're *in* with her, she'll fight to the death to keep you. She's the most loyal person I know."

I cocked my head. "Do I detect a crush on my little sister?" I meant it to sound playful, but my words came out choked, leaving a sour taste in my mouth.

Caspien didn't speak for a long while.

"No," he finally said, "not Hallie."

My phone rang, Jared's photo appearing on the screen.

"You can't be serious." The heat drained from my body. Was he angry about my fight with Michael Kay? Or embarrassed about my love confession in the video?

"You don't have to answer," Caspien said, but if I didn't answer now, I'd just have to face Jared later.

"Hello?" I put the phone on speaker and set it in the center of the table, but I motioned for Caspien to be silent.

"Lauren?" Jared's deep voice echoed tentatively in our booth. At least he had the decency to sound ashamed.

But all my pent-up emotions welled inside me at once. "*Where the hell were you?*" I screamed. "You were the guest speaker! The keynote!"

I'd yelled at plenty of people before but never Jared. The second I opened my mouth, my fury erupted like a pressurized volcano.

"*You* were supposed to go on for me," he shot back. "Why did you let Michael Kay take your spot?"

"You think I *let* him? And did you think to ask me *before* you shoved the assignment into my lap? *You* always give speeches, remember? Not me. And why didn't you warn me about your affair with Nicoleta? I wasn't prepared—how could I have—the whole thing was—ugh!"

"Damnit, Lauren," he spit back, "this wouldn't have blown up if you could just speak in coherent sentences. Lucas Croft was *right there.* You couldn't shut off your brain long enough to have one decent conversation?"

Connie scuttled over, shushing me with a hiss, her eyes narrowed, one finger to her lips.

I shot her a glare, and she froze in place three steps away. Her gaze darted to Caspien, searching for support. He just shrugged and whispered, "Now's not a good time."

She gasped at the same moment that I sucked in a breath, staring down at my phone. "Jared, that's not fair—"

"We don't have time for you to be a loose cannon right now. Tomorrow's meeting is too important. Lucas is the only one who can keep us afloat. I need you to come through for me—*without* embarrassing us."

My blood froze. "*Come through*? What does that mean?" Every vein became an ice cube. No, a glacier. He wouldn't do that to me, would he? "Jared, you're getting on a plane right now, right? You're at the airport?"

He said nothing.

"Right, Jared?"

Caspien grasped my arm across the table, and I tried to take a breath. I tried, really, I did—but then I stopped. Jared didn't deserve the calm version of me. Instead, I gave my mouth control of my actions.

"Answer me!"

"There's trouble with ZBC."

"The network? Your last remaining paid gig? Let me guess, they saw the videos."

"They want me to smooth things over with Lily, convince the press that we're better than ever."

My strength finally gave out, and I dropped my forehead onto the table. "Let me guess, they need you tomorrow morning?"

"I'm sorry, Lauren, you're going to have to do this one on your own. So much is riding on me over here, I can't leave."

It was like he'd punched me in the lungs. "You can't leave this in my hands. I'm drowning."

"Me too. You know better than anyone what the media's doing to me. It's ruining my life; I'm hardly functioning. I need you to handle tomorrow's meeting, then when you win me the showcase, I'll fly in for it. I'm so sorry, but I'm counting on you. Please?"

Caspian rubbed my arm, but I couldn't make myself look up at him—because I knew exactly what words Jared would say next, and I knew exactly how I'd respond. The shame of it burned me alive.

"Trust-fall," Jared whispered.

"I know," I replied. "I'll find a way."

Chapter 11

Still $173.09, but not for long

Jared ended the phone call. Instant anxiety exploded through my body, like bottle rockets launching into the ceiling and burning down the walls. I shot to my feet and paced the pink restaurant carpet.

"Shit! Shit, shit, shit. What am I going to do? I never considered that he might not show up at all!" Pain lanced into my chest, a spear of fiery metal. "I can't breathe," I gasped, reaching for Caspien. "Help."

The room dimmed to black, then Caspien was there, scooping up my limp body and pulling me against his chest on his side of the booth. "Just breathe," he said. "Come on, Lauren, stay with me. I've got you."

His heart pounded solidly against my forehead, slow and strong. His arms engulfed my fragile body, holding me in place, slowing the spinning of the room. Air trickled into my lungs, and I opened my eyes.

"You okay?" His breath tickled the hair on my forehead.

"Don't let go." One move, one inch of space between his steady heart and my skin, and the blackness would win.

"I promise, I'm staying."

It took five minutes for the room to hold still, and another ten for the pounding in my head to slow. But at last, I crawled from his arms and squeezed my legs up against my chest beside him.

"This is so embarrassing," I said, all my energy depleted. I shoved tomorrow's meeting into the darkest corner of my mind.

"Why?"

"You've hardly known me twenty-four hours, and you've witnessed every one of my worst traits. Next time, it's your turn to have a panic attack. Or at least toss me my Xanax."

Caspien nudged me with his shoulder. "I don't mind. You're the first person since Maddie that I feel like I genuinely know."

"What about Hallie?"

"Nah. She's a good friend, but she's layered with secrets. Too many for me to peel back."

Secrets? What was Hallie hiding? But I dug through my purse and pulled out my prescription bottle. The final pill was reserved for tomorrow, but it seemed wise to have it nearby. Just in case.

"I know you like the Xanax," Caspien said, "but maybe it's a bandage when you need a real solution."

"This isn't like your wife," I said carefully. "My pills are prescribed, from a real doctor—it's not like I'm buying drugs off Michael Kay. Have you ever had a panic attack? Or lived with chronic anxiety?"

"No. I'll be the first to admit that I know nothing about how you feel—and medication can be lifesaving. But tell me honestly, does the Xanax help the panic attacks?"

I only ever took them when rapidly spiraling. By that point, they wouldn't have time to get into my system. "Maybe, or maybe not. But I don't have a better solution. The only other thing that calms me is the Green Fizz."

"That stuff calms you down? Even with all the caffeine?"

"Makes no sense, right? But it clears my head."

Caspien studied me for a long moment, then pulled his phone from his pocket and opened to an article. "Read this. It's about ADHD being misdiagnosed as anxiety."

I burst out laughing. "It's a Fearless Felicity article—I remember when she wrote that one. But I'd never considered it might apply to me."

"Sometimes caffeine reacts differently for people with ADHD than it does for everyone else. It calms them, instead of energizing. Maybe you just need different medication." His gaze dropped to the Xanax bottle in my hand. "If I get you the number of my aunt's doctor, will you call him when you get home? He's in St. Louis. I'm only pushing it because he helped her so much—I promise not to bug you about it again."

He looked so earnest, so concerned, though there was no chance I was addicted to Xanax. I paused, scratching my cheek. Could I be? Nah. But it was clearly important to Caspien. After learning about his wife, I couldn't blame him. And what if this doctor could answer my questions . . .?

"Sure, I'll call as soon as I get home—though you may need to remind me. But I promise, I'm not addicted."

"I believe you," he said, the corners of his eyes creasing as he smiled, "because you didn't hyperventilate when you said it."

My phone beeped with a text, and I lurched away from it, banging my head on the back of the booth. I shoved the phone at Caspien. "Please tell me it's not Jared."

Another text beeped. Then another. Then another. They kept coming through as Connie stalked toward our table with our bill in her hand. She dropped it in front of us, then folded her arms, her feet planted.

But Caspien kept his gaze on my phone as more texts arrived, then smiled, passing me the phone. "It's not Jared."

Kindy: *O MY HECK!!!*

Kindy: *Lauren ur brilliant!!!!*

Kindy: *Its Kindy btw*

Kindy: *These plans for me and Cam? Flying out to the factory? Streaming the whole thing?*

Kindy: *Ur a Genius. Literally genius.*

Kindy: *OMG!!! We just made the deal. Hes writing up the contract right now!*

Kindy: *Im dying over here!!!*

Kindy: *U just exploded our careers! I owe you everything! Seriously everything!!!*

Kindy: *Also, Michael Kay was garbage tonight, so cam and I are for real on ur side.*

Kindy: *If u need anything just hit me up luv!*

"Oh my heck?" I read. "Who says, 'oh my heck'?"

Caspien laughed, pressing his arm against mine as he read over my shoulder. "Mormons."

"I have no idea what the rest of that says."

"Time for you two to go," Connie interrupted. "You're too loud, scaring the other customers."

There were no other customers.

But Caspien rose from the table and slid his arms into his black jacket. He held out his hand to help me up. My clothes were still wet from the rain, and when I put my hand in his, the warmth of his fingers sent a shiver up my arm. Caspien dropped a pile of cash onto the table for the meal as I slid into my coat.

"I can pay for that," I said.

"I already did." Caspien opened our umbrella, then we stepped out into the deafening rain. This late at night, no cars passed us on the street, and with the sky full of storm clouds, our only light came from the occasional dim streetlamp. "Now, don't be mad," he shouted, "but remember when you were helping Cameron and Kindy with the protein bar guy? I wrote down your ideas as you spouted them off. While you were working on your speech, I typed them up and emailed them to Kindy. Apparently, she was impressed."

I stopped at the corner and faced Caspien. Under the umbrella, we were inches apart, so I leaned back to see his whole face.

"You pieced my incoherent thoughts together?"

He propped the umbrella handle under his arm, swiped through his phone, then showed me the email. I took his phone and skimmed the words, line after line of my own thoughts, written in perfect order and complete sentences.

Deep inside my chest, another piece of my puzzle clicked into place.

"This is incredible," I whispered. Rain rattled loudly onto the umbrella above us.

"What did you say?" He leaned down, putting his ear near my mouth, so our cheeks brushed together.

Without thinking, I tucked his phone into his jacket pocket, grabbed the front of his jacket, and pulled him closer beneath the umbrella. Our bodies pressed softly together. "I said, you're incredible."

He leaned back just enough to search my face, a question in his eyes. Our breaths mingled together, visible in the cold air. Then his gaze dropped to my lips. My stomach fluttered, and I released his jacket to rest my hands flat on his chest. Did I want to push him away or pull him closer? I wasn't sure. But he carefully placed one hand around my hip, and my breath came out in a ragged sigh. Was Caspien going to kiss me?

Did I want him to?

I inched my foot closer—stepping on his toe. My ankle twisted awkwardly. I stumbled in my heels and fell sideways, out from under the umbrella, into the pouring rain.

"Lauren!" Caspien shouted. He lunged for me, but my arm slipped through his wet hands, and I fell backward, landing hard on my butt in the gutter. Water poured over me like a river, covering my legs, my torso, up to my chest, saturating my coat and my hands and arms.

"It's so cold!" I screamed, but laughter bubbled up inside me. Could this night throw me *any* more surprises? Caspien grabbed my hand and hoisted me up, back under the umbrella. "Are you laughing at me?"

"No," Caspien said, but his body shook as I peeled off my soaked coat and draped it over my arm. The jacket, and the umbrella, were pointless now. My nice jeans were saturated. Water squelched between my toes. Were those turquoise stains on the shoulders of my blouse? And why was it so *freezing* out here? "Come on," Caspien laughed. "Let's get you home."

We trekked back up the road in a comfortable silence. I dared a furtive glance at his face, his jaw, his lips. No one had kissed me in years. Anytime I'd gone out with a guy, they'd fled after the first date.

But Caspien wasn't running away.

What would Jared think?

It made absolutely no sense, but my maybe-almost-kiss felt disloyal to Jared. Was it? He was *married* for crying out loud! He'd had plenty of sex with his wife—they had kids together!

Caspien walked quietly, no longer laughing at my watery fumble, but his eyes danced in a way that warmed me from the inside. So, when the wind blew the rain onto my exposed shoulder, and Caspien tucked me under his arm to pull me into his warm body, I didn't argue.

In fact, I scooted closer.

Eventually, we escaped the rain into the plush lobby of my hotel, and Caspien closed his umbrella. We were soaked to the bone, with water dripping off our noses.

"Come upstairs? There's hot tea and coffee in my room, and a heater I can crank full blast."

"For a minute," he said, and I hooked my arm into his as we stepped into the elevator. I'd never acted so boldly, never once touched a man uninvited. And Caspien didn't push me away.

Three minutes later we entered my hotel room. This wasn't his first time, of course, but our relationship had shifted since then. To *what* exactly, I wasn't sure. But it was also possible a bomb had exploded in my room. Thanks to my frantic attempt to write Jared's speech, papers scribbled with notes lay scattered across the floor, empty Green Fizz wrappers and stray water bottles clogged every counter, and my suitcase, clothes, towels, and hair accessories were strewn everywhere else.

"Sorry about the mess," I muttered. "Every time I leave it's because I'm racing off, late to the next place."

Caspien stripped off his coat, and I cranked the heater up, up, up, dropping my phone and purse on the small coffee table.

"You can put on dry clothes," he said. "Pajamas or something."

"I'll dry quick enough. Have a seat. Can you believe I'm hungry again?" I dug through the pile of powder packets on my counter and chugged down a Neon Nutrition.

Caspien cleared himself a spot on the couch, replacing the rest of the cushions from when I'd dumped him off yesterday. "Now tell me, what are you thinking for tomorrow morning?"

"Ugh," I groaned, slumping on the couch beside him and letting my head fall back. The hotel clock said 1:00 a.m., which meant only nine hours until my meeting. What plans did I have? I glanced at my papers, but my words laughed at me from the pages. Half sentences scribbled sideways over the top of the previous notes. How would any of this help me woo Lucas? I'd had strokes of brilliant ideas as I wrote them. But where were they?

"I know how Jared would handle it—he'd revive our glory days."

Caspien frowned. "What does that mean?"

"He'd probably throw on 80s exercise gear and perform a full retro-workout for Lucas. And honestly, he'd impress him with his charisma. If all else fails, I could try something like that."

Caspien cocked his head. I knew what that meant—he was skeptical. Good. Because I was too.

"Listen," Caspien said, "you did a brilliant job with Kindy, Cameron and the protein guy, so I know your plans are solid. So, tell me, if Jared was out of the picture completely, if old-school routines didn't exist, how would *you* handle tomorrow's meeting?"

"Me?"

"Without Jared."

The room spun. But not in the anxiety-inducing, I-can't-breathe sort of way. It spun with a whirl of undiscovered possibilities. People rarely asked me what *my* way looked like. I was only ever the information-gatherer, and Jared vetoed most of my real ideas. But all those *real ideas?* They still lived in my brain.

"I'd use a PowerPoint."

Caspien paused. "Seriously?"

"It would be a brilliant PowerPoint, full of genius ideas." I laughed, tapping on my skull. "They're all in here."

"Excellent," he said. "Then tell me, between Jared's retro idea and yours, which one gives you anxiety when you contemplate trying to explain it to Lucas?"

My idea, or Jared's? One of them made me lighter than air, and one made me want to vomit. Somewhere, deep inside the expanse of my chest, a third piece of my puzzle clicked into place.

Rising from the couch, I scooped up that garbage bag of puke-covered, vintage fitness clothes. Then I crossed the room and dropped the entire thing straight into the garbage can.

Caspien clapped. "Bravo! That deserves celebrating. But first, we have a meeting to plan. What ideas are you considering?"

Two feet from the couch, I stopped. "You're going to help me? This goes way above and beyond babysitting."

Caspien crossed one foot over the other knee and frowned. "Has no one ever helped you plan Jared's shows? Not even Jared?"

"Never. Though I'll admit I tend to scare people off. But why would you stay? I doubt you care this much about Jared's career."

"You're right. But the more time I spend with you, the more I care about yours."

I studied his expression. The sincerity in his brown eyes, the earnestness in his brow. Had Jared ever looked at me that way? Like he believed in me? Like he would take me seriously no matter what idea I threw at him? Like he'd help sharpen it into a viable plan without doubt or ridicule? My heart skipped a beat, my insides melting into a puddle of goo. How could I possibly thank him? Not just for this, but for the past two days of support.

"I'll make you a deal," I said. "You help me organize my ideas, the way you did with Kindy's sales plan, and I'll help you run your first non-profit fundraiser for kids."

"That is not an equal trade," he protested. "You'd be doing miles more work than this. And I'm not helping you to get something out of it. I'm helping because I want to."

Jared never helped me *because he wanted to.* It was only to repay a favor, or to earn one for the future. "After everything you've done for me this week, it's the least I can do."

He hesitated, then he ran both hands through his dark hair. "You know how to run a fundraiser?"

"I've produced hundreds of shows, and more than a handful of them raised money for one charity or another. This is right up my alley. And it would mean a lot to your daughter."

Caspien's eyes widened. "How do I thank you?"

I gathered the few papers within my reach then dropped them between us. "Organize me?"

"My pleasure." Caspien and I scoured the room, collecting notepads, loose pages, sticky notes, and a few scribbled-on receipts. I compiled the papers into a neat stack, then ceremoniously handed the pile to Caspien. "What exactly is all this?" he asked.

"My notes."

Slowly, he flipped through the papers, scanning page by page until he pointed to the words scrawled across the bottom of one. "A lot of these aren't complete sentences."

"Most are, look." I riffled through them until I found the paper I needed. "Here's the rest of the idea, I forgot to write the second half until later, but by then I couldn't find the beginning."

"It's written over the top of another sentence."

"I know, but in a different direction to separate them."

"These are like a puzzle, but the pieces are printed on top of each other."

I lounged against the far arm of the couch and crossed my ankles on the cushion between us. "Welcome to my brain."

Caspien read through the pages again, taking longer this time, until he finally set them down on the table. "Why don't you tell me your plans? Even vague ideas. Let me hear them in your words, and we'll piece it together from there."

"My ideas are all over the place," I warned.

"I'm not afraid."

With a grin, I started talking. "Lucas is awarding the winner a live showcase, right? That means I need to convince him that Jared will put on a good show. What if we made a video montage of Jared's best TV moments? In fact, Jared always scores with his vintage performance. What if we made a series of highlight videos from that throwback program he made a few years ago? Or better yet, we fill the presentation with his stats. Show how much he can lift and his strength gains over the years." I paused. "Scratch that, everyone knows he's strong. No one cares about the numbers on his dumbbells."

I expected Caspien to be lost already, but he patiently watched me.

I jumped back in. "But what about viewer numbers? Slides with graphs. YouTube stats. Subscriber rates. We'd have to stop at six months ago though. No one watches him anymore, since he started cheating. Well, he always cheated. But the numbers dropped when the secret got out." I paused again. "Hang on, we're going about this wrong."

New ideas flew through my brain until I was vaguely aware that my complete sentences had stopped. "No one wants to see Jared anymore. What if he showcases *other* people . . . A competition? No petting zoos, but make it a triathlon? Or everyone lifts blindfolded? That's stupid . . . What if they all face their greatest fear while lifting? Or drink a two-liter and then lift? Wait! What if we build an entire show around making a fool of Jared? Flood the internet with stupid videos . . ."

My mouth kept moving, a steady stream of who-knows-what. At some point, Caspien scooped up my pile of papers and scribbled his own notes over mine. Then he found my laptop and furiously typed, swapping frantically between the computer and the papers. While I was lost in thought, a pair of glasses appeared on his nose.

Around 3:00 a.m., I ran out of ideas. My mouth just stopped.

"You okay?" Caspien asked. We sat facing each other while leaning against opposite couch arms, our legs stretched out side-by-side between us. He'd perched my laptop on his thighs and peered at me over his glasses. "You stopped."

"That's all."

"You're done?"

"Finished. What do you think?" I chewed on the skin around my nails, a habit I didn't have but found surprisingly comforting.

Caspien pulled off his glasses and rubbed his eyes. "You have enough material for twenty brilliant proposals. The struggle will be picking one."

"Can we pull it off by tomorrow?"

Caspien moved my computer to the coffee table and ran one hand along the top of my bare foot. Somehow, both of our feet had melded into the others' laps, but I hadn't noticed it happen.

"I think so, but I typed over forty pages of notes. Why don't you sleep while I sift through it all?"

I glanced at the clock—we didn't have long before my meeting. "You must be exhausted. It should be me staying up."

"You're the one who has to do the actual presentation. Climb into bed, I'll wake you when I've got it ready."

"Are you sure?"

Caspien rose, stretching as he yawned, then offered me a hand up. When I stood, he pulled me into him, wrapping his arms around my body in the gentlest hug since Mom said goodbye at the airport.

"Thank you," I whispered, resting my cheek against his chest. He smelled like the rainstorm. Like clean air and overcast skies. The hug lasted for several peaceful moments, and when he tried to pull away, I stopped him, slipping my phone from my pocket and snapping a selfie of the two of us. I wanted to capture this moment, this feeling, remember it forever. "I'm so glad Hallie forced you to babysit me."

He rested his chin on the top of my head. "Next time I see her, I'll tell her to come visit you."

I pulled away until I could peer into his eyes. "Really? You will?"

"I've been thinking about it since the restaurant. Once she understands you, I think she'll forgive everything." I squeezed him tighter. "She's deeply afraid of rejection. If you want her back, she needs to know that you love her, and that you always will."

That I love her? That was easy. I loved her more than anything else.

"Can I ask you something?" His voice dropped to barely a whisper.

"Of course."

"If I let you help me with my foundation, my first big event, what happens if something comes up with Jared at the same time? Would you ditch me and run off to help him?"

A horribly complicated question.

I let it hang in the air, swinging heavily between us. Thank goodness he couldn't see my face as I cringed. "I guess I don't know. Jared's been my compass for so long, it's hard to imagine anything else. But I'm getting tired of running his race when he keeps moving the finish line."

Caspien sighed into my hair. "Thanks for being honest."

"I don't know how to be anything else."

After a moment of quiet, I reluctantly pulled away, too shy to look directly at him, then I ducked into the bathroom to brush my teeth. It didn't seem possible that I could fall asleep with him still in my room, but he flicked off the lights and returned his glasses to his face, busying himself behind my laptop on the couch.

I'd never felt so comfortable around a man. I'd never felt so comfortable around anyone.

Within seconds of climbing into bed, I fell asleep.

***

I woke up with a lurch, shooting upright in bed. The sun streamed through the window illuminating every corner of my exploded hotel room. Someone had cracked the window and the air smelled fresh, the sound of a faint drizzle echoing from outside. Caspien slept on his back on the couch. He snored softly, his chin tilted toward his chest, one arm draped over his eyes. My laptop sat closed on the table beside him.

What time was it?

8:15 a.m.

Less than two hours until my meeting. But how much work was left to be done? If Caspien had organized my ideas and picked the one Lucas would like most, I still needed to gather videos of Jared, make the presentation, and practice my speech. What would I say? What would I wear?

Shooting out of bed, still in yesterday's clothes, I toppled over a pair of shoes on the floor and landed, wrists first, on the edge of the table. The corner gouged into my skin.

"Yeow!" I hissed as silently as I could manage, shaking one hand wildly while fumbling for my laptop with the other. Caspien still dozed, so I dropped onto the floor in front of him. I never should have slept. How could I pull this together in an hour and a half?

While my computer powered up, I rubbed the sleep from my eyes. *Ow!* I opened the selfie camera on my phone. Yup. A black semi-circle marred the tender skin below my lower lashes. It swelled slightly, keeping my eye from opening all the way. At least my shoulder no longer ached.

Finally, the computer screen blinked awake, and a program opened.

PowerPoint.

A thirty-two-slide presentation.

Jared's profile filled the screen. He wore full 80s gear, a crown on his head, and I stood beside him.

It was my polaroid.

Caspien had taken my photograph and turned it into the cover slide. We could no longer wear the clothes, but we could still celebrate what they meant.

An explosion of warmth turned cartwheels in my belly. Caspien had listened, really *listened,* then created what I'd asked for. I pressed my hands to my cheeks and squealed. It took all my strength not to shake his legs and wake him up, tackle him with a hug, climb on top of him and kiss him silly.

Instead, I clicked to the next slide. The second page was a full outline of the showcase I'd designed for Lucas and Jared. Well, I'd described a dozen options, but this one was my favorite. Somehow, Caspien had known. I rose from the floor and perched on the arm of the couch, as close to him as possible without waking him.

The next page began the logistics: who we'd need to perform and their specific jobs. Page four covered the unique stage crew, since this wouldn't be your everyday show. Pages five through seven were filled with equipment, images, prices, complete with links to my favorite suppliers. I kept clicking, every page loaded with details, as if Caspien had taken my scrunched-up brain and stretched it out on display in the most beautiful way.

Deep inside the cavern that held my chaos, more of my puzzle clicked into place.

But not just one piece this time, a heap of it. A mountain. Like Caspien had dug and dug until he found all four corners, then aligned every edge piece until they clicked perfectly together, one PowerPoint page at a time.

Caspien lifted himself up, then rested his chin on my shoulder. "What do you think?" he said, his voice still scratchy from sleep.

"I think you're a genius."

"You're the genius, I just sifted through your ideas."

I faced him, my throat tightening. "Caspien, I can't believe you did this for me. I might actually have a chance to win. It's like you took these slides straight from my brain."

Caspien's smile split his face. "I'm glad you like it. We have some time. Want to get breakfast?"

Usually, I was so filled with nerves before big meetings that the thought of food flipped my stomach over. But today? Nothing about this gavc me anxiety. Spending more time with Caspien sounded lovely.

"Let me get dressed," I said. "Do you live close? We could swing by your place for new clothes too, if you want. Do you need to feed your dog?"

"Dakota's with a sitter, but I live in Queen Ann, not too far."

After the fastest shower of my life, I threw on my favorite slacks and my softest cream blouse, styled my turquoise hair, then took a good look at myself in the mirror. A purple bruise clung under my eye, and the muscles around my jaw were sore, but I didn't have the right makeup to cover it up or the time to buy any. But a purple eye and blue hair seemed fitting—each were a part of me, my puzzle pieces on display. If Lucas wanted to work with me, he deserved to know exactly what he was in for.

Lauren in pieces. Take it or leave it.

With a slow breath, I opened a text to Hallie. What had Caspien said? Hallie was afraid of rejection. She needed assurance that I loved her.

Lauren: *Hey Hallie, I think I need to explain something. When I left Seattle, it wasn't because I didn't love you or didn't care about you. I was young and reckless and madly in love with Jared. But after fifteen years, we're still not together . . . I understand why you're afraid to talk to me. Rejection sucks. Loving someone who doesn't love you back sucks. But I promise, that's not me. I love you. I always have, I always will. I'm sorry I wasn't here for you, but if you'll meet up with me, I can try to explain. I miss you.*

I hit send, then closed my phone. Hopefully that would be enough.

By the time I walked out of the bathroom, Caspien had donned his jacket, fixed his hair in the sink, and was slipping on his shoes. When he smiled up at me, my heart triple thumped. My hands clammed up—where should I put them? In front of me? On my hips? Fold my arms? Why was I so nervous?

Almost like he could tell, Caspien laughed and headed over to hold the door. "Ready?"

All I needed was my morning Green Fizz. I grabbed a water bottle and a packet from my dwindling heap of powders. I grabbed my bottle of Xanax too, but then I stopped. If the caffeine already kept me calm, was Xanax counteracting it? Perhaps a conversation with a doctor was what I needed.

I left the Xanax on the desk and floated past Caspien through the door. He stopped me in the hall with a hand on my arm, then pulled me into his chest, engulfing my tiny body with his.

"Have I told you how much I like you?" he asked.

I wrapped my arms around his waist. "Maybe you should."

Caspien pulled away just enough to look at me. His eyes bounced back and forth between mine—was that uncertainty? Was he nervous? Then they dropped to my lips.

Mine dropped too. The air crackled between us. I lifted onto my tiptoes, my head fuzzy, and I leaned toward him.

The elevator chimed at the end of the hall. The door slid open and we both turned. A man stepped out, six feet tall, black hair with silver streaks and a yellow tank top that accented his rippling arms. His blue tights matched his blue 1980s sweatband and he carried a vintage boombox on his shoulder.

His entire body perked up when his gaze raked over me.

Caspien sucked in a breath.

Mine rushed out.

No freaking way.

It was Jared.

Jared DiMaggio was here.

Chapter 12

$173.09 since Caspien paid for those delicious grilled cheese sandwiches

Jared!" I took a sharp step away from Caspien. "You came!"

He came? Why did he come? I'd spoken to him only eight hours ago and he was still in St. Louis, still grappling with ZBC, still faking a happy marriage.

"Of course I came; you needed me."

He walked straight up to me and wrapped his arms around my waist, lifting me in the air and spinning me around.

"You smell amazing," he muttered in my ear. "Damn, I missed you. Is this your room?" He lowered me to my feet but locked his fingers in mine—he'd never done that before. He might as well have lifted a leg and marked his territory for the effect it had on Caspien.

Jared pulled me toward the door that Caspien still held propped open.

He watched us, tense, quiet.

But as Jared tugged my hand, I pulled back. My feet stayed solidly in place, though nothing inside me felt solid.

"Why'd you change your mind?" I asked.

Jared faced me, slipped both hands onto my hips, then bent down to meet my gaze. "I quit my contract with ZBC for next year. You don't earn commissions from the deal, which means you're struggling even more than me. How could I do that to you?"

"You quit for *me*?"

Jared raised one finger to brush under my chin. "We started this crazy business together; we should *still* be in it together. What do you say, are you ready to make a few deals and resurrect our careers?"

My head nodded before my mouth could formulate a response. Jared laughed then escorted me into my hotel room.

His gaze swept over the mess, and he laughed again. "Still the Lauren I love."

Love?

He riffled through my stack of papers. Caspien must have put them in their neat pile on the desk because I certainly hadn't. "Are these your notes for today's meeting?"

"Sort of."

He pulled me into another hug and lingered. Never, in fifteen years, had Jared held me like this. My stomach fluttered, but it didn't feel quite as I'd expected. There was an edge to it. I pressed my fingers against his back. All these years I'd dreamed of running my fingers down his back. Was this finally happening?

"Never change, Lauren. Stay exactly like this."

I pulled out of his arms and took a step back. "What's going on? Is everything fine at home?"

"It's perfect. I re-watched Michael Kay's video a dozen times. When you admitted how you feel, I . . ." He grinned widely. "I had to come see you."

Caspien slipped into the room then leaned quietly against the door. Jared took him in, blinking rapidly, like he'd only now registered his existence.

"Oh!" Jared said, turning back to me, "these are for you." From a small duffel bag, he retrieved a sleeve of individually wrapped cinnamon taffy.

I stared at the offering in his hand. "You brought those for me?"

"Of course. You've been here totally alone for two days; I owe you way more than a bag of candy." He opened the taffy and handed me one. My heart pounded—they really were my favorite. Then he searched around the room, poking through my things. "But where's your gear?"

"My gear?"

"Your vintage clothes. We're going to be late!"

I glanced at the clear bag holding my vomit-covered leotard and leggings. It still sat in the garbage on top of a heap of empty water bottles. Jared followed my gaze, scooped up the bag, and tossed it to me.

But he knew what had happened in those clothes, right?

"I can't wear that."

He spun me around and nudged me toward the bathroom. "Wash it in the sink, no one will know."

"I'll be soaked."

"If you get the whole thing wet, there won't be water marks. Hurry up, clock's ticking!" He bumped me the rest of the way into the bathroom. I craned my neck, searching for Caspien's face, but Jared closed the door behind me.

He wanted me to wear *these*? He had to have seen the video of me puking on them, the entire world watched that video. What did he think would happen, the purple stains would magically wash away?

And what were his plans for the presentation to Lucas? Would we still use my PowerPoint? Lucas wasn't like everyone else. Caspien said Jared's methods wouldn't work. Lucas liked numbers, not schmoozing.

But Jared had never met someone he couldn't schmooze.

My fingers tapped a frantic rhythm against my thigh. One leg bounced, then the other, until my entire frame shook. When did I last feel this much anxiety? Last night with Caspien, I'd floated on a sea of calm. But with Jared here, my body fell instinctively into old patterns.

Shove it down, quiet the voices.

Jared could do this, right? He'd even convinced the family network to broadcast his workout program after admitting to the world that he'd cheated on his wife. Jared never lost.

He never lost.

Never.

With careful fingers, I untwisted the top of the garbage bag and dumped my workout gear into the sink. The stench of sour wine erupted through the bathroom.

Take a deep breath. You can do this.

My yellow tights, blue leg warmers, and green leotard filled most of the basin. I spun the faucet. Purple water ran through the wrinkles, marring the white porcelain, strings of slime clinging to the fabric.

I gagged.

Don't puke.

I squirmed out of my jacket, rolled up the sleeves of my blouse, and stuck my hands into the water.

Everything felt gooey. As fast as I could, I rinsed each piece until the last of the slime washed away. Then I plugged the drain and dumped the entire bottle of complimentary hotel shampoo onto the fabric. I scrubbed and scrubbed until my arms ran out of strength. Then I kept going with the bar of soap, attacking the lingering spots of purple until the sink overflowed with white bubbles. Finally, I rinsed it and wringed out the fabric.

It was still purple.

But I had no more soap.

And the odor . . . it still lingered, clinging to the clothes like a virus.

Not wanting the smell to escape, I cracked open the door and peeked outside. Caspien had slipped the rest of the way into the room. He'd glued his gaze to my bathroom door, and when I stepped out, he raised both eyebrows. Jared hadn't moved. He stood in front of the couch, his back to Caspien, his arms folded across the front of his neon tank top.

"The stains won't come out." My voice wobbled.

"That's fine," Jared said with full confidence. "No one will be looking at you, I'll be front and center."

"You still want me to wear it?"

"Hell yes!" He held up the Polaroid—*my* Polaroid. He must have found it on the desk. Or the floor. Or the bed. "Today's our comeback! Now hurry, I want time to mingle before we see Lucas."

Pointedly avoiding eye contact with Caspien, I slipped back into the bathroom and took a heavy breath. Scratch that, no breathing. It smelled too awful. Holding the air in my lungs, I stripped down to my bra, then shoved my body into the soaking wet exercise gear, one freezing limb at a time. The green sweatbands were the final touch, one around my head and two around my wrists. Never mind, one was missing, so I only donned one on the right, then took in my appearance in the small hotel mirror.

I was purple.

Not purple, brown. Everywhere, splotches of wine that had darkened over time. My entire body shivered from the cold, wet clothes. And the smell? Like someone had spilled milk on a cloth and forgotten to rinse it out for days. Not overpowering, but lingering.

Steeling my nerves, I pushed open the door and returned to the bedroom. Both men reacted instantly. Caspien's jaw dropped, Jared's split into a grin.

"Perfect!" he said, taking my hand again. "Shall we go?"

"Let me grab my things."

I found my purse then pulled two water bottles from my case—it was almost empty. While Jared perused my room, I twisted the lids off both, poured two packets of Green Fizz, then chugged them, one at a time. In minutes, my body felt it. I could survive this. Really, I could.

Caspien finally darted from his post near the door. In a low voice, he said, "You don't have to do this."

My gaze flicked to Jared, then back to Caspien. "Yes, I do."

"Dressing like retro trainers isn't the way to impress Lucas. You know this. Tell Jared."

The Green Fizz tingled into my hands and my cheeks. My skin buzzed. I'd never taken two at once, maybe it wasn't the smartest idea.

"Jared always wins with routines like this." Both my hands were tapping now. "He knows what he's doing."

"By dressing you in stained clothes, freezing your butt off? Is reviving your glory days worth all this? It isn't *you,* Lauren."

Wasn't it, though? Was there a *me* without Jared? Without following his lead as he captained our ship? For a few hours, maybe I'd found something more. Another path forward. But Jared was here now, and we had a way of doing things: I hid behind a desk while he starred in the programs. Today wasn't any different.

"Yes, this *is* me. It always has been." But my insides shriveled at the words.

"Then why are you panicking? It's obvious you hate this. You're brilliant at conjuring extravagant plans! Why are you humiliating yourself?"

Jared poked his face between us, his eyes narrowing. "Who are you again?"

Caspien folded his arms, matching Jared's glare. "Lauren's sister asked me to show her around."

"Right, the babysitter." Jared pulled a ten-dollar bill from the back pocket of his tights and tucked it into Caspien's jacket. "Here's a tip, we won't be needing your services anymore."

I couldn't breathe. I teetered backward, careening wildly. Caspien grabbed my arm and slid me carefully to the floor until I sat with my back against the wall. He pressed my palm against his chest, directly over his heart. How did he know that this rhythm steadied me?

But Jared knelt beside us with my bottle of Xanax perched between two fingers. He unscrewed the lid. "Only one left? You've had a bad week." He glared at Caspien like he was the root of my problems, but Caspien refused to budge.

When Jared placed the bottle in my hand, I stared at it, my mind numb.

"That's my girl," Jared said. "We don't have time for you to get panicky right now. Save all that for later when we don't have people to see. Shove it down, quiet the voices."

His mantra grated down my spine, down the seams of these disgusting clothes. Save *what* for later? My personality? My flaws? All the screwed-up pieces of my brain? I curled into a smaller ball, folding in on myself.

"Swallow the Xanax quick, we have a big day ahead of us."

I stared at the bottle, but I hesitated. Was Caspien right? Did I have better options than *this?* "Before we go," I whispered, "do you want to see my presentation for Lucas? It's on my laptop. A PowerPoint."

But Jared laughed. "A PowerPoint? Like we're business dweebs? Way too boring. Come on, I've got this thing in the bag." In one swift movement, he pulled me to my feet, then strolled out, boxing the air like he was pumping himself up for a workout.

But Caspien stopped me before I could follow. "This is a terrible idea."

"What else am I supposed to do?" I shot back. "You heard him, there's no talking him out of it."

"You don't have to tag along. What do *you* want to do?"

What did I want? I had no idea. I didn't want to wear these clothes, but my partnership with Jared had spanned half my life. This was our one shot to salvage everything we'd built. Could I walk away from that now?

Caspien frowned, his lips pursed, then he held out my laptop. "Just in case?"

Jared scooted back into the room and bumped my hand away from the computer. "She won't be needing that." Then he pulled me into the hall and closed the door behind me, with Caspian still inside. "Shall we?"

Jared whistled as he walked toward the elevator, but the sound moved in slow motion. The elevator door opened, and Jared stepped inside. I stood painfully still, hovering between him and my hotel room.

Between Jared and Caspien.

Caspien *saw* me, he knew me, he accepted all my quirks without adding a layer of shame. But there was still one riddle that Caspien couldn't solve. One question that gnawed on me, slithered through my chest and ate away my confidence. *Why was Jared here*? Did he love me? Was this finally our chance to be together? Or was it something else? No onc could answer those questions except the man waiting for me in the elevator.

For fifteen long years I'd wanted him to chase after me. He wouldn't have hugged me like that unless he'd finally left his wife, right?

"Are you coming?" Jared asked, holding the elevator door open.

This was the moment I'd waited for all my life. Jared and me, together at last. Us against the world. Everything I'd ever dreamed of was right here, in that elevator.

All I had to do was step inside.

"Lauren?"

"I'm coming," I whispered, and I followed him into the elevator.

We reached the ground floor in seconds and Jared led me into the lobby, intertwining his fingers with mine. "Weird smell in there," he said, and I put a few extra inches between him and my clothes.

Outside, the rain fell steadily, more than a drizzle but nothing like the downpour last night. Jared ignored the cold. I tried to, but failed miserably. Frigid wind leached through my soaked leotard, cut into my exposed arms. The wine stains burned my skin like acid—or maybe that was the sharp raindrops. Either way, I could smell myself every step of the two blocks to the convention center. When we stepped into the lobby, raindrops had speckled Jared's yellow tank. My leotard hadn't changed. A perk of already being wet, I supposed.

"Where is everyone?" he asked.

I pointed to the grand French doors that led to the banquet hall. "Most will be off in classes, but a few might be lingering in there."

He opened both doors at once and then beamed. I, on the other hand, shrank back. Why did I never remember to look at the schedule? Hundreds of people milled about. Vendors, influencers, convention staff. The tables had been cleared and some sort of crew scurried around the stage setting up weight racks and microphones.

The showcase.

Everyone was gathered to watch it come together—and to see my repeat of this awful outfit.

Jared strolled right in and started shaking hands. Then a few influencers I didn't know—maybe he didn't either—took quick videos for their feeds, then gawked at him behind his back. Jared knew how to play the game. He spoke to a few, only a moment each, then moved on. By making his attention sparse, he made himself more desirable.

After chatting with ten, maybe fifteen people, he pulled me directly through the center of the crowd, toward the far exit.

"That was perfect!" Jared high-fived a random staff member as we hurried down a long hall. "They all got a chance to see me, so they know I'm raising the stakes in this competition. But they also saw our gear, which will make them worry. This showcase is ours. Okay, you ready?"

"For what?"

"For our meeting with Lucas." He motioned to the door we'd stopped in front of. "He should be in there."

"Wait, it's time?" Everything was happening too fast. I peered at my watch and shrieked. 9:55? We hadn't spent a single minute discussing our sales tactic. What the hell were we walking into?

"Hang on," Jared said, pointing to a vending machine. "Buy me a water? I spent the last of my money tipping your babysitter."

"It's five dollars!"

"I need a Green Fizz." He unzipped my purse, swiped a bill from my wallet, then slid it into the machine. "Thanks, Lauren, I owe you."

I gaped at him, my mind reeling. How could . . . he . . . just . . . what? Was this how he'd always treated me? Like I was just an extension of his property? Like he could spend *my* money as if it were his?

Once he'd downed his energy drink, he pulled his boombox out from a nook beside the vending machine.

"Where the hell did that come from?" The surprises were too much on my system.

"I bribed the hotel concierge to carry it over, didn't you see me?"

"No!"

"Why else would I be running low on money?" He said the words as if there were logic to them. How did he stay sane when he functioned this way? Spending money he didn't have and jumping into essential meetings without a plan? He put his hand on the doorknob, excitement dancing across his face. "Ready?"

"No!"

He recoiled like I'd slapped him. "Why not?"

"You can't just run in there!" Each word squeaked louder than the last, and I yanked on my hair with both hands. "What's your plan? What will you say? At least give me *something* so I don't ruin this for us both."

A group of four women pressed against the wall as they skirted around me.

"You've got to act more normal in public," Jared hissed. "We've talked about this. Don't act crazy where people can see you." Then he winked and planted a heavy kiss on my forehead. "Besides, isn't it more fun not to know my plan? You'll get swept up in the moment, same as Lucas."

Jared lifted the boombox onto his shoulder and hit play. *Rocky* theme music blared from the speakers, then he burst through the door.

He ran in like a cheerleader, hooting and hollering, jumping with every step. I crept in behind him as he set the boombox in the corner, then performed a series of front handsprings—he could still do those?—to reach the center of the room.

It was a typical convention center classroom, complete with ugly carpet, a projector screen, and the lingering smell of fast food. Lucas sat wide-eyed behind a small desk in the far corner. A weight rack stood against the wall, the vertical kind that takes up minimal space but doesn't easily tip over.

And Jared?

Jared's enormous presence filled every inch of empty space.

"Are you ready to PARTY?" he hollered as if to an enormous crowd.

Lucas flinched the tiniest bit. Jared didn't notice, but I did.

The music morphed into a *Bon Jovi* song and Jared grabbed the heaviest weights on the rack, transitioning into a lifting routine that he was clearly making up on the fly.

"Squats!" he called out, demonstrating three reps of a half-dozen variations. "Shoulders!" He pressed, then punched, then struggled through shoulder-raises, since he hadn't decreased to lighter dumbbells. Each time the song jumped back into the chorus, he rolled the dumbbells to the side and handspringed across the room again. As the song drew to a close, he finally swapped out his weights for ones a bit lighter and curled them both up beneath his chin, his biceps quaking, veins popping, sweat dripping onto the carpet below.

When the song ended, Jared dropped the weights with a crash before strutting to Lucas's desk and flipping him a business card through the air. Where had that come from? Had he tucked it inside his tights?

"Now you know what to expect from Jared DiMaggio," he said. "Have your people call my people, we'll make this thing happen." Then he swaggered straight past me, out of the room. The door snicked shut behind him.

For a long moment, Lucas's silence reverberated off the walls like a gong. I closed my eyes, dreading the reaction on his face. I felt like someone had run me over with a bus. Or hit me with a dumbbell.

"This wasn't what I expected," he finally said, and I had to open my eyes. The way Lucas lounged back in his chair contrasted sharply with his pressed, gray suit.

"Me neither."

"Caspien called me last night, told me to keep an open mind about you. He said he helped with your presentation."

"Caspien and I prepared something different. But Jared arrived at the last second, we had to . . . adjust."

"You have a different plan?" He circled the small desk and crossed half the room before tucking his hands into the pockets of his suit pants and leaning one shoulder against the wall. His jet-black hair fell lazily over one of his raised eyebrows. "Caspien said it was good."

Caspien had offered me my laptop. *Just in case,* he'd said. Why didn't I listen? He knew I did better with notes. I'd make a fool of myself if I tried to remember all the details of my plan.

But there was one thing I could explain without screwing up. "I know Jared's reputation is bad, and I know most of it is deserved. But *my* reputation is squeaky clean. For fifteen years I've produced Jared's programs, and if there's one thing I know, it's that he always delivers an exciting performance."

"So does everyone else here," Lucas said. "But they don't have the ticks against their reputation. What sets Jared apart?"

"Can I be upfront?"

Lucas nodded and I took a deep breath.

"Jared's the only one who needs this. There are so many wonderful fitness instructors here, and they're already all leaving with a dozen signed promotional deals or affiliate contracts. Their plates are full, they'll succeed no matter what. But Jared? His is empty. When we leave here tomorrow, he has nothing lined up next. If you pick him, you'll get both of us—not just him—and you'll have our undivided attention."

"You really believe in him?" Lucas asked.

"If I didn't, I wouldn't have put on these awful clothes."

"Your loyalty says a lot."

"I was thinking we could pull together a few other influencers and make the showcase a charity event. It could be the start of your non-profit foundation. It would draw a huge crowd."

One of Lucas's eyebrows tilted a tad higher than the other. The expression was familiar. Somewhere, I'd met him before. "Now I understand why Caspian insists you're brilliant. He's wanted to found a non-profit for as long as I've known him."

"Does that mean we're still in the running for the showcase?"

Lucas nodded. "I'll give you fair consideration. I trust Hallie and Caspien more than anyone. You're her sister, right? I think you moved out around the time I moved in."

"You and Hallie were friends?" His black hair, the freckles over his nose, the way one eyebrow raised slightly higher than the other . . . "You're the boy who moved in next door? The one with the horror films?"

Lucas laughed. "Nice to meet you, again."

"You've come a long way since White Center. Wait—you trust Hallie more than anyone?"

Lucas's laughter dimmed, something like sorrow casting a shadow over his features. "I think you need to catch up with your sister. Anyway, nice work today." He headed back toward his desk and packed up a narrow, black briefcase. "I need to go upstairs and catch up on work. I'll announce the winner tomorrow morning. Best of luck to you and Jared."

Fortunately, he hadn't inched close enough to smell me. "Thanks."

When I left, Jared waited for me at the end of the hall, outside the back door to the main ballroom.

"What did he say?"

How to answer honestly? Sure, he didn't immediately disqualify us. But would we win? Lucas would have to be in an overly charitable mood—or willing to take a risk. The uncertainty dragged me underwater until each thought felt like slogging through molasses. This morning I'd awoken so confident, when I'd had my own plan and my own presentation.

"Well?" Jared pressed.

"We're in the running." It wasn't technically a lie.

"Yes!" Jared boxed the air like a punching bag, then wrapped one arm securely around my waist. He pushed us through the door into the busy banquet hall. Was I ready to face real people? Not even a little bit. But what choice did I have?

Expectant eyes landed on us immediately.

The twins approached first, of course, followed by a swarm of influencers. Sheila marched straight toward me, ignoring Jared altogether.

"Did it go okay?"

"Nailed it," Jared said, pulling me closer. "We've got it in the bag."

Other people crowded in, and this time Jared gave them more attention. He spoke into their cameras like his career was back on track, told long stories about filming with ZBC, even went so far as to claim that my outbursts the last few days were intentional publicity stunts.

With every word he spoke, I listened less.

Caspien appeared in my peripheral, chatting with the twins, laughing at Kindy's jokes. He'd claimed he didn't like people, preferred staying behind the scenes, but apparently, he'd found exceptions.

Anytime they came to speak to me, though, he didn't join them.

Sherry was the one who finally pried me out from under Jared's arm. "Tell me the truth, away from Jared. How'd it go?"

"In the bag," I whispered, looking at her, but not really looking. This was worse than a panic attack. Worse than anxiety. This was nothing.

Numb.

Empty.

"She's not okay," Sheila said.

"What do we do?" Kindy asked. When had she arrived?

Nothing. No one could do anything. For fifteen years I'd fumbled through life with Jared.

And now? Today?

Everything relied on Lucas's decision, including whether I could afford a plane ticket back to Bailey and JD Fitness. Without this showcase, my life was over.

Lucas had been noticeably absent for hours. Everyone speculated—was he back in his office, making his final decision? I knew where he was, but I told them nothing.

No one else's lives hung in the balance.

No one else was drowning in not knowing.

Not even Jared.

Hours later, Caspien found me alone at an empty, round table. The others had stopped checking on me, probably because of my meaningless responses to their questions. Or the odor.

"Do I smell that bad?"

He didn't laugh. "Do you need anything?"

And then it occurred to me—someone as sincere as Caspien deserved so much better than a mess like me. I'd dragged him into my drama and wasted three days of his time, his energy, his talents. Had I even thanked him? All I'd done was make an empty promise to help his non-profit, then I abandoned him at the first sign of Jared.

Exactly what Caspien had feared.

"I've loved him all my life," I whispered, staring at a brown stain on my tights.

"And it's killing you, can't you see it? Stop clinging to him and move on. Make new glory days. Better ones."

He shrugged at someone over my shoulder, then he rose, and Hallie stood in his place.

"Hey big sis. I got your text. Did you mean what you said?"

I nodded, then she slowly, tentatively lowered into Caspien's empty chair. Her nose wrinkled as she breathed in. But she scooted closer. "Are you okay?"

"No."

Hallie sighed. "I brought you something." She slid a paper grocery bag between us and pulled out jeans, a sweater, and white sneakers. "I heard you needed an upgrade."

My heart leapt into my throat. "You brought me clothes? After everything I've done to you?"

"Of course. You're my sister."

I pulled her into a hug, her hair tickling my nose and smelling faintly like cinnamon. My favorite. Hers too. She didn't even gag from my putrid stench. "Thank you, Hallie."

"Now, will you please come home and see Mom? She's dying to hug you."

I sucked in a breath. "She is? She's not totally embarrassed by me?"

Hallie shrugged, tossing back her ponytail at the same time. "She's pretty mad that I didn't bring you home the first day."

Home. To see Mom. And they *wanted* me there? I felt like Hallie had wrapped my frozen body in a heated blanket, thawing my insides until my cheeks turned pink.

"Let me change, then we'll go."

I sprinted into the bathroom. Stripping off my clothes felt better than eating the best cake of my life. Hallie's jeans were a size too big, but the brown fuzzy sweater hugged my body like a teddy bear and smelled like cinnamon. Like my sister. And the sneakers fit like a glove. I dropped the gross clothes into the trash as I ran out—and crashed straight into Jared.

He clenched my hand in a vice grip and pulled me into a dark corner, then glanced in both directions before speaking in low tones. "Lucas is back."

"So?"

"So, he's mingling again. Talking to the competition."

"Is that important?"

Jared put both hands on my shoulders and shook me. "Important? This is it! The meeting after the meeting. Our final chance to convince Lucas to pick us! And to sway him *against* everyone else."

"Then shouldn't you be talking to him?"

Jared groaned, like I was missing the obvious. "That's where I'm headed, but I need you to figure out who he picked."

An ache settled in the back of my throat. "How can I do that?"

Jared grinned and held up a rectangular, plastic badge with Hallie's face on it. Her Croft Power ID card. "We're only borrowing it for a minute. I need you to run up to Lucas's office and peek at the name on the contract."

I couldn't swallow. "*We* are borrowing it? You want me to break into his office? That's insane!"

"You're being dramatic," Jared huffed. "It's not like you're stealing anything. I'll keep him distracted, you just slip in, peek at the paper, and slip back out."

"Jared . . ."

He cupped my face with his warm palms and rested his forehead against mine. "This is how we get our lives back on track. If we do this, we fix everything. You and me."

But as he said those words, as he clumped us together, my nervous system recoiled. My fingers flexed, both legs bounced, and I exhaled with a shudder. "You and me?"

I didn't want that.

For the first time in fifteen years, I didn't want that.

Jared must have seen it in my face because he exhaled his next words in a whisper.

"Trust-fall favor."

The world slowed to a crawl, and for once, I saw right through Jared's confidence. He stood before me as a man with nothing. Desperate. He'd lost his family, his career, his reputation. He'd ruined every good thing he'd ever had until all that remained was me.

Me.

And now he was losing me too.

But he was also the man who'd given me a job when I'd failed at everything else. He gave me a couch to sleep on, a career to hyper-focus on, a salary to keep me from starvation. And purpose. Fifteen years ago, when I'd stood on the brink of epic failure, Jared had saved me from myself. I didn't want to see him fail.

Trust-fall favor.

A favor reserved for life-or-death situations.

Our tables had turned, and now Jared was the one struggling to float. Beneath all his confidence, all his swagger, Jared was as desperate now as I'd been all those years ago. I didn't want *us* anymore, but could I leave him to drown?

"This is your last one," I said. "Then I'm done."

He exhaled heavily, then nodded. "Text me the winner's name and I'll take care of the rest. Okay?" His eyes searched mine. "Okay?"

"Sure."

"That's my girl. Lucas's office is on the top floor of the skyscraper." He kissed my forehead, then dropped Hallie's key card into my hand before strolling confidently toward Lucas.

Hallie found me a minute later. "Ready to go?"

My gaze stayed trained on Jared's back as he pushed into Lucas's circle.

"Almost, but I can't leave yet." My face flushed with shame as I hid Hallie's ID card behind my back. "Jared needs me to grab something, then we'll go. It'll only take a minute."

Hallie tugged on the end of her long ponytail. "Sure thing, let me know when you're ready."

"Sorry, Hallie," I whispered as I hurried away. "Don't hate me for this."

The Croft Power skyscraper was technically the back half of this building, but I had no clue which halls would take me there. I jogged outside into the pouring rain, then around the perimeter of the building instead. My hands shook from adrenaline, or terror, but I tried not to think about it.

All I needed to do was find a name, text it to Jared, and let him work his magic.

And I needed to do it quick, before he lost Lucas's attention.

Chapter 13

$173.09
-$5.00 for Jared's stupid water bottle he could have taken free from my hotel room
$168.09

When I reached the top floor of Croft Power Company, the elevator gave a high-pitched ding. I shivered from my cold, wet clothes as the door slid open, revealing a long, dark hallway smelling faintly of a lemony cleaning solution. Instead of walls, the hall was lined with floor-to-ceiling windows. Dimly lit workstations filled the office space on both sides. For an ultra-modern, New Age energy company, it appeared so . . . normal.

Now, where to find Lucas's office?

Doors dotted the hall between windows, every twenty feet or so. I picked the first one on the right, swiping Hallie's card until the electronic lock flashed green. But when I stepped inside, the entire floor's automatic lights flicked on, and I ducked. Was there security? An alarm system? Cameras? Lucas's office was probably loaded with proprietary information.

"You'd look less suspicious if you didn't crouch," Caspien said, "and maybe don't glance over your shoulder like a criminal." He was seated at a sturdy, rectangular table in the middle of the room. He leaned forward, elbows on the table, palms rubbing his eyes. "What the hell are you doing here?"

"What are *you* doing here?" I'd left him back at the conference with Hallie.

"I saw you sprint out of the convention center, and I chased after you. I yelled your name, but you didn't hear me over the rain. When I realized where you were going, I walked through the inside of the building. It's faster." He eyed my wet clothes. "And drier."

Behind Caspien's chair, a glass door rose from the floor to the ceiling. The name *Caspien Martell* was etched into a plate at eye-level. Beside it stood a matching door that said *Lucas Croft*.

There it was.

But Caspien's gaze bore into my skin, and the importance of Jared's *trust-fall favor* grew lighter. Less urgent. Caspien would never agree if I told him my plan. But Jared was positive this was the key to saving his career, and I'd promised to help him this one last time.

I slid past him and twisted the smooth handle to Lucas's room.

"Lauren, *stop!*" Caspien lurched to his feet and placed his body between me and the door, knocking me backward. "What's gotten into you?"

"Somewhere in that office is a contract for whoever Lucas picked." No matter how hard I shoved, he didn't budge. "I won't touch anything; I just want to look at it."

"Do you hear yourself?"

"Of course. You're making a big deal out of nothing. Now move!"

Caspien took both my shoulders and held me perfectly still. "Think about this. Trespassing? Into the office of someone like Lucas? It's a felony. You could go to jail."

"Not if no one finds out." I squirmed away. Couldn't he see how important this was? Jared's life would get back on track, and I could finally move on without his failing career hanging over my conscience. "You said it yourself, I'm good at matching people together. The Mormons with the protein bar guy, the twins with Doug. Jared is the perfect partner for Lucas, I just need a chance to prove it. If I can figure out who he picked, I can go back into that ballroom and explain exactly why Jared is the better choice."

Caspien stared at my face, his gaze darting between my eyes. Then he exhaled, like a heavy blanket of understanding was melding onto his bones. "You believe what you're saying." He didn't ask it like a question.

"He needs me."

"You love Jared this much? Enough to risk jail?"

I froze. *Love?*

That word, from Caspien's mouth, pierced my chest like a needle. Every speck of confidence I'd carried into this room deflated. I'd followed Jared everywhere, across the country, across the internet. But he'd *never* asked me to do something as reckless and stupid as this.

But then again, what about the years we'd spent imagining opportunities like this showcase? The countless college nights walking through the streets of Seattle, planning our future? We'd built dreams as big as the universe—then he'd ruined them all with his affairs.

Sure, I'd loved him.

But now?

I didn't want my future tied up in his anymore. That was why I'd come here. One final favor.

But before I could answer, Caspien shot me a fiery glare and swung open Lucas's door. "Search quickly so we can get out of here." There was no kindness in his voice, none of the patience that had carried me through the last few days. Only frustration. Maybe even disgust.

Disgust?

Holy shit, what was I doing?

Reality crashed around me like an avalanche. I'd betrayed my sister by using her keycard, trespassed into a skyscraper, then forced Caspien to break the law with me—all so that Jared could con Lucas.

Would Jared have done this for me?

Not in a million years.

Caspien spun on his heels and stalked into Lucas's office.

Inside, bookshelves lined the wall to my left. A wide desk with six computer monitors covered the exterior window in the back, and an oversized, half-dead plant sat in the corner. Everything was messy. Engineering books lay open in heaps, sticky notes poked out between the pages, and papers and files were piled high on the floor. Did Lucas print *everything?* But the most bizarre item on the shelves was an ornate pair of pink-and-gold, bedazzled heels.

"You don't have to do this," I stammered.

But Caspien shuffled through a pile of manilla folders, then shoved one against my chest.

My anxiety exploded. My hands, my knees, my heart, all trembled with adrenaline. "Let's just leave." But Caspien yanked the file from my hands and opened to the first page. It was a series of printed emails between Lucas and my sister.

Lucas,

I know Jared's a wildcard, but you have a dozen of these conventions coming up to draw more publicity. Caspien says my sister needs the business.

Hallie,

I'm torn . . . I know Cass says Lauren's brilliant, but I haven't seen it. Seems risky.

Lucas,

Remember that street hockey game when I let you score on me? Just so you could look cool in front of Jack and his high school friends? You owe me.

Hallie,

WE WERE THIRTEEN! But fine, okay, so long as she doesn't puke on my shoes again.

I inhaled sharply. "He was already going to pick us?"

"Hallie and I made sure of it." Caspien folded his arms. "But that wasn't enough. You had to be reckless and go through all *this* to prove some misguided devotion to Jared."

He plucked the file from my arms and returned it carefully to Lucas's desk, disturbing nothing. Then he swept past me into the main office.

"Caspien, wait." I grabbed his arm. "I'm sorry, I shouldn't have dragged you into this. I shouldn't have come here at all."

"Too late for that." He squirmed out of my grip.

Then every light in the building shut off, drenching us in black. Not even the city lights down below reached through the windows.

"Shit," Caspien hissed.

A door creaked open and closed. Then a dozen flashlights flicked on, blinding lights shining straight into our faces.

"Freeze!" a deep voice barked. "Don't move, keep your hands where I can see them."

A scraping sound, and then someone grabbed me from behind, twisting my arms behind my back and slapping something cold and hard around my wrists.

Handcuffs?

Were those *handcuffs?*

Someone grunted to my left, followed by a crash, then the lights flipped back on. Caspien was on the floor, on his stomach, his hands cuffed behind his back with a police officer kneeling on his spine. Another stood above them, his hand on the gun at his waist. Two stood behind me, each holding one of my elbows, while six more faced us from the far side of the cubicles, guns drawn and pointed at our faces.

"I work here!" Caspien yelled, but the blue carpet muffled his voice.

"You didn't sign in through security," an officer said. "You'll have to prove it at the station." He grabbed Caspien's bicep and hoisted him roughly to his feet.

"He didn't do anything," I insisted. "We scanned ourselves in."

But the officer to my left swiped Hallie's badge from Caspien's hand. He glanced at the picture, then back at him—when had Caspien picked up her ID?

"A stolen badge?" He tucked it into his pocket, then pulled me toward the elevator, yanking my elbow at an awkward angle. From Caspien's grunts behind me, he was receiving the same treatment.

The elevator door slid open just as we stopped in front of it.

Lucas and Hallie stepped out.

"*You* set off the alarm?" Lucas's eyes widened. Then he addressed the closest officer. "Caspien works here, you can let him go."

But the officer pulled Hallie's badge from his pocket and held it before him, comparing Hallie's face to the one in the picture. "He used this badge to break in. Employee or not, we'll have to sort it out at the station. It's procedure."

Hallie slowly reached for her badge, like it might bite her if she grabbed it.

"This isn't what it looks like!" I stammered. "Hallie, I'm so sorry!"

"It's exactly what it looks like," Caspien mumbled.

Hallie's entire demeanor darkened, her hands clenching. Could I blame her? She'd brought me her own clothes. Offered to take me home to Mom. Then I'd done the exact thing she'd feared the most—I'd betrayed her trust.

But that didn't stop me from begging.

"Tell them!" I cried, the handcuffs digging into my skin. "Tell them I'm your sister, that they don't need to arrest me!"

But Hallie and I looked nothing alike. Complete opposites. And Hallie said nothing to convince the police as they ushered me past. Lucas either. They observed in silence, Hallie's accusing gaze gouging a black hole in my chest.

The door closed between us with a thud.

Chapter 14

$168.09. Not enough for bail.

Of course.

Of course, the quickest route to the street was through the conference center. And not through the maze of hallways and classrooms, but directly through the grand ballroom.

When our police entourage swung open the doors, Jared stood in the center of the room surrounded by an adoring crowd, telling a story with so much animation it took both arms, his head, and one of his feet. He froze mid-sentence when he saw me. His entire audience did, twisting around to gawk and point at my handcuffs.

"Jared, help!" I called. "Can you get me out of this?"

Jared blinked, slowly. Two times. No, three.

Then he returned to his story.

His audience whipped back around, immediately engrossed. What difference did *I* make so long as Jared remained to entertain them?

"Jared?" I said, feebly this time. "I need a *trust-fall favor!*"

He didn't look up again.

The noise in the room faded away. The people fizzled out. Everything disappeared except the back of Jared's head. He'd ignored me. Refused to help. What did that mean? He was supposed to come running when I used those words. I always had for him—every single time. Did it not mean the same thing to him that it meant to me? No, he knew exactly what weight those words carried.

But still . . . he'd ignored them.

That was it. I stopped fighting. I allowed the officers to trudge me out into the rain where a long line of police cars had blocked off the street. One put a hand on my head and shoved me into the back seat of the middle squad car. I slid across it to make room for Caspien, but they shoved him into the car in front of me.

We drove in silence except for some code words on the radio that I didn't understand. At the station, someone took mug shots of my face. *Mug shots!* How could this be happening to me? Then they plopped me in a chair in a room with nothing but a table.

Was Caspien somewhere nearby?

Every time I blinked, his face burned deeper into the back of my eyelids. His hurt, his fury, his disgust.

Eventually, a female officer entered with a black bun and wide shoulders. She looked like she knew her way around a gym. Perhaps she'd heard of Jared. Perhaps she'd call him for me.

But would he come?

Did I want him to?

I had no one else to call.

She introduced herself as Officer Torres and asked me endless questions. Why did I break into Croft Power? Where did I get Hallie's badge? What was I trying to learn? Did a competing power company hire me? Did I have a secret relationship with anyone who worked for one? Did I find Lucas's safe? Did I know the combination? Did I have a hunch about what numbers *might* be the combination?

She asked them again and again, and I answered them honestly, again and again. Couldn't she tell my kryptonite was telling lies? It was impossible. We could have finished this interrogation in under five minutes because I told her everything! But she didn't believe me. Or didn't care. Eventually though, I couldn't keep the panic at bay and my entire body shook.

"Do you need a doctor?" Officer Torres asked. "Are you on any drugs?"

I shook my head to both, and she finally led me down a long hall through the heavily occupied jail cells that reeked of foul breath and unwashed bodies. She opened the cell at the far end then removed my handcuffs after I'd entered. As soon as she closed the door behind me, I rubbed my bruised wrists

"You get one phone call," she said. "Let me know when you want to make it."

She retreated the way she came, and I spun around. One other person shared my cell, a woman whose hands quaked as violently as mine—though hers was clearly drug induced. She rocked back and forth, her thin hair brushing against the shoulders of her worn purple sweatshirt, talking to herself in incoherent sentences. The unexpected smell of raw onions wafted off her. I sank onto the bench as far away as I could, trying to ignore the men gawking through the bars.

One phone call? Who would I call?

Bailey? Marco? Stella? What could they do for me all the way in Missouri? Obviously not Caspien. Could I plead my case to Hallie? Definitely not.

Mom.

I could call Mom.

But even if she'd reconnected her landline, I never would, not for ten million dollars. I'd rather live in this jail forever than face her this way.

The cell beside mine opened and Caspien entered. Our eyes met and I ran to the bars between us, but he turned his back toward me and dropped stiffly onto the nearby bench.

"I'm so sorry."

I reached between the cold metal and touched his shoulder. He flinched, like I'd seared him with a branding iron. He didn't turn around. I pulled my hand slowly back, a deep ache settling into my empty fingers.

Caspien. He'd driven me around, reconnected me with Hallie, written down my incoherent thoughts, then stayed up all night turning my dreams into real plans. And what had I done?

Ditched him the second Jared arrived.

Ignored his PowerPoint.

Gotten him arrested.

And all for what? To prove myself to the man who'd ignored me for fifteen years?

I began to pace, back and forth. It only took six steps to cross the cell, so I switched to walking in a circle, around and around, reversing directions when I became too dizzy.

How would I get out of here?

Who did I need to beg?

Hallie? The twins? Where the hell was Jared?

The way he'd watched me when the police marched me past him. My plea for a *trust-fall favor*. He'd ignored me like I was nothing. Nobody. A disgraced skeleton from a long-locked closet.

The shame of it bounced inside me, zinging through my skull like a bullet. It shattered me from the inside, until I was a glass vase webbed with fractures—one tap and I'd explode into a million fragments. It couldn't stay trapped inside forever, so I spoke out loud as I paced, sounding as crazy as the lady on the bench.

"Maybe Kindy would come get me," I mumbled, "though Cameron wouldn't like it. But jail scandals always draw viewers. Maybe he'd like the publicity."

"Do you hear yourself?" Caspien asked. His voice sounded empty, hollow. He still sat with his back against the bars, his body facing away. Half of me wanted him to spin around, to show me the face that had brought so much comfort this week. But if his expression matched his tone? It would kill me.

I continued pacing in a circle. "Can you blame me for trying to find a solution to this mess? All you're doing is sitting there."

"Because I have no one to call."

"Neither do I. I just want to fly back to St. Louis and forget this whole trip ever happened."

"Are you kidding me?" Caspien launched to his feet and twisted around, gripping the bars with white knuckles. He spoke through his teeth like he was holding back a snarl. "How can you run and hide from all this mess when you've ruined so many lives with your lies?"

I stepped closer. "Who's telling lies?"

Caspien leaned into the vertical bars, one pressing into his cheek, a raging storm building behind his eyes. "I trusted you. Look where it got me!"

I recoiled like he'd slapped me, my entire body turning cold. "I just wanted to save Jared," I snapped.

"He doesn't need you to save him!" Caspien shook the bars, but they were too solid to rattle. Even still, I flinched. "If he wanted to fix his life, he wouldn't keep digging more holes to fall into. If he wanted a better reputation, he'd stop sleeping around." Caspien's voice grew louder, sharper. "If he wanted a happy marriage, he'd spend every weekend at home with his wife. If he wanted to leave her for you, he wouldn't have married her in the first place."

Was this true? Was Caspien right? "I know *all* of those things!" I shouted. But admitting it gouged a hole in my stomach, ripping out my insides.

Caspien released the bars and dropped his arms to his sides, as if defeated. "Clearly, you don't. He's done nothing, *nothing,* to earn your loyalty, yet you keep giving it. Why are you so willing to die on the hill of his career, when he's doing absolutely nothing for you in return?"

I stormed up to the bars, inches from Caspien's face. "I told you about the situation with his wife." But I choked on the words as I spoke them. "She provided the money, which came with specific obligations."

"So, he's a prostitute now? He can't leave her because she's paying for their marriage? He's a world-famous superstar, Lauren. He made millions in his heyday. That was more than enough to walk away from her and her daddy's checkbook years ago. So why didn't he?"

I didn't answer. I couldn't. I'd asked myself those same questions hundreds of times. Thousands. The answer was something I'd refused to face for over a decade. But now? It screamed in my ear. Jared didn't love me. Perhaps he never had. Perhaps to him, I was just a tool in his work belt doing the dirty work he didn't want to do.

A strangled sob clawed its way up my throat.

Could that be true?

"We've worked together our whole lives," I whispered, more to myself than Caspien.

But deep down, I couldn't deny it. Not anymore.

"Fine, don't answer," Caspien said, pacing his small cell. "But I'd bet Lily hasn't helped with money in years, but Jared's still married, right? And he's been stringing you along, the sad puppy who cleans up all his messes and hides his dirty laundry. He treats you like shit, Lauren. Why do you keep following him?"

"I don't!" I raked my hands through my hair, tugging desperately at my scalp. "I'm done following him! I told him today that it was over. *We* were over. No more favors, no more humiliation. But after everything we've built together, I couldn't leave him stranded. Finding that name in Lucas's office was supposed to be my last favor. One final boost so he could take his career into his own hands."

Caspien threw his arms in the air with a cynical laugh. "You think you built JD Fitness *together*? No, *you* built it, while Jared filled his weekends with women and drugs. But you're so blind to it that you've not only sacrificed fifteen years for him, but now you've sacrificed me and

Hallie too. We vouched for you. We put everything on the line for you. Then you did *exactly* what Hallie was afraid of. You abandoned her again!" He pointed directly at my chest, his own rising with each panting breath. "How can you be so selfish?"

What—how dare he? "Selfish?" I stumbled toward the bars that separated us, my voice raising an octave. "Everything I do is for other people!"

"No, everything you do is for *Jared.*"

"How is that different?"

"You're hurting the rest of us *for him*. Was it worth it? Does he at least cater to you the way you do to him? What does he do for you in return?"

"Everything!" I screamed, not caring one bit that everyone in the next three cells watched me. But I twisted around and dropped onto the bench, hiding my face from Caspien. Jared did *everything* for me, just like I did for him.

Didn't he?

Except earlier tonight, when he'd stayed silent as the police carted me away. He watched me pass by then acted like he didn't know me.

Why would he do that?

He knew exactly where they'd caught me. He'd begged me to break into that skyscraper. He'd said it would be easy. But then why hadn't he gone up there with me? In fact, why wasn't he with me this entire weekend? And why didn't he listen to my plan for our meeting with Lucas? He didn't even pause when Caspien offered me my laptop on the way out of my hotel room. Jared had brushed it off like crumbs on his sleeve.

Who needed my ideas when he had his own?

But what ideas had he contributed?

I'd developed our YouTube brand—he'd just smiled for the camera.

I'd developed our marketing plans—he'd just . . . smiled for the camera?

I'd developed every business partnership we'd ever had. He'd just . . . married into enough money for our first set of camera equipment.

In fact, Jared's father-in-law had only contributed enough to get us through our first year. We'd paid it all back with interest during our second. After that, Jared had enjoyed the spotlight while I hid behind a computer and built him into a superstar.

I could have done that for anyone.

"Oh no," I whispered. The truth hung in the air before me, shaped dangerously like a boxing glove. Then it punched me square in the nose.

What had Jared ever contributed? *Really* contributed?

It punched me again.

Nothing but drama and messes.

It punched me a third time.

Every time he'd messed up, he'd pleaded for me to help, claimed he needed me, said he couldn't do it alone. He wasn't lying—he *couldn't* do it alone. He couldn't survive one day in this industry without me.

Because I did everything for him.

And he knew it.

But he didn't want me to realize it.

A sob hiccupped from my chest. Could this be real? Could this be happening? How did I not see this sooner—fifteen years sooner? Every time I'd found a sliver of independence, Jared reeled me back in. Like how he showed up in Seattle this morning, right as I was taking my life into my own hands.

Did the whole world know? Were they laughing at me, shaking their heads, murmuring behind my back?

What did I have to show for my fifteen years of grueling work?

No relationship with Jared. No job, no career, no money. Nothing.

I'd sacrificed everything . . . for nothing.

My breathing escalated into gasps, but at this point my panic attacks were old news. I didn't bother trying to stop it; I scooted off the bench and slid to the floor and let the room spin. The air disappeared, the stars erupted in my peripheral.

I let it come. Let it consume me. The only thing that had ever brought me back to the surface was the steady heartbeat of the man in the cell behind me. But after what I'd put him through, he'd never speak to me again. He'd been interested in *us*, that was obvious. He'd almost kissed me—maybe twice. He'd given up days of his time, gone well beyond the requirements of a standard babysitting gig. He'd *seen* me without shame, put my chaos in order, worried about my well-being. He'd reunited me with my sister.

And I'd sacrificed it all for Jared.

I'd left my family, my home, my friends. Moved across the country on the wings of a promise Jared had never technically made. Grown the business he'd hardly contributed to. Allowed his ego to explode.

For what?

For a ruined relationship with Mom?

For a sister whose childhood I missed out on?

For a life spent as the third wheel to his picturesque family?

It was . . . I was . . . pathetic.

I was nothing.

I was a person with no life of my own, living on the edge of someone else's.

How had I turned into this?

The clock on the wall said 8:00 p.m. when a familiar voice echoed down the long row of jail cells. Hallie and Lucas trailed in after Officer Torres. I jumped to my feet. Caspien, on the other hand, didn't move from his spot on his bench—but it was his cell they stopped in front of.

"They're not pressing charges," the officer said. "You're free to go."

Caspien rose, but Lucas stopped him with a hand on his chest. "Security will escort you back to Croft Power. You have until midnight to clear out your office."

What?

No. No, no, no, no, no.

"You can't fire Caspien!" I gripped the bars until bumps in the metal pierced my hands. "This job is everything to him. This was my fault, not his."

But all three of them ignored me.

"Understood," Caspien said, his voice devoid of emotion.

Lucas stepped out of his way, but Hallie replaced him, stabbing her finger into Caspien's ribs. "I needed you in that job," she hissed. "I *needed* you and you knew it."

Caspien's eyes grew heavy. "I know. I'm so sorry, Hallie."

"Your police escort through the ballroom made every news channel," Lucas added. He sounded exhausted. They all did. "Tonight was too much bad press. I'm shutting down the entire series of conventions."

All of them?

But Caspien only nodded, and Hallie moved to face me.

"I'm sorry too," I said. I couldn't look her in the eyes, so I stared at her necklace, a tiny gold ring with a heart on top, strung onto a chain. I knew that ring from a million years ago. "If you'll drop me off at the airport, I'll get out of your hair forever."

Hallie stood there a long time. Silent. The longer she stared, the more shame heaped over me, like I'd been naked all my life but hadn't realized it until that moment. Why couldn't I disappear into the cracks in the floor?

"We're not taking you with us," Hallie finally said.

My gaze sprang up to hers, "You're leaving me here?" Then I leaned into the bars and touched Caspien's shoulder. "Please, you can't!"

He took a heavy breath without meeting my eyes. "I'm done, Lauren. I'm not babysitting you anymore."

"Someone else is on their way to get you," Hallie added.

Without another word, Lucas led the three of them down the long hall. Officer Torres opened my door and waved for me to follow. When I reached the crowded lobby, Caspien was still signing his release paperwork. His attention darted to the door the same moment mine did.

Jared strolled in, a grin stretching from ear to ear. "You say *trust-fall,* I come running." He boxed with an invisible opponent in the air. "And I've got to say, no one has *ever* gotten themselves arrested on my behalf."

Then he did something he'd never done in the fifteen years I'd known him. He strode across the room, pulled my face to his, and kissed me.

Chapter 15

Still $168.09. It's hard to spend money in jail.

Jared didn't hold back. He pulled me hungrily against him, his fingers sliding under the back of my shirt, all the way up to my bra. He moaned, then brushed his tongue along my bottom lip.

In a room full of people.

For fifteen years I'd waited for this moment, prayed for it, begged for it. I'd dreamed it so many times, playing scenarios out in my head. Would he finally kiss me on the set of our show, at the end of filming an episode? Everyone would cheer and applaud and pat us on the back and say, *It's about time!* Or would it be on a trip, at a convention like this one? We'd close an enormous deal, and he'd walk me to my hotel room, praising me for all the work I'd done. He'd hesitate at the door, his lustful gaze would drop to my lips, and when he finally kissed me, fireworks would erupt outside at that exact same moment. No matter the scenario, one thing was always certain: when his lips touched mine, it would feel like the final two puzzle pieces united at last.

But never once did I imagine him accosting me in jail.

Or that he would taste like watermelon gum and cigarettes.

But that couldn't be. He'd done an anti-smoking ad campaign last year and vowed to a room of sixth graders that he'd never touch a cigarette for the rest of his life.

His scent said otherwise.

I pulled away, lurching back far enough that it forced his hand to drop from under my shirt and cling to my waist instead. I didn't want his first time touching me to be in a jail waiting room crammed with people.

"What was that for?" I asked.

"We're over."

"Who's over?"

"My wife." His voice rose. "We're officially divorced, Lauren. Finally!" Then he leaned away, his energy fading into uncertainty. "This is what we wanted, right? Or was it only me?"

Three days ago, my heart would have throbbed. Butterflies would have danced in my stomach. But when he kissed me? Our lips hadn't fit together like puzzle pieces—it felt like he'd eaten my face. My mouth tasted like cigarettes. And Caspien watched me, listening, his pen hovering above his paper. Hallie and Lucas remained silent behind him.

"It's really over?" I asked, keeping my voice low.

Jared did the opposite, doubling the volume of his words. "Forever. Let's start over, you and me. We'll leave everything behind and go back to the beginning. A fresh start, but this time we'll do it *our* way—how we should have all along." He pointed to my release papers on the desk, but I hesitated.

This was what I'd waited fifteen years for, right? This was why I'd betrayed Hallie and Caspien? To remind Jared that he'd once loved me? He seemed to finally remember, but was a smoky kiss in a police station worth all that?

No. Not even a little bit.

But I'd hurt everyone important to me just to help Jared, and now he was all I had left. Hallie had already refused to take me with her. Caspien couldn't even look at me without seething. My only options were to rot in jail . . . or leave with Jared. This was my fault; I'd chained myself to him.

He pressed a pen into my hand. I stared at it for a long moment. Then I signed the papers quickly. Officer Torres returned my purse and my watch—when had she taken them? By the time she said I was free to leave, Caspien and Hallie had already gone.

Gone.

Leaving me alone with Jared.

He intertwined his fingers with mine then pushed open the police station door with his other shoulder, swinging it wide to let me pass through first. I stared at our hands as we walked. I couldn't find the energy to yank mine away. Soon, this would all be over; for now, I just needed to endure it. He led me to the passenger door of a black Camaro.

"Where'd this come from?" I asked.

"Rental. How else could I come get you?"

With what money? I tried to slide into the dark car, but takeout wrappers filled my seat. The whole car smelled like fried fish. My stomach growled. When did I last eat? The greasy air made my stomach churn. So did this car. And Jared's fingers still twisted into mine. Was I imagining the fast-food grease between the lines of his fingerprints?

"Sorry about that." Jared dropped my hand to wad up the trash, and he threw it into the can outside the police station door.

I wiped my fingers on Hallie's jeans. "Did you get takeout *before* bailing me out of jail?"

Jared beamed as he circled the car and slid into the driver's seat. "You have to understand, I hadn't eaten in a few hours. These muscles require constant nourishment. Are you getting in?"

Every instinct screamed *no*. But what else could I do? Sit on the curb until a stranger picked me up? Jared was all I had. I slid inside, and Jared tore out of the parking lot, revving the engine at the first red light.

"Are we in a hurry?" Jared's fast driving was nothing new—he'd exclusively owned muscle cars as long as I'd known him. But my nerves dangled off the edge of a crevice. I could only handle so much.

"I used my reward points to book us the last flight home to St. Louis. But it leaves in three hours, and we still need to pick up your things."

Home. To Bailey and Marco and Stella. Had my disastrous weekend here hurt JD Fitness? Probably, but Bailey would understand. Even without a job to return home to, their memories soothed my aching limbs.

As soon as we entered my hotel room, Jared unzipped my suitcase and laid it open on the bed. I shoved everything inside. Papers, clothes, my laptop, toiletries. Nothing fit well, but I couldn't miss that flight. The only thing I kept out was the bottle containing my final Xanax—I'd definitely need it.

"Ready?" I asked. This night couldn't end soon enough.

"Not quite." Jared wrapped both hands around my waist, then he leaned down and kissed me. This was nothing like the kiss in the station. He moved slowly, deliberately, pulling me gently into him.

My index finger tapped against his back. My thumb too. "Aren't we in a hurry?"

He kissed me with more urgency. "What if we changed our flights to tomorrow morning? I've waited a lifetime to finally do this."

He had? This was the first time he'd admitted it out loud, so I let him coax my lips open, then he teased his tongue into my mouth.

That's when I tasted it.

Fried fish.

The food he'd needed so badly that he let me sit in jail while he ate it. Had I waited fifteen years to be second priority to fast food? And how had he paid for it? Hadn't he spent all his money before I bought him that water bottle?

"Don't you still need to return the rental car?"

"You're doing that thing again," he said against my lips, "where you say the words in your brain without thinking about them first. Shove down those thoughts, remember?"

The voices in my head roared to life.

I pulled out of his reach and slung my purse over my shoulder, grabbing my suitcase. "We don't want to miss that flight."

Jared's broad shoulders drooped into a pout. "We have the hotel room all night. What if we reschedule the flight for tomorrow?"

"I just want to go home."

Thc fish smell wafted as we climbed back into his rental car. It took all my strength to keep from losing my stomach—not that there was anything in there to throw up. But instead of heading toward the freeway, Jared drove around the block and parked in the underground lot beneath Croft Power.

"What are we doing? I'm positive I'm not allowed back in here."

"This'll be quick. No one will ever see you." Jared hopped out, then circled the car and opened my door. The faint echoes of dance music vibrated through the ceiling of the packed parking lot. The conference folk were still partying upstairs. Jared glanced over his shoulder twice, like someone might be watching. He led me across the dark parking garage toward a sign that read *Employee Gym.* The same gym where Caspien taught me to box.

"What are we doing?" I asked again.

Oddly, the door was unlocked. He led me down a familiar hall that smelled like chlorine. The gym would be at the end. But Jared followed the signs for the locker room. He still didn't answer my question, and when he stopped outside the door, he scanned both directions. Nausea crept into my gut. Not the usual anxiety, but an instinct, an alert. Jared was up to something suspicious.

"We don't have time for a workout." I whispered the words, though I wasn't sure why. "We need to go to the airport."

After checking the empty hall one last time, Jared put both hands on my shoulders and gazed deep into my eyes. "I love you," he said. "I always have. I'm so sorry it took this long for me to come to my senses."

He paused, like he was waiting for me to return the sentiment. Did he say *love?* All I could do was squeak.

He laughed and brushed his thumb across my chin. "I love the way you tense up when you're nervous. Soon, we'll be together so often that you'll be relaxed every second."

He brushed his lips softly against mine. I couldn't make mine pucker—I really did try—but he didn't seem to notice. He pulled open the door behind him. Something scraped against the back of my mind, something unsettling, but I couldn't place it. Perhaps it was his overly doting behavior, or the way he checked over his shoulder again. "Let's go."

"That's the men's locker room."

"I know." He slid my purse off my arm, then dug through it for my wallet. "Oh good, we have plenty of money."

"Why do we need money?"

"I spent the last of mine on takeout. Tell you what, you wait here. I'm going to run in there, buy something from Michael Kay, then come back out. Quick and easy."

"You're meeting Michael Kay?" Even hearing his name made my stomach twist. Why was he stupid enough to come here? Wasn't he banned from the property?

Then again, I was probably banned too. Yet, here I was.

"Just keep watch," Jared whispered. "If anyone comes my way, shout."

That unsettling feeling roared into sirens that blared—no, shrieked—in my head. "Why? What are you buying?"

"It's nothing, just a new product his company's selling."

I stepped away until my back hit the wall. My brain could hardly form words. "What product?"

"Nothing interesting, a new supplement. He offered me an early sample. Think of it like a partnership; he'll sell it to me at a discount, then I'll recommend his brand. He's going to help us get our new business off the ground, that's all."

"You can't seriously think Michael Kay wants to help—"

"Don't worry!" He tucked my wallet back into my purse then slung it over his shoulder. "Stay here. I'll be back in a second."

"Is it drugs?"

Jared shushed me, scanning the dark hallway again. "Of course not. Just his new steroid. It's not technically legal, yet, but it will be. It's fine, Lauren. Everything's fine." Jared moved closer and cupped my cheeks. Why did such a simple gesture feel so manipulative? "Besides, nobody's getting caught. Soon, we'll fly back home, and we'll start our new life together, just like we always wanted. It'll be perfect."

He lowered his fingers then pulled open the heavy locker room door. The bright lights inside blinded me. He was serious. He wanted to walk in there and buy illegal drugs with the last of *my* money?

What would happen if I said no?

Nothing. He wouldn't hand that money back no matter how hard I begged. And would he also leave me behind? Without Jared, I was stranded in Seattle. No car, no money, no way to get home.

As much as I hated it, I needed him.

Once we returned home, I'd figure out the rest.

"He's expecting you?"

Jared nodded. "We're a little late, but he should still be here." He inched away, still squeezing my purse. "In and out, I'll be back before you know it."

"In and out," I breathed.

Jared kissed my forehead, then ducked into the locker room. The door swished quietly closed behind him, leaving me alone in the dimly lit hall. The only sound was the thumping of my frantic heart. *In and out.* Any second, he'd return and this whole nightmare would be over. Any second, we could go home.

But Jared didn't come back.

The seconds ticked by into minutes. Ten, fifteen. My heart raced. It thundered painfully against my lungs. Why couldn't I breathe? *It's fine,* he'd said. *Everything's fine.* I blocked his words from my mind. In fact, I blocked everything out. My fears, my doubts, the risks, the what-ifs. I pushed every single voice into a tiny box in my head and sealed the lid. If I couldn't hear them, they didn't exist.

But those were all lies.

When thirty minutes had passed, I couldn't wait any longer. Our plane would depart in two hours and Jared still had to return the rental car. Could I leave without him? No, he still held my purse. And what if he was injured? Had Michael Kay attacked him too? What if he were bleeding to death while I lounged in the hallway like a fool?

Too much time had passed. I needed to find him.

I swung open the locker room door. My sneakers scuffed on the rough floor as I crept down the hallway that smelled of shampoo and chlorine. I peered down each row of lockers without any sign of other people. Even the air stood still, like nothing had disturbed the room in ages.

At last, voices echoed quietly from a distance.

I followed the sound until I found them. Jared lounged casually against a locker, laughing at a story from Michael Kay. The fake Frenchman glanced over his shoulder and took me in. His grin deepened. He strolled my way and clapped me on the shoulder, much too hard. I stumbled and he cackled. The sound echoed off the walls and grated up my spine.

"No hard feelings about our little spat, right?" he said. The sword at his belt bumped against my leg, and every instinct told me to run. If he picked another fight, I had no friends here to protect me.

"Should you be here?" I whispered, even though the men spoke in full voices. "Weren't you banned from Croft property?"

Michael Kay lifted both hands out wide, a grin lighting up his face as he laughed. "Come on, Lauren, this is a fitness convention. I'm royalty around here! No one would turn me in." He dropped both hands to rest on the hilt of his sword. "Besides, there's a party booming upstairs, which means plenty of business for me. I go where the money takes me."

I scooted around him and hurried to Jared's side. "Our plane leaves soon. Are you done? Can we go?"

"Almost." Jared continued lounging against the lockers, no trace of urgency.

I checked my watch and shifted my weight. Time was running out. "Do you have to buy from Michael Kay of all people? We hate him. Can't we do this another time?"

Jared waved a hand, brushing me off as Michael Kay strolled over. "Of course we hate him. But we also have an understanding that goes way back. When I need certain . . . items, he supplies them for me." He winked at Michael Kay, who dug into the pocket of his joggers. He held up a tiny clear bag. Inside were five capsules filled with faintly blue powder. He raised them to my eye level.

"Aren't steroids usually liquid and a syringe?" Jared asked.

Seriously? They hadn't dealt with the drugs yet?

"Technology has improved. These babies are twice as effective, but completely undetectable in blood tests."

A door opened in the distance, and my entire body tensed. Michael Kay's did too, though Jared stayed perfectly calm. As usual.

"Pay me, quick," Michael Kay hissed as the footsteps drew closer.

Jared dug through my purse and pulled out three, crisp fifties. He dropped the cash in Michael Kay's hand, and I swiped the pills—right as someone came around the corner, a brown box overflowing with files and personal items.

Caspien.

His gaze dropped instantly to our hands, the pills in mine, the cash in Michael Kay's. "You're buying drugs?"

"It's not what it looks like!"

But it was. It was exactly what it looked like. I was buying illegal drugs from a dealer in the privacy of an underground locker room—and we all knew it.

Caspien didn't say another word. He opened a locker, pulled out his gym clothes, then left back the way he'd come. Michael Kay sprinted off in the opposite direction. Jared tugged on my elbow, but I couldn't move. All I could do was stare down the hall where Caspien had disappeared.

Jared wrapped his fingers around my wrist and yanked me through the lockers, down the chlorine-filled hall, into the parking garage. He clicked the button to unlock his rental car, and we climbed into the seats as the vehicle came alive, roared through the parking garage, then out into the safety of Seattle's busy streets.

Away from Michael Kay, from Caspien, from all of it.

Suddenly, my body shook so violently I couldn't buckle my seatbelt. The metal square wouldn't go into the plastic hole, even as I tried again and again. A groan lurched from my mouth as I tried it a fifth time.

Jared took the seatbelt from my hand, clicking it into place, laughing. "That was a rush!" he hollered, rubbing his hands together and steering with his knee.

"A rush?" I shrieked. "Do you hear yourself? We just bought illegal drugs!" He tried to clasp my hand, but I yanked it away. "Do you not know me at all? In what world am I okay having any part of this? Or breaking into high-security offices? How could you ask it of me? I got arrested today, Jared, because of *you*!"

He relaxed on the gas pedal and eased the Camaro onto the freeway. "You're right," he said, sobering quickly. "You're absolutely right. I never should have sent you into Lucas's office. But how else could I find out who the competition was?"

Fire exploded inside my brain. I twisted in my chair and punched him in the shoulder with all my strength—which wasn't much. "You would have known if you were *here* this weekend. But you weren't!"

Jared flinched, gripping the wheel with both hands, the silence stretching thin between us. I folded my arms tightly across my chest. After a while, he relaxed and snaked a hand onto my thigh, massaging gently. He'd caressed his wife's leg like that plenty of times, right in front of me. It had struck me as so intimate, so sensual. How many times had I dreamed of him touching me that same way? But now his hand felt dirty. Greasy.

"I'm sorry," he said softly. "It was out of line. I *do* know you better than that, and I shouldn't have put you in that spot."

He inched his fingers up my thigh, massaging my tense muscles, his hands creeping higher and higher. This was what I'd wanted. For fifteen years, I'd waited for this exact moment. To be the one he took on adventures, the one he kissed, the one he caressed in the car.

But now?

I dropped my hand onto his, freezing it in place. If I stopped him altogether, would it offend him enough to leave me stranded? My plane tickets were on *his* phone; and Jared became a loose cannon when he was mad. It wasn't worth the risk. I set our hands firmly on my knee until we reached the airport.

After a quick trip to the rental car return, the enormous airport was relatively quiet. At 9:00 p.m., most flights had left for the day and only a few stragglers lounged on benches or waited for their lost luggage. By the time we passed through security, our plane was boarding.

"Hey Lauren," Jared said, pointing to a café across the terminal. "Can you grab me a sandwich? I spent the last of my money on takeout, but I'll starve if I only have peanuts for the next three hours."

"I only have eighteen dollars left," I said. "It's all the money I have in the world."

"More than I've got. I want a turkey sandwich if they have one. Tuna's my second choice. Grab me a water too. I'll drink one of your Green Fizzes so I can stay awake for a movie." He joined the end of the line of waiting passengers.

I just stood there, staring at his back. When he saw I hadn't moved, he waved me toward the café. Caspien's voice echoed in my head, *When did you last eat, Lauren?* I had no idea. But Caspien wasn't really here. He wasn't looking out for me. Jared wasn't either. No one was.

For the second time today, my anxiety dropped from crippling to nothing.

I was numb. Empty. A vast ocean without the tiniest ripple. Both times I'd felt this way today, Jared had been responsible.

Before him? Yesterday? When my life revolved around me and Caspien and putting my ideas out into the world? I'd felt calm—maybe confident—for the first time in ages. But today? Jared had dropped my puzzle pieces through a shredder and then shaken up their remains. I didn't know who I was or what I wanted. Everything had flipped upside down.

My phone dinged with a text.

Kindy: *WATCH THIS NOW.*

She sent a link to her Instagram feed. I shoved my phone back into my pocket.

At twelve dollars per sandwich, we could only afford one, and the café was out of turkey. Tuna would make the entire airplane reek, and there was no way Jared would share, but I was a zombie, and zombies were beyond caring. The sandwich cost twelve dollars, and a water bottle was seven. *Seven dollars?* I didn't have enough money for both.

My phone dinged again, vibrating against my hand as I paid for the tuna.

Kindy: *Did you watch it!?!*

I clicked the link and a video opened, time stamped late last night. It was already viral with twelve million views.

The video showed Jared's back, with the arms of a woman curled around his neck. She'd wrapped her legs around him too, clinging to his waist as they kissed. He hoisted her up, both of his hands gripping her rear, her back pressed against the wall.

Then Lily appeared through a door, flanked by two men—the one on her right I recognized as an executive for ZBC. Whoever was filming ducked behind a long black curtain, then poked their phone out to continue recording.

"Jared?" Lily said, her voice eerily calm.

He leapt back, releasing the girl, who crashed to the floor. "This isn't what it looks like."

The videographer zoomed in on the girl's face. She couldn't have been more than twenty, perhaps younger.

To Lily's credit, she stayed perfectly calm.

The man to her left handed Jared a large yellow envelope. "Are you Jared DiMaggio?"

He shifted his weight, blocking the girl from view like they might not notice her. "Yes."

"I'm your wife's attorney. She's asked me to serve you with these divorce papers. She also requested that you not return home tonight. You can call my office tomorrow to schedule an appointment to pack up your things. My card is in the envelope."

Jared lurched forward and swiped for Lily's hands, but she slid back, allowing the attorney to scoot between them.

The ZBC executive moved closer to Jared. "I'm sorry, man, we wanted this to work. But now that we're done filming for the season, we're not renewing your contract."

Jared fumbled backward like the exec had punched him, stepping on the fingers of the girl who huddled on the floor. "You'll still pay me, right? I'll take my check right now."

"We pay JD Fitness. Your salary is between you and your CEO."

Jared was a statue for the next few moments, then he turned his back to them and shoved through a metal door, screaming curse words until his voice faded.

The video ended.

So did any remaining fragments of my pride. My self-respect. Of any surviving tendrils of hope that perhaps, this time, romance could finally bloom between me and Jared.

He had still been married? All this time, he'd never even filed for divorce?

And ZBC? He'd claimed that he quit. But in reality, they straight-up fired him?

Last night.

All of this happened *last night?*

In a daze, I returned to the line of boarding passengers.

"Where's my water?" Jared asked when I handed him the mushy sandwich.

"We couldn't afford it." I hated the word *we* and how it lumped us together.

He frowned as we neared the front of the line. Then the corner of his lip rose into a smirk. "Next time you publicly embarrass us at a conference, I'll make sure you have more money before you make me fly out to rescue you."

Words fired from my mouth before I could stop them. "Rescue me? Tell me, Jared, what happened between you and ZBC?"

He waved his other hand in the air, brushing off my question. "It was a bad fit."

"You've worked for them for six months. You only *now* figured that out?"

He hooked one thumb onto the lip of his pocket, his wedding ring still glistening on his finger. "The red flags were there all along, I just didn't want to face them. They have a nursery downstairs below the recording studio, you know, for the employees' kids. There's always toddlers running up for diaper changes or begging their moms for food. Stepping on crackers and stray bottles gets really old, really fast."

Was this the lie he wanted to feed me? He didn't flinch as he spoke. Didn't track my response for signs that I might be suspicious. Did he lie to my face like this so often that he assumed I'd always believe him? "They're a *family* network."

"Sure, but the camera lady would breastfeed on set during dress rehearsals. Breastfeed! Sure, babies need to eat. But couldn't she go someplace else? Nobody wants to see that."

My brain shot a million responses toward my mouth, but none of them conveyed a sufficient level of loathing. "What about your wife?"

"It's over." He said it matter-of-factly, like there were no other possibilities. Then he pulled my fingers to his lips, kissed the back of my hand, and trained his attention on the gate. Then at his watch. Then back to the gate, only ten people away, like this whole process was cutting into his movie-viewing time. The line moved forward, but I stayed in place until it was our turn to board. Jared scanned our tickets, but stopped at the door when I didn't follow him onto the plane. "Come on Lauren, it's just you and me now."

Something inside me snapped.

A tidal wave of fury crashed through my veins. "You and me? *You and me*?"

I stomped up to him and shoved my phone in his face, letting the video replay for him to see. "What's this, Jared?" He studied my screen, recoiling with every passing second. "She served you divorce papers? *Last night?* You told me you'd filed months ago! That we were just waiting for them to go through. That I was the only one in on the secret. You lied to me, all this time?"

"Where did you get that?" He lunged for my phone.

I swiveled back, stuffing it into my pocket. "Kindy sent it to me. If she's watched it, the whole world has."

"Shit." He ran both hands through his hair, breathing heavily, as if the vents had sucked the oxygen from the room. The airline attendant announced *last call* for boarding. Then slowly, the tension drained from his shoulders. He looked up at me with a lopsided grin that made my stomach roil. "What difference does it make when the split happened? She's gone for good, and we can finally be together."

"If she hadn't filed for divorce, would you have come here today? Would you have finally kissed me? Or told me you loved me?"

Jared didn't answer. He stared at my forehead—not my eyes.

"And ZBC? Would you have come to my meeting with Lucas if ZBC hadn't fired you? Have you ever once spent time with me simply because you wanted to? Because I was your first choice?"

"Of course." Jared sighed, exasperated. "You're twisting it all around. Blowing this out of proportion." He spoke those words with a swish of his hand, like he could wave this all away, sweep it under the rug, move on like he hadn't thrown his flaming life into a vat of gasoline, then stood idly by as the entire world watched him burn. "Let's get on the plane."

I stayed firmly in place.

Jared sucked in an impatient breath, like he was a parent and I was his obnoxious toddler. "We've talked about this." He slowed his words, annunciating them one at a time. "You can act neurotic and distracted when you're home alone, but not in public. You're making a scene." Then he leaned toward the airline attendant and asked, "Will there be movies on this flight?"

Was this the real Jared?

Infuriatingly calm, never losing a minute of sleep by worrying about the future?

Yes, but I knew that already. Even last year, when JD Fitness had teetered on the edge of bankruptcy, he'd never dropped one hair from stress. This was nothing new, he'd always been this way. What I hadn't realized was *why* he acted so comfortably everywhere he went. Jared never worried about anything.

Why?

Because he had me to fall back on.

When his company went bankrupt? He left it to me to fix.

When the media smeared his name? He sent me to save him.

When he quit his job and walked out on his wife? I was there waiting.

Me.

His fallback plan.

Never his first choice, not even his tenth. I was the contingency, the final resort, the safety net when he had nothing else. Why would he stress when he had me, building him a castle and asking nothing in return?

"You coming?" he asked, motioning toward the plane with his head.

But I stepped back, away from the gate. Away from him. "*This* is what life married to you would feel like? Constantly worried that you're with another woman. Constantly fighting for your attention. Wondering when the next lie will surface. How did Lily put up with you all this time?"

Jared swooped forward and took my left hand in both of his. "I'm here now, aren't I? You're the woman I've wanted for fifteen years." But a sliver of fear etched into his eyes.

I shoved my phone into his face. "Look at the timestamp, Jared. 2:00 a.m.—only nineteen hours ago! Were you thinking about me when you were squeezing her ass? Were you thinking about your wife? Or your kids, or your job, or *anything* other than your dick?"

"Lauren!" he snapped, dropping my hands. "You know that's not true."

"Or did you come here because I'm the only sucker pathetic enough to hang around while you buy drugs?"

"That's ridiculous," he scoffed. "That girl meant nothing to me. Why should you care?"

"Because I'm tired of being your last choice. You said you *needed* me to come to this convention, to fix your reputation and save our careers. You said our entire lives relied on me. If it was that important, why weren't you here with me?"

"I was filming, you know that."

"No, you were sleeping with groupies on the ZBC set. Why did you finally show up here *this morning*?"

"To help you out with Lucas."

"Liar!" The answer blew through me like a gale force wind, breaking down my walls and tossing me through the air. "Your wife kicked you out, your day job fired you, then you dropped your girlfriend on her ass and now she'll never want you back. You came here, Jared, to me, because you had nowhere left to go."

"Do you hear yourself?"

"Yes, I do. I'm tired of being your last choice. Why couldn't I be your first? Why couldn't I be *anyone's* first?"

Caspien.

The name fluttered through me like a wisp of a breeze.

I was Caspien's first choice—the first person he'd opened up to in years, the first person he'd trusted. He'd helped me, he'd put me before everything.

But I'd put him last.

Just like Jared always did to me.

"You're fired," I said.

His nostrils puckered into a snarl. "You can't fire me. I hired *you.* You're *my* agent."

"Then I quit." My own snarl bubbled up inside me, and it burst from my chest in a strangled screech. "I want no part of your mess, ever again."

"No one will hire you after the shitty job you did for me."

"*I* did a shitty job? *Me?*" My temper roared, and Jared cowered the tiniest bit. "For fifteen years, you and I had an effective system. I researched potential partners, and you closed the deal. But six months ago, it all fell apart. Don't get me wrong, I still kicked ass at my part, but no one trusted you anymore."

People stared, but I didn't care. I stepped closer, pointing at my own chest with one finger. "I tried to be understanding, and I wanted to be on your side. I wanted to believe that the media was blowing everything out of proportion. I stood up for you, over and over again. Except that you *kept cheating* on your wife! You gave nobody any reason to give you another chance."

Jared raised both hands defensively. "Hang on, Lauren—"

The airline attendant raised her hand to interrupt, but I ignored her. I couldn't stop now.

"No, you hang on—because it gets worse. Yesterday, with no warning, you changed the game again. You shoved your work in my lap and told me I had to do it—when we both knew that I would be a complete trainwreck. And guess what? I was! Not only did I fail miserably, but my anxiety skyrocketed so high that I couldn't do my half either. I failed at everything. No amount of notes or lists or alarms could make that level of anxiety go away. You knew this about me, Jared." I poked him in the chest, my voice rising to a shout. "You've known for fifteen years, but you threw it at me anyway. You let me make a fool of myself in front of the entire world, all so that you could have one more night with your secret girlfriend."

"That's not what happened—"

"The video has a timestamp! The whole world knows exactly where you were last night!"

Jared shoved his hands deep in his pockets, as two more attendants joined us at the gate. He eyed them then lowered his voice to a hiss. "You can't possibly put all of this on me. We're a fifty-fifty team here."

But I threw my hands into the air and shouted, "I know we are! But yours is the half that's failing, because no one wants to work with a guy who can't keep his dick in his pants!"

The attendants exchanged a glance. The one on the left smirked.

"That's not fair. You know what the media's been doing to me."

"They've told the truth. You're a public figure, which means that if you make the public hate you, you can't do your job. I, on the other hand, have done a damn good job. So yes, Jared, I quit. In fact—"

I yanked the little bag of steroids from my purse and stormed to the drinking fountain, pressing the button with my hip and dumping the pills into the water. I lowered my voice to a whisper. No sense in getting arrested twice. "Next time, don't piss me off then expect me to carry your drugs."

Jared lunged toward the fountain, scooping up the capsules as they melted between his fingers. The powder dissolved into mush, then washed away.

"Those were mine!" he bellowed, glancing anxiously at the airline employees.

An airport security guard strolled up, leaning against a nearby pillar, watching us, eyes narrowed.

"Technically, I paid for them." I kept my voice low. "But if you want to fight me on it, go ahead and call the cops. In fact, ask for Officer Torres, we're already friends. Feel free to tell her all about how I destroyed your illegal drugs. I'll be sure to post about it on Instagram."

"You crazy bitch!" he growled. Then his fingers curled into fists, just like Michael Kay's had before he attacked me. Was Jared going to do the same? His knuckles turned white. His jaw tensed.

Yes. Yes, he was.

But what had Caspien said? Throw the first punch? And make it count?

I could do better than that.

I pulled back my foot, then swung it forward, slamming it straight up between Jared's legs. He screeched like a strangled chicken, hunching over and grabbing his privates.

Then his whole body sagged, like the reality of losing me was finally sinking in. Where would he go? Who would pull his life together? How would he make a living?

I didn't care.

Not anymore.

"Goodbye, Jared. I hope I never see you again."

The last thread of my binding attachment to him snapped. I spun around and marched through the terminal, nodding to the security guard as I passed. The farther I walked, the lighter my feet became. The chains around my shoulders lifted. The weights strapped to my ankles dissolved. I'd dragged around a two-hundred-fifty-pound dumbbell all these years, and suddenly the burden disappeared. Why had I thought my happiness was utterly dependent on him? Without Jared dragging me under water, I could go anywhere, do anything.

Jared, on the other hand, would choke down that soggy tuna sandwich and somehow blame me for ruining it. He'd mutter a string of curses when he realized he'd never swiped a Green Fizz from my purse. He'd watch a movie anyway, then he'd fall asleep halfway through and blame me again.

At the far end of the terminal, I glanced over my shoulder. Jared stood in the center of the walkway, watching me, his mouth open, arms limp at his sides. Even his perfect hair was awkwardly mussed. Was he not boarding his plane? Or could he not even make a simple decision without me? Did his overbearing confidence require someone to double-check each of his choices?

The old me would have gone back.

The old me would have told him exactly what to do.

But the new me didn't care.

He wasn't my responsibility anymore.

He could hop a plane to France, and it wouldn't affect me at all.

I turned away and resumed walking. Eventually he must have climbed aboard his plane, but I didn't turn around to check. Not once.

As I backtracked through security, though, a different sort of heaviness settled onto me. Once I exited this airport, what would I do? With only a few dollars left in my wallet, I couldn't hire a cab. I had no job, no prospects, no friends—at least not here in Seattle—and no vendors at the convention would ever hire me. Even if I could get back to my hotel, we'd technically already checked out.

So where did that leave me?

Stranded at the airport, that was where.

I couldn't call Hallie—she'd never speak to me again. I couldn't call Caspien or Lucas. I couldn't even afford dinner.

For the first time since entering this dismal city, the rain had stopped. I tilted my head back and stared up into the dry, clear sky, inhaling a deep breath of fresh air. One heavy drop of water fell from the eave above and went straight down my throat. I spluttered and coughed, leaning forward until my hands rested on my knees.

A rain-free night, but I still choked on water. Figured.

My life had spiraled, but one glittering truth remained. Leaving Jared was the first decision I'd made entirely for myself in fifteen years. My one silver lining in all this. No matter what this world had in store for me, the next decision was mine to make. Mine alone. And the decision after that. And all the ones that followed.

And right now, I had an important one to make.

I sank onto the curb, parking my suitcase against my legs, and pulled out my phone. I'd hit rock bottom. There was no one left to call. I scrolled through my contacts, reading name after name. None of them could help, none of them would come.

Except one.

Holding my breath, I tapped on one name, then pressed the phone to my ear.

Would the call even go through? Every time I'd tried in the past three years, the phone service had been disconnected. But what if . . .

"Lauren?" a voice said at the other end.

Should I laugh? Or cry.

Maybe both.

"Yeah, Mom, it's me."

Chapter 16

$168.09
-$150.00 steroids
-$12.07 soggy, mushy tuna sandwich
$6.02

My watch said just past 10:00 p.m. when Mom's car pulled up. I recognized it instantly—she'd had the same grey Honda Civic since we were kids. How was it still running? Though by "running" I meant "spluttering along."

I had to summon all my courage to stand. So many years had passed. How would she react when I climbed into her car? Did she hate me? Would she forgive me? She'd sounded okay on the phone, but she'd clearly been sleeping because her voice sounded groggy and slow.

When I could delay the inevitable no longer, I dragged my suitcase to the dented trunk and hefted it inside, then slid into the passenger seat. The car smelled exactly as I remembered—Mom's soap mixed with too much engine oil. The fumes had saturated the seats. As a kid, it had seemed edgy. Now, it smelled like home.

"Mom, I'm so sorry—"

My breath froze—my sister's profile filled the seat beside me, her small nose, her high ponytail, the gold ring with a heart that she wore on a chain around her neck.

"Hallie? What are you doing here?"

But Hallie didn't answer. Silently, she drove us away from the airport.

Even at 10:00 at night the Seattle traffic hadn't let up, but we only needed to drive six miles. We trudged along until her silence rang in my ears like a whistle. Her keychains tapped against the ignition each time the engine revved, and the brakes whined anytime we slowed. But Hallie's silence haunted me.

My fingers started tapping.

How could she sit there so quietly? She hadn't looked at me once.

My knee bounced too. It shook the entire car, but I couldn't make it stop. I had so many things I wanted to say, apologies I wanted to give, explanations for my behavior. Why had I left? Why hadn't I returned? Why did I break into Lucas's stupid office? But how to say it . . . where to begin . . . how to keep from making a fool of myself . . .

I had no notes on my phone for a conversation like this.

At last, we spluttered into our neighborhood, the small suburb called White Center, and the memories roared to life around me. My high school, with its barbed-wire fence and metal detectors, then the elementary school that often had a giant penis spray-painted on the wall. The little grocery store where Mom would take me shopping once a week, but I could only pick cereals that WIC would pay for.

Hallie turned again, creeping deeper into White Center. One-story houses lined the road, drowning in weed-filled yards and rusted, decrepit vehicles. The siding had peeled off most of them, the roofs splintered, shingles missing. A black rottweiler with a chain tied around his neck tensed under a streetlight. He jumped to his feet as we drove past, snarling and barking at our car.

At the end of the road sat a worn-down café called Mimi's. The lights glowed through the windows, teenagers crowding the tables, two tossing a turquoise football between booths. I remembered those times—I'd spent plenty of winter nights drinking hot chocolate at Mimi's with my friends.

Hallie turned again and my thoughts slowed to a crawl. Our street. The small houses shrank to dilapidated trailers—some double-wide but most single. Boards filled the spaces that used to be windows. Duct tape held walls together. Busted-up bicycles dotted the yards with weeds growing around the tires. Three elementary-age kids watched us drive past in the dark, no sign of their parents.

"Was it always like this?" I asked, staring out the window.

Hallie scratched absently at her wrist. "Yeah."

Mom had always made our street so happy, made home a welcoming place. She'd usually worked two jobs, but she spent every extra second treating me like the most special girl in the world. We'd bake cookies on Saturdays, plant seeds in leftover jars and line the back porch, stay up all night studying for my tests.

She never said no. She always made time for me.

Then I abandoned her.

Our car slowed and I sucked in a breath.

There it was.

Home.

A familiar red trailer near the end of the street. The paint had peeled, most of the red had faded, and they'd replaced the kitchen window with heavy plastic. The shoulder-height chain-link fence was gone, though the posts remained, and the overgrown yard had turned into pebbly dirt marred by clumps of weeds. Two broken bikes leaned against the house half-buried in blackberry vines.

The house was so small, so broken. I closed my eyes and did my best to remember. The plastic in the window was new, but the neighborhood was never nice. Still, the reality of it squeezed tighter. All these years, maybe they'd needed more help than an occasional check in the mail. Hallie stopped the car. She grabbed my suitcase from the trunk, then headed toward the house without looking back.

"Wait!" I climbed out, tripping over the crumbling curb and falling hard on my knees.

She paused, one hand on the knob.

"It wasn't Caspien's fault."

Hallie met my eyes for the first time since the airport, so I spoke quickly, before I lost her attention.

"He tried to stop me from breaking into Lucas's office. He followed me, then he begged me not to do it. You don't have to trust me. I won't blame you if you ignore everything that I say all night tonight. But believe this one thing—Caspien was on your side all along."

Hallie still didn't respond, but maybe the tension in her jaw relaxed the tiniest bit. It was hard to tell in the dark. But she nodded then pushed open the door.

Memories whirled around me as I climbed to my feet and followed her inside. The smell of dryer sheets and Mom's favorite soap. The blue corduroy couch filling up half the tiny living room. New holes had ripped through its fabric, and the wooden feet were gone, but I knew exactly where the softest spots were. A box television used to live on the shelf to my right. Now there was a bookshelf with no books, only worn picture frames and piles of mail.

My gaze darted to the kitchen to my left. The same wooden table filled most of the space, one leg replaced by something plastic and yellow, attached with copious amounts of silver duct tape. A stove, an oven, and just enough counter space for two people to work side-by-side. The window above the sink was covered in plastic. Cold air seeped steadily into the room.

Behind the kitchen was the door to the master bedroom. Last time I went in there, Mom's queen bed had filled the entire space, with barely enough room for a dresser in the corner. Tonight though, her door was closed.

To my right, past the living room, was the second bedroom, my bedroom—at least it used to be. Now the room didn't have walls. A mattress was shoved into the corner, pressing against the arm of a couch draped in a familiar pink blanket. It was mine once, pink and plush. Now it had more holes than fabric.

Home.

Coming here, standing in this room, this place, a piece of my soul relaxed that had stood on edge for too long.

But where was Mom?

My fingers brushed a tall stack of mail on the table. Red stamps covered the front of each one. *Past due.* Hallie swept them up in one fluid movement and stuffed them onto the bookshelf. The way she hid her face as she did it was like a clichéd scene from a movie.

"Were those medical bills?"

"Don't worry about it."

How could I not worry? If Hallie worked with Caspien at Croft Power, she should earn a decent salary, right? So why did they still live here? Why not fix the window? Why the beat-up car and unpaid medical bills?

The rain started falling outside. It thundered against the roof like we were trapped under a metal bowl. Hallie dove for a stack of buckets and lined them around the room, just in time for water to drip through leaks in the roof. "Mom keeps putting these away," she mumbled, then she busied herself in the kitchen, hand-washing the single bowl and spoon someone had left in the sink.

Once she'd dried and shelved them, she washed the counters and swept the floor, then when the heater stopped blowing, she banged it with her fist until it roared back to life. Even then, it couldn't compete with the frigid air streaming through the plastic window. Then she moved on to smoothing the perfectly straight covers on her bed.

All this while I stood in the doorway, watching.

But she never returned my gaze. Not once.

Was she . . . nervous?

"Hallie?"

She didn't stop moving.

"Hey, Hallie?"

She kept cleaning, this time attacking the walls with a wet cloth. Lightning lit up the sky and the lights went out down the entire street. Through the one functioning window came only blackness. Hallie muttered under her breath and pulled a lantern from somewhere in the dark kitchen. She flipped on the small light and then resumed washing the wall.

"Hallie? Where's Mom?"

My kid sister whirled around, storming toward me, poking her finger in my face. "Don't you dare say my mother's name. You don't deserve to call her *Mom*."

The blood left my face. And my hands, and my lungs. Suddenly, she was fourteen-years-old again, crying at the airport all those years ago, begging me not to leave.

"You're right," I whispered. My voice mingled with the raging storm outside. "I left you—I left both of you—and I'm so sorry."

Her entire body sagged as the dim light of the lantern cast shadows across her face. "Then why did you go? And why did you never come back?"

"I have reasons, but they're all stupid. None of them will make you less mad." Without any sort of notes or prior planning, my rambling brain went into overdrive and took control of my mouth. "I meant to come visit, but life got so busy. Jared's show went viral, and that kind of growth just takes over your life, you know?"

The air seized in my lungs.

Not another panic attack. Please, no.

But I was lying. To Hallie, and to myself. Lies always brought the panic back.

Hallie pressed her fists to her hips. "Jared had time for a wife and kids. Are you telling me he never took a day off to be with his family? He worked on Christmas and Thanksgiving?"

"No, but—"

She lurched forward and crossed her arms. "Mom made me promise to wake her up when you arrived. She's begged me to bring you here all week. But how can I go back there and get her when all you can say is, *I was too busy*?"

I panted, hyperventilating. Hallie's eyes widened, watching me fall apart.

"I wanted to," I gasped. The room slowly spun. I clutched the edge of the cupboard near my face, but the entire cabinet door fell off, medical bills spilling out onto the kitchen counter below.

Hallie ignored them. "That's bullshit, Lauren. For eleven years? Where the hell have you been?"

She wanted to know the real reason I'd stayed away. But where to start? First, because I believed in Jared. I believed in his—our—company. I wanted to be there from the ground up. How could I leave, even for a short time? What if he partnered with a new client, and I wasn't there to plan the deal?

I'd also hoped someday he'd leave Lily for me. What if they got into another fight? What if he needed a place to stay? He'd slept plenty of nights on my couch, but what if they finally had *the* fight? The one where he came to his senses and realized he loved me more than her—but I wasn't in town when it happened? What if I missed my chance to be with him because I'd visited Seattle the exact day that he needed me?

My panic attack revved and my stomach churned. I clutched my belly with one hand, the other still clinging to my chest, my lungs. All these reasons, they sounded so pathetic. So desperate. If I spoke a single one out loud I would puke, because all of them were true—

—but none were the real reason I'd stayed away.

The truth clawed its way from my belly to my chest. A reality so dark and grim I'd denied it to myself all these years. Refused to face it, even as it ate me alive like a cancer. As it manifested through my panic attacks and anxiety and my relentless drive to rescue Jared's career.

How could I face it now, with Hallie watching it unravel me from the inside?

When I didn't speak, the cold anger in Hallie's expression morphed into shock, then hurt. Her disappointment killed me. Like I'd betrayed her. Mom must have concocted an elaborate story to convince her I hadn't abandoned her. To make her believe her big sister had good reasons for leaving. All her life, Hallie had probably clung to that story.

But I'd just ripped it away.

"Why?" she asked, voice cracking.

Why? Why did I avoid my mom and sister all these years? Why did I make excuses and use my devotion to Jared as a cover story? What, deep down, was the real reason I'd stayed away?

"Because I wanted to protect you," I blurted. The words in my mouth tasted like death. Like mustard gas. Like acid burning away my soul, one shameful inch at a time.

But those words were the truth.

"From what?"

"From me!"

Hallie froze, hands on her hips. "What does that mean?"

"I couldn't face you, Hallie. Ever since I moved to college, I've been a wreck. A mess. My anxiety cripples me, and I have panic attacks until I puke or get myself arrested. The people around me get hurt too, like when I got Caspien arrested. I've lied to you over and over again to cover up the real me, because what if I let you see me and I screwed up your life too? I'd never forgive myself."

"Lauren, hang on—"

"No, you have to understand." The words went wild in my head, fighting their way out. "I forgot to call. Every single day, I *forgot.* I don't know what's wrong with me. Caspien thinks it's a symptom of ADHD." Hallie folded her arms, her rag wetting the front of her shirt. I threw my hands up in the air. "I know, I know! I *meant to* call, then all of a sudden five years had passed, and I was too ashamed that I'd let you grow up without me. I should have boarded the plane both times I bought tickets. I should have done so many things differently, but I genuinely forgot."

"You *forgot* to come to my college graduation?"

"Yes! When I remembered, I tried to call and apologize, but wouldn't go through!" Each word pounded a nail deeper into my lungs. Of course, she didn't understand. How could anyone forgive me for abandoning them over and over? "I know how terrible it sounds." I dropped my hands limply to my sides. "But it gets worse. I followed Jared to St Louis because he promised his marriage was a sham. It was temporary. I was terrified that if I left—even for a weekend—he'd finally be ready for *us,* and I wouldn't be there!"

"A fake marriage?" The frown in her eyebrows drove home the ridiculousness of my words. It punched me in the stomach, twisted my insides up like a snake. Was I so desperate for his approval that I'd never stopped to question all of this? No, somewhere deep down, I'd known the truth about him. But I was too ashamed to come home and face it.

"Sometimes, I *did* remember to call you—but I'd left you guys for the biggest scumbag on the planet, lying to myself every day for fifteen years that it'd get better, *he'd* get better. I was waiting for him to open his eyes and love me instead. Then, I'd have the perfect husband, a glamorous job, I would have had everything! And I wouldn't be embarrassed to come home and confess all my lies." I sucked in air as the humiliation rolled over me in waves.

Hallie pressed a delicate hand against her chest. "The entire world knew Jared was manipulating you. You can't put all that on yourself."

"That's even worse!" I groaned. "Everyone knows how stupid I've been! Can't you see why I couldn't make myself come home? Couldn't let you see me like this? Let Mom see me? How could I face you when *this* was what I'd become? I thought I needed more money, a ritzy husband, some tangible proof of success, so that I could walk back in here and prove that it was all worth it."

"You're worth millions, aren't you? You used to send us checks."

"On paper, I was. In real life? I'm a wreck! A mess. And completely broke. I dropped out of college my first semester, Hallie. All those times you wanted to sleep over in my dorm? I was living on Jared's couch, pretending like I was still a student. I've spent fifteen years chasing a man who never loved me, and now I have less than seven dollars to my name. Forget about having a successful career, I can barely speak in coherent sentences anymore! I have nothing to show for all the years I lost. Nothing to justify the way I treated you. I abandoned you for . . . nothing."

I held my hands out, away from my sides, palms up. Empty.

Empty like me.

I had nothing left.

Hallie raised an eyebrow. "Honestly?" she said, the venom gone from her voice. "Your sentences sound perfectly coherent to me."

I dropped my hands. "*That's* what you took from everything I said?"

But her words echoed in the empty space inside me.

Empty.

Why was my head empty? Five minutes ago, hundreds of thoughts had spun their circles, so chaotic I couldn't possibly sort them out. But now?

They'd all come out. One at a time. Hallie had called them *coherent.*

I'd made sense. How had I made sense?

The answer settled, peaceful and quiet, like the calm of an early morning snowstorm. It was this place. It was White Center. It was this house. The couch, my pink blanket, the cupboard door that hadn't been fixed since before I left.

It was Hallie.

The fact that she'd still picked me up from the airport after everything I'd done, all the ways I'd embarrassed her. The way she stood here now, listening, concentrating, wanting to be convinced. She didn't cringe at my confession, she didn't pull away, draw back, send me packing, even after I told her I might ruin her life.

Jared would have told me to shove it all down, hide myself away.

But Hallie inched closer.

This was what family looked like.

"I'm sorry I didn't call."

"I missed you," she whispered.

"All I wanted was to come home."

Hallie ran forward and collapsed into my arms, her chest heaving as a sob climbed out of her throat, her arms clinging to my neck. "We wanted you back. Every single day."

I squeezed her waist and pulled her close, and suddenly she was fourteen again, so small and innocent, refusing to let go as she hugged me at the airport.

Call me every week, she'd begged.

How about every day? I'd pried her off me, then lifted her hand that wore my ring, painted gold and cheap, with a heart on top. *You'll keep this safe? Until I come home?*

I promise.

But today, I didn't pry her off me. I held her as she cried then gripped tighter when my own tears joined hers. Her necklace pressed into my collar bone, the gold ring with a heart.

Why would she still have it if she didn't want me home?

This was the reason I could speak coherently here. Because in my home, with Hallie, I didn't need to prove myself. Didn't need to impress anyone, or show off, or put my best self on display. Here, I could be the greatest failure on the planet, and she'd still love me.

That ring proved it.

"I'm so sorry, Hallie."

"You're already forgiven."

Then the door at the end of the kitchen creaked open and footsteps shuffled across the floor. "Took you two long enough to make up," a familiar voice said.

I sucked in a breath, and a new wave of tears began.

Mom.

Chapter 17

$6.02 remaining

Hi, Mom." Had she heard everything? All my shame? Would she want me in her house after all that? But the look in her eyes answered my question. Her forgiveness, her love. They sparkled in the dim lantern light as brightly as they had when we'd said goodbye in the airport.

"Come give me a hug," she whispered.

I bolted across the room, pulling her into my chest. She smelled the same, but her frail body trembled slightly. She'd always been soft, with loose, warm skin. But today she felt fragile. Like she'd lost half her weight. Was she shorter?

"Careful," she croaked, and I loosened my grip. Her beanie fell off her head.

No hair.

I pulled back to study her face. Her features were the same, blue eyes like mine that sparkled with happiness. But her face had thinned out and sunken in around her cheekbones. She'd penciled lines where brows should have been, the skin too wrinkled for a fifty-five-year-old woman. Her hands shook in mine. Why did her hands shake?

"Your cancer's back." I whispered the words, like I could wish them away and they wouldn't come true. They couldn't. She'd already beaten this, ages ago.

"It's just a little flare up, no big deal." But she edged around the water bowls on the floor, walked slowly to the kitchen table, and lowered herself carefully into a chair. Hallie supported Mom with one hand on the back of her robe, then draped a blanket over her lap.

The air thinned, barely filling my lungs. I crept closer. "Cancer doesn't *flare up,* Mom. How long have you known? Why didn't you tell me?"

"I tried to call, hundreds of times. It wouldn't go through."

"I couldn't call you either," I replied, though I hadn't tried a fraction as many times.

Hallie shied away, backing against the kitchen sink.

"Spill it," Mom sighed, without even looking up. "What did you do?"

"I might have . . . blocked Lauren's number on the landline."

My gaze snapped toward my little sister. "What? Why?"

She stomped the four steps across the kitchen to the table. "It was hard enough losing you once. What if I told you about Mom and you came back, then as soon as Mom recovered, you left again? I couldn't face losing you twice. Worse, I couldn't put Mom through it. Can you blame me?"

I sucked in a breath. No, I couldn't blame her at all. To Hallie, I'd only ever been unreliable.

"I'm sorry," she said. "It was wrong. Last night, I called the phone company and unblocked you."

That explained why my call from the airport had gone through. I had bigger concerns, though. "Mom, how bad is your cancer?"

But she just waved a hand then patted the chair beside hers. "I'm not dying tonight. I want to hear all about your adventures, every second of the past fifteen years."

Hallie brought us each a cup of warm tea then fetched a third chair and a stack of worn blankets. Cold air seeped through the plastic on the window, and water trickled steadily into the bowls on the floor, making a symphony of drips as they filled. Once I'd wrapped a blanket around my shoulders, and Hallie had settled into her chair, they both peered at me, expectantly.

"My story doesn't have a happy ending," I warned.

"Nonsense," Mom said. "It brought you home—that's happy. And just because you're here, doesn't mean your story's finished."

So, I started at the beginning. I told them about college and my struggles in classes, how my anxiety—or maybe ADHD—kept me from making it to the end of the first semester.

I told them about meeting Jared and the idea we hatched in the campus gym. He was everything I'd wished I could be—smart, confident, and articulate. I told them how we spent every minute together when he wasn't in class. How our obsession with growing JD Fitness shoved away my other failures. Then I explained his out-of-the-blue engagement to Lily, how devastated I'd been when he announced he was moving across the country.

"He told me that *I* was the one he really loved. Like a fool, I believed him. So, I packed up my things and moved to St. Louis."

"The company grew fast though, right?" Hallie asked. "Jared's face is plastered all over the internet."

"Yeah, the first decade in Missouri was amazing. He hated his wife, spent all his time at work with me. I could hide behind my desk and work whatever hours I wanted with no one to answer to. It didn't matter if one week I was way ahead, then the next week I was way behind, as long as I kept Jared busy with new projects. And he did all the in-person meetings himself, so I didn't have to remember to return phone calls or dress up for important people. He only got frustrated when I forgot things. Like, if he needed a contract and I'd forgotten to write it up, or if I got so immersed in a project that I totally spaced something else he needed. But for the most part, so long as my quirks didn't interfere with his superstardom, Jared ignored them. Then he started cheating."

"Not with you, though?" Mom said, her forehead creased.

"No, never. Though I'd be lying if I said I wasn't jealous of those girls. But then his cheating became public, and no one wanted to work with him. The last six months, I've had to take his place holding meetings and selling our brand, but all he did was ridicule me for not hiding my flaws well enough to fix *his* ruined reputation. He insisted I could just silence all the rapid thoughts in my head. Like, like if I snapped my fingers, I'd magically change into something I'm not."

Mom patted my arm with her slender fingers, but she didn't interrupt.

"In half a year, we went from millionaires to flat broke. When I arrived here on Wednesday, I had nothing left—no money, no job, no prospects. This was my last-ditch attempt to salvage our careers."

"Oh dear," Hallie said, wrapping her hands around her chipped mug. "No wonder you tried so hard all week."

I filled them in on every mortifying moment of the past three days, until I reached the most important part. "I kicked Jared in the nuts and left him alone in the airport. That's when I called you, Mom."

She put one warm hand over mine, rubbing my fingers. "I'm so glad you did."

"I just wish that, when I finally came home, it was with better news. I wish I could have brought you guys the world instead of crawling home with nothing. I was so in love with him, I ignored all the ways he was using me. How he led me along, dropping just enough breadcrumbs to give me hope, to keep me coming back for more. It's humiliating."

Mom pulled my hand closer to her, so she could wrap her fingers around it. "You spent half your life with him. Walking away took more courage than I've ever had. I'm so proud of you."

Hallie nodded. "It sounds like he manipulated you more than he did anyone else. That's a hard web to untangle yourself from."

Their words soaked through my skin. "You're not embarrassed by me? By all my pathetic mistakes?"

"Never," Mom said. "In this house, I only want you to be exactly who you are—no matter what that looks like."

"Even if I lied for *years* about dropping out of college? I was ashamed to face you every single time I came home. But you were so proud of me succeeding, and you were so sick from chemo, how could I admit that I'd failed? I thought that if I stuck with Jared, I could be successful in another way, and it would make up for all the other failures." I dropped my forehead onto the table then peered up at Mom. "But I failed at that too."

The edge of Mom's mouth lifted into a smile, creasing the lines around her lips. "You think I didn't know you weren't going to class?"

My thundering heart stilled. "You knew?"

"I'm your mother; of course I knew. I also knew that every person has to find their own path in life; sometimes you don't know you're on the wrong one until you try it. College wasn't for you, and neither was a life with Jared. Hallie and I don't love you for your degrees or your resume or your fancy boyfriend. We love you for the kind of person you are."

I grimaced. "A failure?"

"A person who'll do anything for the people she loves."

Hallie nodded again, taking my other hand—and something inside me shifted. Not a storm of emotions, not even a puzzle piece clicking into place. It was the board *underneath* the puzzle, the foundation that the pieces rested on, the rock that kept them from falling into oblivion. Here, in this place, my foundation returned. Here, I knew exactly who I was and where I belonged.

"I was so scared that you'd be too embarrassed of me. Or that I'd come home, and everything would feel different, like you'd moved on without me."

Mom laughed and pointed to her wrinkled face. "I haven't aged a day."

"Never," I said with a wink. "But you?" I turned to Hallie who'd grown a foot since I moved away. "You're a whole different person. I missed your school dances, and your graduation, and staying up all night cleaning a shotgun so I could threaten the boys who took you on dates. I'll spend the rest of my life trying to make up for it."

Hallie reached behind her neck and unclipped her necklace, then she handed me her gold ring. "I promised I'd keep this safe until you came back."

The cheap metal warmed my palm, warmth from her skin, from the spot above her heart where it had rested. Warmth from the love she'd put into it.

"Keep it," I said, "until I come visit again. When this week ends, I'll have to go back to St. Louis. Half my life is here, but the other half is there. I can't walk out on Bailey."

But she folded my fingers over the ring and pushed them against my chest. "We'll switch off. I'll take a turn when you come back next. And it had better be soon because I love that ring."

"You really forgive me?"

Hallie circled the table and hugged me from behind, a tear dripping off her chin and landing on my hand. "Just don't wait another decade to visit, or I'll block your number for good. You're my idol. The brilliance behind hotshot Jared DiMaggio. Of course I forgive you. You make me cool by association."

All three of us laughed.

"I don't know if I count as *cool* anymore though," I said, draping my blanket over the back of my chair and rising to refill everyone's mugs with another round of warm water from the tap.

Cold air from the window hit my skin like a barrage of bullets. Hallie rose too, pulling a bowl of salsa from the fridge and a giant bag of tortilla chips from the cupboard. My stomach growled.

"If you had seen our meeting with Lucas," I said, "you would have croaked dead of embarrassment right there. We were wearing our vintage gear."

Hallie closed her eyes and shook her head in the dim lantern light. "His career . . ."

"Down the drain. I know."

"If it makes you feel better, no one else did amazing either. Lucas had me sit in for most of the contenders' pitches. Normally that's Caspien's job, but he was too occupied with you the last few days."

Caspien had spent almost every second with me since I arrived. But where was he now, after watching me buy drugs with Jared? Would he talk to me? Let me explain what had happened? Let me tell him everything I'd done since we crossed paths in the locker room?

No. I'd given him no reason to listen.

"First was a set of twins," Hallie continued. "Two muscley women with deep voices."

"Sheila and Sherry," I said, sliding back into my seat and crunching into a salty chip. "I've known them for years."

"They had the best interview, but they don't do much online anymore. They only have a cult following. Then there was this young couple, super cute and bubbly. They took turns performing while the other filmed."

"Those were the Mormons. They were probably streaming it live to their millions of followers."

Hallie's jaw dropped. "Seriously? That whole interview was televised?"

"On Instagram, yeah. They're nice kids."

"Are they always so . . . cheerful?"

"All Mormons are, I think. At least that's what Caspien says."

"Huh. Anyway, they were doing great until they got in an explosive fight and the girl ran out crying. But then the last interview was with the Frenchman who attacked you." Hallie shook her head like she wanted to erase the memory. "His accent was cringy, and he brought a spare sword and made Lucas duel him. Lucas was not thrilled. I heard the police arrested the guy for selling drugs a few hours ago—*inside* the convention center."

I perked up. "Arrested? Really? He's been selling illegal steroids this whole week. Jared bought some from him using the last of *my* money." I'd skimmed over that part in my story. "The whole thing was a mess." I hung my blanket over the back of my chair, the cold air soothing my prickly thoughts. "I don't know why I didn't walk away from Jared right then. But I'd hurt everyone else I cared about; he was the only person I had left."

"What finally changed your mind?" Hallie rested her chin on her hands above the table. Mom sat quietly, her gaze bouncing between us.

"A sandwich. I was down to my last few dollars, and I hadn't eaten in over a day, then Jared spent my money on a soggy tuna sandwich. Seconds later, Kindy sent me that video that proved Jared was lying to my face, and it hit me like a semi. He didn't want me, he wanted what he could *get* from me. Every time he touched me or kissed me, I felt . . . used. And gross, like I needed to take a shower. Or scrub a layer off my lips. Just the thought of him touching me again makes my skin crawl." I shot Hallie a sideways grin. "I dumped those steroids down the drain in the airport."

"You know," Hallie said, scooting her chair around the table so our shoulders touched, "we have a lot to catch up on, but there's one thing we have in common." She laid her head on my shoulder, curling her knees up into her chest the same way I often did.

"What's that?"

"The plague of unrequited love." Her gaze wandered toward Mom's bedroom—toward the next house beyond ours.

"You mean Lucas?"

She didn't answer, just squeezed into a tighter ball. "That was the real reason I brought you clothes this afternoon. And why I came to the ballroom to find you last night. I saw the video of you admitting your love for Jared, and suddenly all those years you spent chasing him made sense."

"We do stupid things when we're in love."

"Yes," Hallie sighed. "We do."

"I didn't realize Lucas was the boy from next door until this morning. I assume he doesn't still live there, being a billionaire and all?"

"No." Hallie's sleeve muffled her voice. "He still technically owns it, but he doesn't come around much. It's empty."

"You're still friends though, right?"

"We've talked more this week than we have in years."

I turned slightly, studying her more closely. What had happened between them? "Want to tell me about it? You two were inseparable before I left."

She shrugged then moved her arms so she could chew on her nails.

"Did he become a jerk, like Jared?"

Hallie shook her head. "The opposite. He's perfect. I'm just . . . not his type."

Ah yes, the European blonde with sparkling, four-inch heels. Hallie only ever wore sneakers.

"I'm sorry, Hal."

"It's okay. But enough about me. What will you do now that you're free of Jared?"

The question crashed into me like a mound of dirt from a dump truck, and my anxiety revved its engine. That was a good question. What *would* I do?

"When I stormed away at the airport, he said no one would ever hire me after working for him. He might be right." My nerves kicked up another notch as my bleak future spread out before me. "I've never done anything but this. If I can't sell for Jared, what can I do?" My fingers tapped on the table, both hands in rapid succession. "I've depended on him for my identity for so long, who am I without him? What am I? Who else will put up with me?"

Then Mom swooped in like a hawk.

She knelt before me, clasping my hands and stilling my fingers. "Look at me, Lauren. Do you remember your AP History test, right before you graduated?"

I nodded, and she held my gaze.

"Remember all those long hours we stayed up studying together? How I sat with you until dawn, every night?"

I nodded again.

"I helped you because your brain moved faster than your hand could write."

"I was screwed up like this back in high school?"

"*Not* screwed up," she said earnestly, "your brain works differently. I always knew this about you; it was part of your brilliance. When you would set your mind to something, you could focus hard enough to think twenty thoughts in the time I could think five."

"That's why you helped me study?"

"Of course. I knew your potential, but you needed someone to take notes for you, to organize your thoughts when they popped up out of order. When you moved off to college and met Jared, I hoped he would see your brilliance too, and help you the way I did."

Shove it down, quiet the voices. "He did see my brilliance . . ."

"I know, but he didn't help with the rest. He wanted you to magically change, to be more like him. When you dropped out, I knew I'd failed you. I didn't give you the tools to channel your knowledge in an effective way."

"No, Mom." I pressed my forehead against hers. "You gave me everything you could. You gave me the confidence to jump into the ocean of adulthood. It's my fault I climbed onto a boat full of holes."

"No, Lauren, listen." She gripped the table and carefully climbed to her feet, then she retrieved a black paperback with pink writing and placed it in my hands. The letters ADHD jumped out in bold font. "I found this recently and devoured every word. It's you, Lauren, inscribed in its pages. I would give anything to go back in time and read this when you were a child, to have had the tools to better help you back then."

I traced the pink letters with my fingers.

"Look at me." Mom gently lifted my chin, but I couldn't pull my gaze from the book. Could this contain the answers? Could it explain *me*? "The way you forgot to call us? It wasn't because you didn't care. It was because people with ADHD forget that people exist outside their everyday lives. It's called *object permanence.* If I'd known sooner, I would have explained it to you. I would have made a point to be the one to always call and check in."

Could this be true? Was it possible I wasn't a terrible sister and daughter, my brain just worked differently than other people's? "Caspien said the same thing."

"There's more."

Finally, I raised my eyes. Mom's had glossed over with unshed tears.

"The way you obsess over projects, but drop the ball on everything else? Like when you became obsessed with JD Fitness but couldn't focus on classwork? That's called *hyperfocus.* It doesn't mean you're a failure. It means you have a superpower."

Ten minutes ago, I would have scoffed. But now I clung to every word.

"Have you ever become so obsessed with researching something that you forgot to go to an important meeting?"

I nodded. I'd spent so much time preparing to give Jared's keynote speech that I forgot to set an alarm to remind me to show up.

Mom lowered her voice conspiratorially. "Or focused so hard on work that you forgot to board a plane to visit your family?"

"Yes," I whispered.

"You're not broken, Lauren. You should not feel shame for the way your brain works. You simply need to learn effective tools to manage it."

Her words slipped over me like a balm, seeping into my cracks, smoothing my sharp edges. Could that be true? Could there be a reason why I function like this? A way to harness it? To use it to my advantage? I'd excelled in high school, but I'd failed in college. What had changed?

The people I spent my time with.

Jared had always told me to hide those pieces of myself away. *Shove it down, quiet the voices.* But Mom had helped me organize my chaos. She called this a *superpower.* Was she right? Maybe what I'd needed, all these years, was to surround myself with people who would support me in my differences—instead of chasing a man who made me hide them.

"Take this." Mom pressed the ADHD book against my chest. "Read it, learn about yourself, then you'll see what I mean."

It was too much to hope for, a perfectly frosted cake that I'd ruin if I sliced into it. Yet, my fingers wouldn't relinquish the book. The way Mom had given names to my quirks. *Hyperfocus. Object permanence.* Were there more? If these traits had names, that meant people had studied them, researched coping skills, developed strategies for becoming more productive.

An endless stream of possibilities erupted into existence in front of me.

Perhaps I could finally stop *shoving it down.*

Perhaps I wasn't something to be ashamed of.

Perhaps, after all this time, I could finally embrace my superpower.

That puzzle inside me trembled, an earthquake shaking the foundation of how I viewed myself. But the puzzle? Held in place by my mother and my sister?

It held strong.

"Thank you, Mom." I wanted to say so much more, but the words wouldn't come.

She seemed to understand though, because she climbed slowly to her feet and sank back into her chair. "The nice thing about life is that there are an endless number of do-overs."

The humiliation of the past three days slammed back into me, washing away my peaceful moment. "Are there though? Who would hire me when the whole world is laughing at me?"

"You're wrong about that too," Mom said, settling back under her blanket. "Your shame wants you to think that there's no way past this. But the truth is, what you do from here on out is completely up to you. You can stay in the past and let Jared's sinking ship pull you down, or you can build your own boat and navigate your own future. Today, right now, is your perfect chance to start fresh. So, the real question is, who do you want to be? What do you want to do?"

A flurry of arguments flushed through my head, so I stood and paced while I sorted through them. Within seconds, I kicked over a bucket.

"I'll clean it," Hallie said.

While she grabbed a blue towel with frayed edges, I wrapped my blanket around my shoulders and resumed walking.

"Ever since I got here," I said, "I've been trying to be someone else. I strolled into the opening banquet in the vintage outfit Jared picked. I tried to channel Bailey's confidence. I tried to toughen up and face my fears head-on, like Marco with his cane. Hallie, I'm even wearing your clothes! I've done nothing *my* way this week—except one thing. For the first time in fifteen years, when I was prepping for my meeting with Lucas, one person shook me from my chaos and asked me how *I* would solve my problems."

"Who?" Mom asked.

A grin split Hallie's face. "Caspien."

"The Caspien you work with?" Mom asked.

"I made him keep an eye on Lauren for me, when I was too mad to face her myself—sorry, Lauren."

"I don't mind. When Jared bailed on me, Caspien saw what kind of help I needed. He took my scattered thoughts and organized them into a brilliant proposal for Lucas. I've created hundreds of proposals, but never anything so detailed. He drove me around all week, calmed all my panic attacks, kept me from murdering Michael Kay, then stayed up all night helping me plan my presentation for Lucas."

"Wait, he stayed up all night with you?" Hallie asked. "I only asked him to spend one day following you around, he did all the rest of that on his own. In all the years we've worked together, I've never seen him take off a single day, until this week."

Wait, she hadn't asked him to do days two and three? Then why had he?

"Either way, I treated him like trash. He'll hate me forever, and I don't blame him. I had a million panic attacks, I popped Xanax every five minutes—"

"He hates that," Hallie said, wincing.

"Sure does. Then I puked twice, got him arrested, and he caught me buying drugs for Jared. He'll never be in the same room as me again."

I stopped pacing abruptly, facing Mom and Hallie.

"Being with him felt like being here. No stress, no anxiety. Jared always told me to squash down my ideas when they ran wild. But you know what Caspien did? He told me to let them loose so he could write them all down. I didn't have to hide myself, never felt ashamed. I was just . . . me." I tilted my head, zeroing in on Mom. She held a notebook and a pen, her hand scribbling furiously as I spewed words from my mouth, just like Caspien had.

She smiled knowingly. "You know what that's called, darling?"

I shook my head.

"Love."

"No, it's not."

"Pure and simple."

"That man's been glued to his miserable routine for years," Hallie snorted. "You're the first person who's ever pulled him out of it. And I've *never* seen him stick his neck out like he did for you to Lucas."

The entire earth stopped turning.

Caspien loved me?

Sure, we'd almost maybe kissed. But that was different than falling for a girl he barely knew. But did he *barely* know me? We'd only met three days ago, but he'd witnessed both my best and my worst. I'd held nothing back, hidden no flaws, laid every scattered piece of me on the table.

But he hadn't run away.

He'd stayed.

He'd *stayed.*

I had to get him back.

He had no reason to come, though. No reason to listen, no reason to forgive me. But what if I gave him one? What if I could save his job, and Lucas's showcase, in one giant swoop?

I dashed to my suitcase and dug through it, then I searched through my purse until I found what I needed. I hugged Mom, then Hallie, then kissed them each on the cheek.

"I have an idea," I said, excitement bubbling out the top of my head. "But to pull it off, I need a favor. Can I borrow your car?"

Chapter 18

$6.02 remaining

Hallie gave me Caspien's address, and I sped the twelve miles to Queen Ann as fast as her ancient car could take me. The streets were empty, but her Civic neither accelerated quickly nor slowed without the brakes squealing. I only made one stop, connecting my laptop to a kiosk in a drug store and printing a photo. Then I bought a gift box the size of my hand, wrapped up the item I'd brought with me, and resumed driving.

The night was getting late, well past 11:00, and if I could convince Caspien to forgive me, we had so much to do.

The map on my phone brought me to a neighborhood lined with high-end condos—perfect for young couples or bachelor pads. When I reached Caspien's street, I cranked the music as loud as the ancient radio could go. If I couldn't hear my thoughts, they couldn't convince me to chicken out.

I still didn't know what I'd say after I knocked on his door, or how to begin. Did I jump right into begging for forgiveness? Did I lay out my plan to save his career? Or show him the video of Jared's wife finally leaving him?

In the end, it didn't matter. When I parallel-parked into the only available spot, Caspien was walking out of his building. He dragged an oversized suitcase with one hand and led a gray-and-white husky with the other. I ducked and turned off my headlights. He tucked his suitcase into the trunk of his Tesla, two cars in front of mine, stowed the dog in the back seat, then climbed into his driver's seat.

By the size of his suitcase, he wasn't coming home anytime soon.

This was it, my only chance before he disappeared from my life forever.

When he started his Tesla and the headlights flipped on, I inhaled deeply. Then I dove out of Hallie's car and wrenched open Caspien's passenger door. He froze, but I jumped inside, holding out the box containing my gift.

"What the hell are you doing?" he growled. "I almost punched you."

I responded with the first thing that came to mind. "I'm getting your job back."

"Get out."

"Five minutes. Hear me out for five minutes."

He didn't agree or accept my present. But he also didn't kick me out. His hair draped sloppily over his forehead, like he couldn't find the energy to fix it, and he stuffed his hands under his legs like he didn't trust himself not to fidget. I, on the other hand, couldn't stop moving. If I told him my plan, would he listen? Would he help? Would he ever forgive me for being so stupid? And where was he headed with his giant suitcase and his dog?

The husky sniffed me from the back row, and I held out my hand for her to sniff. Then I slid the gift box onto the dash and matched Caspien's posture, miserably uncomfortable. It felt exactly like our first afternoon leaving the airport, when I'd thought he was a hired driver. But this time, we both knew exactly why he wanted me out. Somehow, I had to convince him otherwise.

But I still didn't know what to say. Where was PowerPoint when I needed it? I always did better with notes.

"Jared kissed me," I blurted.

Caspien's head swiveled my way. "I know. So, you two are together now?"

"No, I took your advice and kicked him in the balls. Then I quit. Forever. I sent him on an airplane alone."

Caspien returned his gaze forward, staring out the window. Now that I'd started talking, ten possible follow-up sentences crashed through my brain. But which to choose?

"I'm sorry about the steroids—but he kissed me—it was oily—he was my only option—but he never loved me—"

Caspien turned his head the tiniest bit, just enough to track me from the corner of his eye. "Slow down," he said.

I took a heavy breath, reorganizing my thoughts to come out one at a time. Somehow, I had to finish speaking each idea before the next shoved its way into my mouth.

"Jared kissed me at the police station."

Caspien nodded. "I saw that."

"Then he told me he'd left his wife for me, that he'd always wanted us to be together and now we finally could."

"That's what you wanted, right?" Caspien asked.

"I thought so. But then he dangled our relationship over my head to get me to buy him steroids and tuna."

Caspien raised an eyebrow, but he also cocked his head in the way that I loved, so I pressed on.

"For years, I've dreamt of Jared finally wanting me, but he's always expected favors in return for his attention. That's all I ever knew. I had to constantly prove my worth while hiding my real self. I had no idea a relationship could be anything other than that until—"

Caspien held perfectly still, his eyes wide, jaw set.

"—until the last three days with you."

He opened his mouth but closed it again. Not one sound came out.

"I liked the idea of him," I said. "He was so confident and so famous. All these years, I couldn't believe he'd stuck with me! Or that he was on the cusp of being mine . . . But once I had him, once he kissed me, I hated it. I hated who I was with him, I hated the way he treated me. All I wanted was to rewind the clock to yesterday when life was just . . . you and me. The last three days I've been more myself than the previous fifteen years with Jared. You make me feel comfortable, you make me feel safe, you make me feel like I don't need to pretend to be something I'm not."

I smiled. No, I laughed. The desperate, pleading, high-pitched squeak of a woman with nothing left.

"More than that, I liked seeing *you* open up. The day I met you, you were so grumpy. You hated everything about my life and all the people in it. But I think you started to trust me—until I blew it."

Caspien held up a hand, maybe to interject, maybe to stop me all together. I didn't let him, though. Too many thoughts still zinged through my head.

"I want the chance to try again. Besides my family, not one person in this world knows the real me—except you. You looked close enough to see the authentic Lauren under all my anxiety and chaos. Jared was always my first choice. But when I finally got him, I hated him. I was so wrong. He's not my first choice, Caspien. You are. I'm sorry I had to make a terrible mistake before I learned how to make the right one. I know this is fast and we live in different states and have separate lives, but I want to at least see where this goes, whatever that looks like."

Caspien finally put a hand on my knee, shaking his head slowly. "Lauren—"

But I dug through my purse and pulled out a photo—the one I'd printed at the drug store kiosk. It was the selfie I'd taken of me and Caspien, late last night in my hotel room. We both looked frazzled and exhausted from a long night of work, but our smiles were genuine.

"You challenged me to stop living in the past. To make new glory days." I held up the old Polaroid of me and Jared, then ripped it to shreds. Then I propped the new one up on his cup holder. "These are them. Last night is one I want to look back on and cherish forever. And I want to make a million more—with you."

Caspien gently lifted the picture, rubbing his finger over the spot where our foreheads angled together.

"Lauren," he said, so quietly I had to lean in to hear him. "I want to believe you . . ."

"But I'm telling the truth! Look, no panic attacks, no throwing up in your car. If this is about buying drugs from Michael Kay, I'm so sorry. It was the stupidest night of my life. It'll never happen again."

"I'm leaving Seattle, forever."

Every sound in the world faded away. The occasional car driving by, dogs barking, the steady rain on the roof, they all poofed into nothing. "Where are you going?"

"To my sister's house in New York, at least for a while." His voice sounded heavy, sorrowful, like he spoke through a thick fog.

"You're not going home?" In St. Louis, at least I'd be able to track him down, talk to him, try to convince him.

Caspien shook his head. "You know I can't face that place. But I can't stay here, either. Everything I wanted was wrapped up in this job, in the non-profit Lucas promised I could run. Without it, I don't know what to do with myself."

This was my fault. He'd saved my life, but I'd ruined his in the process. His job was supposed to rescue him from his grief, but instead I'd gotten him fired. Of course he didn't feel the same way I did. Why would he connect himself to someone who broke everything she touched?

"What if I could save your job? I have a plan. Hallie said she'd help. But I can't do it without you."

He didn't meet my eyes as he leaned across my seat, across my lap, and opened my car door. Rain pounded down on my exposed arm. He held out my picture of the two of us.

So that was his answer?

"Keep it," I said. It meant nothing without him, anyway. I hoisted my purse onto my shoulder, then stepped into the rain, not caring that it instantly flattened my turquoise hair and soaked Hallie's sweater.

When I moved out of Caspien's way, he put his car in reverse and pulled out, turning onto the next block, then disappearing.

Forever.

I'd failed.

The rain soaked through my jeans, saturated my frozen toes until they ached. But none of that registered.

Even if Caspien didn't want me, even if he rejected my feelings and sent me back to St. Louis alone, I'd counted on him wanting his job back. I'd assumed, without a doubt, that he'd jump on board to save his career. Never, in all the ways I'd imagined this conversation panning out, had I pictured a version where he flat-out refused.

What would I do now?

Without Caspien, I couldn't pull off my grand plan. Hallie and Mom could support me for a while, but they clearly had no money to spare. Eventually, Bailey would call about my empty office in the JD Fitness building. Should she pass it on to someone new? What about my apartment? My angelfish? Someone would need to feed Francine.

My whole life was back home in St. Louis, but I couldn't even get there.

My feet walked on their own, with no idea where I was headed. I wasn't familiar with the neighborhoods in Queen Anne, but I kept going anyway, in the rain, in the dark, as the clock passed midnight. The longest day of my life. It felt like three weeks ago that Jared had shown up in my hotel, though that happened only this morning. It felt like three months ago that I'd hopped on the plane to come here.

A sedan swerved around the corner behind me, plowing through the puddle built up on the edge of the road. It sprayed water high above my head, soaking me to the skin. I peered into the sky and laughed.

“Thank you, fitness gods,” I yelled, “for the reminder that things can always get worse.”

The black car screeched as it slammed on its brakes, then zoomed backward in reverse. When it reached me, it stopped. The door swung open and Caspien jumped out. He held my gift in his outstretched hand. He must have opened it after I left. He jogged toward me, rain dripping down his face, until he stopped on the sidewalk three feet in front of me.

“What’s this?” He opened the giftbox, then raised my prescription bottle with my final Xanax in the bottom.

“It’s my medication.”

“I know what it is,” he said, wiping the water from his forehead. “But why did you give it to me?”

Wasn’t it obvious?

“Because I don’t need it when I’m with you. The half of me that’s anxious and disorganized? You pieced it back together. You and Mom and Hallie. You made me whole again.”

He took a shaky step forward on the gray sidewalk. “I believe you,” he said.

“You do?”

His gaze bore into mine. “You’re a terrible liar. Which means you were telling the truth about all of it.”

“I’ll never lie to you, Caspien. I don’t know how.”

He stepped forward, until he stood so close we’d bump together if he moved again. “I know. That’s one of the reasons I want to be with you.”

“Because I can’t lie?”

A hopeful smile spread across his face.

“Wait, you want to be with me?” My brain went haywire. I wasn’t his third choice or his tenth—but his first?

“There are more reasons.” He wiped the water off his brow. “You’re driven and you’re selfless. I’ve lived here three years and only ever thought about myself, about how to convince Lucas to let me start his foundation. But you've only been here three days and you spent that time fighting viciously to help other people."

"Jared?" I said, cringing.

"Yes, Jared. But also the twins, and Doug, and the Mormon kids, and the protein bar guy. You push and push, long after anyone else would have given up. You've worked ten times as hard as anyone else here this week."

"I'm also ten times more scatterbrained."

He lightly touched my shoulder then slid his hand down my arm until his fingers twisted into mine. "Another reason I like you."

My frozen insides melted into a puddle of warmth. My whole body trembled. I wanted, *needed*, him closer. I yanked him toward me and kissed him. A symphony of glowing lanterns erupted around us. He tasted like fresh air and frozen rain. Every inch of me heated to scalding. Like dipping into a hot bath. Like two pieces of a puzzle clicking perfectly together.

A low rumble vibrated through Caspien's chest.

"Sorry!" I jumped back. "Sometimes I act before I think. If you didn't want to kiss me . . . I'm an idiot. Or should I have let *you* do that? Was it okay? Please, say something." I gripped his arm, searching his eyes.

Dark heat filled his gaze as it swept over me. "Come here," he growled, and he pulled me toward him, pressing his lips hungrily against mine.

All my anxiety calmed, like it had since the day I met him. My heart slowed, matching his rhythm, and for the first time in a long time, I allowed myself to just exist in the moment. To enjoy the feel of his lips on mine, his arms wrapped protectively around me, his whiskers tickling my face. With Caspien, I felt whole.

"You taste good," I whispered, and he cradled my cheeks in his palms, so my entire body melted into his, warm in the freezing rain. He kissed me long and slow—until I pulled barely away, peering up at him. "Have you been driving around looking for me?"

He nodded, brushing his lips softly against mine until my entire body glowed from the inside out. I never wanted him to stop.

But I couldn't hold still forever. I had too much I still wanted to say.

"I think you're onto something," I said, "about the ADHD."

Caspien leaned his head back and laughed. "I think so too."

"I'll schedule an appointment with that doctor on Monday. But first, as much as I love kissing you in the rain—and I *really* do—why don't we save your job? And mine. And rescue the showcase, and every other convention Lucas has lined up?"

"Tonight?" Caspien glanced at his watch. It was well past midnight after an extraordinarily long day.

"When else?"

Caspien's face transformed as he nodded, focused and alert. "You honestly think you can save my job?"

My heart double-jumped. For Caspien, I'd do anything. "I think so."

"What do you need me to do?"

At a jog, we both hurried back to his car, still parked in the middle of the road.

"My mom said that one of the attributes of ADHD is," I squinted my forehead, searching my brain for the right word, "*hyperfocus.* I have a million ideas zinging through my brain, all ready to go, but can you help me organize them?"

He grinned across the roof of his car. "I'd love to."

Caspien dropped his dog off at his apartment, then drove us back to White Center as quickly as the slippery roads would allow—we'd come back for Hallie's car later.

He must have never visited Hallie's house because, when I pointed to our street he said, "Are you sure it's this one?"

"This is where we grew up."

Mom was asleep on the couch, and Hallie read a book at the table under the lantern.

"No power yet?" I asked as I entered. The temperature inside had dropped, or maybe I was just wet. Caspien stopped inside the door, taking it all in—the ragged couch, the plastic-covered window, the buckets catching rainwater. He said nothing, but surprise spelled across his face. He ran back outside for a change of dry clothes from his suitcase, and Hallie gave me new jeans and a sweater from her closet. Soon, we all sat around the table, huddled in blankets, with lukewarm cups of tea.

"Okay," Hallie said. "What next?"

I handed Caspien my laptop, but he clenched his jaw. "It's dead." With the power out, we couldn't charge it. Hallie grabbed two spiral notebooks and gave one to Caspien. Then he handed me a packet of powder.

"Green Fizz?"

"You take this every time you're trying to focus. Do you need one now?"

I knew Caspien's concerns about these, how he didn't believe I needed them. My stomach fluttered that he'd offer me one anyway. That he'd offer me whatever I thought I needed to succeed.

"When I'm overwhelmed, I use this stuff to calm the chaos inside me. It settles the voices screaming in my head. But tonight? I don't want to block them out. I want to listen to every single one."

Caspien grinned while Hallie watched us both, eyes darting back and forth, sparkling. But at last, we were all ready.

"Why are you both staring at me like dead fish?" I asked.

"It's time to do your thing," Caspien said.

"My thing?"

"Where the ideas pour out of you, and we try to catch them before they swim away."

Suddenly, with Hallie there, my face grew hot. "This feels weird. I can't do it on command."

Hallie frowned but Caspien shrugged. "That's fine. Hallie and I will start planning. You can chime in if you want to add anything." He turned his entire body to face Hallie, blocking me out of their conversation. "I'm thinking we stick a plush couch on the Convention Center stage, then have Lucas interview Jared, plain and simple."

Sirens screamed in my head.

"Sounds like the past showcases," Hallie said. "What if they both interview each other, back and forth?"

Were they serious? This was the lamest idea I'd ever heard.

"That's a new twist, I like it. But let's keep them focused on exercise. They can take turns sharing their fitness journeys with the camera. They'll need scripted questions, though. I'm not sure we can trust Jared with a live camera."

"No!" I groaned. "Just stop, both of you. We're not doing anything like Lucas's past showcases, and no one is ever, *ever* allowed to hand Jared a microphone on live TV. Besides, he's not invited. He's on his way to St. Louis. The goal is no longer to promote his career, it's to save all of ours. I'm thinking of a multi-influencer showcase where all the top contenders from this week get their chance on stage. They all had ideas, right? Let's let every one of them take their turn to show off for the camera, then let the audience back home decide who earned the long-term partnership with Lucas."

"A live vote through our app?" Caspien asked.

"Exactly."

The ideas exploded inside my head. This time, I didn't shove them down. They washed over me, filling my arms and my legs, filling every strand of my turquoise hair, until they overflowed from my mouth. Caspien and Hallie scribbled furiously on their notepads.

"We'll bring in the vendors too," I said. "Catch them before they pack up and fly home—There were dozens . . . sixty seconds on stage each . . . people can call in to buy products—OH! Let's make it a charity event. We'll need phones. Dedicated numbers for each charity, and each influencer picks their favorite. Forget the live vote, what if whoever's charity earns the most money, that influencer wins the contract. Vendors can *give away* their products too, one each. We'll need the stage. Phones, people to answer them."

This would be the grandest showcase in Croft Power history. Never had anyone done something like this, never had anyone pulled together so many fitness superstars, and never had they had *me* behind the scenes. Forget my life as an agent, I could produce fitness shows in my sleep. I'd done hundreds, maybe thousands, for Jared—

—but he'd vetoed most of my best ideas.

Now, I would combine the grandest pieces of all of them. This was simple. Like breathing. How much anxiety did it give me?

None.

Not one bit.

Now that I had the basic framework in place, it was time to fill in the details. Caspien and Hallie would need to know exactly what equipment to gather, how many stagehands to hire, who to call to set up donation accounts.

I placed both of my hands on the table and let them tap to the beat of my thoughts, then I bounced both my legs. All that fidgeting should be enough to distract my subconscious.

Then I let the ideas flow.

Eventually, Hallie set her phone to record in case they missed anything important. Caspien nodded his approval, then they resumed scribbling. I spoke for forty-five straight minutes, maybe longer, as each idea took its turn to fill the air in the kitchen. They didn't come in order, but they each danced their way out of my mouth—

—until suddenly only one thought remained.

"We'll need a Master of Ceremonies. Someone who will draw a crowd and entertain the audience, but who isn't in the show."

"Lucas?" Caspien asked.

"No," Hallie said. "He's not charismatic enough. On this short of notice, we'll need someone local. Lots of famous people live in Seattle, right?"

Caspien chewed his lip. "Do we know anyone well enough? Someone famous, who would drop everything and appear tomorrow morning to help?"

To help *me?*

Maybe that was my problem. Maybe I'd spent the past fifteen years trying to do everything on my own. When Hallie needed help, she'd asked Caspien to move across the country and come work with her. When Jared needed help, well, he'd asked me for things every day.

But when I needed help? I'd tried to carry the entire world on my own.

Until it crushed me.

But now, I needed someone famous who would drop everything to star in my show. Did I know anyone who might fit that description?

Yes.

I knew the most famous fitness influencer in the world. But every time I'd tried to give her a job, she'd refused.

But this wasn't just a job, this was my life. My future. And she was my friend. Friends were supposed to help each other when they were in a mess, right? Perhaps it was time to stop pretending my life was in order and tell Bailey the truth about my situation.

"I know someone," I said with a deep breath. "I'll make the call."

The question was, would she come?

With that, the last of my ideas ran out. Hallie stopped her recording. My watch said 2:00 a.m., and Mom sat up on the couch, smiling proudly. She must have woken sometime during my onslaught of thoughts.

Hallie shuffled through her piles and piles of papers. "All this was inside your head?"

"It was, but not anymore. I hope you took good notes. And that you're extraordinarily good at organizing them."

Hallie and Caspien exchanged grins then dove into the job of piecing my ideas back together. Caspien pulled ten blank pages from his notebook and laid them in a line across the floor—like the slides in a PowerPoint.

He wrote the biggest pieces of the puzzle across the tops. One said *Performers,* one said *Vendors*, one said *Charities*, and so on. This event was similar to the one we'd outlined yesterday, only much grander and with far more people and moving parts. But at least he already had an idea of how to make it flow. Then the two of them danced around each other as they worked through their notes, one line at a time, rewriting their bullet points onto the appropriate page using their phones as flashlights. This took nearly an hour. Then they went back again and organized each page into to-do lists, supplies lists, and personnel requirements.

While they worked, I settled onto the couch. Mom threw her blanket over my body until she'd snuggled me against her. She'd become so small, so weak, but she glowed with the same strength that had always radiated from her heart.

"I knew you could do it," she said, nodding to the long flow chart that Caspien and Hallie had filled with rows and rows of tiny words. "But I don't think you were meant to be Jared's agent."

"No?"

She tapped her head against mine. "You're much better at event planning."

The truth of her words settled into me without a hint of anxiety. "Only took me fifteen years to figure it out."

"Fifteen years, and just the right helpers. You were lucky to find Caspien this week."

Lucky, yes. But her words were a double-edged sword. After tomorrow, after the showcase, where would we be? Caspien would hopefully have his job back, and I'd be on a plane returning to St. Louis. Even if I wanted to stay, I owned half of JD Fitness. But since Bailey took over my old job running the company, where did that leave me?

After tomorrow, Caspien and I would live in different states.

"You're right," I said. "I was lucky." Caspien glanced up at me with soft eyes that made my stomach flip like a pancake.

He and Hallie stood back and announced our project finished, right as the power flicked back on. The heater roared to life, and there, across the narrow rectangle of floor, was my entire chaotic world in an organized line.

"You guys," I gasped, climbing out from under Mom's blanket. I took each of their hands and squeezed. "You put me in order."

"It was kind of fun," Hallie admitted. "You gave us the weirdest jigsaw puzzle, and we had to piece it together. Your ideas are brilliant."

"I can't thank you enough."

"Final step," Caspien said, sliding around us in the tiny space to snap a picture of each page. "Someone has to convince Lucas to let us do this. It'll cost a fortune, and Lauren is banned for life. Not to mention I'm already fired."

We both looked at Hallie.

She groaned, then she slumped onto the couch beside Mom. "You both know I don't like talking to him. We're not friends."

"Baloney," Mom said, taking Hallie's hand. "You were practically siblings growing up. Maybe this is exactly what you two need."

"Trust me, it's not." Hallie chewed her thumbnail. But she was our only option. "Fine. I'll go see him in the morning."

I exhaled loudly, and Caspien nodded.

At last, the exhaustion hit. The others felt it too. Red veins filled Caspien's bloodshot eyes and Hallie stopped talking altogether. We cleaned up our papers in slow motion, then I walked Caspien to the door.

"Do you think he'll go for it?" I asked.

Caspien only shrugged. "No way to know. Tomorrow will either be the busiest day of our lives, or a quick drive to the airport."

"To fly away in opposite directions . . ."

Caspien's smile didn't reach his eyes. Despite the suitcase in his trunk, he'd waited years for Lucas to fund his foundation.

And what did I want? To go home to Bailey and my company? To produce fitness shows? Yes, I wanted to be with my work family.

But what did that mean for me and Caspien?

Neither of us had an answer.

Caspien rubbed his eyes then glanced at his watch. "See you in four hours?"

"Try to get some sleep."

"You too."

He leaned down and kissed me with infinite softness. My entire body melted into a puddle.

"See you soon," he whispered, then he slipped out the door.

Hallie helped Mom to her bed while I finally pulled out my phone and stared at Bailey's number. Would she pick up in the middle of the night? Would she be willing to send Fearless Felicity on a last-minute trip, right in the middle of launching Stella's new show? Or had I embarrassed the company so much this weekend, that she'd see my name and refuse to answer?

Only one way to find out.

Bailey picked up after the first ring. "Is everything okay?" The worry in her voice overpowered her middle of the night grogginess.

"I need help."

"What's wrong?"

But where to start? With my crazy story of the last three days? Announcing that I fired Jared? Begging her to put on her Felicity costume and bail me out of trouble *again*?

"I think I have ADHD."

"I know," Bailey said.

"You do?"

"We've worked together for a long time."

I stilled, holding my phone to my ear with both hands. "And you don't care?"

"Why would I care? You're brilliant at what you do, and you work harder and longer than anyone I know. Doesn't bother me that you organize yourself in your own way."

"Really?" Her words hardly made sense. "Because I need help, and I've been too embarrassed to ask. I keep ridiculously detailed notes, thousands of them, but when I'm forced to speak in public, my ideas come too fast. Jared keeps shoving me into the spotlight, and I keep making a fool of myself! I need to work in an office again. Off stage. Behind the camera, not in front of it, where I can research and work without having video cameras in my face—

"Oh! And I forget to call people. I've been here three days and I forgot to call or text every single vendor I'd planned to reach out to. I got too focused, and I just . . . didn't. I think I need help with reminders. Or an assistant who can make calls for me when I get too focused on something else—which reminds me, I also lose track of time when I'm working. I used to be able to work all night if I needed to, but in this job? With Jared? I missed giving a speech because I was too busy writing it."

Bailey's breathing echoed through the phone, but she remained quiet as I composed myself. I relaxed my clenched hands, sank onto the couch, and pulled my knees to my chest.

"I messed up this weekend. I humiliated myself in front of the whole world, and I ruined the career of someone important to me. But I'm trying to make up for it. Jared always told me to pretend to be 'normal', that my ADHD symptoms were something to be ashamed of. But I'm tired of hiding who I am while I'm drowning on the inside. So, I'm asking for help. I need people in my life who understand me and aren't embarrassed of me—and will remind me to set alarms for meetings when I get hyper focused."

Slowly, I rose from the couch and paced Mom's small living room. This was it. Either she'd help, or she'd run away screaming.

"I also need help saving Caspien's job, and all of Lucas's future conventions. We're putting together a huge fitness showcase and charity auction tomorrow afternoon. Caspien and Hallie helped organize all the details, but I need someone to host the show who can draw a big enough crowd. I'm sorry to ask this. I know you keep your life private for a reason, but . . . I need help. I need Fearless Felicity."

Bailey stayed quiet for a long time.

I clenched my phone, breathing carefully to slow my racing heart. "Bailey?"

"How soon do you need me? I found a flight, but I won't land until 1:00. Will I make it in time?"

"You'll come?"

Bailey's laugh echoed through the phone. "You're my family. When you ask for help, I'll always say yes."

"Even when I'm scatterbrained and anxiety-ridden? And my career is a dumpster fire?"

With her steady voice, Bailey calmed every one of my frazzled nerves. "We'll figure all of it out. Together."

Together.

Nothing could have sounded more perfect.

"Send me your flight details, I'll pick you up. Er, I don't have a car. I'll send someone."

Bailey chuckled. "You'll be busy getting ready. Don't worry about me; I'll catch an Uber."

I thanked her a million times before we hung up, then I used my jacket as a pillow and buried myself in the couch. It smelled like home, like Mom's soap and Hallie's cinnamon gum, like everything I'd forgotten to miss. *Object permanence.* Giving it a name made all the difference. For the first time, I didn't feel ashamed of it.

Chapter 19

$6.02
-$4.09 crappy cardboard gift box
-$1.87 printed photograph
Six cents left

Morning came far too soon. The sounds of someone stirring and the smell of coffee pulled me from a deep sleep. A note waited for me on the kitchen table, along with a key fob to Caspien's car.

Hallie and I went to meet with Lucas. Get some rest, then join us. Fingers crossed!

I picked up his key with two fingers. He'd trust me with his car? Beneath it sat the photo I'd printed of the two of us. *Our new glory days,* he'd written on the back, and I pressed it against my chest.

What time was it? 9:30? I shouldn't have slept so long.

I took a quick shower and put on my only remaining outfit. It was my favorite one I owned, comfy slacks and a cream collared blouse. This suit always made me feel powerful, and I'd saved it especially for yesterday. Of course, Jared had made me change into my puke-covered vintage clothes. So today, it felt meant to be.

Today, I would earn back my crown—*my* way.

Mom sat me in a chair and fussed over my eye until the purple bruise had mostly disappeared. When I finished loading my things into Caspien's car, she took my hands. "I'm so proud of you." Her blue eyes sparkled. Even at my worst, she'd always believed.

"I love you, Mom. If I don't see you again today, I'll visit Seattle soon, I promise. And I'll ask Bailey to remind me to call."

She reached into her pocket and pulled out Hallie's necklace, the long chain with our gold ring. "For good luck," she said, clipping it around my neck. "May it bring you more than it brought Hallie."

"What do you mean?"

Lucas had said something similar after my interview, something about Hallie needing my support.

"It's a story for another day. Now get going." She hugged me again, then shooed me out the door.

Caspien's car came quietly to life when I started it, the electric motor nearly silent. It drove smooth and calm, exactly like my thoughts—

—until I reached the conference center. My nerves began to jingle, but not with my typical anxiety. This was the thrill of confidence. I knew how to do this; I knew how to blow Lucas's mind. All I needed was his permission.

I parked Caspien's car next to a black Camaro in the convention center's underground lot, then checked my phone. No word from Caspien or Hallie. So, I tiptoed up the stairs and opened the back door to the banquet hall.

My heart stopped.

Dozens of people scurried around the stage, filling every inch of air with movement. Stage crew were setting up a squat rack and the camera crew was installing lights—rows and rows of stage lights. Two women in jeans carried small tables and chairs up to the left side of the stage, with a man in a suit fumbling behind with an armful of laptops. A woman with pigtails sat crisscross in the center, testing microphones.

On the ground below the stage, a string of men lined up rows and rows of audience chairs. Behind them, directly in front of me, were two distinct groups. On one side stood dozens of vendors, each with an armful of their products, receiving instruction from a woman in a pantsuit. On the other side were performers—the twins and the Mormons—lifting weights and practicing skits.

And in the center of it all, conducting the madness like a symphony, stood Caspien and Hallie—with our handwritten flowchart spread over a long table before them. The only person not moving was Lucas. He slouched in a chair with his arms folded, stoic, watching it all develop.

The hair on my arms stood on end.

Did this mean we got his approval? They'd convinced Lucas? He didn't act thrilled, but this was clearly my show, my idea, coming to life around me.

Caspien sprinted over, scooping me up by the waist and spinning me around. "He agreed!"

"He doesn't look happy."

"He's not, but he will be. Give him time. The more pieces we put into motion, the more impressed I am. How did you pull this out of your brain in the middle of the night? Every detail, every hiccup we come across—you put the solution into our notes."

I laughed. "This stuff is easy."

"Come see." He took my hand and pulled me to their table.

Hallie hugged me with one arm, while she drew a checkmark onto my flowchart with her other. "The phone company gave us temporary numbers," she said. "Five lines for five different charities. They're sending a rep out with the phones, already loaded with sim cards. They'll be here in a couple of hours."

"Do we have anyone to answer the phones?" I asked.

"Yes. They offered the option of automated answering services, but you wrote in our notes that people prefer to donate to a real person. Makes them more comfortable sharing their credit card number. There's also an online donation option."

"That's perfect," I said. "Did you talk to the bank and set up accounts? And credit card processing services?"

"My assistant is at the bank right now," Caspien said. "Well, my former assistant. I'm not technically employed anymore."

"You will be soon."

"The vendors are writing their sixty-second pitches," Hallie continued. "We gave them the lady who writes our commercials, she's brilliant with that stuff. She's working with them one-by-one so they can memorize their speeches by this afternoon."

"Good thinking," I said, my heart pounding. It was coming together. It really, truly was. "And our performers?"

Caspien pointed to the corner of influencers, where Cameron and Kindy were practicing a swing dancing routine complete with booming music and acrobatic flips. Behind them, a broad-shouldered man wearing a black polo slipped through the crowd. A sliver of neon blue flashed beneath his collar.

Was that . . .? No, he wouldn't be that stupid.

"Two groups have agreed," Caspien continued. "We're still waiting for one more." This new Caspien was nothing like the grim man I'd met four days ago. He'd come alive—today more than ever.

"This is perfect." I squeezed both their arms. "You're the most amazing people I know."

Then, something entirely unexpected happened: my stomach growled. Never, in fifteen years in this job, had I been hungry while working. Never once had my anxiety let me put food in my stomach until the show had ended. But this? Putting together a show of my own creation? This was unlike anything I'd ever built. This wasn't anxiety-inducing, this was fun.

"Want to get lunch in a bit?" I asked Caspien. "We could go to Marigold's Splendid Sandwiches."

Caspien leaned his hip against the table and hooked his fingers loosely through mine. "I think I'm done going there. I'm tired of living in the past. But this?" He motioned to the flurry of movement around us. "This showcase feels like a way forward."

A way forward? It felt like that for me too. This felt like *me.* Like a future I could step into.

"What if we did another one?" The ideas trickled into my brain . . . and then erupted like a volcano. "If this goes well, we could hold more charity events. Balls? Auctions? And not just fitness people, we switch it up every time. Annually? Better yet, quarterly. Monthly! Use Lucas's past conventions to drum up ideas—"

"One thing at a time," Caspien said, laughing as he took my other hand in his. "First, we need to pull this off. But I like what you're thinking. If you planned the showcases, I could manage the business side."

"You'd do that? With me?"

Caspien pressed one of my hands against his chest, his eyes softening. "If Lucas doesn't give me my job back? I'd want nothing more."

The ideas stopped erupting, settling into a steady flow, a peaceful rhythm. A way forward that shined so brightly, it dulled every memory of my past glory days. "When this is over, let's talk. I have so many ideas."

Caspien kissed my fingers and my heart raced again. "I bet you do."

After that, we all got to work. Caspien hopped on the phone with his assistant at the bank, Hallie helped the vendor crowd with their pitches, and I inspected the stage, moving cameras and adjusting lights. By lunchtime, energy rippled through the air. Even Lucas left his corner and now strolled through the busy ballroom with his European girlfriend on his arm, chatting with the performers. When Lucas wandered off to the next crowd, he nodded at me.

Was I winning him over?

Sandwiches arrived for a late lunch, courtesy of Croft Power, and after a quick break, everyone returned immediately to work. The showcase would stream live on the internet at 3:00 p.m., then would stream again at 7:00. Between the two, we hoped to raise a million dollars for charity.

As the clock passed 1:00, I found Sheila and Sherry tucked into a corner, deep in conversation with Lucas. They took turns speaking quietly. Lucas folded his arms, deep in concentration, then he ushered them out of the ballroom. Was everything okay? I moved to follow when Caspien tapped my shoulder, a nervous tension in his hands and jaw. All thoughts of the twins fled. "I have a question," he said. "Or more of a favor."

"Anything."

"We have five phone lines, but only ended up with three acts. How would you feel if we dedicated one to people like my daughter and my wife? People who need help before it's too late?"

He didn't meet my eyes when he asked it. Like it meant so much, he couldn't bear to look if I said no. But my heart swelled at the idea.

"This is *your* project as much as it's mine," I said. "We could dedicate all five lines to this, if that's what you wanted."

He pulled me against him, enveloping me in his arms as his voice turned hoarse. "One is enough. Thank you."

But something didn't add up. I scanned the corner of performers, counting each act. The twins, then Cameron and Kindy.

"Who's the third act?" I asked.

Caspien pointed to Hallie, who was chatting animatedly with a short woman in the doorway. Her jet-black hair was braided down her back, and tattoos laced one arm from her shoulder to her wrist. Muscles filled out every inch of her fitted long-sleeves and leggings.

Stella?

My Stella?

JD Fitness's new superstar trainer?

"What's she doing here?" I gasped and Caspien laughed.

"Ask her yourself. She just arrived."

I sprinted down the stage stairs and across the room. Stella was *here*, she came for *me*. She brought a little slice of St. Louis, of home, into this dizzying city.

"Stella!" I squeaked.

"There you are!" She laughed, twisting the end of her braid. "Your sister was telling me about all the planning you put into this showcase. Looks like a huge production."

"What are you doing here?" It didn't feel real.

"Bailey called me at the crack of dawn, said you could use reinforcements. I wouldn't have missed this for anything. And my new show drops in three weeks, this is the perfect chance to market it. Sounds like we'll have a huge audience."

"Let's hope so." I couldn't stop smiling, giggling, in the most ridiculous way. With Stella here, I cared infinitely more that we pulled this thing off. "Is Bailey here yet?"

Stella shifted out of the doorway to reveal another woman. She wore clothes from JD Fitness's latest line, the Avalanche Collection. Black leggings that sparkled like diamonds in the light, and a maroon, form-fitting, long-sleeved shirt with thumb holes. We'd designed them for outdoor training during cooler spring weather, and they'd only been released two months ago. She was tall, or at least taller than me, and her long hair tumbled down her shoulders.

"Bailey!" I shrieked. She grinned, and I tackled her, knocking her back as I pulled her into a hug. "You're here!"

"I wouldn't miss this for anything. But even if you hadn't called last night, Hallie wouldn't have let me stay away."

"What do you mean?"

My little sister shrugged, tugging on the end of her ponytail. "I've finally figured out that you sometimes forget to call people, so I reached out to her, just in case."

Bailey held out her hand and Hallie dropped a microphone into her fingers. "She called ten times while I was in the shower this morning, claiming her big sister needed an MC who could draw a crowd."

I still couldn't believe she was here. "Fearless Felicity doesn't do shows or events. Deep down, I worried you wouldn't come."

Bailey nudged my shoulder. "What's my number one goal with Fearless Felicity articles?"

"To uplift people?"

"Exactly. To make them feel confident in themselves. First and foremost, that applies to my friends. Besides, what better event could Felicity appear at than a charity show featuring the world's best fitness stars, the world's cleanest energy inventor, and a bunch of vendors I'd love free samples from. I'll write reviews for every single one." She pointed to a man sitting in the back row with a fancy water bottle in his lap. "Especially that guy."

When I finished laughing, I hooked my arm in hers. "How's Francine?"

"Your angelfish? She's perfect. She misses you."

Warmth filled my chest, then a man entered our hallway whistling a tune, his black metal cane clinking. His black hair matched his black slacks and dark button-up, and he'd rolled his sleeves up to his elbows in a classy-casual way.

"Marco? You came too?"

"Hallie was very convincing." He slapped his hand on my back. "Plus, I've been talking to people backstage. Sounds like this production will be the biggest in Croft Power history. Glad you took my advice and faced your fears."

"Funny story," I said. "That backfired. After we spoke, I made a fool of myself and fought a man twice my size."

Bailey whacked him on the arm. "Marco, that fight on YouTube was your fault?"

But Marco laughed. "Are you sure it backfired? Think about it. I suspect you were never afraid of those crowds, or Michael Kay, or any of the hard work this job requires."

No, none of those things ever scared me. Every goal I'd set this week, I'd jumped in with two feet. It wasn't the work, or the people, who had erupted my anxiety. "You're right."

"Then what were you really afraid of?" he pressed.

The answer came easily, sliding from my lungs like an exhale after holding my breath for too long. "Letting go of my dependency on Jared. I'd spent so many years clinging to him, I didn't know who I'd be if I walked away. What would I do with myself? But I faced it, and I did it."

"And look at you now," Marco said proudly, motioning toward the production inside the banquet hall. "Those days are gone. The best are still coming, just wait and see."

His words filled me up like a balloon, like a ball of shimmering glass, a new shell, a new foundation for my future. But one thing still remained.

"Don't be mad," I told Bailey, "but I fired Jared. Well, I quit. We don't work together anymore. If that messes up anything at JD Fitness, I'm so sorry."

All of them burst out laughing.

"That's the best news I've heard all year," Bailey said. "We couldn't get rid of him until you were ready to cut ties."

"Get rid of him?"

"He's a PR and HR nightmare. If you're done with him, I'll fire him from JD Fitness first thing Monday morning."

"Can you do that? If he still owns half the company?"

"Absolutely, I'm the CEO. In fact—" She stepped back, then motioned to a tall woman at the end of the hall. The woman tentatively approached our group, her forest-green pencil skirt reaching two inches below her knees, coupled with a cream sweater and matching purse and heels.

"Hey, Lauren," Lily said, giving me a small wave.

Lily was here? Hours after serving Jared's divorce papers? She had to have seen the videos over the past few days, what could she possibly want from me? My stomach clenched until I realized Lily's eyes danced with the same excitement as Bailey's.

"Lily is working to get half of Jared's shares of JD fitness in the divorce, making her a quarter-owner. You own fifty percent of the company. What would you think if I offered to buy out Jared's other quarter? He's desperate for cash, I'm sure I can convince him. The three of us would own the company together. Want to come back to JD Fitness? All three of us, partners?"

A hundred thoughts raced through my head, a thousand ideas, millions of possible futures. Bailey would support me in ways Jared never had. But Caspien peeked his head into the hall then joined our circle, introducing himself to my family from St. Louis. Returning to JD Fitness would mean abandoning my ideas to help Caspien with his foundation. Both options pulled at me.

"It's 2:50," Caspien said, sliding his fingers into mine. "Time to take our places. The showcase starts in ten."

Bailey winked at me then kissed Marco and headed toward the stage. Her unspoken message settled into me like a bandage over a cut—I didn't need to decide right now.

Marco joined the rapidly growing audience as thousands of people filled the chairs. Vendors dominated the first three rows, holding their products on their laps and mouthing their pitches quietly to themselves. Stella hurried backstage to wait for her turn to perform. Hallie followed her, acting as stage director. Caspien and I sat at a table facing the stage, front and center, with headsets and mics. Everyone wore earpieces, but hopefully we wouldn't need them.

And there, in an aisle seat two thirds back, sat Jared. Arms folded, mood dark, pointedly avoiding looking in my direction. His neon tank top glared beneath his unbuttoned collar.

My whole body recoiled, scuttling backward into Caspien. "What's he doing here?" If he wore his vintage clothes, he must be planning something.

"I'll alert security," Caspien muttered.

But the lights dimmed, and a hush fell over the large room. Dealing with Jared would have to wait.

I shoved him from my mind and focused on the show. Butterflies rumbled in my fingers and feet. This was it. This was my chance to prove myself. But not to Jared, not to Lucas, not even to Bailey or Caspien or the entire fitness community.

I would prove to *myself* how far my ideas could go.

The stage lights flipped on, the curtain closed, and everything went silent.

Chapter 20

Six cents left.
One nickel and one penny.

Bailey's Avalanche Collection outfit glittered in the light as she and Lucas stepped on stage. The cameraman counted down with his fingers.

Five, four, three, two, one.

"Here we go," I whispered, and the television cameras went live. So did Lucas's YouTube stream, and a scattering of cellphone cameras in the packed audience. Perhaps people came hoping for another embarrassing moment, or maybe they had friends in the show. Either way, our virtual audience had to be huge.

The crowd cheered and Bailey smiled for the camera, then Lucas raised his microphone, his hand trembling slightly.

"Welcome to this month's showcase." He cleared his throat. He must have been nervous, but he did a decent job hiding it. "Rather than our usual talk-show-style showcase, tonight we've put together a fitness demonstration with multiple acts and two dozen sponsors."

Bailey raised her mic. "To make things interesting, we turned this demonstration into a competition. Three fitness stars will be showing off their skills to earn money for their favorite charities. You viewers at home may call in at any time to donate money to their charities of choice. Whichever raises the most money wins our little competition—*and* a long-term publicity contract with Lucas Croft, CEO and Founder of Croft Power, the fastest growing clean energy company in the world."

"There are also two bonus charities," Lucas said, "hand-selected by Croft Power employees." He pointed toward the floor. "If you look at the bottom of your TV screen, five phone numbers will scroll continuously throughout our entire show. Call any of those lines to make your donation."

Caspien nudged me, then pointed to a monitor displaying what everyone at home was currently seeing. I couldn't read the words from here, but I could read a larger number printed on the top of the screen, rapidly rising. Three hundred thousand, four hundred thousand, then six hundred thousand.

"What's that?" I asked.

He motioned to a man on a laptop, furiously searching social media accounts. "He's following everyone in the audience, trying to track our live viewers. Though the real number is probably far higher." By the time Caspien finished explaining, the number had jumped to one million.

"Shall we introduce ourselves?" Bailey said to the camera. "Of course, you all know Lucas Croft, the host of this fitness convention and founder of Croft Power."

Lucas nodded thanks to the applause. Once it had settled, he grinned at the camera like he held a secret, and pointed at Bailey. "Does anyone know who's co-hosting with me tonight?"

The entire audience stayed quiet. Had enough time passed since her one day on the JD Fitness stage that no one recognized her? Bailey looked as surprised as I felt.

Lucas's grin widened, his visible nervousness disappearing as he laughed. "Then I am thrilled to introduce, in her debut public appearance, my good friend Fearless Felicity."

It took a moment for the audience to register what he'd said, then the entire room went wild. They screamed, they cheered, they yanked out their phones to snap pictures, to film, or to stream her into their social media feeds. In seconds, the number on the monitor jumped to five million, then eight million, then ten.

"Look at that," Caspien whispered. "We've never had more than a couple hundred thousand viewers."

"Let's hope it's worth it."

Caspien squeezed my hand as the cheering died down. "It will be."

Lucas gave a quick introduction to his company and how they were trying to revolutionize the world with environmentally clean power. Afterward, Bailey rubbed her hands together in excitement.

"Our first act tonight are fan favorites. They were among the pioneers of contemporary bodybuilding competitions. Please welcome my life-long heroes and everyone's favorite twins, Sherry and Sheila Templeton."

The crowd cheered as the black curtains drew back, revealing a stage loaded with lifting equipment. In the center stood the twins, atop a tower of boards and oddly shaped objects. They wore competition bikinis, one silver, one gold, which showed off the defined muscles that laced every inch of their bodies.

But the real focus was on the five desks to the side of the stage. Three men and two women filled them, each with a cell phone in their hands and a laptop on their counter. Hanging off the front of each desk, for the entire audience to see, was the name of a charity and a large black screen. At the moment, all five screens read $0.00.

"Can you tell us a little about your charity?" Bailey said, holding the mic up high.

Sherry leaned down to grab it. "We love our fur babies, so we're supporting the Humane Society. Every animal deserves a good home."

After a large applause, quick-tempo music blared through the speakers, and they began their performance. Sheila laid a board across the back of her shoulders and Sherry stepped on top of it, then posed like a bodybuilder while Sheila did a set of squats. After dismounting, they switched spots. Sherry gripped the pull-up bar with Sheila in a graceful piggyback, and she did ten pull-ups while Sheila waved to a laughing audience. They switched again, their tricks becoming progressively more elaborate, until they blew everyone away when they made Bailey and Lucas stand in the center of the stage while they team-juggled bottles of protein shakes back and forth. Lucas didn't look thrilled, but Bailey didn't flinch once as the audience laughed and cheered.

After a final bow, Sheila peered at the number on the desk that said *Humane Society*. It read $115,674 and continued climbing.

Sheila took Lucas's microphone as she wiped her forehead with a towel. "Thank you for all your support through the years. We lived amazing careers because of wonderful fans like you guys." Sherry wrapped an arm around her sister's broad shoulders as Sheila went on. "We have a confession. Tonight, we are both sad and happy to announce that we are officially retiring from our public fitness lives."

Bailey's jaw dropped. Mine did too. The twins had stood with me my entire adult life, held my hand as I first navigated into this crazy industry. It wouldn't be the same without them.

Sheila handed the mic to Sherry, who wiped a tear from her cheek. "When we were approached about performing in this showcase, we considered turning it down. It didn't seem fair to compete for a prize that we couldn't accept." She sniffled, taking a moment to regain her composure. "But after a long conversation with Lucas Croft, he encouraged us to use this as a final goodbye to our fans."

"And to raise money for the Humane Society," Sheila piped in. "To thank our incredible fans, we will personally match whatever donations you give. We're so grateful for all the years of fun. Thanks again, everyone. We love you all!"

I joined in with the loud cheering, and every member of the audience rose to their feet. The live viewers jumped to fifteen million.

The curtain closed, leaving only Lucas and Bailey on stage. Bailey still looked shell-shocked by their announcement, so Lucas moved the program forward.

"While the next performer sets up the stage, we have eight vendors with incredible products who would like to show the fitness world what they've got."

The first man walked onto the stage, his hands trembling as he hugged his fancy water bottle to his chest. Bailey recovered from her shock and eyed the water bottle with a wide grin.

"As a bonus," Lucas continued, "anyone who gives a free sample of their product to Fearless Felicity will receive an honest review on her website." The water bottle guy's eyes doubled in size. "You have fifteen million viewers right now," Lucas told him. "Make it good."

The man dropped his bottle into Bailey's hands, then he stumbled backward and fainted at her feet.

Two people rushed out from backstage and carried him off, while Bailey poured a disposable bottle of water into the fancy one. She took a drink, thought for a moment, then nodded.

"Shiftry Bottle Company gets five stars," she said into the camera. "Since our poor friend was a bit overwhelmed tonight, I'll give his pitch for him. I collect water bottles, I have hundreds, and I can already tell this one's a winner."

After that, seven more vendors took their turn on the stage, delivering their well-practiced sales pitches and offering a free item to Bailey. A stagehand was brilliant enough to collect them down below, so no one tripped on the rapidly growing pile.

"I think we're ready for our second act," Bailey finally said.

As the curtain opened, Caspien leaned in close. "Is it going the way you'd planned?"

"Besides the guy who fainted? And the twins retiring? It's exactly how I'd imagined it." It felt like viewing the movie of a book I'd written, but someone had added surprises to every scene. My gaze darted briefly back to Jared. He leaned forward, elbows on his knees, his eyes trained intensely on Bailey.

"Our next performer," Bailey said, "is one of my personal best friends. She works with me at JD Fitness, and it's been exciting to watch her career take off. We're especially thrilled because in three weeks, her new YouTube workout program will drop. I've seen it, it's extraordinary."

The room cheered again, and the curtain opened to reveal a stage that was empty apart from a squat rack, Stella, and nine muscular men in gym clothes. Scratch that; the Polynesian in back wore a sharp, gray suit. When Stella came forward to join Lucas and Bailey, her swarm of men came with her. Bailey raised one eyebrow.

"What is your charity?" Lucas asked. Stella's Avalanche Collection outfit mirrored Baileys, except she wore it in all-black to match her hair, with a brown lifting belt strapped around her midsection.

Stella eyed Bailey then glanced away quickly. "My charity is to finance extracurricular activities for children of single moms."

Bailey's hand flew to her mouth, and her eyes turned glassy. Before she became famous, Bailey had struggled to make ends meet for her daughter. Stella couldn't have given her a better thank you for everything she'd done for all of us the past six months. The donation amount for Stella's charity jumped instantly.

Lucas pointed to the squat rack behind Stella. "Tell us about your performance."

The man in the black suit joined them at the front of the stage. "This is Kekoa Tihoni," Stella said, "CEO of the Pacific Powerlifting Federation. Today, I will attempt to beat the powerlifting record for the women's raw super-heavyweight squat."

Lucas raised both eyebrows, while Bailey burst out laughing. "You didn't tell me you were planning this!"

Stella grinned while she rubbed chalk on her hands. "More fun when it's a surprise." She circled the squat rack where the bar was already in place. While she tightened her belt and stuck a pouch of smelling salts under her nose, four of the men loaded giant plates onto the bar. "The record's six hundred and four pounds," Stella said. "I'll be squatting six ten."

Kekoa inspected each piece, then nodded.

The other eight men circled Stella, three as judges, five as spotters. She moved under the rack, shaking with adrenaline, and positioned the bar onto her shoulders, adjusting her hands to maintain a solid grip. She took an enormous breath, then lifted. Silence fell over the room. We all held perfectly still as she took two steps back, tensed her stomach, and dropped into the squat. When her thighs reached a horizontal line, Stella clenched her teeth, straining, pushing, climbing back up to a standing position. She reached the top and thumped the bar back onto the rack. The spotters locked it in place.

"Did I do it?" she panted.

The first judge raised a small green flag. Then the second. Then the third.

Yes!

Kekoa reached out his hand to shake hers. "Congratulations, Stella, you set a new world record."

The entire room exploded, everyone jumping up and down and screaming. Stella leapt off the stage with a whoop and merged into the crowd, people patting her back and snapping selfies.

"Brilliant," Caspien said as the curtain closed, but my heart pounded too hard to reply. Her performance was better than I could have dreamed up on my own.

"How could Cameron and Kindy possibly beat that?" I asked.

Caspien shook his head. "I have no idea. How did she get the federation guys here on such short notice?"

"I don't know either," I said. "But we sure know how to put on a good show!"

Bailey tapped the mic, and everyone found their seats, then she introduced the next round of vendors.

Soon enough it was time for the final performance.

But Jared's seat was empty.

"Alert security," I whispered, and Caspien mumbled quietly into his headpiece. He wouldn't try anything stupid, right? He'd already lost his shot with Lucas. He must have finally given up and headed to the airport. But I glanced again at his empty chair.

"Our final act," Bailey said, "is a young couple from sunny southern California. They're relatively new to the fitness industry, but over the past year they've taken it by storm. You all know them, please welcome Kindy Young and Cameron Pratt!"

The curtain opened as big band music blared through the loudspeakers. Cameron stood in the center of the empty stage in baggy pants and suspenders. Kindy wore a poofy black dress with orange polka dots, her hair in a high ponytail. Without a word, she launched herself at Cameron, who caught her in mid-air, flipping her in a full circle, then pulling her into a twisting, spinning, kicking, swing dance routine. The room erupted into cheers—Bailey included. Their dance ended as Cameron spun her around and around his body, her head gliding shockingly close to the floor. But she landed perfectly on her feet, and they bowed . . . and then she swiped Lucas's microphone straight out of his hand.

"I'm Kindy!" she panted. "And this is Cameron." Her adorably infectious smile spread across every face in the ballroom. "Our charity is to raise money for foster children." She pressed her hand against her heart and sniffed, her words sticking in her throat. "That's how Cameron and I met, in a foster home after we both lost our parents. If it weren't for the loving families who took us in, we wouldn't be here today."

She handed the mic to Cameron, wiping a tear from her eye.

"Before we finish our performance," he said, "I have one more thing to do."

He dug into his pocket and pulled out a black velvet box, then dropped to one knee. Kindy gasped, covering her mouth with both hands.

Caspien leaned over, his mouth close to my ear. "Did you know about this?"

I shook my head. "Aren't they only like, twenty? I didn't know about a single thing that's happened on this stage tonight."

"We're just brilliant at picking performers, I guess." Caspien wrapped his arm around my shoulder as Kindy said yes and the whole room erupted. Again.

And if I didn't think one more thing could surprise me after all this, I was dead wrong. The second they stopped making out on the stage, another round of upbeat music burst through the speakers. Kindy ripped off her dress to reveal turquoise leggings and a pink sports bra, and Cameron ditched the suspenders and procured a set of pink dumbbells for each of them. Then almost every person in the audience pulled out their own dumbbells from their purses or gym bags or who knows where, and they all performed a weightlifting flash mob right there in the ballroom. Somehow, Cameron and Kindy had packed the entire audience with their followers, and somehow, they'd convinced them all to learn a lifting routine in advance.

They surged through the room to fill every bit of extra space, each person lifting with one hand while streaming the show with their other. The number of viewers on the monitor jumped to twenty million. Then twenty-five.

Kindy and Cameron had packed the room with influencers.

For the next five minutes, I couldn't stop laughing.

Then the song ended, and every dancer/lifter/influencer returned to their seats. The dumbbells disappeared like they'd never existed.

"I won't lie," Lucas said from the edge of the stage, "never in my entire life did I imagine a moment like that one. Brilliant. Absolutely brilliant."

Finally, the chaos settled, leaving only Lucas and Bailey on the stage. "Before we announce our winners," Lucas said. "I have a few final items. First, thank you to all of you at home who viewed our show and donated money. If you missed my announcement at the beginning, we've talked about three charities, but we have five options for donations. Please take a moment to read about the other two and consider contributing."

The donation numbers on the desks continued to rise; Kindy and Cameron's Foster Care number more than tripled the others.

"Second," Lucas continued, "I'd like to thank Fearless Felicity for joining me tonight. And our three incredible organizers. Hallie Cross, Lauren Cross, and Caspien Martel. Will you please join us on stage?"

Caspien and I looked at each other, but I shook my head; nothing good ever happened when I put myself on camera. But he pulled my hand until I obliged, and when I reached the stage, Bailey wrapped her arm around my shoulder. Yes, this time would be different.

The bright lights blinded me, and I blinked hard to refocus. Hundreds of faces beamed up at us, their phone cameras streaming, but I could barely make them out through the stage lights. Hallie, however, did not join us. For a brief second, I saw a flick of her ponytail and sneakers just off stage, then she disappeared.

Lucas blinked twice as she retreated, but he recovered quickly. "These were the brains behind this incredible show. Without them, I would have canceled my entire line of conventions. But Caspien convinced me otherwise." Lucas put his arm around Caspien's shoulder. "This man has volunteered to start the Croft Foundation, a non-profit organization to raise money for an assortment of charities." Lucas motioned to the fourth desk with its donation number slowly rising. "This one is Caspien's, a foundation to support the children of those suffering through addiction. So please, keep the donations coming in. One hundred percent will go straight to the organization, we're not keeping a penny."

The audience cheered again, then Lucas turned serious as he faced Caspien. "This event was incredible. Let's meet on Monday to formally organize our foundation."

Caspien vigorously shook his hand, mumbling an awkward *thank you*. But my insides twisted. If Caspien ran Lucas's foundation, and I returned to JD Fitness with Bailey, when would we see each other? With two enormous companies to run, we'd never start our own non-profit. We'd never run another event together.

But now wasn't the time to think about it. Lucas had refocused his attention on the camera.

"Shall we announce our winners?"

The audience roared, but before he could speak again, *Rocky* theme music blared through the speakers.

Jared DiMaggio appeared at the edge of the stage.

Then he performed a series of handsprings that brought him right to the front.

"Hell-oooo Seattle!" he yelled into a tiny mic taped sloppily to his cheek. He scooped up a dumbbell and pressed it above his head. "Who's ready to *party?*"

Nobody said a word. Not one audience member cheered. Even Lucas froze in stunned silence.

Only Jared remained unphased. "Let's go, everyone. Pull out those dumbbells and follow me. It's time to get our sweat on."

Jared's music screeched to a halt.

But Jared kept going.

"Come on guys!" He squatted ten times, then moved to shoulder presses, counting out loud with each rep. He didn't slow down, but his voice turned to pleading. "Anyone? Someone?"

His mic cut out. Whatever he said next, only the front row heard.

"Jared," I shouted in the silent auditorium, "just stop."

He lowered the dumbbell to his side, forehead creasing. "I don't understand. Everyone loves my workouts." His gaze met mine like a lost child at a carnival, his thoughts spelled plainly across his face. This life was all he knew, what else was there for him?

"It's over," I said, softer this time. "All of it."

Jared glanced at the audience, at the hundreds of cameras, millions of viewers, then back at me. "But what will I do? You'll help me, right?"

With this final embarrassing moment in public, he'd lost the last of his dignity. Ruined the final shreds of his reputation. I knew exactly what that felt like—I'd lived it this past week when I dug myself into a deep, dark hole. Just like Jared, I'd needed to ask for help.

But I hadn't blamed my friends for my mistakes.

I hadn't shamed them for being themselves.

I hadn't spent half my life manipulating the people I loved.

"Please, Lauren?" Jared begged.

When I'd needed help, I planned this showcase, then I asked my family to lend a hand. But Jared? He wanted me to bail him out. Again. To justify his shitty behavior. But I'd been doing that for too long.

"No. Not this time."

Empty, heavy silence filled every crack in the room.

Then Jared's nostrils flared. His lips curled, and his fists clenched in a way that was becoming too familiar.

"Stay cool, Jared," one of the twins warned, as they stepped out onto the stage behind me. Cameron came too, with Kindy huddling behind him, peeking over his shoulder.

"You're siding with *her*?" Jared shouted. Caspien shifted his body, angling his shoulder protectively in front of mine. "What's *she* done for any of you? I've boosted your viewer numbers, visited your shows, sold your products. Without me, you're all *nothing*!"

"We built our careers ourselves," Sherry argued.

"And Lauren's nice," Kindy squeaked, then she ducked completely behind Cameron.

"She's a freak!" Jared roared. "She spews things totally out of order." He glared straight at me. "Look at you, you're making a spectacle of yourself *again.* Haven't you had enough humiliation for one week?"

Caspien slid his hand into mine, a silent offering of comfort and support. For once, my body remained perfectly calm. "It was never *me* that made a spectacle. It was you, every time. Even when I puked on Lucas's shoes—though I really do feel awful about that—it was your fault. *You* put me in that situation. *You* insisted I step into the spotlight when *you* knew it would torture me. But I refuse to be your scapegoat ever again. And did you notice that I spoke every one of those words in perfect order? No spectacles, not a hint of spewing."

A vein bulged on the left side of Jared's neck. "Just wait," he bellowed. "Once you all get to know her, you'll see."

"We do know her," Bailey said. "She's a genius."

Then Hallie, my beautiful sister who'd avoided every camera the last three days, slipped onto the stage and stood solidly by my side. "She doesn't need you anymore." Hallie took my other hand in hers. "She has us now."

Jared blinked. Twice. The entire audience held perfectly still. Dozens of phone cameras pointed our direction. Nobody spoke.

Then Jared launched himself across the stage, headed directly toward me.

I pulled my hands free and braced for impact. "Throw the first punch," I whispered to myself. "Make it count." I balled my hand into a fist—

—and Caspien threw himself at Jared.

The audience erupted into cheers.

Jared tumbled backward. He crashed onto his back, and Caspien knelt on top of him, pinning him down. Jared wildly swung his fist. Caspien caught it, then trapped it with his other knee.

"Don't *ever* touch her," Caspien hissed.

Lucas dropped to the floor and pinned Jared's other arm. He stopped thrashing, groaned, then rested his head back on the stage floor.

"Security, take him now," Lucas shouted, and within seconds a swarm of men and women in uniform grabbed Jared and hoisted him to his feet.

He snarled as they struggled to yank him off stage.

"Jared Quinton DiMaggio," a stern voice said, "stop making a fool of yourself." The crowd hushed as Jared's ex-wife stalked onto the stage with her pristine suit and sharp glare. Jared's entire body wilted. "Get outside, now." Without another word, Jared trudged off the stage with Croft Power security at his heels.

He was gone.

Forever.

I blew out everything in my lungs, and any remaining shards of my attachment to Jared blew away in the breeze.

Lily immediately approached me, taking my left hand in both of hers. "I don't know how you put up with him all these years."

Someone in the crowd shouted, "Amen!"

Awkward laughter slithered up my throat. "You either."

Lily rolled her eyes, then she lowered her voice so the audience couldn't hear. "I'll make sure he's gone. Then once we're all back home, I'll reach out about reorganizing the company." She stepped closer. "Are you okay?"

Okay? Could I be *okay* after my third almost-fight in three days? But Caspien slipped back to my side and wrapped his arm tightly around my waist. Instantly, my jaw loosened, and my stomach unwound. On my other side, Hallie hooked her arm in mine, squeezing gently. Behind me stood Bailey and Lucas, Sheila and Sherry, even Stella and the Mormons. I'd needed help, and they'd come. And Mom was out there too, watching through one of the many live streams, sending her love and acceptance.

They all wanted to be here.

They all loved me exactly the way I was.

"I'm okay," I said, nodding to Lily. More than okay.

Lucas cleared his throat, then strolled to the center of the stage, lifting the microphone to his mouth. Bailey hurried after him.

Oh yeah, live TV show.

"Now that we've taken care of the uncomfortable stuff . . ." the audience burst into laughter, "shall we announce our winning act?"

The rest of us huddled at the edge of the stage. Kindy and Cameron crossed all their fingers. Stella covered her eyes with her hands. The twins scooted to the back of the crowd—they *had* just confirmed their retirement, after all.

"I'm happy to announce," Lucas continued, "that I'm awarding my publicity contract to Kindy and Cameron! Lucas tried to continue speaking, probably to explain what this partnership meant, but Kindy and Cameron screamed and jumped, hugging in mid-air until they both toppled over. The rest of the room erupted too, drowning out Lucas's words.

Hallie disappeared, then returned carrying a tray with four flutes of champagne. She'd resumed hiding her face from the camera, but she gave one each to Lucas and Bailey, then offered the other two to Cameron and Kindy.

"We don't drink," Kindy said.

But Hallie handed them the glasses anyway. "They're sparkling cider." Then she slipped off stage.

I'd included the cider detail in my notes, in case we reached this point. But after the show, I'd have to ask Hallie why she always hid her face. What was she hiding from?

When the cameraman officially ended the show, the audience swarmed the participants as the convention center staff wheeled in drinks for everyone. Someone closed the giant black curtain, and me, Bailey, Caspien, and Lucas were separated from the noise and chaos down below. Hallie materialized a moment later, grinning from ear to ear.

Lucas raised his glass again. "To you four," he said, "for putting on the most unexpected evening of my life. I won't lie, I thought this would flop."

"We can't take credit for a lot of it," I said. "We never expected Stella to bring the power lifting guy."

"Or the twins to announce their retirement," Caspien added.

"Or Cameron to propose."

"Or a flash mob."

"But you built the framework," Lucas argued, "then put the right people on the stage. I'm glad I was here to see it."

"Thanks for giving us a second chance," I said. "Sorry about the whole 'breaking into your office' thing. It was"—I cleared my throat—"a bad idea."

Bailey frowned, like maybe she hadn't heard about that particular decision of mine, but Lucas shook his head. "You more than made up for it."

A mob of fans opened the curtain and cajoled Bailey out into the crowd, snapping selfies with the one-and-only Fearless Felicity. Hallie, however, wrapped me in an enormous hug, then tapped her finger against the ring around my neck.

"I knew it would bring you good luck," she said.

I unclipped it from my throat and clasped it around hers. "I filled up its battery, now it's your turn. Find your dreams and chase them."

Hallie frowned. "Does that mean you're not staying? You could work with me and Caspien. There's always room in Lucas's sales department."

From our spot above the throng, I tracked Bailey as she laughed with her fans, giving each of them the time and attention they deserved. She'd done the same for me. She'd taken over my job at JD Fitness when I couldn't handle it anymore. She'd let me work independently for Jared, even though it took profits directly from the company. She'd let me keep an office in their building, and when I came here and fell apart, she flew out to support me.

Without Bailey, my company would have run into the ground. We'd be nothing, and I'd still be chasing Jared like a lovesick puppy.

"I can't," I said. "I have my own company to run. I've abandoned it for too long. It's time to step up and build it into the company *I* want it to be, not whatever Jared wanted on a whim."

"We'll miss you," Hallie said, but she turned to Caspien and poked him firmly in the chest. "But you're not allowed to leave, *ever*. Sure, help with Lucas's foundation. But I brought you here to run sales and marketing. If you abandon me, I'll kill you." She stabbed him with her finger again. "*Kill. You.*"

He laughed and raised both hands defensively. "Don't worry, I'm sticking around."

Someone called Hallie's name, and she whisked away, leaving me with the two men. Lucas leaned casually against the fifth donation desk.

"What's that one for?" I asked. "No one's mentioned it."

The man holding the fifth donation phone inched closer. "Hallie asked me to include it." He nervously straightened his thin, purple tie. "It's financial relief for low-income families who are in over their heads with medical bills."

Lucas and Caspien exchanged a long look, then both pulled their wallets from their pockets and took turns donating. I didn't see how much they gave, but hopefully it would find its way to my sister.

When Lucas was called away to deal with paperwork for the Kindy and Cameron deal, at last Caspien and I found ourselves alone backstage. Suddenly, my gaze grew too heavy to meet his. If he stayed in Seattle, and I returned to Missouri, what did that mean for us?

"That guy with the cane was right," Caspien said. "We'll remember this day forever."

"It topped any show I've ever put on." I forced myself to look at him and found him watching me. "Thanks for believing in me and unlocking the idea behind my craziness."

Caspien held my gaze for a long moment. "Stay," he pleaded, taking my hand in both of his. He pressed it against his warm shirt, against his chest the way I loved. His heart pounded steadily beneath my fingers.

For the first time today, my anxiety crept back up my neck, down my arms, and laced its way into my fingers. But Caspien only squeezed them tighter.

"Let's find a place to talk," he said.

But when we reached the bottom of the stairs, I paused.

"Hang on," I said, and I dropped his hand and raced back up, digging through the junk at the bottom of my purse.

It took some searching, but at last I found them.

One nickel and one penny.

Six measly cents—all I had left in the world. I kissed them both, then pressed them onto Hallie's donation desk. They weren't much, but those coins came with my promise. Somehow, I'd find a way to give more.

When I returned to Caspien, he reclaimed my hand and led me through the winding hallways, into a quiet classroom filled with a dozen chairs and one couch. We both sat, and he angled his body to face mine.

"Stay," he said again, his eyes pleading.

Never in my life had two futures torn me so violently down the middle. "What would I do?"

"Work for me. For Lucas's foundation. Or Hallie's marketing team. Wherever you want."

His words felt too perfect, too heavy, too impossible. "He liked our show," I said, "but he'd never put up with the real me. Only three people have ever survived me for more than a few days. You, Bailey, and my mom. I'm too screwed-up."

"You are *not* screwed-up." Caspien grabbed both of my arms, just above my elbows. "You're not broken, you're not even *different.* Do you know how many adults are struggling because their ADHD is undiagnosed?"

"Are there a lot?"

"Millions. And now that you know what it is, we can work on it together. We can work *here* together." He motioned to the walls, the building, the place that he and my sister called home. But resignation echoed in his voice. I wouldn't stay, and he knew it. And he couldn't leave, now that Lucas had offered him the job he'd waited so long for.

"For the first time," I said, "I can go home and run my company the way I want, without Jared wasting all our money. Bailey wants to buy out his shares, become my new business partner. With him gone, I can turn it into something I'm proud of."

Caspien nodded slowly. "You two are good for each other. But I'll miss you every day. For the first time in years, I feel like more than a shell of a person. You saved me."

"Enough to fly home and visit sometimes?" I held my breath. Caspien hadn't gone home in years. Not a single time.

He held perfectly still too, gazing off into the distance. "Maybe I should finally visit Maddie's grave. Face those memories."

"And visit me too?"

Caspien dropped my hands and caught my face instead. "I'd visit you every day if Lucas would allow it. But I'm thinking May sounds like a nice time for vacation."

"That's only two weeks away."

"My niece is getting married. I hadn't planned to go, but I'm having a change of heart. Can you wait that long?"

"Two weeks sounds like forever." But if the alternative was never, I would take whatever I could get. My heart hammered against my ribs as I leaned my forehead against his. Slowly, the too-familiar ache of anxiety crept its way into my chest, curling around my ribs to compress my lungs. "Before you commit to this, there's something you need to understand. When we're apart, I'll probably forget to call. You might need to be the one who initiates that part."

"I already know this about you. I don't mind."

I met his eyes. "Really?"

"I also know you lose track of time when you're focused. And that you're brilliant, but you struggle vocalizing your thoughts if you haven't written down organized notes. None of these things affect how I feel about you."

"They don't?" His words loosened the coil around my ribs, freeing my lungs, softening the ache that had shadowed the past fifteen years.

Caspien brushed one thumb across the bottom of my jaw, leaving a trail of goosebumps down my neck. "Not for one second. In fact, the thought of you flying away makes me miss you already. But I can't wait to hear about all your new adventures with Fearless Felicity as your business partner." He dropped one hand to press a button on his watch.

"The second you're ready to host your first charity event, I'll catch the next plane to come help."

Caspien swallowed, his voice catching as he said, "Thank you."

"You know what's strange?" I asked. "I don't feel like a shaken-up puzzle anymore. I think you pieced me back together."

Caspien pulled back, just enough to meet my eyes. "Maybe you should still talk to someone about the ADHD, though."

I laughed. "I promise, if you remind me, I'll call that doctor."

"And maybe get more of these too." He handed me my bottle of Xanax. "Even without Jared around, sometimes anxiety is out of your control."

"You wouldn't mind?"

He smiled, a soft one. "Your mental health is more important than my paranoia. I trust you to be careful."

I dropped the bottle into my purse, then I wrapped my arms around his neck and pulled his warm lips softly against mine. Caspien sighed, deepening the kiss as he wrapped one hand around my waist.

All that existed was Caspien. And me.

And one little voice in the back of my head.

Then two.

Then two hundred.

"What I'm thinking," I said, pulling away as the ideas cranked up their volume, "is to design JD Fitness's next show after what we did here. What if each quarter Bailey and I pick a charity, and we donate a percentage of our profits? Celebrity guests! Michael Kay did this once and I hated it—but if they donated their time to charity, it wouldn't be cheesy like his was. Bailey just hired a new trainer. She'd be a great face for this. We could bring in live bands for background music—can't afford them long term—but a live band? I'll run it by Bailey—"

I froze. Somewhere in there, I'd risen and started pacing. I didn't remember standing. Caspien watched me, barely holding in his laughter.

"I ruined our perfect moment!" I gasped. "I'm so sorry!"

He pushed another button on his watch then held it up for me to see. "Twenty-two seconds. It took only twenty-two seconds after I mentioned your new job for your brilliant brain to start ticking. It still baffles me that Jared didn't appreciate your genius."

Mortified, I hid my face behind my hands, as if it would hide my quirks where he couldn't witness them.

But then I stopped, dropping my arms to my sides. With Caspien, I didn't need to hide who I was. I didn't need to be ashamed.

Over the past four days I'd laid all my pieces out for Caspien to see, and he hadn't fled, hadn't shied away. Instead, he'd showed me how priceless each of those pieces were, then helped me put them back together in whatever order I'd wanted.

For the first time in my life, I felt whole.

A completed puzzle.

Yes, I would miss him fiercely when I went back home, but Caspien had opened my eyes to what was happening in my brain, pointed me toward the tools to help me function with ADHD, helped me find the answers I'd searched for my whole life.

I wasn't broken.

I wasn't flawed.

I was *me,* and that was enough.

Epilogue

---*Three weeks later*

Hallie Cross

My entire adult life, I'd earned my paycheck from the same place. I pointedly ignored the glowing, blue-and-red *Croft Power Company* logo that hung far above me as I steered my musty car into its dark, underground parking garage. Lucas's corporate office filled the top seven stories of the tallest skyscraper in downtown Seattle. His executive team filled the top level, and his beloved scientists spanned the next floor down. Beneath them were the attorneys, then the accountants, then the IT department and Human Resources.

But on the seventh level down, on the floor dubbed *the dungeon,* lived the sales and marketing teams.

That was where I worked.

Our offices hadn't always been there, but I'd moved us down two years ago while Lucas was vacationing on his yacht. We used to fill the cubicles right outside his office—but I couldn't stand one more eyeful of his talented, gorgeous, European girlfriend.

Irina.

I hated her.

And she was *always* around, hanging on his arm, lounging in his conference room, giggling in the break room.

So, I took matters into my own hands and moved our department to the dungeon. Lucas was furious, of course, but he hadn't pushed the subject too hard. Deep down, I think he knew it was for the best. Friendships never lasted when one person was madly in love.

And the other was not.

So now I came to work every day and did my job from a place where I could pine over him in peace—without the risk of passing him and Irina in the hall. Or the bathroom. Or the elevator.

When Lauren showed up two weeks ago, I'd gone nearly six months without crossing his path. Before that, the last time was in the parking garage. He'd hooked his Tesla to the charger when I climbed out of my thirty-year-old beater. I didn't even say hello. How could I when just the sight of him had my heartbeat reverberating through me like a bass drum? Who could make small talk over noise like that?

The whole thing was silly. We'd lived next door our entire lives. Best friends, practically siblings—until "feelings" happened. Or hormones. Or whatever. And I became the lovesick tomboy-next-door while he discovered a liking for exotic blondes in designer clothing.

Love was stupid.

Realistically, I should have found a new job. Moved on from Croft Power, moved to a new city, stopped torturing myself with the possibility of bumping into him.

But like I said, love was stupid.

Lucas worked inside this building, and no matter how much I wanted to escape him, I yearned to be near him more. So, here I stayed, deep in my dungeon, the smallest fish in the pond of the sales team, with seven floors of wood and concrete providing a barrier between my dingy cubicle and Lucas's glass-walled office.

And when Lucas needed something from the marketing team? I had Caspien, our fearless director, to descend into the dark to ask us for it.

Which was why, every single day, I arrived to work an hour early to help him do his job. I wasn't sure anyone realized the true extent of my help. But if Caspien continually impressed Lucas, then Lucas would continue to pay him, and I'd win in my quest to keep Lucas at just the right distance.

Plus, deep down, I loved this company. I'd worked here since its beginning, since day one. It felt too much like home to not do all I could to keep it going.

And there was more, another reason I could never quit. A darker one. But I'd banished that memory to the back of my mind where no one could ever reel it back in—not even me. It was the same reason I would never let Caspien promote me, and I'd *never* let Lucas know my true worth. That secret would . . . destroy him.

So today, I parked my soaking wet (and leaking) car in Croft Power's underground lot and rode the elevator upstairs. Alone. It smelled like lemon-fresh cleaner and played elegant piano music. When the door opened to the long hall, I strolled inside like a woman on a mission.

My favorite pink sneakers squeaked on the shiny tile floor. I didn't stop at my desk long enough to turn on my computer. I just dropped my purse onto my chair and collected the sales reports everyone had left out on their desks for me. By the time they arrived at 8:00 a.m., I would have already compiled a full summary, with historical graphs and future projections for the next quarter and the next year. My data would be in Caspien's inbox before he arrived, so he could deliver it to Lucas at their morning meeting and claim the credit for himself.

That was our deal.

I made the reports if he'd promise not to tell Lucas where they came from. Caspien would look good, the sales team would look good, and I'd stay off Lucas's radar.

Everybody won.

When I'd collected the sales reports, I dropped into my tall black chair at the corner desk. As the tiniest nobody on the marketing team, they paid the least attention to me back here. My computer booted slowly. I'd needed a new one for a while now, but it seemed like a waste to ask for a replacement before this one died.

So, while I waited, I ran my fingers over the photo of my family, the sole decoration on my desk. I couldn't have been more than ten, my long ponytail hidden under a baseball cap, dirt smudges on my cheeks. Mom had one arm around me and the other around Lauren. My sister's blond hair had reached her shoulders back then, but she was the only one not posing for the camera. Something had distracted her, though I couldn't remember what.

Back then, she was always distracted. Still was.

I hovered over Mom the most, though. Her hair matched Lauren's, blond and straight. Until she got sick, she'd worked two jobs to keep the three of us fed and clothed, but she'd never once complained.

My heart ached for that version of her. The version that was healthy enough to leave the house.

My computer finished booting and I rubbed my eyes with my fists, refocusing on work. Thanks to rainstorm traffic, I'd arrived late, which meant I needed to rush through compiling this data. I'd collected twelve reports from my coworkers' desks, so I laid them across mine in three neat rows, skimming the numbers.

My mouth went dry. Something was wrong.

These numbers didn't look right. Sales had dropped, despite the insane level of publicity we'd earned from Lauren's showcase two weeks ago.

They'd dropped significantly.

I called Caspien's cell, but he didn't answer, and my stomach twisted. Lucas wouldn't be happy about this. I googled Croft Power to check for any bad press I wasn't aware of, but I found nothing. Caspien would have an explanation, right? Something to placate Lucas so he wouldn't come to my dungeon searching for answers?

Because I had none.

At least not yet.

At last, my email loaded, and I scanned the subject lines of everything unread. Caspien's name jumped out at me. My entire body crumpled with relief. I double clicked the email and read the first few lines.

Dear Hallie,

Please don't hate me. I tried to give my notice to Lucas, but he said to take it up with you. I know I promised I'd stay, but Lucas has a different vision for his non-profit foundation than what I was hoping for. As you know, I've spent the last week in St. Louis for my niece's wedding. This is the first time I've visited home in years, and my daughter's memories are everywhere. I was supposed to fly back last night but . . . I've decided to stay. It's time to stop running from my past.

Lauren offered me the Marketing Director position at her company, and I've accepted it. She's turning a branch of JD Fitness into The Cinderella Foundation, a charity organization for the children of addicts. How could I possibly turn that down?

Please, please don't hate me.

In fact, think of this as an opportunity to stop hiding away in the dungeon! I promise, Lucas is not that scary. Perhaps it's time to admit that you're the one putting together all my sales reports. You deserve a raise. If nothing else, maybe he'll let you help hire my replacement. I think it's your turn to step out of the shadows and let him see how valuable you are.

Good luck with everything, Hallie. I'll miss you.

Your friend,
Caspien

I gasped, my breath piercing the icy stillness of the dark office.

He was already gone? Without even hiring his replacement? Who would orchestrate sales for each sector of the US? What about our expansion into Canada—that would start next week! Who would manage marketing campaigns and online ads and hire our next batch of sales reps?

Lucas would want me to do it.

"Shit!"

I scooped up the rows of sales reports and wrinkled them into a massive ball, then chucked it as hard as I could. My aim failed and the ball crashed against my laptop screen. It toppled backward off my desk, then crashed onto the floor, cracking the screen.

"Shit!"

Caspien thought I stayed down here because I was *afraid* of Lucas? Because I didn't see my own value? No. There were so many secrets beneath the surface of our ex-friendship, so much that Caspien didn't understand. No one did—not even Lucas. Those secrets could never get out.

What I needed most was to stay invisible. To bury myself so deeply in the dungeon that Lucas couldn't find out what I knew.

It would hurt him.

Destroy him.

But without Caspien here, how could I keep Lucas away? He would come looking for marketing and sales help!

I needed to make sure he regretted it.

Yes, that was exactly it.

I scooped up my cracked laptop and returned it to my desk. Only the top half of the screen still worked, but I opened my email into that rectangle of visible space and typed out a quick farewell to Caspien. Then I steeled my nerves for what came next.

I loved this company. I loved Lucas. I desperately wanted both to succeed. But since quitting wasn't an option, what other choice did I have? Even if it went against everything I stood for . . .

"It's for the best," I whispered into the empty office.

Starting now, I'd become the worst employee Croft Power had ever seen.

The End

Acknowledgements

The inspiration for Lauren in Pieces came when I spent a weekend at a wedding with my sister Brenna. She had recently been diagnosed with ADHD, and we spent the evening discussing how life-changing her diagnosis had been. Since that conversation, I have met dozens of women who struggled with the same thing, suffering and alone, having no idea that there were others out there like them. I've spent the past few years collecting their stories and learning from their experiences. While the character of Lauren is not based on any of them, I hope that her story touches the hearts of all the people out there who are still struggling. You are not alone.

Now, I have many people to thank. While I wrote this book, I listened to nothing but *Panic! At the Disco*. Thank you for your brilliant music, it inspired my creativity and set the mood for every scene. Without those songs, this book would have turned out completely different. Brendon Urie, to show my appreciation, I gave you a cameo in chapter six!

A huge and heartfelt thanks to Richard Pink and Roxanne Emery at @ADHD_LOVE. I read your book *Dirty Laundry,* and it changed the entire scope of my novel. Thank you for teaching me about how it feels to have ADHD, and how to help someone else with ADHD. Your book and TikTok videos made all the difference.

Thank you to my early readers who stumbled through my first draft. Allison Anderson, Michelle Henrie, and KayLynn Flanders, thank you for pointing out the glaring issue in the first half of the book. I was too close to the story to see it, but that revision meant everything! And KayLynn, thank you for pointing out how much deeper I could dive into the world of ADHD. It changed the whole story. Keri Newport (my amazing mother!),

Breanna Trost, Kelly Wilson, and Nikki Seigel, a million thanks for your revisions and comments! They were invaluable!

I have the two best editors that ever existed. Andrea Robinson-DiNardo, the hours you pour into every line of my stories . . . there are no words for the depth of my gratitude. You're never allowed to retire. Sally O'Keef, I hope you already know exactly how much you mean to me. If you don't, I'll send you some more Instagram videos to remind you. Thank you for both your editing help and your friendship. My life changed when you walked into it.

To my final round of readers, thank you for reading quickly, for your encouragement, and for all the screen shots and texts telling me your favorite parts. You really know how to make a girl feel loved. Amber Weston, Kelsey Larson, Kayla Tillotson, Tarry Perry, Linda Peterson, and Aimee Hall. Thank you from the depths of my soul.

A huge shout-out to my writing groups. To the Sisters Prim/Sisters Grimm and Writing Flirty. You guys mean everything to me. *Everything.* I've never known a group of women more encouraging or uplifting. To the TypeWriters chapter of the League of Utah Writers. When we started meeting every week, my consistency and goals completely changed. Your friendship and encouragement are what keep me writing!

Thank you to Dustin Hansen for my fantastic cover art. I'm always excited when I see your name pop up in my email. Your art is incredible, and I'm endlessly grateful that we met.

A huge thank you to all my ADHD friends for sharing your stories and helping me understand your lives. And thank you for reading my drafts and encouraging me to keep going. I couldn't have done this without you.

The biggest thank you goes to my family. My husband Jake, who always believes in me and supports my crazy writing dream. And to my incredible kids who let me hide out behind my computer. Our family is everything. You are the reason I do this.

Most importantly, to my Heavenly Father, thank you for the gift of words. I'm trying to use them well.

About the Author

Lindsay Hiller lives in Utah with her husband Jake and their six children. When she isn't writing, Lindsay loves reading, growing food, and Disneyland. She also loves chatting with fans, so please reach out to her via social media! www.LindsayHiller.com

BOOKS BY LINDSAY HILLER:

Fearless Series

Bailey in the Corner

Lauren in Pieces